DEATH OF THE MOON

SECRETS OF THE MOON
BOOK 1

S.A. PAVLIK

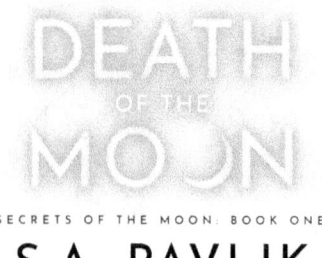

SECRETS OF THE MOON: BOOK ONE

S.A. PAVLIK

Paperback: ISBN 979-8-9857876-1-0
Ebook: ISBN 979-8-9857876-0-3

First paperback edition April 2022.

CONTENT ADVISORY: MC with PTSD, past torture implied through flashbacks, dealing with grief

A werewolf with secrets.

Alec Channing has lived a long life, and he's just going through the motions, lost in his troubled past, until fellow werewolves and shifters start dying around him. An increase in werewolf attacks only adds to Alec's problems. As his past closes in, his only hope lies in one man—an unaware human whose vanilla and spice scent and easygoing attitude draw Alec in. However, Alec can't help but worry about what will happen when that man uncovers the truth about Alec's preternatural world.

A homicide detective who is out of his depth.

Detective Damien O'Connor joined the Columbus Police Department to bring closure to victims and their families—closure that he never got for himself. But when none of the evidence adds up for what should be a routine death investigation, he's floundering. As the bodies continue to pile up, the sweet man who has caught Damien's eye is at the center of the storm. When closely guarded secrets start to emerge, can Damien reconcile himself to an entirely new reality—and solve the case that might also save the man he's come to care for?

Death of the Moon is Book One of the Secrets of the Moon trilogy, an 84k-word M/M, paranormal crime/mystery romance, with an HFN ending. While there is a complete story arc in this book, there are plot threads that will carry on throughout the trilogy. There is language and explicit intimate scenes not suitable for readers under the age of 18. Warnings: MC with PTSD, past torture implied through flashbacks, dealing with grief.

ACKNOWLEDGMENTS

First I have to thank my husband. Without his support, this book never would have gone from the early stages of free writing to 84k words. Thank you for being my alpha reader.

Thank you to Kaje Harper, my sprint partner, for encouraging a newbie author. Your consistent cheerleading kept me coming back to my chair day after day.

To the team that came together to make this happen, thank you from the bottom of my heart. I want to thank my crit reader, Eden Winters, and my beta reader, Megan Dischinger of LesCourt Author Services/Blue Beta Reading, for your invaluable feedback. Cate Ashwood, you *blew me away* with your cover design. Never in my wildest dreams could I have imagined my world come to life like this. You outdid yourself on this one. Lisa Lakeland, thank you for fitting me into your schedule and your hard work. I owe you that chocolate.

Finally, to my friends and family, thank you for encouraging me and supporting me throughout this adventure. I love you all.

1

ANOTHER WEREWOLF ATTACK.

This marked the fifth in as many months. Alec sat back and rubbed away the tension in his neck. A few Irish Gaelic curses slipped out under his breath as stress thickened his all-but-forgotten Irish accent. "She didn't make it?"

The Alpha of the Redwood Pack sighed. The grim resignation in his voice carried over the phone. "I'm afraid not. I understand that only your Oliver has survived the change out of the attacks so far this year."

Alec bristled. Oliver was not *his*.

Not pack, though the young wolf certainly wanted to be. Alec didn't belong in any pack, and he preferred it that way. No wolf would accept him if they knew his secrets, and a pack of wolves wouldn't take long to sniff them out. Not that Oliver had noticed anything yet, but he was still too young as a werewolf and not used to his heightened senses.

"We appreciate the update, Alpha. I will pass the information along to Ari as soon as I am able." Alec set his cell phone on his desk after ending the call. With any luck, the leaders within the preternatural community would track down the wolf or wolves responsible for the attacks across the country and put a stop to them before they drew too much attention.

Of any kind.

Alec's phone rang again. Oliver. He briefly considered not answering. They needed to make plans for their run on June fifth, but Alec had been hoping that he or Ari would've found someone else to take Oliver under their wing by now, or that Oliver would feel comfortable going alone. There was a pack in Cincinnati, but Oliver had established his life here in Columbus and didn't want to leave.

Alec tugged self-consciously at the fingerless leather gloves he was wearing. He didn't mind running with others, exactly, but keeping his guard up all the time was exhausting. Forcefully pushing down his instinct to check the scarf tucked around his throat, he swiped his phone off the desk instead. Avoiding the call was useless. "Hi, Oliver."

"Hey, Alec. So I was thinking we could go for a drive this month. Full moon's on a Friday night, and I don't work that weekend. How about you show me the national park you're always on about? The new temp worker at the storage facility keeps talking about it too."

"It's a national forest, not a park."

"Tomato, tomahto. How about it? We could camp. It'll be fun. You're too young to be cooped up in that apartment all the time."

Always so eager and upbeat. Just the thought of spending three hours in the car with the man was exhausting. And while Oliver thought Alec was young, he was a bit older than the thirty-one years he appeared to be. "I'm not so sure—"

"Hey, there's another call coming in. I think it's work. I gotta take this. Think about it. We can talk more tomorrow? I'll come by after lunch."

"Sounds like a plan." Alec leaned forward and cupped his face in his hands after the call cut out. Why couldn't they run somewhere nearby? Wayne National Forest was Alec's sanctuary. A private place where he went to be alone, far away from the noise of the city. Something about the forest called to him, with a sense of rightness he felt in few other places.

Though he hadn't been there in some time.

The sweet scent of caramel announced a visitor at the door to his Vine Street apartment. Alec frowned, hackles rising, as he followed the scent out of his office and into his kitchen, picking up the subtle aroma of autumn leaves under the caramel as he got closer. Startled, he stopped short. "Ari? I wasn't expecting you today. Is that a ... doughnut?"

Ari so rarely indulged in sweets that for a moment, Alec had thought someone else had bypassed his security.

"Hello, Alec." Sliding onto a stool at the kitchen counter, Ari hummed her approval around a mouthful of doughnut. "They were giving out samples at North Market today. It doesn't hurt to try new things now and then, does it?"

"And you didn't bring one for me?"

"Why would I do that?"

That was more like Ari. Her kitsune nature rarely allowed her to share her meal. Why do that when she could eat everything herself?

But that didn't stop Alec from trying.

Leaning against the counter, Alec waited until she had finished her snack. "So what brings you by tonight? I thought you weren't coming until tomorrow."

"I was in the area and thought I would drop by. Is that so unusual?"

She had a point there. Typically, Ari would call ahead to give him a little notice, but as Alec rarely had much of a social life, dropping in unexpectedly wasn't an issue. Besides, she probably knew he would have news for her tonight. Might as well open with that. "There was another wolf attack. In Oregon this time."

Ari stilled. "Did they survive?"

"No." Alec's heart broke for every person who lost their lives to senseless violence. In today's preternatural community, there was no need to force the change on anyone. While their numbers were few, no single species was considered endangered, and they had to be more careful these days.

Every member of the community had one survival goal: keep the humans unaware. Attacking humans senselessly did not align with that goal.

Ari cursed softly under her breath. "Did the Alpha who called have any idea who is doing this?"

Alec shook his head. The attacks were too random and spread too far apart to believe they came from any one person. However, the fact that many of the local Alphas had reached out to Alec or Ari about the matter suggested that they all suspected an Independent. After all, the rogue couldn't be one of their own.

He and Ari had become advocates of a sort for the Independents over the years. Word had quickly spread about the work they did here in Ohio. They'd done similar work back east, but Columbus housed the largest Independent preternatural community in the United States.

"Hmm. Well, there's not much we can do about it right now. Perhaps I should stop and see Oliver to ensure he's safe."

Alec tilted his head. "You think he might still be a target?"

"It's a possibility."

Until now, they'd had no reason to believe Oliver wouldn't be safe on his own. Had Ari seen or heard something that gave her an impression otherwise? If so, she clearly wasn't in the mood to share.

But she rarely was.

It was a burden she often bore alone out of necessity.

"Do you want me to come with you? Protect you from the hellhound next door?" Alec was only half teasing. Although the Pomeranian that belonged to Oliver's neighbor usually turned into a hyperactive, vicious ball of terror around Ari, it didn't take much for Alec to get the beast to roll over and show its belly.

"Hellhound?"

Alec laughed at Ari's bewildered tone and held the door open for her. Surely this wasn't the first time he'd used that moniker. Oliver loved it. "Oh, come on, you know who I mean."

"Right, of course. You're sweet to offer, Alec, but no. That isn't necessary tonight." Hesitantly, Ari patted Alec's arm in farewell before stepping into the hallway.

Something about her seemed off tonight, but he couldn't put his finger on what it was. Perhaps she had seen something after all.

And it had shaken her.

2

FRESH ROASTED COFFEE IN HAND, Damien stood in line to grab a hot-from-the-fryer doughnut from his favorite shop in North Market before heading into the office. They even had his favorite flavor today. Damien's mouth watered in anticipation of gooey caramel and spiced apples.

When his phone rang with the tone reserved for work, Damien sighed and stared longingly at his doughnut. Someone out there was laughing their ass off at him, taking great pleasure in dangling his one guilty pleasure in front of him before yanking it away.

Damien turned toward the nearest door and pressed the phone to his ear as he headed back outside. "O'Connor."

The cool voice of Captain Katarina Saunders of the Columbus Police Department skipped right past a greeting and straight to the point. "I need you to head out to Mount

Vernon. The victim is a John Doe, discovered by the neighbor's dog. Officer Jones will fill you in when you arrive."

A quick glance at Damien's phone confirmed that Kat had hung up on him without waiting for a reply. Hell would freeze over the day she finally did wait. Shaking his head, Damien climbed in behind the wheel of his SUV and took a sip of coffee while waiting for the ping to come in with the location.

At least he had coffee.

It took ten minutes on I-670 to arrive in Mount Vernon and another ten minutes to find somewhere to park. Damien ended up a few blocks away, having to walk back. Most of the houses on Graham Street were carriage lane style, with an alley between the homes and rear entry garages. CPD's crime scene unit and medical examiner vans had already claimed the precious few parking spaces near the front of the house where the victim had been found. Granted, CSU had more to lug around than Damien did.

Officer Andrew Jones stood off to the side, interviewing the neighbor as Damien passed him on the way in. Andy had his hands full with the woman, who couldn't seem to keep hold of the chirping little ball of fluff she called a dog as it fought to get back into the house with or without her.

Damien flashed his badge at the gatekeeper—some rookie he didn't recognize—and stepped inside. A CSU tech pointed up the stairs, where Franklin County Medical

Examiner Emily Whitehall had already started her examination of the body. He took in the seventy to eighty-year-old man lying in the bed. The victim almost appeared to be sleeping if Damien ignored the pallor of his skin. "What, they're calling homicide for old men dying in bed now, Em?"

"Good morning, Detective. I *am* doing well. Thank you for asking." Emily glanced up as he approached, ignoring Damien's question with a sparkle in her bright blue eyes. She nodded toward the bedside table, pulling off one of her gloves to tuck a stray auburn curl behind her ear. "The neighbor didn't recognize our John Doe, and so far, no one has seen the homeowner. We found his wallet on the nightstand, though. You should take a look."

Damien raised an eyebrow and pulled a pair of gloves out of his pocket before he picked up the wallet. The driver's license tucked into the clear outside pocket belonged to Oliver Stone, age thirty-seven and a resident of the house. Aside from a few credit cards, the wallet contained assorted dollar bills with odd folds in them and a dried leaf stuck to a crumpled note with what looked like PIN numbers scribbled across the page. "What am I looking for here?"

"Take a look at the license photo again. Notice anything?"

An attractive young man? "Aside from the fact that Oliver is pretty damn cute?"

Emily stared at him, unamused. "Nice. Damien, you need to get out more."

"I get out plenty." Damien shrugged and returned his attention to the license. Oliver was Damien's height at six feet, with blue and green streaks highlighting his dirty blond hair and making his dark blue eyes pop. Only a year younger than Damien, Oliver possessed the type of facial structure Damien usually found appealing, but what drew the eye was a thin scar bisecting his left eyebrow.

After Emily stepped back, Damien inspected the John Doe more closely. The similarities to the photograph floored him, right down to that same little scar. "Christ, if this guy wasn't clearly an old man, I'd say our John Doe *was* Stone."

"If you look closely, he even has the same blue and green highlights, though they're faded now. That license was issued in December, according to the dates. When I get him on my table, we'll take some fingerprints and see if we can figure out who this guy is."

"So maybe a stalker situation? John Doe fixates on Oliver and mirrors his appearance. Goes as far as replicating the scar on his face. Dementia maybe?"

"You know I can't—"

A cacophony outside drew their attention. Damien glanced out the window to see what was happening as the spitfire of a Pomeranian made a beeline for the front door. The owner shouted uselessly as she ran after it, and Andy chased after them both. A crime scene tech tried to grab the slippery devil dog but missed by a mile.

Within moments, the dog launched itself into the bedroom, growling and barking at the John Doe on the bed. Fur flew everywhere. The frenzy had happened so fast that the dog managed two or three laps around the room, knocking things over and causing an overall disaster, before Damien could do anything but stare at it in disbelief.

The neighbor shot into the room and scooped the dog up in her arms. "Fluffy! What has gotten into you? I'm so sorry, Officers, she's not usually like this." She turned her attention back to the dog in her arms, cooing at it despite the dead body not two feet away from her. Damien suppressed an eye roll.

Dog people.

Andy reached for the woman's arm and herded her back toward the stairs. "Come on, Mrs. Stevenson, how about we take Fluffers home? I can finish taking your statement there."

After Mrs. Stevenson followed Andy back outside, Damien took in the devastation that Hurricane Fluffball had left in its wake. He and Emily blinked slowly at each other for a few moments before they both burst out laughing. "Well," she said between gasps of air, "at least CSU already took their pictures."

Since Andy had his hands full with Mrs. Stevenson, Damien headed downstairs to talk to the officer's partner, Candice Lawrence. The petite blonde grinned at Damien from her new gatekeeper post at the door, replacing the rookie from earlier. "Hey there, handsome. Quite the morning, huh?"

"Would've been better if the call came in just two minutes later. Two minutes, Candice, and I would've had my doughnut." Her grin turned into a knowing smirk at his plight. "Since your partner is busy playing dog sitter, what've you got for me?"

"Well, Mrs. Stevenson told us Fluffy was acting strangely this morning. Kept scratching at the door, eager to get outside. When Mrs. Stevenson opened her back door, Fluffy raced right on over here and through the wide-open front door. She chased Fluffy up into the bedroom and discovered our John Doe.

"So far, we haven't been able to locate the homeowner, but his car is still in the rear garage. Mrs. Stevenson told me she hadn't seen him leave the house since yesterday." Candice gave Damien a knowing look. Seems Mrs. Stevenson was the Mrs. Kravitz of the neighborhood. A quick glance next door as Andy stepped out of the house, and sure enough, one corner of the kitchen curtain drew back.

"That ridiculous excuse for a dog hasn't quit barking since we got here." Andy shook his head, grumbling to himself. "From what Mrs. Stevenson could tell me, Mr. Stone doesn't have many visitors. He mostly keeps to himself, but he apparently has a lady friend who stops by occasionally after he gets home from work."

"Did she have a name for this 'lady friend'?" Damien asked.

Andy rubbed the back of his neck and ran a naturally tanned hand through his dirty blond hair. "I get the feeling that Mrs. Stevenson never actually spoke to Mr. Stone."

Of course not. That would be too easy.

"Well, there's not much more we can do here. Em is wrapping up, and CSU is working the house. Stick around and make sure we don't have any more excitement. Let me know if Mr. Stone comes home." Leaving Candice and Andy to their tasks, Damien started back toward his SUV.

The pair of officers both had plans to take the detective exam in the fall. Since Damien didn't have a partner, it worked out well for him to mentor the two of them, and they were often assigned as liaisons for his cases. While he didn't know them well outside of work, they worked effectively with him, and he considered them not only colleagues but friends.

By the time Damien arrived at the station, it was already early afternoon. He gave Kat a quick update then stopped briefly to ask their techs to pull together anything else they could find on Mr. Stone. With that out of the way, Damien settled in at his desk to hunt down the man's employment records.

Damien called the storage facility listed in the records and immediately groaned when an automated system answered. Could they interest him in a storage space today? These damned things were the bane of his existence. "No."

Pinching the bridge of his nose, Damien glared at a water spot on the ceiling, as if the stain could help him find the answers to all of life's questions. Jerry Sorensen and Thomas Young, two detectives from special operations, snickered at their desks a few rows over. He didn't know the pair as well as Candice and Andy—despite having worked with them just as long—as their undercover work took them away from the precinct, sometimes for months at a time.

"Still no!" Damien didn't need a rental truck either. He pressed the heels of his palms into his eyes, attempting to stave off an oncoming headache.

"No, I don't have an account." Damien jammed his finger repeatedly on the zero key on his desk phone, hoping the trick would get him out of robot hell and into talking to an actual person. It didn't.

"I want a person. A per-son!" Maybe enunciating would help. Phone systems like these were designed to prevent any sort of human interaction. Automation was nice, but what happened to good old-fashioned customer service?

Christ, he was getting old.

Damien responded to the poorly disguised snickering behind him with a one-fingered salute. *Glad I could be so amusing today.*

Just about to give up on this waste of time, the not-very-pleasant robot voice finally relented and said what he'd been waiting to hear. "Please wait for the next available associate." *Oh, thank fuck.*

"Good afternoon! This is Trish. How may I help you today?" The bubbly woman's voice made Damien twitch. Regardless, he straightened his spine and injected a smile into his voice. It wasn't this woman's fault their phone system was asinine.

"Hello, Trish. This is Detective O'Connor with the CPD. I'm hoping you can help me. I'm trying to locate an employee named Oliver Stone, and I understand he works at your facility. We just have a few routine questions for him."

"Oh." Trish's voice became more subdued now that she knew Damien wasn't a customer. "Well, I'm sorry, Detective, but Oliver didn't show up for work today. I can certainly take a message for you. Would you like me to have him call you back the next time he's in?"

Now he was getting somewhere. "Is it normal for Mr. Stone not to show up for work?"

Trish made a sound of discouragement, her professional mien slipping further. "I'm sorry. What did you say you needed to speak with Oliver about?"

So much for his smile. "Can I speak to your supervisor?"

"Just a moment."

The phone clicked over to the robot voice again ... and restarted its prompts. "Son of a bitch!" Damien's shout echoed off the walls, much to the peanut gallery's continuing amusement—if the riotous laughter was anything to go by. Damien hung up and rubbed his temples. Later. He'd deal with the damned robot again later.

"Problem, Damien?" Kat called from her office, abruptly cutting the laughter short.

Damien winced. He didn't need to get on Kat's bad side today.

Or any other day.

Ever.

A slow grin spread across Damien's lips as Candice and Andy stepped into the bullpen. "Candi! Perfect timing." He grabbed the file with the employment information and handed the headache to her. "Would you be a doll and call Mr. Stone's employer for me?"

"Um, sure." Skepticism laced her words as she took the file from him.

Andy raised his eyebrow, noticing Sorensen still shaking in silent laughter at his desk. Damien shook his head, to which Andy chuckled and shrugged. "Your funeral."

Damien pulled up the preliminary medical examiner's report and skimmed it while waiting for Candice. In the ME's report, Emily had tentatively determined that John Doe had died of natural causes, citing no signs of a struggle or indications of malicious intent. But he knew she would wait until the body was on her table before officially signing off on anything.

"Damien." The cold calmness in Candice's voice, directly behind him, sent an involuntary shudder through him. Damien glanced over his shoulder, quickly wishing he hadn't. "I am going to kill you." Candice smacked Damien across the back of the head with the folder.

"Any luck?"

"I finally got through to a supervisor, Mr. Parsons. Mr. Stone neither called in nor showed up to his shift today, and Mr. Parsons sounded concerned when he told me this hasn't happened before. He's been trying to get hold of Mr. Stone all day." Candice set the file neatly on Damien's desk and threw up her hands as she turned to go. "Oh, and I complained about that bubbly bitch on the phone. Get this. She's a temp worker. What temp worker acts like that?"

Young watched Candice stalk back to her desk before sharing a knowing glance with his partner. "So what do you want on your tombstone, O'Connor?"

"Yeah, yeah. Laugh it up. Don't you two have a drug bust you're supposed to be planning?" Damien shook his head and started shutting down his computer.

With nothing left but the waiting game, Damien headed home to his small studio in the Arena District. One of Damien's downstairs neighbors arrived at the same time he did, with a white Labrador retriever mix on a leash. "Hey, Tim, is that a new dog?"

Timothy Singer was an investment banker in Uptown. Damien had met him last year when Tim moved into the apartment below Damien's, and they often ended up in the building's gym at the same time. Tim didn't really strike

Damien as a dog person, but he could've been projecting his own distaste for the animals onto the other man.

Tim waved in greeting. "Damien! Come here and meet Frosty. He's a rescue. One of our secretaries at the office told me about him, and I just couldn't resist."

Damien knelt and held out his hand to the animal. With no hesitation at all, Frosty sniffed and licked his fingers. Compared to Fluffy, this dog was downright mellow. The big tail thwacking back and forth did not bode well for Tim's apartment, however. Such a large dog didn't really belong in a 640-square-foot studio.

Damien looked up with a raised eyebrow. Tim laughed, correctly reading the expression. "I'm looking to move soon. City life just isn't for me. Need to stretch my legs more, you know?"

"Going to be quite the drive to get to work."

"Actually, I'm moving out of state. Total fresh start."

There was a story there. Damien struggled to turn off his inner investigator and shrugged as they both stepped inside and upstairs in companionable silence. Tim split off on the second floor and headed toward his apartment, warmly greeting the woman who stood patiently waiting near his door. "Ari! I wasn't expecting you."

The tiny Asian woman had long, white-blonde hair separated into several sets of braids pulled together in an intricate twist on top of her head. She took a few startled steps back when she saw Frosty but quickly recovered.

Damien chuckled, catching her attention. When she

locked her ethereal eyes on him, it was almost as though she were staring *through* him. Unnerved, Damien continued up the stairs to his apartment on the third floor.

THE SCENT of veggie shoyu from the ramen place in North Market announced Ari's arrival at Alec's apartment that evening. While he didn't particularly care for tofu, the rich scent of the sauce still made his stomach growl, reminding him he hadn't eaten in hours. How was it evening already?

"Did you bring anything for me this time?" Alec asked, standing to help her with the takeout bags as she entered the kitchen area. He promptly got his hand swatted for his efforts. He knew she hadn't, but he still had to ask. Sometimes he got lucky.

"Paws off, this is mine!" Her indignant huff made Alec smile and divert his hand to ruffle her hair instead, fingers tangling in the nine braids piled on top of her head. The extra height of the braids brought her head nearly to Alec's shoulders. Ari pushed up for an indulgent second then slipped out from under his hand, nudging him back through the French doors into the den where he'd been working.

Knowing the danger of getting between Ari and her food, Alec sat back and waited while she ate in relative silence.

As the slurping gave way to a contented sigh, she got

down to business. "I just left Tim a short while ago. Still no decision, and I have to keep reminding him that the pride in West Virginia does not tolerate Independent shifters. He either has to negotiate joining them or pick somewhere else."

Last month, Timothy Singer had requested help with moving out of the city. Once he settled on a destination, Ari would facilitate territory negotiations with the local shifter community. A Pack Alpha, like the Alpha of the Redwood Pack on the west coast, or a Pride Leader would normally handle the transition, but Independent shifters and werecreatures usually ended up getting the short end of the stick.

"You know how stubborn bobcats can be. They're independent by nature." Both in the literal and figurative sense. Bobcat shifters like Tim rarely joined a pride. Even in the wild, the creatures weren't often found in a pounce.

"They are indeed. Oh, and you will not believe this." Ari huffed out a sudden breath, her melodic voice filling with disdain. "Tim got a dog. A giant beast of a dog!"

Alec held back a smirk, imagining Ari around an unexpected dog. "You know what a bleeding heart he has for abused animals."

"Yes, but a *dog*? The creature is so large it barely fits in his apartment. It is almost as tall as I am!" That really didn't take much.

If he let her, Ari would obsess over the dog for hours. At her age, the chances were minimal that a dog would startle her into revealing her kitsune nature, but she still didn't like the animals.

"Oliver was supposed to stop by today, but he's neither shown up nor answered my calls."

Allowing the change of topic, Ari turned serious. "When did you last speak with him?"

Blinking, Alec frowned as pressure built behind his eyes. Was it getting brighter in here? "Yesterday. Didn't you—"

"Maybe I need to pop in to see Oliver before I head home, then." Ari hummed thoughtfully, carrying on as though she hadn't interrupted him. "He gets so caught up in things sometimes that he does not always answer the phone."

Hadn't she stopped by yesterday? Alec rubbed at his eyes and shook his head to clear it.

Ari's phone vibrated, and she quickly answered. Alec's headache faded as he turned his attention to the call. There was no need to place the call on speakerphone for Alec to listen in as his sensitive hearing easily picked up the other end of the conversation. "Michael?"

"Ari, so glad I caught you. Techs brought in a werewolf today. Thought you should know. I haven't gotten in there to see who it is yet. Checked the reports after I scented wolf. Death is clean, but they're doing a full workup." The voice on the line belonged to their contact in the morgue, Mike Miller. *Clean* meant no immediate cause for concern, but they still needed to prevent any potential exposure.

At least werecreatures started human and would, for all intents and purposes, appear that way to any tests the morgue ran.

"Thank you." Ari huffed out a breath after hanging up —the only sign the call had upset her. "I must go take care of this. You should get yourself some dinner and call it a night. You have been working far too hard, Little Wolf."

She was right. Alec bopped her nose playfully. "I wouldn't need to go *get* dinner if you would just bring me some when you get your own."

"Now, why would I do something like that? Besides, you have such a lovely kitchen. You should use it sometime." Ari nudged Alec's hand in an affectionate gesture with her nose and stood. "Walk me downstairs?"

"You know I don't cook, Ari. The kitchen came with the apartment that you insisted I have." Alec stood and followed her to the door, so he could hunt down some dinner.

Ari bumped his arm with her shoulder in farewell and climbed into the back seat of her private Rolls-Royce Phantom, relaying instructions to her personal driver, an aware human named Vincent St. James, as she closed the door. "Take me to see Oliver if you would be so kind."

"Of course, mum," Vincent murmured from the front seat.

They'd known Vincent's family for as long as they had lived in the States. The family had already been aware when Ari and Alec met them. Even after several generations, the family still spoke like proper Englishmen. Alec shook his head and turned away with a grin.

The May night air was cool on Alec's face as he followed his nose to the heavenly scent of burgers and fries a few blocks away at Sister's Bar and Grill. It didn't take long for the boisterous laughter and conversations from inside the bar to assault his ears.

Alec's hearing could be hypersensitive, and he often used it to remain aware of his surroundings. With a lifetime of practice, his mind could adapt after a few minutes and filter out unnecessary information as white background noise. He took a moment to center himself before making his way back to the bar area to place an order.

"Hey, now, I didn't touch your girl!" Alec's ears perked up at a voice he recognized.

Suppressing a growl, Alec rushed over to the pool tables just in time to grab a drunk thug's wrist before his punch could connect with Collin Wilde. Not realizing he was at a severe disadvantage, the thug instantly tried to follow up with his other fist.

Sidestepping, Alec pulled the thug's wrist tight behind his back and leaned into him from behind, so he could murmur in the thug's ear. "Leave the kid alone, and you won't spend the night getting your shoulder popped back into its socket in the ER."

"Who do you think you are?" The thug struggled to break Alec's hold. "And how are you so s-strong?" The sour smell of the alcohol on the thug's breath made Alec want to gag.

Alec shot his free hand out behind him, intercepting a beer bottle aimed at the back of his head. The thug's girlfriend wanted in on the action.

"Dammit, Collin, what did you take this time?" Alec barely suppressed an irritated growl as he spun the thug around, so both assailants were in front of him. He sidestepped the thug's foot as the idiot tried to stomp down on Alec's.

The crowd around them fell silent one by one. They were drawing attention, and Alec really wanted his burgers before he got kicked out.

"I didn't take anything, Mr. Channing!" Collin swore, his voice high pitched and tense from being caught. Alec could practically hear Collin's fight-or-flight instincts kicking in, leaning decisively toward flight.

Alec snorted. "Right, kid. Return whatever you stole, so our friends here can go home without broken bones, yeah? I'll even buy you a burger."

Collin complied, rifling through his pockets while remaining safely behind Alec. Collin produced several items and lined each one up on the pool table. He paused suddenly when a man approached from behind them and asked, "Everything okay over here?"

With a squeak, Collin dashed off between bodies toward the other side of the bar. Alec stepped back from the thug to address the newcomer. "Just fine." Casually placing his back against the pool table, Alec ensured no one else could sneak up on him.

Alec tilted his head toward the man who smelled like vanilla, spice, and the faintest hint of something else that tickled his nose, but he couldn't quite place it while surrounded by so much food. Not to mention, he could still smell the thug's rancid alcohol breath.

"Detective O'Connor! Are you here for your pickup order?" Deci asked, approaching them. Deci spent most of her time in the restaurant behind the bar, one of three sister witches who ran the establishment that doubled as a safe haven for the preternatural community. The sisters had bought the restaurant from an old shifter couple earlier in the year when they could no longer handle the day-to-day business aspect of it.

Naomi and Marta, the other two witches, rarely made an appearance inside the restaurant proper. At least fifteen years separated each of the women. He'd been surprised to learn that Naomi was only a teenager while Marta had grandchildren to care for. Alec had only met Naomi once, but Marta dropped by from time to time to stir up trouble.

Deci was the middle sister and the main proprietor of the bar. Her arrival diffused the rest of the situation. The thug and his girlfriend quickly gathered their things and turned to go.

Alec cocked an eyebrow. "Isn't breaking up a bar fight a little beneath you, Detective?"

"I thought you said everything was just fine?" A grin laced the man's cheeky reply.

Alec returned the smile then patted his pocket and frowned. *That squirrely little shit.* "Ah, Deci?" he asked, turning toward her. "Did you see the young man who was just over here leave?"

"Oh, hello, Alec. No, I think he's at your normal table by the bar. Did you want the usual smokehouse burgers and a side of fries tonight?"

"Better add one for Collin. Thanks, hon." Alec had to slip past the detective on his way over to his table. He couldn't resist breathing in the detective's vanilla and spice scent one more time before frowning and shaking his head at himself.

Alec stopped short at the table. "I didn't think you'd stick around."

"You said you'd buy me a burger." Collin's mumble was nearly drowned under the ambient noise.

Alec held out his hand expectantly, and Collin reluctantly handed over the wallet. Alec thumbed through the contents and held his hand out again with a raised eyebrow. Collin huffed out a sigh and placed several bills into Alec's hand. Shuffling them quickly with his finger along the edges, Alec confirmed the amount.

"I know you can take care of yourself, but I want you to reconsider Ari's offer. This isn't the first time someone has caught you."

"I know. I just ..."

"Can't help it. I get it, Collin. There are better places to do this than a bar in the Arena District, though. Drunk people are far more aware than you think they are."

Collin sighed, defeated. "I know, Mr. Channing."

"How many times do I have to ask you to call me Alec?" Mr. Channing made Alec sound so ... old. He frowned. *I'm not that old. Am I?*

Collin chuckled. "Probably a few more times, Mr. Channing."

"Punk."

Their food arrived a few minutes later with the heavenly scent of bacon, onions, and barbeque. "I take it you're hungry?" Collin asked with amusement as Alec dove into the burgers as soon as they were in front of him. The first disappeared within seconds.

"Yeah," Alec said after swallowing a bite of his second burger. "Ari keeps bringing food over and not sharing. Want some of my fries?"

He had just started on his third burger when Ari's ringtone sounded on Alec's phone. He lifted the phone to his ear, frowning. "Hey, Ari, did you—"

"The wolf in the morgue is Oliver."

3

DARKNESS.

He could hear water dripping somewhere nearby, but as he turned his head to look around, the fabric covering his eyes pulled tight against his head. He tried to remove the blindfold, but he couldn't move. Shackles held his arms tight above his head.

The cool dampness of stone surrounded him while his body pulsed with agonizing pain radiating from the tips of his fingers down to his toes. The drumbeat of his heart pounded in his head. His eyes burned, crusty against the cloth.

Footsteps echoed around him. The pounding in his ears took on a frantic rhythm.

They were coming back.

He struggled against the bindings.

He had to get away.

He had to—

. . .

"FUCK!" Damien sat up in a cold sweat, breathing hard. He glared at the bedside clock and scrubbed a hand over his face. 3:02 a.m. He'd only managed two fucking hours of sleep. Damien hated the insomnia that came with working a case.

He hadn't had nightmares since ... *No*. Damien packed those thoughts back into the little box in the back of his mind where they belonged.

Taking deep, controlled breaths, Damien willed his racing heart to slow down. He kicked the sheets out of the way with a grunt and stumbled over to his bathroom, turning the shower tap on as hot as he could stand it. No point in trying to go back to sleep now.

As Damien stepped under the spray, his thoughts drifted away from the nightmare and landed on the strange scene at Sister's Bar and Grill four nights ago. He'd gone over there to pick up a quick takeout order and had spent the time waiting in the entryway, appreciating the way a pair of tight-fit jeans cupped the sexy ass in front of him. Then the attractive man it belonged to had suddenly lurched into action. The man had raced to intercept a big bruiser, keeping him from beating up on a scrawny, twenty-something kid.

He'd never seen someone move so fast through a crowd like that. One second the man—Damien later found out his name was Alec—was in front of him, and the next, the echo of Alec's palm slapping against the bruiser's wrist had reached his ears above the low drone of noise in the bar. Alec had deflected a punch aimed toward the lanky kid, whose dark eyes were as big as saucers.

When the bruiser's girlfriend had picked up her beer bottle by the neck, Damien started forward, but Alec caught the bottle with his other hand before the intent to swing even fully formed. The action struck Damien stupid for the second time that day as the lithe, attractive man's movements shot a bolt of lust straight to Damien's cock.

Alec had said something to the kid that Damien couldn't quite make out. It resulted in several items from the kid's pockets lined up on the pool table and a petulant pout on the kid's face. Two wallets, a tube of lipstick, a watch ...

Damien had finally approached after Alec shifted his full attention toward the kid and his haul, and the intent to pull something stupid flashed across the bruiser's drunken face. "Everything okay over here?" Damien had asked.

"Just fine." Alec's voice had held the faint edge of a brogue that could've been either Irish or Scottish—it was hard to tell which, as light as it was.

Damien's breath had caught when Alec turned. The man was *abso-fucking-lutely gorgeous* with messy brown hair he kept long on top and shorter on the sides. He had evening scruff, darkening a square jaw that surrounded full, kissable lips. Damien couldn't help but imagine those lips wrapped around his cock. There was even an adorable little dimple in his chin that had disappeared when a puzzled frown furrowed Alec's brow.

Damien still wanted to lick that dimple.

It was too bad the beautiful man had worn wraparound mirrored sunglasses, and Damien couldn't see his eyes ...

Hadn't it been dark in there?

A flash of cold water startled Damien out of his daydream, effectively dousing the arousal the memory had reignited. He still had shampoo in his hair. Grumbling, Damien quickly rinsed it out and turned the water off. Accusatory steel blue eyes stared back at him from the bathroom mirror as he reached for his towel. Em was right. Damien needed to get out more.

Heading over to North Market the minute they opened, Damien got in line for his favorite fresh-roasted coffee. He groaned when the guy at the front of the line ordered a venti concoction with more milk than coffee. Oh, but make that almond milk. And three pumps of caramel. Why did everyone insist on ordering like they were at Starbucks these days? Stauf's coffee didn't need to be covered up with all that garbage.

Then the guy ordered five more complicated drinks. Naturally.

When the pretentious asshole had finally paid and stepped aside, and the poor barista started making the order, Damien's phone taunted him with a distinctive ringtone. Could he get away with a murder of his own? Although, with his luck, he'd probably end up assigned to solving his own case.

"O'Connor," Damien answered far more gruffly than he probably should've as the barista moved on to the second of the six drinks.

Amusement laced Kat's voice when she responded, and Damien suppressed the urge to look around for hidden cameras. Somehow, Kat always knew. "I need you to head over to the Franklin County Forensic Science Center immediately. Dr. Whitehall wishes to present her findings in person. She has a court case to testify for this afternoon and will need to leave within the next hour. The case will have her tied up for the rest of the week."

A whimper escaped Damien's lips as the barista started on the third drink. There was no time to wait and still get across town in time to catch Em. So much for coffee.

Fifteen minutes later, Damien pulled into the parking lot across from the beige brick building that housed the coroner's office. He had to admit, the unusual request to debrief in person piqued his curiosity and almost made up for the lack of coffee.

Almost.

Emily met him in the hallway outside her office. "Damien, I'm so glad you could make it in on such short notice."

"You owe me a coffee, Em." Damien softened his grumpiness with a grin.

She winced. "I'm terribly sorry. I take it you didn't get your doughnut, either?"

Damien sighed dramatically. "No."

"Well, I stayed late last night when my initial scans started coming in with some curious results. I'll admit, I got a little obsessed. Come on in. I have something interesting to show you." Emily gestured to the wall where she had various X-ray images lined up.

Damien blinked slowly at the images and shook his head. "Remember, I haven't had any coffee. What's the significance here?"

"It's what I'm not seeing that's so astounding. This John Doe presents very few signs of aging in his joints and skeletal structure." Damien stepped closer to the image she pointed to. "The spacing between his joints is more what I would expect to see in a man in his late thirties. Here, I have a comparison for you."

Emily shuffled through some files on her computer and opened another set of X-rays. "This is from the Anderson case from last week. Keep in mind that Anderson was sixty-eight years old. Look here. See the difference? This is more in line with what I expected when I started reviewing the Doe images."

Damien glanced back and forth between the two sets of X-rays and furrowed his brow. The difference was most obvious in the hands and wrists. John Doe still had a very distinct skeletal structure, whereas the bones in the

Anderson X-rays were a more indistinct blob of light and dark.

"Okay, so ..." Damien prompted.

"Really, Damien, do I need to send my intern out to get you a coffee?" Emily deadpanned. She continued, gesturing wildly with her hands, before he could find out if she was serious about the coffee. Was an IV drip too much to ask?

"This John Doe has virtually no arthritis. There's no sign of osteoporosis. By the time a body reaches this one's apparent age of seventy to seventy-five, there *will* be evidence of wear and tear. If his musculature wasn't so healthy, I'd be inclined to believe he hadn't moved around at all for the past thirty years. However, there's no sign of muscular atrophy.

"In fact, there is no way a male in his seventies could retain *this* much muscle mass. He would have to be working out constantly to achieve it. I mean, really, if all his organs were as healthy as the rest of him? I wouldn't believe what I was seeing at all."

She then explained, in grotesque detail, everything she'd found during the internal examination, which only added to the dichotomy of John Doe's age. Heart and liver? Old as fuck. Brain and lungs? Middle-aged and comparable to a man in his fifties. As Em moved on to the stomach contents and showed no sign of stopping, Damien couldn't take any more.

"Emily," Damien interjected. "Emily!" he repeated louder when she didn't seem to hear him. "So what you're saying is John Doe is a medical marvel. How did he die? Do you know who he *is*?"

Emily blinked at Damien like he was dense. "This John Doe had a heart attack, like I told you. I'm running a toxicology with a full spectrum drug panel, but there isn't any evidence that someone drugged him. And no, Damien, I don't know who he is. I sent the fingerprints in as soon as he arrived, though. Oh! Look at the time. I have to get going."

After promising that she would submit her full analysis after the court case, Emily chased Damien out of the office.

4

COLLIN WAS STEADILY DRIVING Alec insane.

The little pickpocket followed him home after another visit to Sister's Bar and Grill. Alec had taken to eating there every night for the past week, hoping to run into Detective O'Connor again after learning the lead detective for Oliver's case was the same Detective O'Connor from the bar.

Alec kept telling himself the only reason he was stalking the man was to ensure the CPD didn't stumble into the preternatural world.

Eventually, he'd believe his own lie.

"This is where you live, Mr. Channing? This place is huge!" Collin squealed and raced inside when Alec opened the door to his apartment.

"Don't move anything, Collin, or I swear I'll find a reason to take up taxidermy!" Alec called when he heard the kid racing from room to room. He frowned. "And will you *stop* calling me Mr. Channing?"

Shaking his head, Alec kicked the door closed and pressed a thumb to the panel by the door to set the security. A single buzz indicated there had been no alerts since he left. The security panel was a custom piece that had been developed for Alec when he moved into the apartment several years ago.

"Alexa, do I have messages?" Ari had bought Alec the device last year and promptly upgraded everything in the apartment to be a "smart" device for him. Some devices were smarter than others, but he enjoyed the freedom that the technology provided.

"You have one new message from Ari Fushimi on Friday, May 29th, at 7:57 p.m.," the device announced. Right after he had left for the bar. "Would you like to play it now?"

"Yes."

"I will stop by later, Little Wolf. I have a job for Collin if he follows you home tonight."

"How did she know I'd be here?" Collin asked, wandering back into the main room from the bedroom as Alec relaxed on the couch.

Alec chuckled. Why hadn't Ari just called his cell while he was at the bar? Alec had almost sent the kid home when he'd realized he was being followed. "Trust me, you don't want to know the answer to that. Might as well get comfortable, though. She's expecting you to be here."

"You don't even have a television." The pout in Collin's voice was rather sad.

Pinching the bridge of his nose, Alec sighed. He didn't really have the need for a television and rarely had guests aside from Ari. He didn't make it a habit to mentor other preternatural creatures in his own home.

Maybe it was time to change that.

He could introduce Collin to one of his favorite radio dramas. "Grab yourself a drink and have a seat. Alexa, play *War of the Worlds* from my library."

When the intro started playing, Collin groaned. "Really? You're going to make me listen to *this*?"

Alec held a finger to his lips. "Just wait."

When the program had first aired, he and Ari had been living in New York City. They'd spent *months* calming down the preternatural community afterward. Every creature that had reached out had been afraid the humans planned to pull together a militia to hunt them down.

Collin's complaints grew silent when the announcer interrupted *La Cumparsita* to describe a series of explosions observed on Mars. As soon as the music started again, however, the kid acted like Alec was trying to torture him.

This generation had no appreciation for the classics.

The scent of miso soup followed Ari into the apartment just as the intermission started. Her sigh was a little dramatic. "Really? Did you not get enough of this nonsense when the trolls started demanding asylum in Canada? Alexa, pause the program."

Alec grinned at the memory. At least he wasn't the one who had ended up dealing with those particular trolls. "I was just trying to broaden Collin's horizons. Not all entertainment comes in the form of TV."

"What about all those audiobooks I got for you?"

Alec made a face. "Did you have to get me books that equate to shifter porn?"

Collin choked on his drink. "She got you *what*?"

"Well, it is not like he has his own love life."

Heat rushing to his cheeks, Alec lobbed one of the throw pillows from the couch in her direction. He smiled when she huffed at him. Served her right for buying him so many fecking pillows.

"I am glad you are here, Collin. I brought some soup. Would you like some?"

Alec frowned as Collin shot up and raced into the kitchen. "Wait, you bring *him* food but not me?"

"I brought enough for both of you." Ari hummed to herself as she rummaged around for dishes. "I can share sometimes, you know."

"When you're trying to butter someone up?" Alec asked, accepting the precious offering from his favorite kitsune. He cherished the rare times she overcame her nature and shared a meal. Even a simple snack. Ari meant well, but she'd already achieved seven tails by the time he met her, each one signifying a century of life. She was quite set in her ways.

Ari booped Alec on the nose. "Not only then. Besides,

Collin will need the energy to break into the funeral home tonight."

"Wait, I'm doing what now?" Collin asked, setting his bowl on the counter with a clink.

"I need you to switch some ID tags around. Preferably without being seen. You will want to go in fur."

"Um."

"The cremation appointment we are borrowing is on Monday, so I need you to go tonight. Our contact at the morgue arranged for delivery this afternoon. It is fortuitous that the medical examiner is out all week."

"Okay ... but why me?" Collin sounded positively baffled.

"Do you not agree this is a better use of your talents than pilfering from drunkards?"

Alec laughed. "I'd stop arguing, kid. She won't give up."

Times like these, Alec had learned to just go with whatever Ari expected. Especially when she spoke as though it were already a foregone conclusion.

It probably was.

Conversation turned to an infiltration plan where Collin would enter in fur through an outside vent. Ari would disrupt the cameras as quickly as possible, but with Collin in fur, no one would realize it was him. The goal was to lift the steel ID tag off one corpse and move it to the other one in the room.

Guilt ate at Alec over disrupting someone else's mourning with the hassle of their loved one not getting cremated on time, but they needed the ashes back before Friday. Ari stopped before him on her way out the door with Collin in tow. "Do not worry, Little Wolf. I shall ensure the family we are inconveniencing is properly seen to."

Grateful to reclaim his own space, Alec headed to the en suite bathroom to take a shower. He swore as he tripped over an open dresser drawer in the bedroom. "Gods dammit, Collin."

He was ready to string that kid up by the tail.

5

DAMIEN THREW his phone into the cup holder of the SUV as soon as the vehicle's Bluetooth picked up the call, slamming his door closed for good measure. "How in the bloody hell does a body just disappear from the morgue?"

Emily's sigh echoed over the speakers. "I don't know yet, Damien. I haven't been in the office all week because of the court case. Mike is checking the security tapes now, but I called as soon as I realized the body was missing."

"Let me know the minute you find something."

"I will," she promised and hung up.

The excessive traffic compounded Damien's foul mood on the way to the station. "I hate full moons on Fridays," he muttered to himself as he parked the vehicle. At least it wasn't Friday the thirteenth on top of everything else. Small blessings.

Candice motioned him over to her desk when he

stepped into the bullpen. "Oh, Damien, come on over here and have a look at this."

"What now?" He tossed his bag on his chair before stomping over to her.

She blinked and backed up a few steps. "Geez, Damien, did someone piss in your coffee this morning?"

Shit, he didn't need to growl at her. "Sorry, Candi."

Candice waved her hand dismissively. "You're fine. What's going on?"

Damien rubbed the back of his neck and took a deep breath before slowly releasing it. "I just got off the phone with the ME's office. Our John Doe is missing."

"What do you mean, *missing*? What did he do, get up and take a stroll?" Andy asked from the adjoining desk.

Nothing would surprise Damien at this point. "I don't know yet. They're still looking into it at the morgue."

Candice shook her head in disbelief. "This case just keeps getting weirder."

"How so?"

"Well, Andy and I have been going over the information that our techs pulled together this past week on Mr. Stone. Something isn't adding up."

Andy handed Damien a file folder. "I had our undercover guys from special operations give us their opinion already. The guy has no criminal record. His driver's license and credit cards were all issued in December. Hell, he just started the job at that storage unit at the end of March."

"Thanks again for pawning that one off on me, by the way." Candice poked Damien in the shoulder. "Between the phone system and the bubbly bitch on the phone, you owe me. Big time."

Damien flipped through the pages in the folder. Sure enough, a bank account, credit and debit cards associated with the account, and an Ohio State driver's license were all issued in December, starting with the license on December 18th. The credit report was rather thin and lacking in detail, with no loans or additional lines of credit over the past ten years.

Andy nodded at the folder. "Sorensen says any measly scraps prior to December that we could dig up read like a manufactured cover—like the ones they build for our guys. We tried digging deeper, but the system got flagged. We found some other files, but they're a bunch of redacted nonsense."

Young poked his head up from his desk. "My money's on WITSEC."

Witness protection was possible, especially if they were getting locked out.

Andy glanced at his computer as it pinged with an alert. Furrowing his brow, he held up his finger, so he could read through the information. "Holy hell, that can't be right."

Damien stepped around the desk to join him and read the screen from over his shoulder. According to the report, the storage company Mr. Stone worked for had taken fingerprints as a part of his background check and registered them. Damien read the next part twice and frowned. "What the fuck? Am I reading this right?"

"What is it?" Candice shoved herself between the two of them to see the computer and sucked in a sharp breath after reading the information.

They stared at each other for so long that Young came over to loom over all of them. "Is your John Doe dancing naked in the streets? I want to see—huh, that's interesting."

Damien glared at him.

"According to this,"—Andy's gaze lifted to meet Damien's—"our John Doe *is* Oliver Stone."

Damien shook his head. "No. No, that isn't possible. Contact CSU and have them send the backup prints they took at the scene to the FBI to run through their database. We'll have to wait longer for the results, but it's all we can do without the damned body."

After dropping the folder off at his desk, Damien headed into Kat's office. Cold, ice blue eyes glared at him when he entered. "Can I help you, Damien?"

"I have an update on the Doe case."

"And?"

He outlined their WITSEC theory for her. Her expression, if possible, turned even stonier when he revealed John Doe was missing from the morgue, and that they had to rerun the fingerprints.

"Keep me apprised of the situation. However, as the autopsy report shows your John Doe died of natural causes, and we no longer have a body, we may need to pass the case on to the BCI Missing Persons Unit soon. We could leave it up to them to locate the missing home-owner and determine Doe's identity. I'll let you know." Kat turned back to her computer, effectively dismissing him.

Damien wasn't sure how he felt about handing everything over to the Bureau of Criminal Investigation. This case had been nothing but a migraine from the start, but it was still his case.

Emily finally called back just as he was about to head out for the day. "Well, the good news is we know what happened."

That didn't sound promising. Damien wasn't sure he wanted to know the bad news. "Oh?"

"There was a mix-up with the paperwork, and they sent your John Doe to a funeral home last Friday in the place of the corpse that was scheduled to go."

While annoying, that didn't sound like such a big deal. They could still have the body returned to the morgue. "What's the catch?"

"That normally wouldn't be a problem, but the body ended up being cremated on Monday in place of another one that was supposed to be."

"Are you fucking kidding me? Don't they need someone to sign off on that?"

The silence on the other end extended so long Damien checked to make sure the call hadn't dropped. "Well ..."

"Spit it out, Emily."

She sighed. "I just sent you the video. You won't believe it unless you see it. Your John Doe is on the left."

Raising an eyebrow, Damien pulled up the video on his laptop. It was surveillance footage from the funeral home's cold storage room, used for intake, time-stamped June 1st at 1:12 a.m. At first, nothing was happening aside from a squirrel scratching away at the grate in the vent above the corpses. Damien chuckled, as it seemed determined to get inside.

The footage went dark two minutes later, like something was blocking the camera, but the video was still running. Unfortunately, the video didn't have audio. The display returned at 1:21 a.m.

A silver glint on top of John Doe's bag caught Damien's attention. It was the steel ID tag used to identify a corpse set for cremation. Damien rewound the footage and watched again. Sure enough, the tag wasn't there before the break in the footage. It was on the other body.

"You've got to be fucking kidding me."

"I wish I was," Emily replied wistfully.

Fuck my life.

"DO we have everything we need for tonight?" Alec asked from his spot on the couch when Ari let herself into his apartment that evening. Alec frowned when the aroma of food didn't follow her in.

"Almost," Ari replied, voice nearly inaudible.

As she came to stand before him, Alec pulled Ari into an embrace, which he probably needed more than she did despite her somber mood. With Ari barely nose-to-nose with Alec in his seated position, he rested his chin on top of the thick pile of braids on her head.

"Not calling his family feels wrong," Alec murmured into her hair.

"Except they already mourned him, Little Wolf. As far as his family is aware, Frank Oliver Stonewell died in December from a hiking accident in Montana. We became his family that day."

Ari had brought Frank to Columbus a few days after the accident to start a fresh life as Oliver Stone. It had been touch-and-go for several days while Oliver's body had fought the changes it was going through. Oliver had taken Alec by surprise and sliced a good strip of skin off Alec's arm when he finally regained consciousness. They ended up having to put Oliver in the holding cell in Ari's basement until the delirium had passed.

It had been an exhausting week for all of them.

"I know, I know. I just ... I remember what it was like. For me, I mean. I just find it hard to fathom that he made it through such a horrific attack, only to die anyway just five months later. He was finally getting his feet under him again, Ari." Gods, why had Alec wanted to foist Oliver off onto someone else for the full moon run tonight? His stomach turned to acid.

Maybe if he hadn't been so fecking reluctant to mentor Oliver ... Alec had let his own insecurities prevent him from making sure Oliver felt comfortable reentering society. Or finding a new family.

Pack.

"It is not your fault, Little Wolf." Ari's affectionate whisper drew Alec out of his musings, almost like she knew where his thoughts had gone. Who was he kidding? She knew far too much and shared only what she could—very little.

"I wouldn't have survived if it weren't for you, you know." If not for Ari, Alec most likely wouldn't even be alive today whether he'd survived back then or not. What would have become of Oliver if Alec hadn't been here? Would he still be alive with whomever would have taken care of him instead?

Words came to his mind that Ari had spoken to him when he awoke that first night. "With every action taken and every choice we make, the Fates' woven path twists anew."

"The Fates are not my biggest fans of late, I assure you." Ari sighed and held him tighter for a moment.

Alec fought not to tense.

She immediately stepped back, and he let out a soft breath. Alec craved physical contact, and Ari knew that, but he hated it at the same time. He hated feeling *constrained*. Would he ever feel safe in someone's arms again?

Ari patted Alec's shoulder and nudged him toward the

door. "We should get going. We have an errand to run before we can head down to the forest."

Their destination was a cemetery near the Archers Fork Trail Head, but it was only a stopping point before they hiked further into Wayne National Forest to a place of power well suited for their needs. Lately, Alec just ran in one of the small woodland areas surrounding Columbus on full moon nights and called it good enough, but what they had planned tonight was far more important. Oliver was more important.

The young wolf would've loved the forest. Regret sank its claws deep. Perhaps the Fates weren't much of a fan of Alec's either, laughing at him as they were. But Ari and Alec would honor Oliver in the best way that they could.

Alec grabbed his duffel by the door and slipped his sunglasses on as he and Ari made their way out of his apartment. The duffel held a quick change of clothes and some other supplies that Ari had stuffed in there. Alec wrinkled his nose at the incense.

"I'm going to need a new bag after this." Ari ignored his complaint as they stepped outside and over to her private car. Alec winced at the bright late-afternoon sunlight despite his dark glasses. "Is Collin coming with us?"

"Yes. He is at the funeral home acquiring the ashes for us now." Ari slipped into the car and waited for Alec to join her. Once they were settled, she tapped her nail against the divider between the front and back seats to let Vincent know they were ready to leave.

Alec leaned back against the seat and closed his eyes. Collin's chipper voice startled him out of a light doze a short while later. "Wow, that kimono is gorgeous, Ari! Pink is definitely your color. But ... isn't it a little fancy for a hike?"

Ari hummed, preening. "Why, thank you, Collin. Normally I would say yes, but we are not just hiking tonight, are we?"

That seemed to subdue Collin a little. "Yeah, you're right."

"Did you have any trouble?"

"Only when I was leaving. I can't exactly carry an urn like this while crawling around on all fours."

Alec chuckled at the thought. The urn would be taller than Collin in fur.

Collin's running commentary during the drive kept their thoughts from turning overly melancholy. "I took your advice and applied for a temp agency. They placed me at the Franklin Park Conservatory along with one of the other temp workers, doing some custodial work and event setup while their full-time employee is out on maternity leave."

Alec nudged him. "Just try to keep your paws out of the customers' pockets, huh?"

No surprise that the comment went ignored. Collin couldn't stop stealing any more than he could stop breathing. It was in his nature to do so.

The moon's song pulsed within Alec as they pulled into the cemetery at dusk. He jumped out the moment the car stopped moving and lifted his face to the sky. The scents of the forest washed over him, centering and grounding him. Whispers of the wind in the trees called Alec home. Fur prickled along his arms while tension thrummed throughout his frame.

Soon, he promised, and the power receded.

Ari bumped her shoulder against Alec's arm as they set off, hiking south on the trail. On a normal night, Alec would start his run near the trailhead, but carrying everything to their destination on foot rather than in fur would be easier.

"How much longer do we have to walk?" A mere ten minutes into their hike, and Collin was already whining.

Alec shook his head and suppressed a grin. The kid was *such* a city boy. "Why don't you change early and ride on Ari's shoulder? Then you don't have to walk. You can even stash your stuff in my duffel since you didn't bring a bag."

Ari huffed indignantly. "He is *not* riding on my shoulder. Besides, we do not have much further to travel and have already passed the cave."

Halfway there.

The trickle of the Irish Run echoed in the distance. They weren't heading all the way to the stream but to a natural sandstone bridge over a nearby ravine. Ari had once told him it was a popular place for photographers during the day, but when the moon rose high, the bridge took on a more preternatural purpose.

As the footing became less stable, Alec grabbed onto Ari to steady them both. Collin remained close on their heels the entire time. When they arrived at the bridge, Alec set his pack down, and Ari rummaged through the bag for her supplies.

"Collin, please place the urn in the middle of the bridge." Ari produced her incense sticks from the bag. Alec fought back a sneeze as the harsh scent tickled his nose. He remained below while the pair climbed up onto the bridge.

"Is that rice?" Collin asked.

Ari hummed an affirmative. The rice was for Oliver to take with him to the beyond. It was one tradition that Ari insisted they follow. Everyone needed food, after all. Even the dead.

Alec slipped into the small cave that had formed at the base of the bridge, taking the duffel with him. While Collin and Ari were busy setting up, Alec undressed. Removing his gloves, Alec tucked them securely in the outside pocket of the bag. He carefully folded his scarf around his sunglasses then tossed the rest haphazardly on top of the bag.

Prickling with anticipation, Alec reached deep down inside and *pulled*.

For a moment, he froze.

His skin was too tight.

The rush of blood pounded in his ears.

Alec's back arched, and phantom pain flared down his spine as he fell to all fours, panting from the exertion.

He was free.

The scents of the forest and Ari's burning incense sharpened around him. Reminded of his purpose, Alec took a moment to stretch out his limbs, bowing low on his forelegs. Carefully, he made his way back to the base of the bridge to stand sentinel as Ari softly began her chant.

Rustling alerted Alec before a squirrel latched on to his tail and scurried up to perch on his shoulder. Alec snorted at Collin, shaking his head to dislodge him, but Collin held fast. Giving up, Alec returned his attention to the task at hand. The scent of the incense grew stronger, mixed with the ashes of the deceased as Ari opened the urn.

Prickles of energy danced along his fur as the forest fell still.

Waiting.

The wind picked up in time with Ari's chanting until it grew into a haunting melody, blowing through the trees. Alec's howl joined the chorus, a mournful cry of loss and regret. Deep in the forest, coyotes added their own somber tone.

They sang for those who came before them.

They anguished for those who had left this world far too soon.

They called out to the ancestors to watch over and guide them.

They stood vigil as the moon danced her way through the night sky.

As the wind grew soft, and the last of the song echoed through the forest, they said goodbye.

6

DAMIEN SLAMMED his laptop closed and rubbed his eyes after staring at cold case files all day. The John Doe file on his desk caught his eye. Damien grabbed the file and wandered over to Candice and Andy's workstation.

Candice smiled softly at him. "You look tired, Damien."

Oh, he was beyond tired. If his insomnia wasn't keeping him awake, the nightmares were making sure he didn't stay asleep. Damien wasn't positive he knew what sleep was anymore. Opting to ignore the comment, Damien held up the folder. "Hey, have we heard from the FBI yet?"

It had only been three days, but maybe they'd be lucky.

Andy shook his head. "No. I tried following up, but I kept hitting brick walls. I'm thinking it would be more efficient to just bang my head against my desk and skip the rest."

Or ... not. Damien sighed. Just great.

"Damien! My office." Damien whipped his head

around at the sharp edge to Kat's hard voice. She didn't look happy as she glared at him from her office doorway. Confident she had his attention, Kat spun and stalked back inside the room.

"Wonder what that's about." Damien didn't dare speak too loudly lest his captain hear him.

Candice leaned in, keeping her voice just as low. "She's been in meetings with the chief of police all day. That's always enough to stick a bug in her craw."

"Ah, best not keep her waiting, then."

"Good luck."

"Close the door behind you," Kat demanded as Damien entered her office. She waited pointedly as he complied and took a seat. "We're closing the John Doe case effective immediately."

Straight to the point, then. Damien blinked in shock. "Wait, we're just *closing* the case?"

"We don't have a body, and, as you well know, the ME report listed Doe's death as a heart attack due to old age. There is no case. The BCI Missing Persons Unit will continue to search for Mr. Stone. You are to hand all pertinent case files over to them before you leave today. Dismissed."

Damn.

The order shouldn't surprise him. She'd all but told him that much on Friday, but why the hell would they just give up on a John Doe? It didn't sit right with him, but he was already pushing his luck by questioning her order the first time.

"Yes, ma'am." He stood and turned to open the door.

Back in the bullpen, Damien strode back to Candice's workstation, where he'd left the Doe file. She glanced up at him as he approached, an eyebrow raised in question. He let out a resigned breath before breaking the news to his officer liaisons. "They shut the case down."

"What? Why?"

"No fucking clue. It makes no sense, but can you pull together your case notes for me? I need to get the information sent over to BCI before I leave. They're at least going to keep looking for Stone." Not that it mattered. The Stone file would end up at the bottom of someone's pile somewhere and would never be seen again.

He hated giving up on cases.

Damien was long past due to go home when he finished collecting and sending the files off. He grabbed his bag and headed out to his SUV. "I need a drink."

Sitting in a bar was better than brooding in his tiny apartment anyway.

Monday nights at Sister's Bar and Grill were typically quiet, with only a few of the area regulars peppered around the various tables. It was also conveniently located across the street from his apartment complex. Damien parked his SUV, headed straight for the bar, and ordered a rum and Coke.

"Tough day?" Deci asked as she returned with the drink.

Damien groaned and dropped his head on his arms. "You could say that again. I feel like everything I've done for the past two weeks was a complete and utter waste of time."

"You sound tired, Detective." Damien perked up a little at the slight brogue that he recognized lacing the words. Alec sat at a table near the bar, smiling shyly at Damien. The late afternoon sun streaming in the windows reflected off his mirrored sunglasses.

Damien lifted his glass in salute. "Understatement of the year. I'm Damien, by the way."

"Damien, then." A faint flush spread over Alec's cheeks. "I'm Alec."

The blush on the younger man was adorable. Damien grabbed his drink and approached Alec's table. "Do you mind if I sit here?"

"No, not at all. I'd love for you to join me. I was just about to order dinner if you want to eat with me?" Alec winced at the end of his rambling.

Damien chuckled softly and sat down across from Alec, who sat in nervous silence. Time to break the ice. "So, do you come here often?"

Smooth, Damien. Real smooth.

Alec tugged at his fingerless leather gloves and nodded silently. Well, that didn't work. Damien reached across the table to rest his hand lightly on both of Alec's. The fidgeting stilled instantly. Alec sucked in a soft breath at the contact before blowing it out with a self-deprecating laugh. "Sorry. Yes. I live a few blocks from here, so it's convenient for me."

"Really? I'm across the street. I'm surprised we haven't run into each other before recently."

An awkward silence fell between them. If only Damien could see Alec's eyes. What color were they? Why did he hide them? There's no way Alec was—

"Are the two of you ready to order?" Deci asked as she set a drink in front of Alec.

Damien pulled his hand away and took a sip of his own drink.

"Wait. Let me guess." She turned to Damien and studied him intently. "You look like you're in the mood for wings tonight, Detective O'Connor. How about the ... smoky chipotle?"

Damn, she was good. Damien always ordered wings when he was having a rotten day. Though the present company had quickly improved his mood. "That sounds like a plan, Deci."

She smiled brightly and turned to Alec. "And for Alec, four smokehouse burgers with a side of fries. Unless you want to change it up for once? You've been here so often the past two weeks. You must be tired of those by now."

Alec's face burned deep red at the teasing lilt in Deci's voice. Interesting.

Wait. *Four* burgers?

"Oh, he always orders that much food. One could wonder what he does with it all. Look at how lean he is."

Alec was not only lean but built like a runner. A hint of muscle teased Damien through the fitted, gray dress shirt Alec was wearing. A spike of lust flashed through him at the reminder of the way Alec's jeans had cupped his gorgeous ass the last time he'd seen him.

When a soft whimper escaped Alec's lips, Damien took pity on him. The poor guy looked like he wanted the floor to open up and swallow him whole. "Thanks, Deci. I think we're good with that."

"Sounds good. I'll be back with those shortly." She quickly bounced back to the kitchen to submit their order.

Damien stretched his legs out under the table, nudging them against Alec's. The other man flinched away from the contact. Damien immediately backed off and leaned forward. "Hey, you okay? I can get my meal to go if I'm overstaying my welcome here."

ALEC HAD LOST himself in Damien's unique scent blend of vanilla and spice ever since the detective had joined him at the table. That mysterious extra scent he had detected the first night was missing, though. Had he imagined it last time? He was also acting like a fecking nervous teenager. He wasn't even this bad when he *was* a teenager, sneaking around on his father's farm with Konnyer.

Konnyer. Alec hadn't thought of Konnyer much at all after he and Ari had left Ireland. The young farmhand had caught Alec's eye early on with his dark brown hair and piercing, steel blue eyes. Konnyer had been a little taller than Alec. But Alec had never tripped over his tongue when speaking with the young man. Although, he hadn't had much of an opportunity. They rarely spoke, too busy sneaking around at night under the silver moonlight or stealing kisses behind the barn.

What was it about Damien that brought out this behavior in him?

Deci hadn't helped matters by revealing how often he'd been eating here lately. Or how much he usually ate. As she spoke with Damien, that tantalizing scent had joined the vanilla and spice, and Alec finally put a finger on what the scent was.

Arousal.

Was Damien aroused because of Alec? A soft, involuntary sound escaped him upon that revelation. While it wasn't the first time since Konnyer that a man had found him attractive, he was rarely brave enough to act on it anymore.

The last time he'd tried had been an absolute disaster.

Alec flinched at the memory and turned his mind away from that cold, rainy night in New York. The last thing he needed was to be caught up in the past. Nothing good waited for him there.

Damien's words finally broke through Alec's musings, and he sat up straight. Wait, what? Go? "No!" he blurted. Alec groaned at himself as heat flushed his cheeks again. This was borderline ridiculous. "Gods, you must think I'm a complete idiot. Can we just, I don't know, start over?"

A bright smile lit Damien's voice. "Hey, no worries. Let's see. How long have you lived in the area?"

Damien's easygoing attitude settled Alec back on even ground. Except, how was he supposed to answer that question? He'd been living in the greater Columbus area for quite a long time now—longer than would be possible for someone who appeared to be only thirty-one years old.

He could take the question literally to mean the Arena District. "Around nine years now, I think. Something like that. My friend Ari talked me into moving here while my building was still under construction. I'm not entirely sure why she thought I needed a two-bedroom apartment with two bathrooms. I ended up converting the smaller bedroom into an office." Now he was rambling again. Alec clamped his mouth shut.

Damien took Alec's babbling in stride. "I moved here five years ago after I became a detective, and I moved into my current apartment two years ago. I'm originally from Milwaukee, but there weren't any homicide positions open in the districts where I wanted to work."

"What made you pick Ohio?"

"My predecessor recommended me for the position here. I went to college with his nephew. Scott's retired now and living down in Florida."

Did Damien mean Scott Abraham? If so, Scott was definitely *not* in Florida. He'd been a useful contact within the CPD for a long time, but because his Fae glamour had given the impression of aging, his detective persona had reached retirement age five years ago. So Scott went home to Underhill. Much of Scott's family was unfamiliar to Alec. He hadn't been aware the Fae even had a nephew.

"Do you like it here?"

"Oh, I love it here. My coworkers are great. Could do without the ice queen I have for a captain, but beggars can't be choosers." Damien took a sip of his drink. "So you know I'm a homicide detective. What do you do?"

Another tough question. Alec fiddled with the glass of iced tea in front of him, stalling by taking a long sip. He didn't drink alcohol or take anything that compromised his senses too much despite how fast he could metabolize most substances. "I guess you could say that I mentor people. Which, given how our conversation started off, must sound ridiculous to you."

"Don't sell yourself short, Alec. What sort of mentoring?"

Alec didn't really want to lie to Damien about what he did. He took a moment to filter his words before responding. "Life and social skills, believe it or not. Ari and I often help others adapt to changes in their lives. We'll help them find a job, coordinate travel, or even coordinate a total relocation."

"That's the second time you've mentioned Ari. Who is she?"

That was easier to answer. "Ari is like the sister I never had. We've been working together for a very long time. She helped me out of a dark place in my life. I guess you could say that she's *my* mentor." Not only that, but she'd saved his life in more ways than one. Alec lifted his hand to the scarf covering his throat before forcefully pushing the painful memories aside. Now wasn't the time for such thoughts.

Their meal arrived, and Alec fought not to fidget. He'd been so caught up in his own head earlier that he hadn't realized Damien had let Deci put in the order for all four burgers. Alec was starving, though. Werewolf metabolism burned through calories at a ridiculous rate, and he expended more energy than most.

This time, the silence they fell into felt comfortable as each of them dove into their meals.

Alec's face burned again when Damien offered to pay for dinner. Unsure how to turn down the offer—Alec was the one who'd invited the other man to eat with him, after all—he just went with it. This was an entirely unfamiliar experience for him. Ari hadn't been joking when she'd told Collin that Alec had no love life. Hell, he had no *dating* life. He was too afraid of opening himself up that way after the last few times and dating in public like this hadn't been possible back in the thirties.

The few partners he'd had in his long life had left for one reason or another. They often grew frustrated and impatient with his hang-ups, among other things. But Damien made him want to try again.

Why?

When Damien rose to head home, Alec stopped him before he knew what he was doing. Words tumbled unbidden out of his mouth. "Wait, before you go, why don't you text me, so I have your number? I—I really enjoyed this and wouldn't mind doing it again."

Why had he asked that?

But now that the question was out there, Alec couldn't take it back. He didn't want to.

Heat rose to Alec's cheeks, but he rattled off his cell number before he could lose his nerve and held his breath, chewing on his bottom lip. When the phone buzzed in his pocket with the pattern of an unknown number, he sighed in relief.

Damien left after shooting Alec a teasing, "Don't worry, sweetheart. I'd love to see you again."

"That went rather well," Deci informed him as she started clearing the table.

Maybe, but it could've gone far better. "No thanks to you," he muttered, softening his words with a grin.

Nothing could stop the distinct bounce in his step as he headed home.

7

HE HAD BEEN HANGING *in the dark for so long that time held no meaning anymore. Minutes bled into hours. Hours into days. Had they imprisoned him for a week? A month? He didn't know. All he knew was the agony that had become his constant companion and the scent of infection rising from his back.*

He rattled the chains above him. The attempt was futile, but he had to do something to relieve the pressure on his shoulders. He rubbed his face against his arm, once again attempting to dislodge the cover from over his eyes.

If only he could see.

A soft scraping in the distance stilled his movements. His captors were returning.

The deep rumbling brogue of his tormenter echoed through the chamber. "Tch, 'e's no fun anymore. How am I ta take me frustrations out on 'im now? More o' me wolves have succumbed to de bastard's father's hounds."

"Oh, I may have some ideas." The menace in the soft feminine voice sent a chill down his spine.

His tormentor laughed, unhooking the chains from the surrounding walls, and dragged him down the hall.

Blood rushed to his ears as he realized where they were going.

No.

Oh no.

Not again.

DAMIEN SHOT up in bed and flailed around for the lamp switch. Flicking it on, he sucked in a deep, gasping breath as his heart beat an erratic tempo in his ears. He glanced around the small studio apartment, taking in the comforting and familiar sights.

Fucking hell.

His eyes landed on the bedside clock, and he fell back into bed, groaning. It was far too early to be awake on a Saturday. With no active cases, Damien had the day off, and he'd planned to spend the free time catching up on some much-needed sleep.

So much for that pipe dream.

He dragged himself out of bed and pulled some gym shorts and a T-shirt out of his drawer, opting to do something productive rather than let his overactive mind wander. Down in the building's gym, Damien found Tim running on the treadmill. While the gym was free for the use of the building's residents, few people took advantage of it.

Tim nodded in greeting. "Hey Damien, it's been awhile."

"Morning," Damien said through a yawn. "You're up early."

"Eh, I have a meeting with my realtor today. Besides, Frosty usually wakes me up pretty early to go for a walk. He doesn't really appreciate the tiny apartment."

Damien grabbed some weights and started on several warm-up reps. "That's right, you were looking to move. How's that going for you?"

Tim shrugged. "Not very well at all. I had a place all lined up, but it fell through at the last minute. Ari might have a solution for me today, though. I'm meeting her for coffee."

There was that name again. There'd been a short Asian woman outside Tim's apartment a few weeks ago. The name was unusual. Was she the same Ari that Alec knew? He shuddered at the memory of that woman's penetrating gaze. It had stuck with him for days.

They fell into a companionable silence as each went about their workout. Damien popped his headphones in and turned on some classic rock. A short while later, Tim waved backward at Damien on his way out.

After several sets of arm and leg reps and an endurance run on the treadmill, Damien headed back to his apartment to shower. His phone pinged at him with an unread message as he emerged from the bathroom, wiping his damp, dark brown hair with a towel.

Damien grinned when he saw the text was from Alec and sat down on the bed to read the message. *So assuming I haven't scared you off by acting like a complete fool on Monday I was hoping you'd like to grab a coffee or something this weekend.*

The man was too adorable. He could just picture the pretty blush that surely must've followed him sending the text. He replied, *I love coffee. There's a place in North Market I like.*

You mean Stauf's?

A man after his own heart. He glanced at the clock. North Market would open soon. *Got it in one. I'm free this morning if you're up to it?*

Damien watched with amusement as the three little dots flashed on and off on his screen for several minutes. While he waited for the reply, Damien pulled on a pair of fitted jeans and a maroon button-down and finished drying his hair.

Grabbing his wallet and keys, Damien headed out. Even if Alec wasn't up to meeting today, Damien still needed the coffee, and all he had in his apartment was emergency fare. His phone finally pinged with a new message as he opened the door for the stairwell. *Sure can I meet you outside Sisters?*

Damien started down the stairs, typing out a quick, *No problem. I'm on my way now.*

Alec had mentioned that he lived only a few blocks away. It didn't take long to spot him walking down Vine shortly after Damien crossed the street to stand near Sister's Bar and Grill. Alec had his head down and didn't appear to be paying close attention to where he was going, but he easily stepped around people standing in his way.

Damien studied Alec as the younger man approached. He still wore those damned sunglasses, but without a cloud in the sky, the sun was nearly blinding. Too bad Damien's were still in his SUV. Alec's dark brown hair reflected hints of mahogany and amber in the bright daylight. His fitted, long-sleeved shirt pulled just enough to hint at strong biceps.

Damien's cock perked up at the sight.

Alec's nostrils flared as he approached, followed by a shy smile. "Hi."

Chuckling, Damien returned the smile. "Hey, you. C'mon, let's go get that coffee. Maybe even some doughnuts."

"Doughnuts sound good. I can't say I've had any there before. Honestly, I've never been inside. Ari goes there a lot, though." Alec gestured for Damien to take the lead.

Damien brushed Alec's arm with his fingers, unsure of his welcome until Alec leaned into the touch. His hand slid down to rest at the small of Alec's back as they crossed Park Street and into North Market together.

The building was bustling with activity, as many of the shop owners were still setting up for the day. Damien directed them to the right toward the coffee stand. He glanced at the doughnut stall as they passed, but the baker was still hard at work making fresh doughnuts and wasn't ready to open yet. "I have to warn you, my track record hasn't been great here lately. Don't get offended if work calls, and I have to leave."

He had probably just jinxed himself.

Alec laughed at the statement, and the rich sound washed over Damien. He missed this. Work kept him so busy all the time that he rarely spent more than passing moments with other people, coworkers notwithstanding. He hadn't tried dating since arriving in Columbus. Sure, he went to clubs occasionally to pick up a quick fuck, but that just didn't do it for him anymore. With a little over a month until he turned thirty-nine, Damien wanted more.

He hoped Alec could be that more.

"So what do you recommend?" Alec asked as they approached the stall for Stauf's Coffee Roasters.

"Their cold brew is good for this June heat. Otherwise, I usually just keep it simple with an Americano, black. Their fresh-roasted coffee is too good to dilute with cream or sugar."

"So you're a coffee snob, then? Sounds good. I'll try a cold brew."

Damien grinned at the teasing tone in Alec's voice. Nice to see him more relaxed today and not overthinking everything.

They ordered drinks and sat down at an open table near

the counter to wait. Motion from the bakery next door caught Damien's eye. Tim stood nearby with the tiny Asian woman from the other day, this time with four individual braids twisted up into one large one. This must be Ari.

Tim glanced over and smiled warmly after handing Ari a cinnamon twist. "Twice in one day, Damien. This has to be some kind of record."

Alec tilted his head. "You two know each other?"

NORTH MARKET HAD SO many unfamiliar and conflicting scents and sounds that Alec hadn't noticed Tim and Ari approach. He sighed. This was not keeping Damien away from the preternatural world.

Though that'd been the last thing on his mind when he invited Damien out for coffee. Ever since their impromptu dinner date on Monday, Alec couldn't get Damien out of his head. He just wanted to be near the man.

Had Ari planned to meet with Tim today to discuss the options they'd found in Montana and Washington? She'd finally convinced him last week that West Virginia was a bad idea. Why hadn't she invited Alec?

Damien's hand rested on Alec's knee under the table as he turned to answer Alec's question. The touch soothed Alec's wandering thoughts. "Tim lives in the apartment right below me, actually."

"Really," Alec said absently as Tim and Ari took a seat

across from him. What was it about Damien that distracted him so completely?

"And you must be Ari? These two both speak highly of you." Wait. Tim had mentioned Ari to Damien?

"Have they now?" Ari asked. Alec winced at the subtle disapproval in her tone. Was her ire directed at both of them or just at Tim? Alec saw no reason for her to be upset, but she seemed a little off again today.

"I understand you're trying to help Tim find somewhere to move." Damien either didn't notice her irritation or ignored it completely. "Make sure the house is big enough for that beast he adopted last month, though."

"Yes, that creature complicates matters a bit, doesn't it?" Ari chuckled, dissipating the building tension. Alec admired Damien's ability to diffuse situations even when he wasn't fully aware of the subtext. It was part of what had drawn him to the man in the first place.

"How do you two know each other?" Tim asked.

"Actually, we kept running into each other at the bar across the street," Damien replied. "You know, this guy has some impressive moves. He rescued a kid from some drunks last month."

Heat crawled up Alec's cheeks at the admiration in Damien's voice. With any luck, it was too dark in the building for anyone to notice.

When their coffee arrived, he and Damien left in search of doughnuts. Damien let out a little cheer as they approached the stand. "Yes! They have caramel apple again today. You've got to try these. They're my favorite."

Alec grinned at the man's excitement. It was cute. "That sounds fantastic."

The items at the stand filled his nose with several conflicting scents. While they waited in line to order, he picked apart threads of chocolate, caramel, apples and ... lavender?

Damien cursed when an obnoxious ringtone blared from his phone. "You've got to be kidding me. Sorry, Alec, I have to take this." He stepped away, but Alec could still hear him. "O'Connor."

There was a woman on the line who had a cold, clipped voice. Alec tuned the call out to give Damien some privacy and stepped aside to wait. It didn't take long.

Damien sighed when he returned. "I have to go."

Alec fought to keep the disappointment out of his voice. "You warned me."

"I'm sorry. I'll call you later. Maybe we can try dinner again."

Smiling softly, Alec nodded. "I'd like that."

Alec frowned after Damien left. The man had been so excited about the doughnuts and didn't get the chance to order any. Approaching the counter, Alec ordered a half dozen of the caramel apple in one container and a few more separately for himself. As an afterthought, he added a few of the lavender doughnuts to his order.

Tim was standing alone near the coffee shop when Alec

worked his way back over to him. "Hey, Tim, could you do me a favor and make sure Damien gets these?" Alec held up the box in his hand.

"Did he get called in to work again?" Tim laughed and grabbed the package. "He will love you for this."

A warm feeling settled in Alec's gut at the thought. "I don't know about that."

"Hey, don't sweat it. Could you thank Ari for me? I'll watch for the details about the Montana Independent community. Kalispell sounds perfect. I'll make sure Damien gets his doughnuts."

"Wasn't Ari just over here with you?"

"She stepped away to take a call. I think she's over by the Park Street entrance."

Thanking Tim, Alec found Ari just outside North Market, eating a salty pretzel. Hadn't she been eating a cinnamon twist?

They walked back toward his apartment together. Ari nudged him playfully after a few blocks. "I saw you with that detective by the doughnut stall, and I wish you had seen how that man was looking at you. I am happy for you, Little Wolf."

Alec fidgeted. "I don't even know what I'm doing."

"You are doing just fine." Soft fingers brushed his cheek. "Have you told him?"

A knot formed in the pit of his stomach. Alec felt cold at the thought, a flicker of panic crawling up his spine. The thought terrified him. "N-no, I haven't."

Damien would leave if he found out the truth.

Ari hummed thoughtfully and patted his arm, seemingly oblivious to the direction his thoughts had taken. "He will figure it out, you know. He *is* a detective."

Before Alec could respond, Collin called out a greeting from the entrance to the apartment complex. Alec had never been so grateful for the little thief. "Oh, hey, Ari! Mr. Channing! I was just trying to buzz in."

"Really, Collin?" Alec grumbled. The kid was such a brat. "What are you doing here anyway?"

There was a slight pause. Alec raised his eyebrow. "Well, I was actually kind of hoping we could finish listening to that show we started two weeks ago."

That ... was not what he had expected. Alec grinned. "I'd love to. Ari, you should join us. I'm sure Collin would love to hear about the trolls."

Ari groaned. "If you insist."

Collin filled Ari and Alec in on his temp work at the Conservatory on the way up the elevator to the fourth floor. It sounded like he was really enjoying himself.

"Oh! The other temp I've been working with? She's beautiful." Collin sighed dreamily. "I'm thinking about asking her out on a date."

"Hey, don't look at me for advice. Not only am I not interested in women, but I can barely navigate dating men. You could try listening to some of my audiobooks, though." Maybe someone could make use of them.

Collin groaned dramatically and smacked Alec on the arm. "That is *so* not happening."

It'd been worth a try.

"Why not, Collin? He does not appreciate them." The warmth in Ari's tone belied her words.

Alec opened the door to his apartment and disabled the security. "Oh, before I forget, Ari. Tim asked me to thank you."

"What ever for?" Ari asked, bewildered.

Alec frowned at her confusion. "He said that you two decided on Kalispell. It sounded like he was expecting contact information for the local Independents."

"I see. How about we start the show, hmm?"

Alec set the box of doughnuts on the counter, pulling out a couple of plates and grabbing a lavender doughnut for himself. "I picked these up in North Market. Do either of you want any?"

Collin squealed and grabbed at least two before taking them into the living room to devour. "Thanks, Mr. Channing!"

Ari hummed a negative. "I cannot say that I particularly care for doughnuts, if I am being honest. I appreciate the gesture, though, Little Wolf. I will have some tea instead."

Hadn't she had one the other day? She'd seemed to enjoy it then. Alec shook his head, rubbing absently at his temple, and sat down in the living room. He queued up the second part of *War of the Worlds* and settled in to listen.

DAMIEN PULLED into the small parking area off Scioto Boulevard behind the city patrol units and several EMT vehicles from the nearby fire station. A teenage girl sat crying in the back of an ambulance, a warming blanket wrapped around her shoulders, while a teenage boy stood nearby speaking with an EMT. He kept glancing back at what Damien assumed was his girlfriend.

An officer whom Damien recognized as the initial rookie guarding the door for the Stone case last month waved him over to the nearby walking trail. "Detective O'Connor! Officers Jones and Lawrence are waiting for you down by the bank."

He followed the officer down the path and through the trees toward the embankment under the Greenlawn Avenue overpass. As they neared the shore, the officer held up a vial of Vicks VapoRub. Damien raised his eyebrow but shook his head at the offer. "That bad, huh?"

"Doctor Whitehall thinks the body had been in the river at least a few weeks and ashore for at least a day. With the heat we've had lately, well ..." The officer gestured toward the body surrounded by CSU techs. Candice and Andy stood a few feet away, looking a little green around the gills.

Emily glanced up and smiled at Damien in greeting, ever the unflappable ME. She stood and pulled off her gloves, stepping carefully around the scene to approach them. "Good morning, Detective."

"What've you got for me, Em?" Damien asked, standing far enough upwind from the body to avoid needing the VapoRub.

"Jane Doe has several superficial lacerations along her hands and feet, likely from scraping along the bottom of the river. There are deeper lacerations on the shoulder and neck and what appear to be defensive wounds on the forearms. I suspect COD is exsanguination from a severed carotid artery. I will confirm with an autopsy, but it's probable that Jane Doe entered the river postmortem somewhere upstream."

"Fuck, that complicates things. Identification?" Any hope for that faded with the grim set of Emily's lips as she shook her head.

"We'll try to dry her out a bit and get some viable prints, but enough skin has sloughed off that we will be lucky to achieve a partial. The techs are going to scour the banks for the crime scene, but given the evidence, Jane Doe has been floating long enough that she could've traveled for miles."

Unfortunately, it could take months before her entry point into the river could be located. With arterial spray from a carotid, chances were high that a crime scene with a lot of blood had existed somewhere. Given how much time had passed, the scene could either be in a secluded area, or outside, where the rain would've washed away any evidence. Hell, it could be somewhere else entirely—probably sanitized by the perpetrator.

The first option was the most ideal, as there would still be evidence to collect.

Which meant reality was likely door number two or even three.

Keeping upwind of the body, Damien circled around for a better look. Scrapes and lacerations covered much of the victim's hands and feet, peppered with small rocks and mud from the river bottom. Long locks of dark brown hair were twisted in an unruly mess around sticks and weeds. Jane Doe had likely been a beautiful woman, her high cheekbones still visible despite the bloating.

Such a waste.

"The kids up by the ambulance found her," Andy said as he came to stand next to Damien. "They were fooling around just behind the trees when the wind shifted."

Damien whistled low at the lacerations across the victim's neck and upper back as Emily carefully lifted the body to slide a transport board underneath. "What the hell? Those almost look like claw marks."

"No animal I've ever seen does this sort of damage and then tosses the body in the river." Candice pursed her lips. "And who would find a body mauled by an animal and decide to throw it in the water instead of calling the police?"

"Well, if they want to avoid attention for other reasons, they might. Why don't you two head back and check with special ops? They might have some idea of places to check along the river." After seeing the officers off, Damien checked in with the teams that were out searching the shore for evidence.

By the time he pulled into his parking spot at home, exhaustion had crept into Damien's bones. The entire day had turned out to be an exercise in futility. Sorensen had provided a list of possible locations, and Damien had met Candice and Andy at the most likely options while Young checked in with some of his contacts in the seedier neighborhoods. Aside from some dirty looks, all access points to the river turned up empty.

It was like finding a needle in a haystack in the dark with mittens on.

With his mind racing through various possibilities, Damien almost tripped over the box sitting next to his apartment door. Snatching it up, he entered the apartment and flipped on the lights. Scrawled across the top of the box was the message: *Alec wanted you to have these. -Tim.*

A slow grin spread across Damien's lips as he hurried to get out a plate and pop a doughnut in the microwave for a few seconds—just enough to make it soft and gooey again. Damien groaned as the taste of caramel and apples hit his tongue.

With any luck, the gesture meant Damien's job hadn't already ruined his chances with Alec. Wiping his hand on a towel, he pulled out his phone and typed out a quick message. *You're the best, Alec. Thanks for the doughnuts. Sorry it's so late. I'll call soon. Goodnight.*

8

ALEC SAT up in bed as the insistent buzz of Ari's ringtone started again. He struggled to shove the grogginess aside and fumbled on the nightstand for his phone. If she was calling this early—what time was it?—it had to be something important. "Hello?"

"Meet me downstairs, Little Wolf. There has been another attack. Pack a bag."

Feck.

The last of the sleepiness fled as adrenaline flooded Alec's system, and he jumped out of bed to pull his duffel out of the closet. While the scent of incense had faded a bit in the past few weeks, Alec still sneezed several times while filling it with essentials. He really should've replaced his bag after that night.

Guilt flooded him all over again. He had failed Oliver.

If this new wolf survived, he would do better.

Be better.

Outside, Vincent had the car idling in a visitor's spot. Alec slid in beside Ari and tapped the partition to let Vincent know he was settled. "Where are we heading?"

"Indianapolis. Diego Ortiz called me a short while ago. He intercepted a patient brought into the ER at IU Health. She is still unconscious, but he believes she will survive." Ari rested a hand on Alec's forearm in reassurance. "We will ensure it."

Diego maintained a private practice, rotating through emergency rooms at several hospitals throughout Indiana and Ohio as a trauma surgeon. Ari had pulled strings to allow the werejaguar to operate across state lines, so he could keep an eye out for situations such as this one. While attacks were typically rare, despite the alarming fact that the community had dealt with so many over the past six months, accidents still happened.

The sun had finally risen by the time they arrived at the hospital, meaning it was just after six in the morning. Alec stretched as he stepped out of the car, stiff from the long drive, and turned his head toward Diego as the doctor approached them. "Alec, Ari, so glad you could come on such short notice. The patient's name is Jessica Harper. Jessica woke up a few minutes ago, and I started a morphine line to keep her pain levels manageable and reduce the amount of attention she draws. It won't last long, but hopefully long enough that we can get her transported."

"The change has started already?" With a purposeful click in her stride, Ari pivoted to head inside. "Then we must hurry. I do not believe she will make it back to Columbus today."

"Unfortunately, yes. They brought her in just after ten last night. I didn't start my shift until midnight and didn't discover her until my rounds at two a.m. I've already arranged a safe house for you, given how much time has passed. The ambulance is on standby."

Alec followed the pair into the hospital as they ironed out the arrangements for transport. This meant they would remain in Indianapolis for at least a week. Sighing, he reached into his pocket for his phone to let Damien know he wouldn't be available for that dinner ... only to find his pocket empty. Did he put his phone in his duffel? Too late to check now.

Inside, they turned down several hallways through a twisting corridor until they arrived at the private room Diego had secured for Jessica. The sharp scent of blood, carnage, and wolf assaulted Alec as soon as they entered the room, and Jessica thrashed wildly on the bed, rattling the frame, her heart thundering in Alec's ears. She was going to hurt herself.

Diego swore. "Shit. Alec, hold her arms."

Racing further into the room, Alec bumped his knee on a piece of medical equipment. Ari steadied him before he could trip. "Go around to the left, Little Wolf. I am just behind you."

"She ripped her stitches and isn't far enough along to heal these leg wounds yet." Diego raised his voice. "Jessica, this is Doctor Ortiz. I need you to calm down as much as you can, okay?"

"It burns!" Jessica smacked Alec in the abdomen before he could get a good grip on her arm, the tangy scent of fear rising from her in waves. "Let go of me, it hurts!"

Finally getting hold of Jessica's left arm, Alec reached for the right. Jessica screamed and tried to twist out of his grip, but he held fast.

Ari stepped up alongside Alec, resting a hand just next to his on Jessica's left shoulder. Sparks of Ari's power tingled along Alec's arm. Finally, Jessica fell still, her heart slowing to a steady rhythm. "This is a temporary calm I planted into her mind. She will begin healing within the hour, Diego. Forget the stitches. Just bandage her up so we can get moving. Her mind is already fighting the suggestion."

"Right, I forgot you could do that. Okay. Stay right here. I'll be back." Diego left the room, presumably to get help with moving Jessica to the ambulance.

"Who are you people?" Jessica asked, much calmer now under Ari's influence.

"Never mind that for now. Can you tell us what you recall?"

"I just got off the closing shift at the diner. The light in the parking lot was out, and it was dark." Jessica sucked in a sharp breath. "Something grabbed me from behind. I ran and ... there was an animal of some kind. It caught me by the legs ... the next thing I knew, I woke up here. Ow, fuck, that burns."

Alec switched his grip on her arms to one hand and stroked Jessica's shoulder as her muscles tensed and her teeth chattered. Frowning, Alec pressed the back of his hand to her forehead. "She's burning up, Ari." Oliver had spiked a fever as well but not this high. The werevirus was just that—a virus. One that would attack her system until it either won, or her body destroyed itself. A high fever was not a promising start.

"That is to be expected, given the severity of her wounds. Do not worry, Little Wolf, this one will pull through."

Diego returned a few minutes later with a couple of orderlies. Moving quickly, they got Jessica situated and secured to a gurney to prevent her doing further injury to herself or those around her. Alec followed them out to the waiting ambulance and climbed in, settling down next to Jessica for the ride.

By the time they arrived at the safe house just outside of the city, Jessica had started thrashing again. No amount of morphine would help her at this point. Alec and the EMT who had driven them—some kind of bird shifter that Alec didn't know—carried her inside and into the first bedroom they came across, with the EMT leading the way.

While Alec hated doing it, they strapped her into soft restraints attached to the bed. Jessica struggled against the bindings, completely lost in the pain and fever as every cell in her body morphed into something new. Something that would allow her to become a wolf on the next full moon.

Ari patted Alec's shoulder as he pulled up a chair to settle in for the long week. "I will sit with her for now and help her through the worst of it. Our bags are still outside with the car. Have Vincent bring them inside and go get some rest."

Nodding, Alec headed outside.

9

ALEC WAS AVOIDING HIM.

Damien sighed and set his phone down without sending a text. It had been a week since the interrupted coffee date, and he tried to ignore the little voice in his head telling him that his job was the reason for the radio silence. Maybe those doughnuts had been more of a "sorry, this isn't going to work out" message rather than an "I'm really interested in you, let's do this again" sort of gesture.

Granted, he'd been busy over the past week with the Jane Doe they'd pulled out of the Scioto River, but he'd reached out whenever the opportunity arose. The potential was there, but it took an effort on both sides to create something.

North Market would open soon, though. Maybe he should suggest trying the coffee date again.

The mocking ringtone on his phone interrupted Damien's thoughts. "Who needs days off anyway?" he muttered to himself as he picked up the phone. "O'Connor."

"A couple found a body on the walking trail in Franklin Park this morning. Just north of the amphitheater parking lot. The ME and CSU are already at the scene. Officers Jones and Lawrence are en route." Kat hung up without a greeting or farewell.

Well, fuck.

So much for that.

Was it any wonder Alec hadn't answered his texts?

It was early enough that Sunday morning traffic wasn't too bad on Broad Street. Damien pulled in behind several police cruisers on Conservatory Drive half an hour after taking the call. Someone had called extra officers in to hold back the growing crowd of gawkers while others strung police tape between the trees. Damien sighed. No doubt the press was already on their way.

Damien spotted Candice first and hurried over to her. "What've we got?" he asked.

"Mr. and Mrs. Daniels' dog discovered the vic this morning. It dragged the body out of the bushes below the decorative bridge a little further up the path. Andy is over in the parking lot speaking to the couple now." Damien followed Candice's gesture at an older couple with a large German shepherd tied to a post next to them.

The animal pulled hard at his leash. Hopefully, they wouldn't have a repeat of the last time a dog was at a crime scene.

Emily glanced up as they approached. "Good morning, Detective. That dog not only found and dragged this body out into the open but shook the ever-loving crap out of it in the process. Look at this."

"Is that your professional opinion, Em?" Damien blinked down at the victim. This John Doe was an older male, likely in his late eighties. There was a large tear in the button-down shirt near the shoulder, where presumably the dog had latched onto him. Several scrapes covered the exposed skin along with dirt and debris.

"Most of the damage appears to be postmortem. Likely from the dog. So far, I'm not seeing anything that could've killed him, but based on the early stage of rigor mortis, I would say he hasn't been here long. Early time of death estimate is between four and seven this morning. I can pin the TOD down further back at the lab."

Damien stared down at the body, taking in the wiry frame and shaggy hair. A sense of familiarity flashed through him. Had he seen this man somewhere before?

Pulling on a pair of gloves, Damien squatted down to slip his hand into the victim's back pocket. He retrieved and flipped open the wallet he found, gaping at the youthful twenty-two-year-old face staring up at him with round, onyx eyes. "No fucking way," he breathed, causing Emily and Candice to glance over at him sharply.

"Collin Wilde," Candice read from over his shoulder. "Do you know him?"

He'd only met the kid briefly at the bar the night he met Alec, but he definitely recognized him. "No, but I know someone who does. I only saw him once during a bar fight, and I think he was the subject of the fight, but he bolted when I approached. I wonder why this guy has Collin's wallet."

According to the license, Collin lived close to the Community College. Damien took a quick picture with his phone.

Checking the remaining pockets, he found a temporary employee badge for the Conservatory with Collin's name printed neatly across the bottom. Some dried leaves had slipped inside the plastic cover. He passed the badge and wallet over to Candice, who stuck each item into evidence bags for CSU.

The other pocket held three watches, a handful of coins, and a tube of lipstick. Damien stared down at the haul, struck by the similarity to the items he recalled lined up across the pool table that night. No other identification was located anywhere on the body.

Shaking his head, he glanced up and studied the victim's face. "This guy looks so much like Collin. It's unreal." Damien held his findings up for Candice to see. "When I saw the kid, he was pulling a bunch of stuff just like this out of his pockets. I think he was a pickpocket or something."

Candice pulled another evidence bag out of her pocket and held it open for him. She raised her eyebrow. "So what are you saying, Damien? You can't possibly be implying that this old man is that kid."

"No. I don't know. This is like the Stone case all over again." He gestured at the badge in her hand. "Why don't you and Andy find out if Collin works there? If we can track him down, maybe the kid can shed some light on who our victim is. I'll reach out to my own contact and see what I can find out." If Alec would answer the phone. Damien clenched his jaw. This was not exactly how he'd planned to reconnect with the man.

"Will do." Candice passed everything over to the nearest CSU tech and stalked off in search of her partner, muttering "no comment" at the press, who had started shouting questions her way from the perimeter.

Back in his SUV, Damien stared down at his phone for a long while before pushing the shortcut for Alec's contact on his home screen. *Here goes nothing.*

The phone rang several times and flipped over to voice-mail. Damn.

Resigned, Damien left a message. "Alec, this is Damien. I'm sorry for running out on you so suddenly last weekend." *Get to the point, O'Connor.*

"Hey, I'm actually calling because I need to talk to that kid from the night we met. Collin? I have a couple of questions for him and would really appreciate it if you could help me get in touch with him. It's important." Damien winced. Yeah, because just calling to talk to Alec *wasn't* important. Foot, meet mouth. "Well, I hope to hear from you soon."

Tossing his phone in the cup holder, Damien punched Collin's address into his GPS. The address turned out to be a small brick apartment complex with exterior access to all the units. Double-checking the ID, he looked for unit eight.

Silence met his two official raps on the first-floor door. He stepped over to the window and peered inside. The apartment was completely empty. "Well, I doubt he lives here." With one last look inside, Damien returned to his car.

He would just have to wait for Alec to reach out to him.

Or hunt the man down himself.

10

ALEC FELL face-first into his bed the moment he entered his bedroom, realizing at the last minute that he'd forgotten to take his glasses off. He slapped his hands out in front of him before he could land on his face and pushed himself over onto his back instead.

Groaning, Alec rubbed grit from his eyes and resettled the glasses.

The past week had been a test of his nerves. Ari's assurance that Jessica would make it through the change had kept him going, but her fever had taken three days to break, spiking to dangerous levels several times.

They'd even called Diego in to help treat the symptoms with fluids not readily on hand at the safe house. While Alec had thought Oliver's change was bad, Jessica's ended up ten times worse. Neither situation was normal for the werecreatures he'd helped through the change in the past.

Of course, his own change had been just as dangerous and painful. Or so Ari had informed him.

Several times.

Alec had also forgotten his fecking phone at home in the rush to get to Jessica.

"Alexa, do I have messages?" he asked, almost afraid of the answer.

"You have twenty-five unread text messages and four voicemails," the device announced through the custom messaging system he used. Fantastic.

"Anything from Damien?"

"Five text messages and two voicemails are from Damien O'Connor. Which would you like to start with?"

"Read the texts first." He would listen to those and then try to get some sleep before dealing with the rest. They'd driven all night to get Jessica settled at Ari's house just before dawn. He'd waited a few hours for Jessica to fall asleep before asking Vincent to take him home.

The texts started out with Damien touching base, apologizing for being so busy with the new case he was on. Alec felt bad and made a mental note to get the sweet man more doughnuts when the shop opened as an apology for disappearing all week. The last text had Alec sitting up in bed, sleep forgotten.

"I'm not sure if you got my voicemail, but it's urgent that you get back to me about Collin."

What about Collin? "Alexa, play the voicemails from Damien."

The first message was fairly vague. *"Hey, I'm actually calling because I need to talk to that kid from the night we met. Collin? I have a couple of questions for him and would really appreciate it if you could help me get in touch with him. It's important. Well, I hope to hear from you soon."*

Alec kicked himself again for forgetting his phone. Damien sounded so unsure. The second voicemail was short. *"Alec, call me back when you get this, no matter what time. I haven't been able to track down Collin or find anyone who can give me his number. Thanks."*

Grabbing the offending device and the Bluetooth earbud off the nightstand, Alec dragged himself out of bed. "Alexa, what time is it?"

"The time is 7:52 a.m."

Perfect. By the time he walked down there, North Market would be opening. "Alexa, compose a text message to Damien," he said, waiting for the tone to indicate the device was ready. "Damien, I'm sorry I haven't gotten back to you this week. Where can I meet you question mark."

It had taken Alec a long time to get used to composing text messages via voice, but it was a useful tool.

Arriving at North Market, he stopped by the doughnut stall. They didn't have the caramel apple, so he picked up an assortment of the other flavors instead. Damien's reply came through while he was waiting for the cold brew coffees at Stauf's. Alec listened through his earbud.

"I'm at the precinct. Ask for me at the receptionist, and she will direct you to my desk."

Well, this would be interesting. He called Vincent to pick him up.

DAMIEN I'M *sorry I haven't gotten back to you this week where can I meet you?*

Damien couldn't help the silly grin on his face as he read the text from Alec. He quickly typed out a reply then sent a message off to Janice at the front desk to let her know to expect a visitor.

"You look like a cat who just got cream," Candice said as she approached his desk with a file. They had all started work early to chase down some kind of lead on the new John Doe case while they waited for the initial autopsy.

This case pushed their Jane Doe from the river lower on the priority list. BCI would continue to track down her identity and next of kin, but they had so little to go on with her that they would have a better chance of predicting the lottery.

"What've you got for me?" he asked.

"Not a lot. Collin is working at the Conservatory through a temp agency. There's one other employee from the agency working there with him, but they're being dodgy when I ask about her or the name of the agency itself. All I know so far is that the two of them are filling in for the maintenance director while she's on maternity leave. Neither one of them showed up for work yesterday."

"Did they have a current residence on file for him?"

Candice pursed her lips. "No, and I swear the information on this kid is thinner than Mr. Stone's, and that's saying something. It's almost like he never existed at all."

Could Collin be a runaway? It would explain a lot. Hopefully, Alec could shed some light on the subject for them. "I haven't been able to track down any previous employment either. My contact is on his way into the office, so maybe we'll catch a break when he gets here."

She raised her brow at that. "Really?"

Damien turned his head at a shout from Sorensen. "Hey, I hope some of those are for us!"

Alec stood in the doorway behind Janice, holding a box of doughnuts and a carrier tray with two coffees from Stauf's. Damien's heart gave a stupid little flip as he rose to greet Alec. "Get your own, Jerry."

Alec stood stock-still at the sudden attention, a faint flush creeping up his cheeks. Damien quickly strode over to him and directed him back into the hallway toward a conference room. "Thanks, Janice," he said over his shoulder.

She grinned and gave him a tiny thumbs-up behind Alec's back.

Shaking his head, Damien gestured at the doughnuts and coffee. "You didn't have to do this. Not that I'm complaining," he amended quickly.

Alec chuckled as they entered the small room and sat next to each other at the table. "I wanted to. Um, they didn't have the flavor you told me you liked, so I got a little of everything."

Damien's mouth watered as he opened the box and selected a peanut butter buckeye. "This is quite the spread here. You really can't go wrong with any of their flavors. Seriously, thank you. I had to come in so early today, I haven't even had breakfast yet."

Shifting in his seat, Alec fiddled with his gloves. "So, you wanted to talk about Collin?"

Right, business before pleasure. Damien pulled out his small notebook. "We found a body in Franklin Park yesterday morning along with Collin's wallet and ID badge for the Conservatory. I was hoping you had a way to get in touch with him."

"Why are you looking for him? Do you think he had something to do with this?" Alec asked worriedly.

"No, not at the moment. But he might be a witness, or at the very least, he might know our victim. There was no ID on the body."

Alec let out a soft breath. "I can try getting in touch with him for you. If he knows you're looking, he might go to ground."

"What else can you tell me about him? I stopped by the apartment listed on his ID, but it was vacant."

"That's not surprising. I actually just got home this morning. We've been out of town all week, and I forgot my phone. There are messages I haven't listened to yet, so maybe he reached out to me. I can let you know after I've checked."

Damien could tell Alec was hedging, but why? Rather than push too hard—he'd been honest that Collin wasn't a suspect yet—he let the topic go for the moment. "Okay. Do you know anything about the work he's been doing at the Conservatory? He has a coworker from the temp agency."

"Not really. I know his coworker is a woman. Collin was gushing over her last week. I think he was planning to ask her out." Alec opened his mouth to say more then clamped it shut. Damien made a quick note to dig further into the coworker. "Is that all, Detective?"

Detective, not Damien. He cocked an eyebrow at the distancing technique, but Alec just stared at him from behind his mirrored lenses. "For now. I might have some follow-up questions for you later. You'll let me know if you get in touch with Collin?"

"I will."

DAMIEN WAS TOO easy to talk to. Alec's penchant for babbling in front of the detective had almost had him saying too much. He'd finally had to remind himself that in that moment, he was talking to Detective O'Connor and not just Damien. Not only that, but an unaware human.

Alec inwardly cringed at the memory of the hardness that had entered Damien's voice, but he needed to get some rest and find out whether this case was of the preternatural or mundane variety before sharing any more information.

After promising to get in touch, Alec made his way back to the front of the precinct and to the car waiting for him outside.

"Alexa, do I have messages from Collin?" he asked the device as soon as he returned to his apartment, setting the security behind him.

"You have one voicemail from Collin Wilde on Saturday, June 20th, at 6:26 p.m. Would you like to listen to it now?" the device responded cheerily.

"Yes."

"Alec, where've you been? I stopped by a few times, but you weren't there. I'm going on a date tonight, and I'm really nervous."

While interesting, the message was not very helpful. He should've known better than to expect the answer to just be magically waiting for him at home.

"Alexa, call Collin." The phone rang several times before flipping over to a voice message. Where the feck was the brat? "It's Alec. Call me when you get this. What have you gotten yourself into now?"

Sighing, Alec stripped out of his clothes and stepped into the shower to wash away the stench of travel. He stood with his face turned up toward the warm water for a long time. He should call Ari and let her know what he'd learned, but the siren song of sleep called him instead. It really had been a long week.

He fell into bed after his shower and immediately fell asleep.

Noise from his kitchen woke him sometime later. Alec sat up in bed and tilted his head at a familiar scent. "Ari, did you get burgers from Sister's?"

"Yes." She spoke so softly that even with his enhanced hearing, he could barely hear her in the other room. "They are for you."

"What's the occasion?" Pulling on some sweatpants and a shirt, he stalked into the kitchen. His stomach growled, reminding him that he'd barely eaten before they left Indianapolis—the doughnut he had on his way to meet with Damien didn't really count.

He leaned against the kitchen island and dove into the first burger, quickly devouring it and licking some of the barbecue sauce off his fingertips. As Alec reached for the second one, he paused. Ari hadn't answered him.

"How's Jessica doing?" he asked instead.

"She is sleeping. I think she has finally come to terms with her new reality." That was good. He'd promised himself he would be a better mentor to her than he'd been with Oliver. Guilt still gnawed at him for the way he'd neglected the new wolf.

"Has she picked her name yet?" They had to get started on rewriting her life before she could leave Ari's home.

"Yes, she chose Harper Johnson."

"That's perfect." Ari always recommended choosing an alternative name that was similar to their original name. It was much easier to get used to something familiar, and it lessened the chance that it would go unanswered.

Maybe he could reach out to Deci about getting Harper a job at Sister's. She could start working during the slower periods and use the opportunity to acclimate to her new instincts. With Alec close by, she would at least have a support system.

A better one than Oliver ever had. Alec shook his head, disgusted with himself.

The conversation had stalled again. This was not like Ari at all. He needed a different approach. "Damien called while we were gone about a case he's working on. He wanted me to help him get in touch with Collin. I wonder what the little shit has gotten himself into this time?"

Tension filled the silence that followed. Alec frowned when she didn't respond after several minutes. Enough of this. "Ari, what's going on?"

She sucked in a shaky breath before letting it out slowly. Another long moment passed before she finally answered. The food in Alec's stomach turned to stone at her whispered words. "I have some bad news, Little Wolf."

He pulled a stool up behind him and sat down heavily, waiting for her to continue.

"It is about Collin." She paused, resting a comforting hand on Alec's arm before turning his world upside down. "He has been killed."

"What?" Alec breathed, stunned.

Did this have something to do with the body Damien

wanted Collin to identify? Damien would've told him if the body *was* Collin.

Wouldn't he?

He couldn't be gone. The young shifter had been so full of life.

"How?" Alec choked out, throat closing up. He couldn't breathe.

He'd failed again.

The deadly conviction in Ari's voice sent a chill down Alec's spine. "I do not know for sure. But I intend to find out."

11

"FRANK OLIVER STONEWELL."

Damien blinked a few times and rubbed his eyes before squinting wearily at Andy. They were getting nowhere fast with the new John Doe case. While he waited for the final ME report, and the techs were still working on tracking down Collin Wilde, Damien was spending time working on old cold cases. Or he was at least staring at them stubbornly and willing them to solve themselves.

"What?" he asked the young officer as the words sank in.

"The FBI finally came through on the fingerprint request from the beginning of the month. The prints came back as belonging to Frank Oliver Stonewell, age thirty-seven. He supposedly died in a hiking accident in Montana." Andy's gaze locked with Damien's. "In December. Sound familiar?"

"That isn't possible." Damien blinked back at Andy. "Doe was at least seventy years old. What the hell?"

"But what if it is?" When Damien opened his mouth to argue, Andy held up a finger. "Hear me out."

Who could fathom such an idea? But ... Frank Oliver Stonewell had died in December. That was during the same time period that Oliver Stone had opened a new bank account and started *existing* in Columbus. Were they the same man?

But what connection did the man have with their victim?

Damien motioned for the officer to continue.

"I'll buy one report coming back inaccurate, but two reports from two independent sources? No way. One of them is the FBI, for fuck's sake. What if they're *both* John Doe?"

Glancing around, Damien stood and grabbed Andy's arm. When Candice glanced up from her desk, he gestured for her to follow them. He led the two officers to the conference room down the hall. Once inside, he shut the door, grabbed a chair, and flipped it around to straddle it.

"Okay, let's say this crazy theory is true. How does thirty-seven-year old Frank Stonewell go from dying in Montana to being reborn as Oliver Stone in Ohio, only to die as a seventy-year-old man from a heart attack, all in the span of six months?" he asked as he sat down.

Candice leaned her hip against the table. "I'll bite. Let's say Thomas's WITSEC theory is accurate. Frank

Stonewell didn't die in Montana but went into witness protection. New life here in Ohio. The redacted documents we found definitely lend credibility to the suggestion."

Andy was quick to point out the flaw in the theory. "Except if it was WITSEC, the FBI would've flagged the prints, and I never would've received this report."

Damien nodded. "I agree. So, either someone royally fucked up preparing Stone's WITSEC identity, or there's more going on. The redacted documents lead me to believe that, at the very least, he had help with faking his death. Let's stick a pin in it. What about the rest?"

This time, Andy slumped in his chair and shrugged helplessly. "He contracted some kind of disease that triggered rapid aging?"

"If it was an isolated incident, I would think that was absurd." Candice cocked an eyebrow at Damien. "But it's not entirely isolated, is it? Let's pretend for a minute that last month's Doe *is* Frank, or Oliver, or whatever you want to call him. Does that mean our current Doe is Collin Wilde? You said at the scene that they looked alike."

"I just find it extremely hard to believe. Let's see what Em's autopsy report says. She found some weird shit with the first Doe, so"—Damien pinned Andy with a hard stare— "*if* she finds something similar this time, we will have to stick a Holmes pin in it and go from there."

Removing all other possibilities, no matter how improbable, whatever information remained must be true.

"In the meantime, the Stone case belongs to BCI. For

now, let's give them the Frank Oliver Stonewell angle, and let them chew on it. Maybe they'll find something. Either way, we can't dig into that."

Andy chuckled. "Not officially anyway."

"Let's focus on Collin and our current Doe for now. Has anyone tracked down the other temp from the Conservatory yet?"

Candice blew out a frustrated breath. "I'm petitioning for a warrant. The Conservatory is refusing to cooperate without one. I just don't get it. What about your contact? Anything?"

Damien groaned and pinched the bridge of his nose. When he texted the other man, Alec was neatly dodging him every time the subject came up, and both of them had been too busy to get together over the past week. "He's still supposedly looking into it, but it's making me wonder."

"When is the autopsy report expected?" Andy asked.

"In the next day or so, hopefully no later than the second. I'll keep you posted." How the hell was it nearly July already?

With nothing else to add, they called it a day.

On his way home, Damien texted Alec. *I'm free this evening. How about that dinner?*

With no response by the time he had arrived at his apartment, Damien sighed and hopped into the shower. His mind spun with the implications of his discussion with Candice and Andy. Was it actually possible there was a connection between the two Doe cases? Were the bodies really the missing men?

The physical resemblance couldn't be ignored. One time was an anomaly, but two instances were a pattern.

What other explanations were there?

A month ago, his first instinct had been a stalker situation, where the older male fixated on Stone and emulated his appearance. A third party could be at play, setting the opening act of a serial case.

But the scenario didn't fit anymore. The similarities in facial and body structure between their current John Doe and Collin were easier to see. How could a stalker emulate that?

The fingerprint results just threw everything they had thought they knew out the window.

Damien considered talking the scenarios out with Emily the next time he saw her, but it would be best to wait until the report came in. The theory was ludicrous, but his mind had latched onto the possibility like a dog with a bone.

When he emerged from the shower, his phone displayed missed text messages from Alec.

I could use a distraction.

Somewhere quiet please.

Damien weighed his options. On Mondays, most places would be quiet, but maybe Alec would open up more in private. *How about you come to my place? I can order pizza or something.*

He watched with amusement as those three little dots

popped in and out several times. He was about to suggest something else when Alec responded, *Okay*.

ALEC STOOD outside Damien's apartment building. What the hell was he thinking, agreeing to this? After spending the past week throwing himself into working with Harper and keeping his mind decidedly away from Collin, this threatened to bring it all back. Tears pricked at the back of Alec's eyes, but he took a deep breath and pushed them away.

All he could do now was move forward.

With Harper keeping Alec's hands full, the responsibility had fallen to Ari to look into the connection between Damien's case and Collin. She was also attempting to track down the young shifter's family. So far, neither investigation had borne fruit.

He sucked in a sharp breath as the pain assaulted him again. He still couldn't believe the kid was gone.

"Hey, Alec. You here to see Damien?" Tim asked as he approached with Frosty. Alec startled out of his thoughts. He hadn't even sensed the pair approaching. Sneaky bobcats.

He pasted on a grin and turned to the other man. "I am, actually."

Tim gave Alec's shoulder a squeeze. "I'll walk with you to my floor. His apartment is directly above mine, 305. I guess we both liked the layout." Grateful for the inadvertently provided information, Alec relaxed a bit. Maybe coming here wouldn't be so bad.

"How's Frosty working out for you?" Alec asked as they started up the stairs.

Tim chuckled. "He hates the apartment but loves going for walks in the area. I hope he enjoys Montana."

"Do you have a date set for the move now? Ari said you settled on Kalispell."

"Yep, I'm all set to move at the end of July. Ari wants to sublet my apartment here to your new wolf. That's a great idea, by the way."

"I want to get her a job through Deci. It works out quite well, in fact."

Tim teasingly bumped Alec's arm with his elbow as they approached his floor. "It will also give you a reason to stop by to see your detective, hey?"

Alec's ears burned, causing Tim to laugh.

"I'll catch you later, Alec."

Continuing up to the third floor, Alec took a moment to steady himself before approaching Damien's door. He knocked after a brief hesitation.

"I wasn't sure if you were still coming." Damien's warm chuckle washed through Alec as the door opened. "You didn't buzz in?"

"Tim was outside." Alec followed Damien into the apartment.

"Ah, that makes sense. Well, have a seat. I didn't order yet since I wasn't sure what you liked."

From the few times he'd been in Tim's apartment, Alec knew the doors on either side of the short hallway led to a closet and utility room on the right and the bathroom on the left.

The kitchen would be on the left just past the short hallway. Alec followed Damien to the right into the open area used as a bedroom and living space. Damien's vanilla and spice scent filled the entire apartment. Alec's nerves settled as the vanilla washed over him.

Until he bumped his hip on a piece of furniture and stumbled into Damien's side.

Heat rushed to Alec's cheeks.

He caught his balance, embarrassed, but didn't step away fast enough. Damien reached out to steady him but ended up knocking his sunglasses off instead. The bright light streaming through the window made Alec flinch.

He froze, the air locked in his lungs at the slight hitch in Damien's breath.

Shame filled him, and he turned his head away.

Get out.

Leave now.

Alec remained rooted where he was. This was it. The point when most of the others left. He was broken. Damaged. And this was only the beginning.

Alec wanted to scream, but his voice remained locked in his throat.

He couldn't stop trembling.

Gentle fingers brushed his arm, and when Alec didn't react, tugged him around the couch. Deft hands manipulated him into a sitting position and pressed his glasses into his hand. The ringing in his ears muted everything around him.

"Alec."

A low whine worked its way free from Alec's throat. He threw his fist up to his mouth and bit down hard to stop the sound. Gods, he couldn't breathe.

"Alec."

He shook his head and fumbled with his glasses, but he couldn't get his fingers to work.

Damien's low, soothing tone slowly penetrated his panic. "Alec, sweetheart, you don't need those here. But wear them if it makes you more comfortable."

"It's too bright," Alec whispered on a shaky exhale. Damien immediately stepped away, and Alec's heart dropped.

Drapes rattled, and the room fell dim. "Is this enough?"

Alec nodded and felt for the table in front of him to set his glasses down. He had to swallow twice before he could respond. "Y-yes. Thank you."

Why was Damien so calm? Why wasn't he disgusted or sending Alec home?

"May I sit next to you?"

"Please."

THE FIRST THING Damien noticed when the glasses flew off Alec's face were his eyes.

Damien sucked in a soft breath, mesmerized by the pale, sage green eyes ringed in emerald that were squinting back at him. It was enough to partially distract him from the light scar tissue around them and the lack of focus in Alec's gaze.

Alec's reaction, however, was harder to ignore. Damien knew the start of a panic attack when he saw one. His dad had been prone to them after coming home from the war.

Damien shoved aside the painful feelings that thoughts of his family always evoked and focused his attention on Alec instead. Alec needed him to stay calm.

He kept his voice low and even. "Hey, calm down. Come on, let's sit, okay?"

Damien's heart broke at the way Alec shook. He tentatively brushed his fingers along Alec's tense shoulder, and when the man barely responded, Damien guided him around the couch. He gently encouraged Alec to sit on the middle cushion, so there were no restrictions on either side of him.

Damien clenched his other hand into a fist. He wanted to hunt down whoever had hurt this sweet man so badly as to trigger such a reaction. Whoever had made Alec feel like he needed to hide this. Damien swiped the mirrored sunglasses up off the floor and pressed them into Alec's shaking hands.

"Alec." Perching on the edge of the coffee table, Damien studied Alec carefully. "Calm down, sweetheart. You're safe here."

A low, animalistic whine started in the back of Alec's throat, and the sound pierced Damien to the core. Alec bit down hard on the back of the gloved hand holding his glasses while the other hand protectively covered the scarf around his throat.

Alec didn't seem to hear him. He tried again. "Alec, listen to me."

Furiously shaking his head, Alec fumbled with the glasses, trying to open them.

"Alec, sweetheart, you don't need those here." Damien frowned at himself. That was a selfish request, and this wasn't about what he wanted right now. "But wear them if it makes you feel more comfortable."

He barely heard Alec's whispered words. "It's too bright."

Damien wanted to kick himself for not noticing sooner how much the light was affecting Alec. He strode over to the picture window and drew the blackout curtains closed. The tension around Alec's eyes relaxed immediately, but Damien had to be sure. "Is this enough?"

"Y-yes. Thank you."

Cautiously, Damien approached. "May I sit next to you?"

Damien sat against the arm of the couch at the whimpered invitation, encouraging Alec to lie down across his lap. Alec buried his face against Damien's stomach and clung to him. Giving in to temptation, Damien carded his fingers through Alec's silky, soft hair and stroked his back until his trembling finally ceased, and his breathing evened out.

"I'm sorry." Damien's shirt muffled Alec's soft words.

Damien shook his head and cupped Alec's cheek. "Hey, now, none of that. Do you still want me to order pizza?"

"You still want me to stay for dinner?" The tentative hope in Alec's voice broke Damien's heart all over again. They would have to discuss this further but not tonight.

"Absolutely." Damien injected as much levity as he could muster into his tone. "I'm starving. What do you want on your pizza?"

Alec pushed himself to a sitting position but didn't move far away from Damien. "I'm not particular. Anything but anchovies."

Damien pulled his phone out of his pocket and pulled up the delivery app to order several pizzas. He could usually eat a whole one himself, and Alec had eaten four burgers and half of Damien's wings at the bar. If they didn't finish it all, he could always take the leftovers in to work.

While they waited, Damien studied the scar tissue around Alec's eyes. Whatever had happened to him was long healed. There wasn't obvious damage to the irises themselves, aside from them not contracting and allowing too much light in, but his pupils were cloudy and more silver than black.

It was clear as day that someone had intentionally blinded the man.

Who the fuck would do that to someone? If Damien ever met the person responsible ... he shook his head and turned his attention back to Alec, forcefully unclenching his jaw to keep the irritation out of his voice. "Food should be here in half an hour or less."

Alec chewed on his bottom lip. "I thought since I'd been in Tim's apartment, it would be fine. He said your apartment had the same floor plan. I mean, I know the general layout, but ..."

Damien glanced around his apartment with a critical eye. He'd sectioned off the studio using a series of bookcases and the couch to give his "bedroom" space a more private feel. Come to think of it, it was lucky that Alec had run into the couch instead of the bookcase.

Based on what Damien had already seen, Alec typically had no trouble navigating without aid. Back in North Market, when Damien had taken Alec there the first time, they'd walked most of the way with Damien's hand on Alec's back. There'd been no hesitation at all. Nothing to give him the impression that Alec couldn't see where he was going.

Damien stood and pulled Alec to his feet. "Come on, I'll give you the nickel tour. What works best for you?"

ALEC STEADIED himself with a palm on Damien's chest. He wanted to kiss the wonderful man. Usually, when people found out about his condition, they treated him like an invalid. It was part of why he kept the blindness hidden as much as he could.

His vision was irrevocably damaged—everything around him was lost in a fog-like haze, leaving nothing but sensitivity to light and shadows behind. But he was a were-wolf and had other tools at his disposal.

The panic attack could've gone so badly. Thank the gods his wolf had remained hidden, and Damien had remained so calm.

But fear clung to him at the thought of revealing the rest.

Usually, Ari was with him when Alec needed to acquaint himself with an unfamiliar environment. Something about her presence always made it easier to perceive his surroundings through scent and sound.

It was also easier when there were several people around, as he could map their paths in his mind and mirror them. The act had become as natural as breathing. Simply having Damien walk around the apartment would be enough. The explanation sat on the tip of his tongue, but ...

That would probably raise too many questions.

Now that he wasn't so caught up in the way Damien's scent permeated the room, Alec was already becoming more aware of the nearby hazards, such as the bookcase filled with a mix of new and old books. New paper didn't hold as many scent memories as cherished older books did, and some of the volumes were very old and loved.

Damien's heart pounded beneath Alec's palm, pulling him out of his musings. The musky tang of arousal quickly mingled with the vanilla and spice. With a soft intake of breath, Alec leaned closer to Damien, his own cock stirring in response to the tantalizing scent.

But he was too raw for that.

Stepping away, Alec cleared his throat. "Why don't you just walk me through the apartment and point out the obstacles."

"All right."

There really wasn't much to Damien's apartment. The large, plush couch sat facing a television with a coffee table in between. He'd partitioned the bed off with four tall bookcases, keeping one opening near the couch and a second opening near the short hallway for easy access from either side.

"Watch for the pillars when you enter the kitchen. I stub my toe on the damned things weekly." Damien walked through the room as he pointed out each appliance and which cabinet or drawer held commonly used items. "There's a small breakfast nook to the right of the dishwasher, but I don't really use it, so it's piled with paperwork right now."

Damien's phone buzzed. "Looks like the pizza is here. I'm going to run down and get it. Make yourself at home."

Alec took a moment to settle himself when he was alone.

He pulled out plates and nosed through the fridge for something to drink. Discovering only milk and beer, Alec decided on a glass of water. It was curious that there were no signs or scents of other visitors in the apartment.

Damien clearly didn't allow just anyone to invade his space. Something inside Alec warmed and settled at the thought.

The rich aroma of the pizza preceded Damien's return. How much pizza had the man ordered? Alec quickly strode over to help him with the boxes. "Are you hungry, Detective?"

"Hey, don't start with me. I saw how much you pack away."

After piling his plate high with pizza, Alec settled on the couch. Damien soon followed and sat close enough to press against Alec from shoulder to hip. Alec leaned further into the warmth. "You need more beverages than just beer, you know."

Damien chuckled. "Why? It's one of the four basic food groups."

"I don't drink alcohol."

"Ah. I'll get some iced tea mix for next time, then."

It pleased Alec that Damien just assumed there would be a next time.

12

IT BURNED.

Fire raced up his spine. The chains rattled as violent tremors trapped him in their throes again.

His back arched as every slash of claws lanced through him, sending more acid through his veins while his tormenter's laughter echoed off the walls.

Twin rivers crawled down his arms to pool at the floor.

Sharp teeth tore into him, flaying him open like so much meat.

This was it.

He would finally die here.

He welcomed the release.

DAMIEN'S SCREAM echoed through the apartment as he came awake, his hands shooting to his stomach as the phantom pain subsided. "Christ." He groaned, rolling onto his side on sweat-damp sheets.

Fucking hell, would this shit ever end? His heart pounded hard in his chest. Laughter still echoed in his ears. Why did his lungs burn? Right. Breathing. Damien held his hand in front of his eyes, expecting to see blood from torn and rendered flesh.

Nothing.

He patted the bed. Soft sheets. No chains. No teeth. No claws. "Just a nightmare," he muttered to himself. Hearing the words solidified reality around him. He sucked in a deep, cleansing breath.

The nightmares were getting more vivid. They'd stopped for nearly a week, and he'd thought they were done, but they'd started up again with his current case. Gradually, his heart rate eased.

What the hell had he ever done to deserve this?

Fuck dreaming.

He'd take the insomnia.

Wiping the grit from his eyes, Damien pulled himself out of bed and stumbled into his closet to pull on some clothes. He might as well go get some work done—it wasn't like he would get any more sleep.

Traffic was light because of the early hour, and he quickly pulled into his spot outside the precinct. There were a few other officers who liked to work early and used the quiet time to get paperwork done until they got called out to a scene.

After booting his laptop, Damien shuffled over to the coffeemaker and popped a pod in. It wasn't Stauf's, but he couldn't get the good stuff for at least another hour. Sipping the bitter brew, he dropped into his chair and pulled up the autopsy report that Emily had posted after he'd left yesterday.

By the time Candice and Andy arrived, he'd read the details twice and was reviewing the first Doe autopsy report again for comparison.

"Morning, Damien. You're here early," Candice said as she approached.

Damien rubbed his eyes and stood. "I couldn't sleep. You two got a minute?"

Andy quirked a brow. "You have something?"

"You could say that. Come on, let's go into the conference room."

The two young officers glanced at each other before following Damien down the hall. "What's going on, Damien?" Candice asked as they gathered around the table.

"Em posted her autopsy results last night. In my pre-caffeinated state, I thought I'd pulled up the wrong report. It reads identically to the Doe from May, barring a few obvious physical differences between the two bodies."

Andy leaned forward. "Holy shit, you mean I could be right? You think the Doe from May is Mr. Stone?"

"I don't know what to think anymore." Damien pinched the bridge of his nose. "The results from this set of fingerprints haven't come back yet. I suspect we won't get anything if this is truly Collin, though."

Based on what Alec had revealed during the interview last week, Collin did, in fact, sound like a runaway. The lack of available background information supported the theory. If the law had never caught the pickpocket, his prints likely weren't in the system.

If only Damien could bring Alec in to identify the current John Doe. Impossible, given Alec's revelations the other day. Besides, how the hell could Damien explain the state of the body? Who outside of this room would even believe their insane theory?

Damien didn't even want to broach the subject with Alec until he was certain. His mind rebelled against bringing Alec any unnecessary pain after what they'd gone through on Monday night.

Why was he was even entertaining the ridiculous possibility?

"This is all kinds of messed up. Where do we go from here? What do we even *do* with this?" Candice rubbed her temples.

A good question.

"I want to talk to Em, present our theory. Hopefully, she doesn't laugh me out of her office. In the meantime, we don't have any solid evidence that points anywhere in the same universe as this. Keep working on tracking down information. Did you get the warrant for the Conservatory yet?"

"I should have it by next Tuesday. Things are a little behind with the holiday this weekend. You know how everyone gets—rushing their requests in at the last minute."

That's right, the Fourth of July was in two days. Which meant fireworks and little sleep. Oh well, not sleeping also meant fewer nightmares. With any luck, the festivities would remain civil, and he'd be able to relax for a day or two.

Fat chance.

Damien nodded and turned to go. "Excellent. Let's regroup when we have more."

Damien glanced at his watch. Emily should be in the office by now. They could discuss this while the reports were still fresh in his mind. He sent a quick text to give her advance notice that he was on his way.

WITH A STAUF'S coffee in hand, Damien entered the red brick building and headed for the morgue. Emily met him outside her office and waved him in. "Good morning, Detective. I assume you read my report. Fascinating, isn't it?"

"These bodies are giving me nightmares, Em." Damien shut the door behind him and took a seat. "I read the report, but I'd like your impressions."

X-rays hung on the wall behind Emily's desk. Damien recognized a few of them from the first Doe in May, labeled

"John Doe 0522." On the second set, while still well defined, the bone structure was far more delicate looking. Which made sense considering how lean their current Doe was. The label for that set read "John Doe 0621."

"JD0621 is remarkably similar to JD0522 in the X-rays, but I saw some distinct differences once I opened JD0621 up." Emily stood and began pacing her office. "As you may recall from last month, while the bone and musculature showed a healthy thirty-something-year-old male, the internal organs were more in line with what I expected given the apparent age of the specimen, albeit still some-what unusual."

Damien gestured for her to get to the point, not wanting to listen to every last, *fascinating* detail about the internal organs again.

"While outwardly JD0621 appears to be in his early eighties, the bones showed even less sign of wear and tear than JD0522. They more closely resemble what I would expect to see from a teenager or young adult."

Damien sat forward. This was getting into the heart of what he wanted to talk about. "Your report mentioned some unusual results from the internal autopsy."

"Yes, it's absolutely astounding. All of his organs are as healthy as those of a middle-aged male. But that isn't the important part. Damien, the organs haven't decayed since I've had him in the morgue. It's unheard of." She stopped her pacing and stared at him.

"What the hell are you saying, Em?"

"It's medically impossible. If we could isolate the cause, the applications would be groundbreaking. It reminded me of research conducted on human hibernation in the early 2000s. I have my intern looking for the article now."

Damien blinked a few times. It was rare for Emily to be so at a loss. "I have a theory I want to run by you."

Emily returned to her seat. "What is it?"

Where the hell did he start? "Is it possible to die of rapid aging? Say these men are actually the age their bones are presenting them to be and not the age they physically appear."

"Well." Emily tilted her chin in thought for a moment. "It's certainly possible. Hutchinson-Gilford progeria syndrome can cause a child's body to age rapidly, but those cases rarely survive into their teenage years."

Not Hutchinson-Gilford, then. "Is there anything else?"

"There's Werner syndrome. It's a hereditary disease that can cause wrinkled skin, baldness, and symptoms of old age. Standard cases present muscular atrophy, osteoporosis, and diabetes. None of which either John Doe possesses, of course."

"What's the likelihood of us having two cases at the same time?" Damien shook his head. This conversation was getting them nowhere.

"Not very. Why do you ask?"

"JD0522's fingerprints came back from the FBI the

other day belonging to a man called Frank Oliver Stonewell."

She caught on quickly. "Oliver Stone."

"Exactly, the same man the first round came back matching. The same man whose home was where we discovered JD0522—along with a wallet left nearby that contained his identification and a photo that looked astonishingly similar to the body. You know we had to stop the investigation shortly after the funeral home incident." Damien still wanted to know why.

Emily pursed her lips at the reminder.

"You were there when I pulled Collin Wilde's wallet out of the pocket of JD0621. Unlike Stone, I met this kid, Em. The similarities were there, plain as day. I haven't been able to get it out of my head since the second fingerprint report came back and Officer Jones suggested the connection."

Biting her lip, Emily's eyes widened. He had her attention now.

"Em, is it possible these cases *are* our missing men?"

Em met his gaze with hard determination in her eyes. "Get me something I can use to identify Collin Wilde, and I'll run every test I can. A DNA comparison, dental records, *something*. In the meantime, I'll have BCI attempt an age regression on both of them. See what we come up with."

"I'll see what I can do."

13

ALEC REACHED out a hand to stop Harper's knee from bouncing. It seemed like the hundredth time he'd done so since Vincent had picked Alec up to take them to High-banks Metro Park at the north end of the city. Since the park closed at eight, Vincent would drop them off from the road and return in the morning to take them home.

Harper let out a frustrated growl. "I can't help it. How are you so calm? I feel like my skin is going to burst open."

Alec chuckled. He could feel the moon's song pulsing against him too, but this was Harper's first shift. "Your anxiety will only make things harder. Try the breathing exercise I taught you last week."

She huffed. "Why is it just us anyway? Don't wolves usually run in packs?"

Alec turned his head away. Harper didn't need to know how much her observation stung. "I usually run alone.

There was another wolf—Oliver—I mentored before you, but ... he's gone."

"I'm sorry. Ari told me about Oliver. I didn't think."

"There are other werewolves in Columbus, but for the most part, they're just passing through. Many who live here have a pack they run with outside Cincinnati."

"Why don't you join them?"

Alec shook his head and turned his head back toward Harper. Did he dare tell her? Oliver had never figured it out, but Alec had kept his distance from the wolf even when they ran together. He'd promised himself Harper would be different.

The events with Damien the other night gave him the courage to reach up with shaky hands and remove his glasses. "Because no wolf would tolerate me in their pack."

"Just because you're blind? That's stupid." She burst out laughing when Alec's eyebrows shot up into his hair-line. "My best friend in high school was blind, Alec. I noticed the mannerisms the minute I was coherent enough. You're great at hiding it, though. I am curious how you get around without help. If you don't mind sharing, that is."

How many others had noticed and never said a word? He was a fool to have thought he could hide such a thing from other preternaturals. "Scent and sound. Our senses are enhanced enough as it is, and something Ari did when I became a werewolf gave me a little extra boost."

Thoughts of the events at Damien's apartment made his cheeks warm. "I have more trouble in private homes. The scent trails blend in with the space, so it takes longer to pick apart. I recently realized I rely on Ari a little too much in those situations."

Harper hummed thoughtfully as the car pulled to a stop. They grabbed their duffel bags and got out. "So where are we going?"

"There should be a trail nearby. We'll follow that deeper in. I usually leave my bag in a hollowed-out tree just off the path."

He couldn't help thinking about the previous month as they hiked side by side. Collin would've hated this park. For a squirrel, the kid really had been a city boy.

And Oliver ...

So much useless waste of life.

This time would be different. It had to be.

Harper startled Alec from his thoughts when she burst out laughing. "Sorry! Sorry. I was just reading the sign. 'Pets and Bicycles Prohibited on Nature Trails.' Guess that means us too, huh?"

Alec shook his head but couldn't help his grin. "We're not in fur yet. I think we'll be fine."

They continued up the path that Alec had walked hundreds of times. He often ran in this park and knew the trails like the back of his hand. The paths of the well-used hiking trail were simple to follow by scent.

He tipped his head back and breathed in the musky forest air.

"Hey, I've been wondering. You said the doctor who

saved me was a werejaguar. We're werewolves. But you call Tim a shifter. What's the difference?"

Alec steered them off the trail as they passed a footbridge. "Shifters are born, not made. The oldest shifter families in the United States have roots back to the early Native American tribes."

"So based on that, I'm guessing they're mostly Native American spirit animals?"

Alec grinned. "Exactly. There are shifters in other countries that have origins closely tied with the spiritual worship in their lands. Japan has the kami, for example. Shifters are also tied to the shamans of Eastern Europe. Of course, you won't see shifters outside of their native habitats. There are no dingo shifters outside of Australia, for example."

They came to a stop next to a hollowed-out stump of a tree. Alec set his bag down beside it, and Harper followed suit.

"Werecreatures, on the other hand, are created and governed by the call of the moon's song. Some call it the werevirus as it appears to transmit through the saliva of the werecreature in their animal form. It only happens with a mortal wound, however, and not everyone is lucky enough to survive."

Alec almost hadn't.

He forcefully pushed those memories aside before they could fully take root. "What I find most interesting is that the virus manifested differently in various parts of the world. The werejaguars originate from South America and tie back to the great jungle cats. Some have traced werewolves back to the Roman empire through tales of Romulus and Remus, and others have found evidence of a werewolf in the stories of Gilgamesh. Werelions and werejackals are from various parts of Africa. I'm sure there are others."

"Can we only change on a full moon?"

Alec snorted. "No. The first change occurs on the first full moon after the infection. The moon's song grows too strong to ignore after that. But you can change any time. After tonight, I'll show you how to control a partial shift."

Harper sucked in a sharp breath, and Alec reached out to steady her. They were wasting time. He could feel the moon's pull and knew it would force her to change before long. "Get undressed. Your clothes won't survive the change. I'll talk you through it and join you after."

He turned to give her the illusion of privacy at the rustle of her clothing, although it didn't really change anything. She chuckled at him. "I don't know why you bothered, but I appreciate it all the same. I'm ready."

Alec shrugged. "Habit, I guess. The most important thing to remember, Harper, is not to fight the change. It can be a painful process if you do. Now, take a deep breath and search inside you for the wolf half of your soul."

The wolf wasn't a separate entity within them. They were the wolf. It was only a matter of letting the other half of their soul out to play.

"Okay, now what?"

"I always visualize pulling my wolf out. It works differently for everyone. Listen to the moon's song, and she will guide you."

Alec could feel the prickles of power dancing along his skin. Harper's scent shifted to something wild and otherworldly. She cried out in pain. "Don't fight it, Harper. Let it happen."

"I don't know if I can—"

"You can. Breathe." Just a little longer.

Another scream ripped from Harper's throat, ending on a painful howl.

"You did it! Take a few minutes while I join you."

Harper flopped to the ground, panting. Alec grinned and undressed while she recovered from her first shift, placing his clothes in the bag. The moon's song grew to a crescendo as he reached inside and *pulled*.

He held in his own cry in response to the phantom pain as the change contorted his spine. Flashes of pain from his memories threatened to consume him, but the shift kept him rooted in the here and now.

As he fell to all fours, he shook out his fur. The scent of the other wolf was strong and foreign to him. Wrong. Alec growled low in his throat, dropping low to attack.

No.

Stop.

This wolf was Harper. She was his charge for this run and didn't care that he was damaged. She was safe.

Alec prodded Harper to her feet instead.

She nipped and growled at him in response.

Yipping a few times, he danced back and forth, urging her to run. He would follow her lead tonight and teach her to hunt.

A bond clicked into place as they charged into the night.

One Alec didn't deserve.

Pack.

14

WARRANT IN HAND, Damien strode into the Franklin Park Conservatory with Candice and Andy trailing on his heels.

He stopped short at the familiar blond man standing outside the director's office wearing a suit and tie and holding a file folder. The man glanced up and beamed at Damien as they approached, silver eyes dancing with mischief.

"Jac fucking Abraham, how the hell are you?" Damien called. Jac's uncle, Scott, had secured Damien's position with the CPD before retiring two years ago. He'd dated Jac for a short stint in college, but they both had quickly realized that there wasn't more than friendship in the cards for them.

Damien hadn't seen the man in years, but it was as if time had stood still for him. He was in his forties now but didn't look a day over thirty. Not a wrinkle or gray hair in sight.

"Goddamn, O'Connor." Jac cackled, his Boston accent coming out thicker than Damien remembered. "My first case in the city, and it had to be yours."

Ah, hell. Damien held up the warrant. "I come bearing paperwork. We just need some information."

Candice blinked. "I take it you two know each other?"

"I went to undergrad with this idiot before continuing on to law school." Jac shook his head, grinning. "All right, let's get the formalities out of the way. My clients wish to keep any further investigation out of the papers. The press has been crawling all over this place after that couple found the body."

Damien held up his hands. "We're just trying to track down the two temp workers the Conservatory hired and the name of the company they work through. I understand neither one has shown up for work since the incident."

Holding out his hand for the warrant, Jac shook his head. "I'm afraid there might be a problem with that. May I see the warrant?"

Damien handed it over and cocked an eyebrow. "What kind of problem?"

Jac turned to the director standing in the doorway behind him after scanning the document. "It looks like everything's in order." He sighed and gestured through the door. "Let's take this inside."

"Mr. Abraham, I do not agree with this." The director

held his ground, arms crossed. The man glared daggers at Damien with narrowed, beady eyes behind Coke bottle lenses.

Damien shared a look with the officers behind him. Andy shrugged. Candice pursed her lips.

Jac backed the director up enough for everyone to enter the office and closed the door behind them. He blew out an exasperated sigh. "Damien, this is Larry Holt. Mr. Holt, they have a warrant. If you insist, we will fight this, but I strongly advise you to cooperate. Let's save everyone some time, hmm?"

"Of all people, I expected you to understand the implications here, Mr. Abraham."

Damien stood by the door and watched the byplay. There was something going on here that went beyond just sharing two simple names. Rather than call attention to himself, he just waited it out. Candice and Andy followed his lead and held back near the wall.

"Let's not forget that Ms. Fushimi is paying my retainer, and she recommended cooperation in this matter. Would you like to call her?"

Mr. Holt sighed and completely deflated. He gestured for everyone to take a seat. "Detective, I'm afraid all I can do is offer the name of the temp agency. The, um ..." He fidgeted in his chair and shared a look with Jac, who made a get-on-with-it gesture with his hand. "The paperwork for the temp workers appears to be missing."

Damien furrowed his brow. "What do you mean, missing?"

Jac set the folder down on the desk and opened it. Inside, there was a crumpled employment agreement with Pack-Force Staffing, but the form was unsigned, and debris and dried leaves clung to the back of the sheet. "It would appear that the agency never sent over the proper paperwork."

"Okay, but why hide this?" Granted, the Conservatory could get into some big trouble here, but it seemed more like the temp agency was at fault. Either way, the issue wasn't part of his investigation. Damien pulled the form closer.

"No one seems to remember the name of the second temp, and we have no other information on Mr. Wilde."

Candice leaned forward. "What do you mean, no one seems to remember the name?"

The director shook his head. "That's all I can tell you."

Damien sighed inwardly. This was getting them nowhere. At least they finally had another avenue to search. If only the Conservatory had released this information sooner.

"Can we speak with the employees that've been working alongside her?" he asked. "It's important that we track both of them down."

Glancing desperately at Jac, Mr. Holt hedged. "I'm not sure that's such a—"

"Let the police do their jobs." Jac slashed his hand, clenching his jaw and glaring at the director.

Just who was the mysterious Ms. Fushimi? Damien made a note to ask Jac as soon as they were alone. Not that he expected to get an answer. Jac wasn't always forthcoming with information, and it surprised Damien how smoothly this was going as it was.

Defeated, the director stood and gestured for them to follow. "How do you want to do this?"

"Can you set us up in a conference room and send everyone in one at a time?" Andy turned to Damien. "Candi and I can handle this."

Tapping away on his phone for the address to the local PackForce office, Damien nodded. "I'll head over to the staffing agency and see if I can find out more. Let's regroup tomorrow back at the station."

Jac stood and followed Damien out. "I'll see you over there, then."

What? *Oh, don't tell me.* "Let me guess. You're representing PackForce too?"

"Got it in one." Jac chuckled and slapped Damien on the back as they exited the building.

Back in his SUV, Damien whistled when Jac climbed behind the wheel of a silver Lexus. The defense attorney must do well for himself. What was he doing in Ohio? Damien plugged the address into his GPS. The map showed his destination was only a five-minute drive away, in the heart of Uptown.

Damien stared up at Chase Tower after parking in the small lot just down the block and blinked at the man exiting the building.

"Damien! What brings you here?"

This must be where Tim's office was located. Damien gestured at the building that Tim had just exited. "I'm looking for PackForce Staffing."

"Ah, they're on the floor above my office. They moved in a few months ago, I believe. We actually just hired a temporary secretary through them. It's unfortunate timing, and it's making it harder for me to wrap things up here for the move at the end of the month. Is there a problem?"

Damien shook his head. "No, just tracking down a lead on a case."

Tim's nostrils flared as Jac crossed the street toward them. He tilted his head curiously as the man approached. "Hello. I don't believe we've met."

Jac smiled warmly. "Jac Abraham, attorney-at-law. I'm here to keep this guy out of trouble. I take it you two know each other?"

"We're neighbors, actually." Damien nodded toward the building. "We should head up. I'll see you later, Tim."

Tim glanced at Jac one more time, a thoughtful furrow in his brow, then continued on his way. What was that all about? Damien watched Tim get into his car before he and Jac headed inside, where the information desk directed them to an elevator that would take them to the eighteenth floor. PackForce Staffing occupied a full quarter of the floor.

The brunette behind the desk glanced up as they entered, setting a pastry down next to her and brushing sugar off her lips. "Hello, and welcome to PackForce. How may I help you today?"

Something about her bubbly voice tickled Damien's brain. Before it could take root, however, Jac stepped forward. "We're here to see Mr. O'Rourke."

She blinked irritably at him, her smile fading. "Do you have an appointment?"

"I'm Jac Abraham, and this is Detective O'Connor. Mr. O'Rourke should be expecting us." Jac turned to Damien and grinned conspiratorially. "I called ahead."

Still frowning, the woman reached for her desk phone. "Let me see if he's available."

Damien shook his head and followed Jac over to the waiting area. He had to admire the tenacity with which she guarded her post. Front desk staff everywhere were the first line of defense against unwanted visitors.

They didn't have to wait long.

The woman—Damien hadn't caught her name and there wasn't a nameplate on the desk—waved for them to follow her and turned down the hall with a bounce in her step, causing the four distinct ringlets at the base of her neck to flick back and forth like little tails. How much hairspray had it taken to keep those separate? "Right this way, gentlemen."

She left a trail of sugar in her wake. Damien shook his head. Anything covered in that much sugar should be banned from the workplace.

They stopped at a frosted door labeled "Tiernan O'Rourke, Regional VP."

Mr. O'Rourke sat behind an extravagant desk in an office with two walls covered completely in windows. Damien raised his eyebrow. He wasn't aware that staffing agencies made so much money. The man himself wore an expensive suit that surely cost him several years' worth of Damien's salary.

They remained standing by the door. After several long moments, the man finally acknowledged them with a terse nod. Damien inwardly groaned at the blatant show of power. He couldn't stand people like that.

"Welcome to PackForce, Detective O'Connor. How may I help you today?" Damien detected a hint of a brogue lacing Mr. O'Rourke's words, similar to Alec's. Something about the man's voice sent a chill down Damien's spine, and he broke out into a cold sweat. *What the hell?*

Jac nudged him when the silence stretched a little too long.

Damien blinked and cleared his throat. "Sorry. I'm here looking for information on two of the temp employees that your company had hired out to Franklin Park Conservatory last month. They couldn't provide the information to us because of an error in the paperwork.

"One of them is Collin Wilde, but we don't have the name of the second employee. I also need the home address and any other contact information you have on file for both of them."

Mr. O'Rourke grinned, flashing teeth, but the friendly expression didn't quite reach his eyes. Damien's heart rate sped up. Why was Mr. O'Rourke looking at him like that? "Of course, Detective. Mr. Abraham, I don't believe we require your services today. We'll be happy to share the information we have with the police."

Jac shrugged and held his ground. "I think I'll stick around all the same."

"Suit yourself."

Mr. O'Rourke pressed a button on his phone. Immediately, the bubbly voice of the woman from the desk chimed through. "Yes, Mr. O'Rourke?"

A sense of familiarity once again washed over Damien, but he was too unnerved by the man in front of him to explore the feeling further.

"Miss Meadows, would you be so kind as to escort our guests to the HR office? Let Suzanne know I have authorized the release of any paperwork the detective may require."

"Yes sir. I'll be right there."

Mr. O'Rourke held out his hand for each of them to shake. A glint that Damien could only describe as predatory flashed in the man's eyes as he returned the handshake. "Can I help you with anything else today, Detective?"

Damien had to resist wiping his hand on his pants, rubbing the back of his neck instead. "I think that's all I need today. Thank you for your cooperation."

Miss Meadows appeared moments later and escorted

them further down the hall. Damien glanced around, curious about how few actual employees he saw. "Regional VP" implied a large enough company to have regions, so maybe this was a smaller satellite office. Damien made a mental note to look further into the company.

They approached a door at the far end of the hallway labeled "Human Resources." Miss Meadows stopped to knock before waltzing inside. "Suzanne, I have a detective here to see you. Mr. O'Rourke said to go right on ahead and give him whatever he needs."

"Yes, I heard." Suzanne swiveled her chair toward the door with a bright smile. "Hello, Detective. Give me just a minute to pull the information up for you."

The fuck? She'd heard their conversation on the other side of the office?

With minimal fuss, Suzanne turned back to her desk, typing rapidly on her keyboard. "This is everything we have on the employees assigned to Franklin Park Conservatory. Give me a moment to print this out for you."

"Let me go grab those quick. I'll be right back!" Miss Meadows flashed a wide grin and bounced toward the door. Who the hell would be that happy to grab paperwork? Everything about this place felt ... off.

"Thank you, Miss Meadows. They should be on the printer just down the hall." Suzanne shook her head. "That girl's had too much sugar today."

After a brief wait, Miss Meadows returned with the stack of papers and handed them to Damien.

"Do you have a folder I can put these in?" he asked, flipping through the pages. The top sheet listed an address for Collin that differed from his ID. Damien recognized the address as one across the Scioto River from the Arena District, near all the new development where he'd worked a few cases last year.

Damien glanced through the other pages. After a moment, his eyes blurred, and a sudden wave of dizziness washed over him. Reaching out, he steadied himself with a hand on Suzanne's desk. Damn, he needed to get more sleep. Despite the fireworks over the weekend, he'd still fallen asleep, only to wake again from another nightmare.

The vicious fucking cycle continued through Monday.

Suzanne produced a large envelope from her desk and handed it to Damien. "Will this work?"

Grateful, he took it from her and stuffed the paperwork inside, shaking off the exhaustion for now. "This is perfect, thanks."

"Do you need anything else today, Detective?"

He handed her his card. "You'll let me know if you hear from either of them?"

"I will."

On the way out to the elevator, Jac turned to Damien. "Now that we're done here, how about we put our professional hats away and have some drinks? For old times' sake?"

Jac always had the best ideas.

"I know just the place."

ALEC SAT at his usual table in Sister's Bar and Grill with Harper across from him. He chuckled at her. "You're fidgeting again."

There were more people at the bar than he would've expected for a Tuesday night. This was a terrible idea. It was too soon.

Harper's breathing picked up for a moment before she got herself under control again. "It's so loud. How can you stand this? I can hear a conversation in the kitchen, for crying out loud."

"You'll adapt. It can take a bit, but you'll eventually learn to filter everything out." He'd planned to talk to Deci about a job tonight, but now he wasn't so sure. Harper needed at least another month. Maybe they should wait until after Tim had moved.

She sighed. "I don't know about that."

"Do you want to leave? We can get our dinner to go."

Rather than respond, Harper hummed appreciatively. "Oh my. I could climb that man like a tree. He is *delish*."

Alec cocked an eyebrow just as the scent of vanilla and spice reached him. He grinned, pulse speeding up. Damien was in the bar. "If you're looking at who I think you are, I'm not so sure he would appreciate that. I know I wouldn't."

She slapped Alec's arm halfheartedly. "Seriously? Damn, boy, you sure know how to pick them. Oh look, he's coming this way."

Alec shook his head at her antics. He turned toward Damien and immediately sneezed at the disgusting scent of chemicals wafting from that direction. "Augh, what is that smell?"

An unfamiliar male voice with a heavy Boston accent spoke from behind Alec. "Well, it can't be me. I'm pretty sure I showered today. Though it looks like I'm still wearing some sugar."

They couldn't smell it?

Damien chuckled. "Yeah, it's definitely clinging to your clothes. I swear she must've eaten an entire box of those pastries before we got there. Hey, Alec, do you mind if we join you?"

Alec tilted his head. "We?"

"How rude of me. Jac Abraham." With a rustle of fabric, Jac held his hand out for Alec to shake, bringing the awful scent closer to Alec's nose. He fought not to gag, grasping Jac's hand firmly, before releasing him and leaning away. Under the chemicals, there was a familiar tinge of something that roused his memories.

"Feel free to join us, but could you sit to my left?" The scents from the kitchen would help dissipate the awful smell. Jac stepped around behind him, and Alec blinked. Wait. "Did you say Abraham? Are you related to Scott?"

"I am, in fact! He's my uncle." The scent was subtle on Jac, but Fae glamour always held a wild edge. Jac's held an earthy flair. It was strange how little Alec could detect it, even given that disgusting chemical smell, but

148

now wasn't the ideal time for questions since Damien was there.

Damien gripped Alec's leg under the table as the detective took the remaining seat, sensation rushing to Alec's groin. He wanted more of that touch. If only they were alone. Leaning closer to take in Damien's vanilla and spice and replace the awful chemicals in his nose, Alec caught the distinct scent of another wolf instead. A low growl rumbled from his throat.

Harper kicked him under the table. "Rude! Don't mind my companion, boys. I'm Harper Johnson. Just moved here recently. It's so nice to meet you both." Harper lowered her voice so only Alec could hear her. "What's wrong with you?"

Huh. What *was* wrong with him?

Alec shook his head and forced himself to focus on his companion. "I'm sorry, Harper. This is Detective Damien O'Connor. He's a homicide detective with the CPD. Jac, I didn't quite catch what you said you did."

"Oh, I'm a defense attorney. I ran into Damien today while he was on a case. We went to college together, so while he's the enemy by day, we're still good friends when the professional hats come off. It's been quite a long time since I last saw him."

Deci approached the table with Alec and Harper's drinks. "Are you okay, Detective? You look rather out of sorts tonight."

Damien cleared his throat. "Yeah, I'm just exhausted."

"Can I get you boys something to drink?"

"I'll just stick with water for now." Damien sounded more than just exhausted, each breath coming out on a weighted exhale.

Jac ordered a cocktail and a round of appetizers for everyone. Alec smiled appreciatively at him before turning his attention back to Damien, leaning close so they could talk privately.

"Not sleeping well?"

"Nothing new when I'm on a big case." Damien squeezed Alec's knee. "I appreciate the concern, though."

Despite his words, Damien's grip loosened a moment later, and a soft groan rumbled up his throat.

"Hey, you sure you're all right, Damien?" Jac asked. "You're getting pale. Maybe you should head home, and we'll do this another time."

Alec gripped the back of Damien's neck, encountering hot and clammy skin. "You're burning up. Come on, I'll walk you home. Harper, call if you need anything, yeah?"

"Do you need help with him?" she asked, sliding her chair back to stand.

Shaking his head, Alec also stood. "I shouldn't."

It took some effort to get Damien out of his chair, and despite Alec's denial, Harper helped anyway. Alec slipped under Damien's arm and grabbed his waist. A few stumbling steps toward the door, and they found a rhythm that worked. "I must be coming down with something." Alec frowned at the slur in Damien's voice. "Sorry about this."

Maybe. Damien's condition was deteriorating quickly enough to concern Alec. It didn't seem normal.

Harper held the door open for them. "Got it from here?"

"Thanks. Yeah, I've got him." Alec readjusted his grip and led Damien out into the night.

As they approached the apartment complex, Alec nudged Damien. "Does this building have a keypad entry?"

"To the left of the door." Damien mumbled a sequence of numbers. After a moment, Alec found the pad and entered the code. The building still had a physical keypad instead of the newer digital interface or a fob.

After a few false starts up the stairs, they finally arrived at Damien's apartment. Damien fumbled in his pocket for his apartment key. Inside, Alec led him straight to the bed. "Okay, let's get you comfortable."

"So tired. Undress later. Sleep now." Damien fell back on the bed, his breath evening out almost immediately. Alec bit back a grin at how adorable it was, but his concern immediately overrode the amusement. He removed each of Damien's shoes and set them out of the way before rotating the man to a better position on the bed.

Alec grabbed a bowl in the kitchen and filled it with cool water. Good thing Damien had given Alec that tour. In the bathroom, Alec searched around until he found the small linen closet filled with towels and washcloths. He grabbed a cloth and returned to Damien's side, dipping the cloth in the water before setting the bowl on the nightstand.

If Damien wasn't better by morning, he would call Ari, but Alec wasn't leaving the man alone like this. He sat on the edge of the bed and draped the cloth over Damien's forehead.

Alec traced his fingers lightly along Damien's strong jawline to lips that were softer than he would've expected. Light scruff tickled Alec's fingers; it was a little thicker around Damien's chin.

Teeth chattering, Damien twisted around in the bed, and low groans of pain escaped his lips. It took Alec a moment to realize the poor man was having a nightmare.

Indecision froze Alec in place.

Should he wake him?

If the detective hadn't been sleeping well, then Alec didn't have it in him to disturb even restless sleep.

But he couldn't let the man suffer.

No one deserved that.

Kicking off his own shoes, Alec crawled into the bed behind Damien and propped himself against the head-board, bumping into a shelf. He pulled the comforter he found bunched along the side of the bed up around them both. Between the comforter and Alec's naturally higher body temperature, Damien warmed quickly.

Damien finally settled, drawing closer as Alec carded his fingers through his short, silky hair.

Several hours passed before Damien's shivering ceased completely, and the fever broke. Alec released a sigh of relief and removed the washcloth, dropping it into the bowl of water.

Setting his glasses on the shelf he'd found above the bed, Alec slid down behind Damien and buried his nose in the crook of Damien's neck, taking in vanilla and spice mixed with sweat. The traces of the other wolf had faded.

Exhaustion tugged at him, and he didn't resist.

"Rest well, *a stór*."

15

A THOUSAND TINY jackhammers were dancing around in his brain.

Damien woke slowly as bright light filtered into his apartment. He blinked at the clock. It was almost eight? Damien never slept that late. He tried to get up but found an arm wrapped around his waist. Warm breath ghosted along the back of his neck. A wall of heat lay plastered against his back, a hard shaft pressing against his ass.

Damien closed his eyes and leaned back, enjoying the sensation for a moment. His suit zipper pressed into his groin as his own body reacted.

He could get used to this.

Maybe with fewer clothes in the way.

Damien frowned at the thought. Hadn't he undressed last night? When had he gone to bed? The panicked thoughts scattered as lips traced his neck. Damien couldn't help but moan. The man's breath caught at the sound, arm tightening around Damien for a moment before disappearing entirely.

Damien rolled over to find sage green eyes squinting back at him, shaded beneath a hand.

With a slow grin, Damien reached out to cup Alec's cheek. "Morning, sweetheart. Not that I'm complaining, but why are you here?"

The adorable flush Damien was quickly becoming fond of rushed to Alec's cheeks while Alec's lips twitched up into a crooked smile. Reaching above him, Alec grabbed his glasses off the headboard shelf and put them on. "Um, I guess I fell asleep. How are you feeling this morning?"

Damien took stock of himself before answering hesitantly. "I have a bit of a headache. I don't remember much after running into you at Sister's yesterday. Did something happen?"

"You had a high fever last night. I brought you home." Alec held the back of his hand to Damien's forehead. "It broke before midnight. You don't seem to have one now."

That was strange. Vague memories of the dizzy spell at the staffing agency yesterday scratched at Damien's brain, but they felt distant and full of cotton. What was the name of the place again? He shook his head to clear it, but the name wouldn't come.

The more he tried to remember, the more intense the headache became.

As Alec pulled his arm away, Damien finally got a clear look at him. The sweet man had fallen asleep in his own clothes, but the scarf he usually wore around his neck had worked itself free. Damien's thoughts fled as he took in the sight. Acting of its own accord, Damien's hand reached out to trace the thick, ropy scars he found circling Alec's neck. He couldn't help the harsh breath of air forced into his lungs.

Alec froze, face draining of all color.

Damien felt sick at causing such a reaction. He jerked his hand away. "You don't have to tell me."

Alec nodded, shoulders slumping. "There's more than just this. Only Ari knows what happened to me. I-I'm not ready to talk about it."

He caressed Alec's cheek with the back of his hand, smiling when Alec leaned into the touch. "I'm here when you are ready, Alec. I'm not going anywhere."

A soft whimper escaped Alec's lips, but a hesitant smile followed, lighting Alec's face. Damien's breath caught as Alec leaned toward him until their faces were barely an inch apart. He cupped the back of Alec's head, closing the distance between them. Their lips brushed, soft and tentative, but before he could follow through on the kiss, Damien's phone screeched at them, announcing a call from work.

Alec fell back on the bed, shaking in silent laughter.

Damien swore as he dug the damned thing out of his pocket and glared at the screen before answering. Seriously?

Cockblocked by a fucking phone.

"O'Connor."

Andy's voice drifted across the line, tinged with amusement at Damien's tone. "Candi and I have to finish up at the Conservatory this morning. We didn't have time to talk to everyone yesterday. Can you come down to help us wrap up?"

Damien glanced at the clock again. "Sure. I can be there around nine."

"Did I ... just interrupt something?"

"Shut it. I'll see you in an hour." Damien hung up and turned to Alec.

"Work?" Alec tilted his head, chewing on his bottom lip.

"Yeah, I have to head in. If you can stick around while I take a quick shower, I should have time for a coffee, though." A slow, wolfish grin spread across Damien's lips. "I'd invite you to join me in the shower, but we definitely don't have time for that."

The lovely blush returned to Alec's cheeks. Damien cackled all the way into the bathroom.

TEASING BASTARD.

Alec palmed his cock as the bathroom door closed behind Damien, attempting to find some relief for the erection that had surged at the mere suggestion of a shared shower. Just waking up with the other man had been heaven.

He itched with the urge to roll around in the sheets and soak in as much of their mixed scent as he could. But he resisted.

Barely.

Damien was an amazing man. Even seeing the scars hadn't been enough of a deterrent for him. Alec's heart soared; he was beyond grateful. Damien was so different from the others.

Maybe this time it would work.

But there was still the issue that Damien was an unaware human. If something triggered another panic attack, and Alec lost control of his wolf, it could be catastrophic. He could even hurt Damien.

A low growl rumbled up at the thought.

The water shut off in the bathroom. Alec had to adjust himself as his imagination conjured an image of Damien on the other side of that door, glistening from the shower and wearing nothing but a towel.

If even that.

Not helping.

Pulling himself out of the bed, Alec straightened his scarf. It would've been nice to have a change of clothes, but there was nothing he could do about that. After coffee, he would go home anyway.

As the bathroom door opened, a burst of vanilla filtered

into the room from either a body wash or shampoo. The spice that followed was all Damien, however.

They headed out as soon as Damien finished dressing.

North Market was busy for a Wednesday morning. The noise assaulted Alec's ears the moment they entered the building. If it weren't Damien's favorite place, Alec would never go there on his own. Harper would hate it there.

As they passed the doughnut stall, Alec leaned into Damien. "They have your doughnuts today. Why don't you grab some while I order our coffee?"

Damien stopped short. "You must have some nose if you can tell that from over here."

Heat crept up Alec's neck. Damien was so comfortable to be around, it was getting harder to remember to filter his words. "Um ..."

Squeezing Alec's shoulder, the other man chuckled. "It was a brilliant suggestion. Do you want anything?"

Tilting his head, Alec sifted through the other scents. They had the lavender doughnuts that he liked. He opened his mouth to suggest them when a sense of loss struck him.

Collin.

He staggered at the memory. They had shared those doughnuts the last time they were together, listening to the rest of *War of the Worlds*. Would he ever be able to listen to that program again without thinking of the brat?

"Hey, you all right? You're swaying on your feet. Maybe you should sit down." Damien pressed a palm to the small of Alec's back, presumably to steer him over to a nearby bench, but Alec resisted and shook his head.

"No, I'm fine. Sorry. I think I'll skip doughnuts this time. Do you want an Americano today?"

Damien started to say something but paused before answering, "Sure, that sounds great."

Alec stood in line, his thoughts drifting. It'd been a while since the detective had brought up Collin. Which was strange, considering he'd been so adamant that first week. Based on the phone call before they left, the CPD was still working the Franklin Park case, so why not bring up the topic again? Was Collin's death connected to the case?

He needed to speak with Ari and find out what she knew.

She could be elusive when she didn't want to talk about something, and now that he thought about it, they'd spoken little over the past week. To be fair, he'd been spending most of his time teaching Harper how to control her shift.

Stepping up to the counter, Alec ordered their coffees. He flipped through his wallet for the money to pay, thumb along the creases to find the right amount.

"Ah, so that's how you do it." Damien stood behind Alec with his doughnut. "I swear I've seen money folded that way before. I wonder where that was."

They moved over to the corner to wait for the coffee. "You have? Ari folds it for me in distinct patterns once a month. I think the treasury is working on some new tactile bills. Eventually, I won't need her to do that anymore."

"I'm surprised they don't have something like that in place already."

"Several countries have done it for years now. Better late than never, right?"

"Looks like the coffee's done. Hey, I have to get going. Thanks for taking care of me last night. We should do this again." Damien pressed against Alec's back, lips brushing against his ear. "Maybe wake up with fewer clothes next time."

Damien's low, throaty suggestion went straight to Alec's cock.

Now he needed a cold shower.

THE INTERVIEWS at Franklin Park Conservatory were a complete bust. Not a single employee could give them any information about the second coworker.

It was fucking weird.

Damien rubbed his temples as he sat behind the wheel of his SUV and stared up at the precinct. The headache from that morning still clawed for attention at the back of his skull. It was enough for him to consider crawling back into bed to sleep the rest of the day away.

Maybe he'd wake up with Alec again.

He still didn't really remember Alec dragging his ass

home last night. There was a niggle in the back of his brain, like he was forgetting something important from yesterday, but it wouldn't come to him.

A fresh spike of pain followed his attempt to remember.

With nothing getting accomplished just sitting in the vehicle, Damien grunted and dragged himself out of his seat. Paper crinkled under his foot as he stepped out. Sticking half out from under the driver's seat was a large envelope with "PackForce Staffing" printed across the top.

That's right. He'd stuffed the envelope in the driver's side-door pocket when he and Jac had gone out for drinks. It must've fallen on the floor when he shut the door.

How the hell had he forgotten the envelope? *I am losing my damned mind.*

Candice and Andy arrived a few minutes later. Damien gestured for the two officers to follow him into the conference room. Closing the door behind them, he tossed the envelope onto the table.

Candice sighed as she took a seat. "What a waste of time. How can no one remember an employee?"

"Because this case is cursed." Damien chuckled at the irritation in Andy's voice as the officer flopped into the chair beside his partner and nodded at the envelope. "What do you have there?"

"I'm not exactly sure." Rubbing his temples, Damien stared at the packet. "To be honest, I forgot all about the damned thing until I found it in my SUV just now."

Andy cocked an eyebrow. "You forgot about it?"

"I don't know. I guess I got pretty sick last night. Some freak overnight bug or something." Not that it was much of an excuse. Damien rarely forgot things, and the disbelief written all over Andy's face was proof of that.

"Well, let's see what you have, then." Shrugging, Candice swiped up the envelope and opened the metal clasp holding it closed. She stared at the contents for a long moment then locked eyes with Damien and bit her lip. "Um ..."

That wasn't a promising look. He gestured for her to continue.

Candice tilted her head, studying him. "Damien, why do you have an envelope full of leaves?"

Wait, what?

"What the fuck?" Damien yanked the envelope out of her hand and peered inside. A handful of dried leaves clung to the bottom of the envelope, mostly broken from when he'd stepped on it earlier. A sunburst of pain flashed behind Damien's eyes. He dropped the envelope, scattering the leaves across the table, and pressed his head into the heels of his palms.

Fragmented shots of memories of shoving papers into the envelope yesterday assaulted him like shards of glass. The contracts for Franklin Park Conservatory were inside, along with the staffing agency's personnel information on the two employees. He'd recognized the address on one of the forms.

What the hell was the address? And where the hell were the papers?

Andy's voice penetrated the pain spiking in his brain as he tried to call up the memory. "Where did you store the envelope last night?"

Groaning, he blinked at Andy. "It was in my SUV from the moment I got back to the apartment and met Jac—the attorney from yesterday—at the bar across the street until I got back here just now. The only two places I've been with the SUV today are Franklin Park and here."

Maybe Jac knew something. Too bad the other man hadn't read through the documents yesterday. Damien pulled out his phone and shot the attorney a quick text. *You saw me put the forms from yesterday in a large format envelope, right?*

Jac replied almost immediately. *Of course, I did. Are you feeling okay?*

Well, at least he hadn't imagined that part.

Woke up with a nasty headache but otherwise fine. The papers are missing, though. Any ideas?

Damien's phone started ringing the moment that "read" showed up on the text. "What do you mean, missing?" Jac demanded as soon as the call connected.

"The envelope is full of leaves."

A full minute of silence met the statement. Damien pulled the phone away from his ear to make sure they were still connected.

When the attorney finally responded, shock filled his voice. "Leaves?"

"Right. The envelope was in my car overnight. Maybe someone pulled some really messed-up prank on me. Thanks for the sanity check. I'll have the camera footage pulled from the parking garage at my apartment and the lot at the Conservatory and see if we can find something. Long shot, but nothing else makes any sense."

"Let me know how that turns out." Thoughtful skepticism filled Jac's voice. "Hey, I need to go back over there on Monday. If you can wait that long, I can get you some extra copies printed. No sense in us both going again."

"Works for me. Thanks, man. We can meet for that drink after."

"Sounds like a plan."

After hanging up the phone, Damien shared a long look with the two officers. "I might as well put in the request for the camera footage right away."

"Like I said, the case is cursed." Andy threw his hands up in the air as they left the room.

16

VOICES on the other side of the door kept Alec from ringing the doorbell as he stood outside Ari's lavish home in Bexley. He frowned. She hadn't mentioned expecting visitors and rarely allowed anyone into her home unannounced. Had she forgotten he was coming to work with Harper today?

That didn't make any sense at all. Ari forgot nothing.

Her agitated voice filtered through the door as clear as day. "Some things just cannot be changed, Jac. You have one responsibility here, and you are already failing at it."

"It was extremely reckless to do that to him, and it's only a matter of time before he stumbles into our world." Jac's voice became muffled as they moved farther into the house.

What was the attorney doing there?

"That is not a concern."

"I lived with the man for four years in college, Ari. His

mind is tenacious when it latches onto a problem that he can't immediately solve. This definitely qualifies."

Were they talking about Damien? Alec knew that Damien and Jac had gone to college together but hadn't realized they'd lived together during that time. An ugly feeling filled Alec at the admiration he heard in Jac's voice. Was there something more between the two of them?

The soundproofing throughout the rest of the house blocked Ari's response.

Harper's teasing voice startled Alec from his musings. "You're growling again. Thinking about Mr. Scrumptious?"

Alec turned toward the other wolf as she stepped around the side of the house. A fresh, wild scent surrounded her. Grinning, Alec approached. "You shifted on your own. That's fantastic, Harper!"

"You can tell?"

He tapped his nose. "I can smell it on you. I'm impressed with the progress you've made this past week."

Humming happily, Harper turned to walk back down the path toward the car park. "Would you mind if we went to your place? If we'll practically be neighbors soon, I'd like to see it."

She had a point. A part of him had been apprehensive about inviting Harper to his apartment. He wasn't sure if the avoidance stemmed from the thought of bringing another wolf into his territory, or if it had something to do with the last time that he'd allowed someone new to invade his space.

Before that thought could sink its claws into him too deeply, Harper continued. "Besides, Ari didn't seem all that thrilled about her guest. I didn't realize the two of them knew each other."

Tilting his head back toward the house, Alec tuned his ears to listen but could no longer pick up any of their conversation. He'd hoped to speak with Ari about Collin today as well, but that wouldn't happen while the attorney was there.

Alec wasn't so sure he wanted to be near Jac at the moment anyway. Just thinking about the other man spiked an irrational irritation in him.

Startled, he stopped walking.

Was he ... jealous?

That was not at all like him. Nor was the frequent growling that Harper kept calling him out on. "What the hell has gotten into me lately?"

"Hmm?"

Realizing he'd spoken out loud, Alec shook his head and gestured for them to continue down the path. "Yeah, let's go to my place. We knew Jac's uncle, Scott Abraham. I didn't personally know any of Scott's family, but I'm not entirely surprised that Ari does."

"What is he? He smells weird."

Harper had picked up on that? She grew more impressive by the day. The scent of Fae was so subtle on Jac. Alec was still curious about him, but it wasn't enough to go in there now and intrude. "Scott is a full-blooded Fae. I'm not so sure about his nephew. There's definitely something there, but it's faint. I'm surprised you caught the scent at all."

"Wait, you mean Fae are real?" The shock in Harper's voice caused Alec to burst out laughing. He ducked quickly to dodge the swipe she aimed at his head.

"What, you thought shifters and werecreatures made up the entire preternatural community? Oh, hon, you have so much to learn." He'd planned on giving her time to adjust to life as a werewolf before overwhelming her with more.

Harper was far more resilient than he gave her credit for.

She pulled a set of keys out of her pocket and jingled them. "Ari retrieved my Ducati from Indianapolis, so I don't have to rely on her driver anymore. Mind if we ride it back to your place?"

Alec could just imagine Harper on a motorcycle. He could not, however, imagine himself on one. "I can't say I've ever ridden one. Why don't we just have Vincent drive instead?"

"What are you, a man or a wolf? C'mon, Alec. Live a little!" Harper laughed and slapped him on the back before shoving a helmet at him. "We probably don't need these, but I'd rather not risk it."

He was not entirely sure how he ended up on the back of Harper's bike after that, but the joy in her laughter made the trip worth his discomfort. Alec tilted his head up into the air as it rushed past them on their way back into Columbus proper.

Maybe this wouldn't be so bad.

That thought lasted until she took a turn like a madwoman, dipping the bike so low he swore he was going to fall off. He had to force himself not to cling to her and risk a wreck. Alec had never been so grateful for solid ground when they pulled into a visitor spot for the apartment complex. "You're insane. What the hell was that?"

"Just testing out those new reflexes you keep telling me I have. It was only the one turn, Alec. That was so much fun. I need to get out into the countryside and really let the Ducati purr. Wanna come?"

The teasing lilt in her voice brought his hackles up. "You won't get me within ten feet of that death machine again. I'm sticking to Ari's driver. Vincent keeps the tires on the fecking road." But if Damien were to ride one, he might learn to love being a back warmer.

Harper took the helmet from him. "So how is tall, dark, and yummy doing anyway?"

"Whatever it was only lasted that night. He was fine when we woke up Wednesday morning." Alec snapped his mouth shut, but it was too late to take the words back. Not that he regretted staying to watch over Damien by any means, but—

"*We* woke up, hmm? Spent the night, did *we*? You two didn't seem that cozy yet."

He'd known that Harper wouldn't waste the opportunity to tease him.

Alec sighed and gestured for them to head inside. "We're not. I couldn't just leave him like that. Besides, I'm not positive, but the fever might not have been mundane. Let's take this up to my apartment."

Inside, Alec flipped on the lights for Harper and set about brewing a pot of coffee. He'd bought beans from Stauf's after realizing just how much Damien enjoyed their coffee, but hadn't tried brewing any yet. Not that he planned on inviting the detective over to his apartment or anything.

Or did he?

Shoving the thought aside, he turned his attention back to his guest. "Coffee? I have some tea packets around here somewhere for Ari if you'd prefer. You can poke around in the fridge. I should have some soda and juice in there. Make yourself at home."

Harper barely held in a laugh as she pulled a soda out of the refrigerator and popped it open. "You don't have guests very often, do you?"

Alec rubbed the back of his neck. "That obvious, huh?"

"Just a bit. Don't worry, it's all part of your charm, sweetie."

Alec took a sip of the coffee and frowned down at the cup before setting it aside and filling a glass with water instead. His sad attempt at making coffee didn't even remotely compare to what they brewed at Stauf's. There was clearly more to this than just using their beans.

Harper picked the cup up and sniffed the contents before dumping it in the sink. "Guessing you've never made coffee before either. Remind me to bring you some things next time I come over. Anyway, what do you mean, you aren't sure the fever was mundane?"

They moved into the living room while Alec considered how to explain. "Like I said, I'm not entirely sure. It just came on so suddenly, and I didn't really detect any illness in his scent."

Not that he'd paid that much attention. He'd been more focused on the scent of the unknown wolf at the time. Alec dropped onto the couch with a sigh. "I had intended to discuss this and some other topics with Ari today. See if she has any ideas. I've seen sudden-onset symptoms like this before when memories were tampered with."

"What do you mean, tampered with?" Harper asked, taking a seat at the other end of the couch.

"There are a few creatures that can alter or replace memories, though the power is limited to short-term memory."

Creatures like the Fae. While the modern Fae's glamour was typically more passive, there were still some old families that retained the powers their bloodline had gained back when humans actively worshipped them as gods. Many of those old families remained in Underhill.

"Depending on how invasive the tampering had to be—

such as if the memory already had deep roots with an existing long-term memory—the human body may respond by attacking it like a virus."

Alec wasn't a fan of coincidences, and having an unknown Fae appear the same day that Damien got sick didn't sit well with him. He didn't trust the Fae lawyer despite Jac's past friendship with Damien. Or maybe it was because of. He probably had a slight bias where that particular Fae was concerned. Just a bit.

He needed Ari's insight. Soon.

"The expressions that crossed your face just now. Never play poker. You'd suck at it." Harper nudged him with her toe from across the couch. "Seriously, though. You said the human body. What about the rest of us?"

"That's a very broad question. The reaction depends on the creature using the power and which denizen of the preternatural community the power is cast on. There's no one-size answer to that. We are all affected to varying degrees. However, we're more likely to notice it's happening and can take measures to stop it."

"Like chomp the bugger's head off?"

Alec burst out laughing. He was growing rather fond of Harper. "Yes, like that. It's generally frowned upon to use the ability for anything other than keeping humans unaware."

"All right, enough of this serious stuff. Let's get back to Wednesday morning. Spill."

Alec groaned and fell back on the couch, covering his face with his hands. "You're like a dog with a bone."

"Or a wolf with some juicy steak."

"There's nothing to talk about. Nothing happened." Frustratingly enough. If the phone hadn't interrupted them, would he have gone through with it? "I'm not so sure anything should."

"Why the hell not?" Harper demanded.

So many reasons. Sure, so far Damien had handled everything with an easygoing grace, but how would he react to the rest? He'd only seen the surface scars and not even all of them. They'd barely scratched the surface of Alec's mental scars with the panic attack that one day.

What if something triggered a full flashback? It'd been decades since he'd last tried to get physically close enough to someone to navigate *that* minefield. The wrong touch could be deadly to Damien.

"Look, I don't really want to talk about it."

A gentle hand landed on his shoulder, and he knew his face had given something away again. "I'll let you off the hook this time."

"Thanks. Enough about me. How are *you* doing?"

Since shortly after Harper had woken up as a wolf, she'd seemed to take to her new life like a duck to water. But the genuine joy in Harper's voice after riding her Ducati today highlighted how much of a front her attitude had been.

"I'm fine." Harper let out an exasperated sigh when

Alec raised his eyebrow. "Growing up a foster brat and being shuffled around all my life, I learned not to let down deep roots. I think the worst part this past month was not having my things, and ... I don't know. With you and Ari, I finally feel like I belong somewhere."

Ah, so that's why Ari had retrieved the Ducati. She couldn't always recover personal items, but if Harper had lived alone ... "That makes sense. Wolves are pack creatures. The full moon run likely helped too, yeah?"

"Exactly. Our little pack of two."

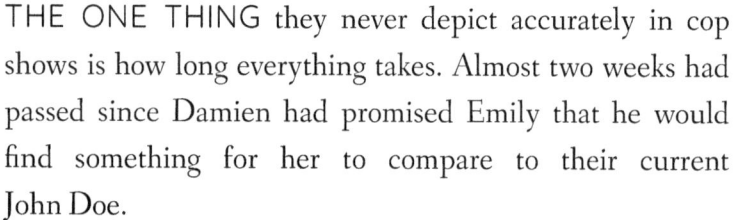

17

THE ONE THING they never depict accurately in cop shows is how long everything takes. Almost two weeks had passed since Damien had promised Emily that he would find something for her to compare to their current John Doe.

And he still had nothing.

BCI had a backlog a mile long. They probably hadn't even started on the age regressions yet.

Frustrated, Damien slumped back in his chair and glared at his phone. Still no word from Jac on the replacement paperwork either. He knew something important was on those forms. An address he'd recognized.

What the hell was it?

A sharp spike of pain burst through his skull. Damien pressed the heel of his palm into his eye, hunching over to reach blindly in his desk drawer. He curled his fingers around the bottle of aspirin stashed there and shook a few into his palm before swallowing them dry.

Why not add a week-long migraine on top of everything else? It wasn't like he slept anymore. He hadn't been entirely truthful with Alec last week—the nightmares that were waking him up at night were definitely not the kind he typically experienced while on a case. He was used to bouts of insomnia but not … this.

Damien cracked an eye open at the sound of approaching footsteps. He glanced up just as Jac dropped an envelope on his desk. The attorney grabbed the chair from the empty adjacent desk, the one that would belong to Damien's partner if the department ever had the budget to hire one—he wasn't holding his breath—and fell into it before eying Damien critically. "You look like shit."

"Tell me how you really feel, why don't you?" Damien dropped his hand away as the headache settled back into the low-level thrum that had taken up residence at the back of his skull. Still irritating, but no longer a debilitating ice pick to the brain.

Gesturing grandly at the envelope, Jac grinned. "Grabbed the papers off the printer myself this time. Ever find out who messed with the last set?"

Damien groaned and scrubbed a hand down his face. "Christ. No. Literally no one touched my SUV but me for the entire twenty-four hours the envelope was inside as far as we can tell from the cameras. The techs think I've lost my shit for wasting their time."

"Hey, you never know. It could've been gremlins. Nasty little buggers, those."

"Like the ones that always ate your homework in undergrad?"

Jac shrugged. "I can neither confirm nor deny."

Always a lawyer.

"Well, I need to take off." Leaning in conspiratorially, Jac lowered his voice. "The vultures have noticed the enemy in their territory."

"Hey, thanks for grabbing these for me. I appreciate it."

"Eh, it didn't make sense for you to waste your time on it. Oh, and we'll have to get those drinks another time. Something came up that I can't duck out of. Sorry." Jac waved a hand behind him as he headed out of the precinct.

Damien shrugged and pulled the envelope over to him. He'd completely forgotten about the drinks anyway.

The top forms in the envelope were the employment contracts between PackForce Staffing and Franklin Park Conservatory. Damien found the page he was looking for next and damn near dropped it after reading the address line. "What the hell?"

"Was that the attorney I just saw in the hallway?" Candice asked as she approached Damien's desk.

He glanced up at her briefly before staring down at the paper in his hand again. He pulled his phone out of his pocket and scrolled back to the picture he had of Collin's ID, staring at it in disbelief. "No, no, this had something else on it the last time. I swear it."

Why couldn't he fucking remember the address?

Damien dropped the papers as his headache flared again. He could practically see the form in his mind, identical to the one now floating to the floor, except that the address listed for Collin most definitely had *not* been the one near campus matching the kid's ID.

Candice bent down and scooped up the papers before rifling through them and putting them back into some semblance of order. She cocked an eyebrow at him. "That headache is still bothering you?"

Damien grunted. "I'll live. I took some aspirin."

She flattened her lips and glared at him but let it drop, perusing and placing the papers in her hand into neat piles across Damien's desk instead. Candice stopped on a form about halfway through the pile, a slow grin spreading across her face. "Mindy Hawthorne."

"Mindy who?"

"The second temp at the conservatory. I have the work contract here." Candice brandished the paper in her hand like some sort of trophy and set the rest aside. "I wonder if this woman knows how much hell we've gone through just to get her name."

Shuffling through the rest of the forms, Damien found the personnel records on Mindy. "Looks like she lives in the South Side, out by Groveport. Grab your partner. I want to head out there now. She ghosted as soon as the body appeared, so the woman has to know something. I don't want to give her a chance to run if she knows we're coming."

Twenty minutes later, Damien parked his SUV in front of a well-landscaped, cottage-style home. Andy whistled from the back seat. Damien agreed with the sentiment. A walkway lined with pink perennials led to a wraparound front porch and the front door.

As they approached the house, Damien held up his hand. The door was slightly ajar, nearly impossible to see from the street, as colorful shrubs and trees mostly hid it. He unholstered his sidearm, pointing it loosely downward as he rapped on the doorframe. "Police! Is anyone home?"

Silence met his shout and a second round of official raps to the door. Damien nudged the door open further with his toe and peered at the devastation inside. Candice and Andy followed him in, weapons also drawn and pointed downward.

They spread out, methodically searching the first floor and shouting, "Clear!" as they combed each room. Damien remained downstairs, studying the tipped-over furniture, as the officers cleared the upper level. After the final all-clear, he holstered his gun and pulled a pair of gloves out of his pocket.

The low drone of Andy calling dispatch to notify them of the crime scene barely reached Damien's ears as he stared at a series of family photographs in the hallway leading to the kitchen. They all starred a young brunette with a radiant smile that lit up her eyes with joy. Another niggle tickled the back of Damien's brain, but his headache stopped the thought from catching any real traction.

He needed to get some fucking sleep.

"Have I mentioned lately that this case is cursed?" Andy asked after completing his report.

Damien chuckled and shook his head. "Every bloody chance you get. Pretty sure you're creating a self-fulfilling prophecy here."

Andy stepped forward, tilting his head to get a better look at the woman in the photos. "She looks familiar."

"Yeah, I thought so too."

"Almost like that Jane Doe we pulled out of the river last month." The young officer pulled out his phone and scrolled back through his photos. "Yep, here it is."

Damien glanced between the bloated face of the woman who'd been pulled out of the Scioto River and the shining beauty on the wall and sighed.

The case had quickly gone cold with no missing person report, no witnesses, and no way of knowing where the body had entered the river despite their efforts and coordination with special operations. The body had been too bloated to get viable prints, and BCI hadn't had enough to work with after CPD had handed the case off to them.

This was the best lead they'd had, and it might well be the break in the case that they needed. Unfortunately, it also spelled a dead end for their current pursuit. "When CSU gets here, we'll have them gather what Emily needs to do a DNA match."

Andy frowned at his phone. "That body washed ashore a week before that couple found John Doe 0621 in the park, according to my notes."

"Which means someone else was Collin's coworker." Not just a dead end but a wrong turn in the opposite direction.

"This case really is cursed."

It was.

18

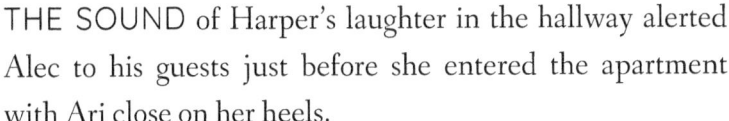

THE SOUND of Harper's laughter in the hallway alerted Alec to his guests just before she entered the apartment with Ari close on her heels.

Alec stood to greet them as the pair headed over to his kitchen and promptly groaned at the scent that followed them in. His nose twisted in distaste at the fried tofu and soy sauce. "Inarizushi?"

He didn't duck fast enough to avoid the swat Ari had aimed at the back of his head. "I was feeling nostalgic."

Of course, she was.

A thunk followed by water filling a canister had Alec curiously wandering over to Harper. "What are you doing?"

Mischief filled Harper's voice when she responded. "I told you I'd bring you some things. When the water heats up, I'll show you how to make real coffee. This is a water boiler for your new coffee press."

His new what now?

Alec stepped forward to investigate the canister. It had a spout pointing downward and several soft buttons on top with slight bumps scratched into the protective lining. He found the release button in the front, and the lid popped up.

"I had to modify this one for you. None of the good ones have normal buttons. The unmarked button is for the temperature, but *don't* monkey with it. The water should always boil then cool down to a hundred and ninety-five degrees, or you burn the coffee. That's where most drip-brew systems get it wrong."

Alec held in a grin at Harper's enthusiasm. The woman was full of interesting quirks. Why not add coffee nerd to the list? "I appreciate it. What do the buttons with scratches do?"

Harper walked him through the inner workings of the device before they left it to heat the water. He found a box on the island and raised an eyebrow. Just how much stuff did she bring? Oh well. He loved learning new things.

"Are you two about done? I cannot stay terribly long tonight." The amusement in Ari's voice belied her words.

"I feel like we haven't spoken in ages. Like you've been avoiding me." Alec ruffled his fingers through Ari's braids. The pile atop her head seemed thicker than normal, as though there were an extra braid.

Her only response was a short hum before Ari skirted away to claim her perch on the couch. So she *had* been avoiding him. Interesting.

Before Alec could say anything, Harper joined Ari on the couch and blew out a deep breath. "I know Tim isn't moving for a few weeks yet, but I was hoping to crash here until then. I'm going a little stir-crazy at Ari's, even with the Ducati. I think I'm ready to try that job you mentioned."

Now that she could shift at will, her instincts would settle down. Still, Alec wasn't sure if she was ready to sort through that level of noise yet. One way to find out, though.

"We can go talk to Deci tomorrow if you want. I'm really glad to hear this, but let's see how you handle the noise first. Thursday nights can get crowded there. It will be an excellent test." Alec bit his lip and considered her other request. He had an air mattress in his hall closet that they could set up in the spare bedroom.

But would it be fair to make her sleep on it? Those things could get awfully uncomfortable.

He could just sleep on the couch for now.

Though he'd rather sleep in vanilla-scented sheets.

Harper's stage whisper pulled him out of his runaway thoughts as heat crawled up his neck. "Have you always been able to read every thought as it crosses his mind, or is this just because of that detective?"

"He has never been able to keep secrets from me." A fond smile colored Ari's voice as she lowered it into her own form of a stage whisper. "But I do believe you are correct that this development has more to do with his detective. He acted this way only once before as far as I can recall."

What did he ever do to deserve this teasing? Time to get

back on track. "You can stay, Harper. I'll think of something, so we can both have some privacy."

"You have a comfortable-looking couch in your office. I can sleep there." Harper raised her voice to cut off any protest he might've made. "It's only for a few weeks, Alec."

He'd see about that.

Knowing they outnumbered him, Alec gave in. For now. "Harper, why don't you run down and get your bag? I assume Ari had you bring it."

"That she did. I'll be right back."

After the door closed, Alec turned to Ari and waited expectantly.

She huffed out a frustrated breath. "I know you believe I have been avoiding you, Little Wolf. I wish I could tell you who stole our Collin away, but ... I will continue to dig into it."

There was nothing but truth in her words, but Alec still felt like she'd left something out. Why was she hiding things from him this time? He couldn't bring himself to ask and knew she wouldn't answer regardless.

Ari had kept things from him in the past. He could rant and rail at her for it, but he knew she had his best interests at heart. Knowing the outcome of one's choices was a burden that he wouldn't wish on his worst enemy.

That his best friend and mentor knew too much hurt his heart. Her silence spoke volumes.

Alec sighed and forced himself to move on. "And his family?"

"I found a shifter enclave in Michigan that claims him. I am having him sent home soon."

An enclave. Also known as a shifter cult. Alec shook his head in disgust but kept his mouth shut.

He wanted to ask why Ari hadn't claimed Collin as theirs. If it'd taken this long to find the enclave, they had likely wanted nothing to do with him in life. Why would they care after death? The young shifter deserved a proper sendoff. One like Oliver's.

But blood and tradition would always come first.

Alec dropped his head into his hands.

Harper paused in the doorway when she returned. "I feel like I should leave and come back later. Is everything okay?"

"Everything's fine. I'm just thinking too hard is all." Alec shook himself out of the melancholy mood that thoughts of Collin often drove him to. He stood to help Harper with her bags, pointedly carrying them into his own room.

"If you say so—Hey! Where do you think you're going?"

Alec hid his grin, dropping the bags on the bed. "You're my guest. I'm not making you sleep on a fecking couch."

"And where do you plan to sleep?" Harper's outrage gave way to a suggestive drawl. "With your detective?"

If only.

Ears burning, Alec shook his head. "I have an air mattress. I'll set it up in the office. It'll be fine."

"Minuet in G major" interrupted Harper's low growl.

Alec raised his eyebrow, and Harper burst out laughing. "The water's ready. Come on, I'll show you how to use the press."

Dispute temporarily forgotten, Harper walked him through the intricacies of using an AeroPress. He was dubious at first, wondering how what essentially equated to a cylinder with a plunger and a metal mesh filter could make coffee, but after tasting Harper's first cup, he understood.

The coffee was on par with Stauf's.

It took him some time to get used to the tool and get everything arranged in a way that made sense to him. By the time he finished, he'd pressed enough coffee for all of them.

Ari hummed happily after taking a sip from the cup he handed to her. "I still prefer tea, but this is not bad."

"Much better than that drip-brew crap he tried to make on Sunday. That machine is going in the trash the first chance I get." Harper pressed against Alec's side and nudged him with her elbow. "Now you can impress Damien with your mad coffee-making skills. How's he doing anyway?"

Right. The other topic that Alec wanted to discuss with Ari. "When I spoke to him yesterday, he was still getting occasional headaches."

"Headaches?" Ari asked.

"Damien came down with a nasty fever last week when Jac came to town. Come to think of it, it only lasted until moonrise." Which only added credence to his theory that the illness was not mundane. "He's complained to me about a headache a few times since then."

"He might have just gotten sick. Summer colds are not that out of the ordinary." Ari's voice lost inflection, and Alec knew instantly she was hiding something again.

"Don't, Ari. Damien didn't smell sick." He barely contained his growl when another thought struck him. "Did you have something to do with this?"

Ari hummed thoughtfully. "Our Little Wolf has become quite growly of late. Do you not agree, Harper?"

Harper laughed. "You noticed that too?"

"Perhaps I should get him more books."

Face burning, Alec sputtered. "What? No. I don't need more shifter porn."

"Well, it has been quite some time."

The floor could open up and swallow him any time now. Seriously. What had he done to deserve this teasing?

"Come on, Alec," Harper said, falling into a fit of laughter. "I'll even listen to them with you."

Ari reached over and patted Alec's arm. "I am happy for you, Little Wolf. Truly. However, I am late for an appointment and cannot stay any longer. We can talk more another time, yes?"

It was only after she left that Alec realized Ari hadn't answered his question.

19

DEATH DID NOT COME *for him.*

The chains rattled a staccato beat as his body contorted, the fever sinking its claws deep. Much like the claws that had finally retreated some time ago, leaving him a ruined mess.

More meat than man.

The pain bled together into a single, excruciating entity, denying him the blessed relief of unconsciousness.

Gentle hands stroked his face, a contrast to his earlier treatment.

No.

He flinched away.

The hands deftly removed the chains binding his wrists. He fell to the floor in a heap, sparking fresh hell throughout his body.

When tentative hands tilted his chin up, he curled into the fetal position, desperately protecting what was left of him. A soothing warmth spread through him, blessedly numbing the pain.

After living with the pain for so long, its absence was pure heaven. He sagged in relief.

Soft, melodic whispers floated in the air. "That is the best I can do to soothe you. I am afraid the respite cannot last. Hold on just a little longer."

A flare of heat washed over him before white-hot agony tore through every muscle in his body. His screams echoed off the walls as a pain unlike any he'd ever felt before pulsed in endlessly growing waves.

Every one of his bones shattered as he writhed on the floor. His vocal cords burst, giving way to harsh panting and little more.

A bitter whisper reached his ears just before he finally succumbed to the pain.

"No good deed goes unpunished. A saying that has never been more true. I am sorry, Lit—"

DAMIEN STARTLED awake to the shrill tone reserved for Kat's personal line. The barest tendrils of dawn were slipping in through the cracks around the blackout curtains. He blinked blearily at the clock, fumbling around for the phone on the nightstand. "O'Connor."

6:02 a.m. Fantastic. He'd slept almost a full five hours.

"Dispatch received a call from your building's security system for apartment 205 three minutes ago and called me.

They've been unable to reach the resident." Damien jumped out of bed at Kat's clipped tone and raced down the hall, angrily ripping the power cord free from his phone when it impeded his progress.

He threw on the first set of clothing he could find and pulled his gun out of the safe in the closet. Not bothering with his holster, he rushed to the door, stopping only briefly to grab his Bluetooth earbud and switch the phone over, so he could safely handle the gun.

Kat continued feeding him information as he rushed down the hall to the stairs. "The resident's name is Timothy Singer. Units are en route, but there was a major accident this morning, and they need to take an alternate way. ETA is still ten to fifteen minutes."

"I'm on my way down now." Taking the stairs two at a time, Damien quickly reached the second floor. He pushed the stairwell door open a crack and peered down the hall. Frosty stood outside the apartment, barking and scratching impatiently at the door. "Tim's dog is in the hallway."

"Damien, wait for backup." Why had Kat even bothered with the warning when he was already this far? She knew full well he wouldn't wait. Disconnecting the call to avoid further distractions, Damien slipped into the hall. Kat could chew him out later.

"Hey, buddy." The whisper-shout was enough to get the dog's attention. Frosty stared at him, anxiously whining and pacing back and forth.

With his gun pointed at the floor, Damien approached

Tim's door. He found the door unlocked and cracked it open carefully. An eerie silence greeted him as he entered the apartment.

The floor plan was identical to Damien's, with a narrow hallway leading to a large open living space and a floor-to-ceiling window overlooking the courtyard pool on the wall directly across from the door.

To his right, the closet door stood open. A quick glance cleared the room—nothing was hiding behind all the boxes piled high and ready for Tim's move. The utility room proved just as empty.

The bathroom door to Damien's left stood closed. He tentatively tried the handle. It opened without resistance.

Damien leaned against the wall, ready to clear the bathroom.

Voices in the next room made him pause.

A woman spoke too softly for Damien to make out any words, but something about her voice was familiar. He lifted his gun at Tim's frantic response as the damned dog charged back into the apartment, directly into the living area.

Cursing under his breath, Damien took a step to follow. He halted when a high-pitched, startled yip—one that under no circumstances could've come from the dog—echoed off the walls.

Still screeching, a blur of orange and black zipped past him through the narrow hallway and out the apartment door.

He wasn't so lucky when the dog followed suit, toppling Damien to the ground with an "oof." Throwing his hands out, Damien shut the door before the dog could escape again to chase whatever-the-hell-it-was down the hall.

With Frosty scratching madly at the door, Damien rolled to his knees and peered around the corner into the living area, gun drawn and ready. Two distinct sets of bloody paw prints, both large and small, covered the room, but there was no one else in the room besides Tim.

All thoughts of paw prints fell away as Damien took in Tim's state, lying on the floor in a pool of blood.

Dropping his gun, Damien raced to Tim's side and clamped his hands down on the gash sliced across the man's neck and into his shoulder. He was still alive but gasping for breath as his lifeblood pumped out to flood the floor. "Hang on, Tim. Help is on the way."

Tim frantically shook his head, attempting to shove Damien away. "G-get out of here!"

"Shh, don't talk. Just hold still."

"C-called. Called Alec. Please, I don't want to hurt you." With a low, inhuman growl, Tim shoved Damien's hands away from him. Damien blinked in surprise as the flow of blood slowed before his eyes. The wound was still gaping but no longer deadly.

He took in the gray peppering throughout Tim's hair, vaguely aware of its wrongness, before the man shoved him again. Rather than tumble onto his ass, Damien *flew* several feet into the wall behind him. His head hit the corner of one of the damned kitchen pillars, rattling his skull.

Damien blinked the blurriness out of his eyes. Distantly, it occurred to him that Tim was the only blurry object in the room as the man collapsed onto his hands and knees. Moments later, Tim disappeared. A bobcat stood in his place. The cat crouched low, hissing and growling, ready to pounce. Shredded fabric covered the animal.

"Oh, fuck." Fight or flight kicked in, and Damien scrambled to get his feet under him, but his bare feet provided no traction on the bloody tile. Crashing back to the floor, Damien's head hit the pillar a second time.

Stars danced behind his eyes, and darkness closed in. *Oh, fuck.*

In the distance, the front door crashed open.

Someone screamed his name.

The last thing he saw before the darkness pulled him under was a flash of white fur crashing into the bobcat.

ALEC RACED out the door of his apartment and down the hall, waving Harper off as she poked her head out of the bedroom. There was no time to explain.

Something was happening at Tim's apartment, and Alec would be damned if he allowed another friend to be harmed. Tim had called him, frantic, but Alec couldn't make out his words, and the call cut out before he could clarify. His calls back remained unanswered.

Arriving at the building, Alec quickly punched in the code to the door, thanking all the gods above that Damien had given it to him a few weeks ago.

A faint, earthy scent followed him in. Alec turned his head to acknowledge the Fae lawyer, only slightly surprised that he hadn't noticed the man behind him before now. "Tim's apartment is on the second floor."

Jac grunted an acknowledgement as they both sprinted to the stairwell door. Sirens sounded in the distance as the door closed behind them.

Alec started up the stairs, only to have a furry bullet crash into him. He twisted his nose up at a familiar, harsh chemical odor that saturated the creature and stumbled back into Jac. "What the hell *was* that thing?"

And where had he encountered that scent before?

The Fae caught Alec with a hand planted between his shoulders before shoving him forward to encourage upward momentum. "I'm not sure, but that isn't our concern right now. Ari sent me. Damien's in trouble."

Alec's heart skipped a beat, and he would've stopped to demand answers if not for the lawyer's insistent push forward. They hurried up the stairs, concern for Damien overriding Alec's worry for Tim. When Alec would've continued to the third floor to get to Damien, Jac grabbed his arm and hauled him through the second-floor doorway. "Ari said he's in Tim's apartment. Tim's badly hurt."

Oh. That was not good.

In no frame of mind to care what Jac saw, Alec pulled off his gloves, scarf, and glasses and shoved them at the lawyer. He reached Tim's door and slammed it open. Frosty took off, barking down the hall.

Immediately, the scent of blood assaulted him, followed by more of that pungent chemical odor. The low growl of a cornered bobcat reached his ears.

They were too late.

"Damien!" Alec's shout echoed off the walls. "Tim, stop!"

There was no conscious decision to shift. No distinct *pull* from one form to the next. In the span of a breath, Alec's shouts transformed into a growl as he dropped to all fours. He shook away his ruined clothes and charged into the living area, aiming directly for the hissing cat.

Tim's attention was fully on Damien; the shifter was completely feral and unaware of his actions. Only life-threatening injuries could turn a shifter's rational mind off so completely. Catching the animal off guard, Alec landed on Tim's back and clamped his jaws around the scruff of his neck.

The cat bucked and growled, attempting to shake him off. A well-placed kick from the animal's claws sliced a blaze of fire down Alec's thigh. He jerked, jaws loosening just enough for the cat to pull away.

"For fuck's sake." Jac muttered something under his

breath and stepped further into the room. "Can we hurry this along? We're about to have company."

Tim's attention briefly split between them, and Alec seized the opportunity to grab him again. This time, he deftly pinned the cat to the floor. After a moment, the animal's body fell lax. Alec released him as fur finally gave way to skin.

Alec turned his attention to the man groaning against the wall. He pressed his nose to Damien's neck. The detective's pulse was strong. He was okay. Relieved, Alec crouched down and rested his head on Damien's lap.

Damien mumbled something, but Alec couldn't make out any actual words.

"Alec, Harper's here." Jac crouched down near them, his voice low. "As adorable as this is, you need to get out of here. The cavalry has arrived, and I'll have a hard enough time explaining where all of this blood came from. There's no way my feeble glamour can hide you *and* make Tim's injuries look like they could've caused all this."

Lifting his lips with a snarl, Alec pressed closer to Damien. When Jac reached for them, he nipped at the air in warning. He still didn't trust this Fae despite his help.

Harper's cooing nearly drowned out Jac's exasperated sigh as she entered the room. A door down the hall opened and cautious whispers between what sounded like officers reached Alec's ears.

Harper gently brushed his scruff with her fingertips. "Come on, Alec. Let's run up to Damien's apartment, so you can shift back and borrow some clothes. Yours, ah, didn't quite make it. Then you can ride with him to the hospital."

Hospital? But Damien didn't seem that injured. There was no blood aside from Tim's and some of Alec's. Alec whined at her in question.

"It looks like he got his bell rung on one of the kitchen's pillars, sweetie. Probably has a concussion."

Reluctantly, Alec left Damien's side. Jac murmured an assurance that he would stall the EMTs as long as he could.

They slipped out the apartment door as Jac's glamour wrapped them up in a tingling wash of power, and they made their way unseen to the stairs on the opposite side of the building. The Fae lawyer quickly approached the arriving officers. "Everything's under control, but there's an officer down and a second injured man inside the apartment."

A female officer sounded like she recognized Jac. Alec let out a tense breath as he and Harper hurried up the stairs to Damien's floor.

"We're in luck. Damien didn't shut his door all the way." Harper stepped inside first then shut the door behind Alec. "You'll have to tell me what happened later. For now, why don't you shift and wash up in the bathroom? I'll see what I can find for you to wear."

Slipping into the bathroom and kicking the door shut behind him, Alec settled down on the floor and focused, so he could push the wolf aside. He rarely shifted outside of the full moon, and he usually found it difficult when the moon song was silent on a new moon like today.

Panic and adrenaline had likely helped the shift downstairs, but now he struggled to pull himself back. Worry over Damien crashed through his mind, making concentration difficult. Pain finally flared along his spine, and his fur receded. His thigh ached where Tim had scratched him, but the wound had stopped bleeding.

Groaning, Alec rose to his feet and felt around for the taps to turn on the shower. Tim's blood covered him from the scuffle. He didn't waste any time standing under the spray. They needed to hurry back downstairs.

Harper knocked and poked her head into the room. "I'm setting your scarf and gloves on the sink. I found a pair of sweats with a drawstring you can tie. I think Damien's other pants would fall right off you."

Alec shut off the water and reached for a towel. The door closed behind Harper as she left to give him some privacy. Along with the pants, he found a thin cotton shirt with long sleeves. He ran his fingers along it and sighed. Harper was too perceptive, but he was grateful that there wouldn't be questions about his scars right now.

Harper handed him his glasses as they rushed back downstairs.

There was an argument taking place in the apartment. Before he could go inside, Harper nudged him further down the hall and shoved a duffel bag into his hands.

"They're leaving with Damien. Go catch up with them. I'll see if I can help Jac out here."

"You're the best." Alec raced down the hall, following Damien's vanilla scent. "Wait! I want to go with him."

One of the EMTs voiced his objection, but a nearby officer spoke up with a knowing grin in her tone. She was the same officer who'd spoken with Jac earlier. "It's okay. Detective O'Connor would appreciate this one's company."

"If you say so, Officer Lawrence. Well, come on, then." Despite the reluctance in the EMT's voice, they started down the stairs. Alec rushed to follow.

"How long has he been unconscious?" the EMT asked his partner.

"He was partially awake when the officers got here, just before we arrived. In and out for the last fifteen minutes, I would guess."

Alec climbed into the back of the ambulance when they had finished securing Damien and took a seat where directed.

Damien groaned and jerked at the bindings that were keeping him still. "What the fuck?"

"Settle down, Detective. You took a nice hit back there. Do you remember anything about what happened?" The EMT's voice took on a warmth that Alec hadn't heard when it was directed at him. He held back a growl. This was not the time.

"I lost a fight with one of those fucking pillars." Damien's slurred voice rose. "Oh, shit, Tim! Is he okay?"

"Tim will be fine." Alec shot the EMT what he hoped was a pleading look then grabbed Damien's hand and leaned forward to whisper in his ear, "Don't say anything else. I promise I'll explain when we're alone."

Damien turned his head toward Alec. "Alec? What are you doing here?"

"Tim called me. Harper and Jac are with him, though. Let's worry about you for now."

The ambulance came to a stop, and the back doors opened again. Alec sat back to get out of the way then followed the group through the ER doors. Damien immediately objected when the triage nurse tried to send Alec to the waiting room. She quickly backed off and started her assessment. Alec hid his grin, grateful they had allowed him to stay.

It didn't take long for them to get settled into a room. Damien put up another fight when a pair of CNAs tried to help him get out of his bloody clothes and into a hospital gown. Alec set his hand on Damien's shoulder. "Let these people do their jobs. Is this what I have to look forward to after we get you home?"

That got Damien's attention. He covered Alec's hand and squeezed. The detective's voice dipped low. "Going to take care of me?"

The tension that Alec had carried since he first found Damien in the apartment with Tim finally eased. Damien already sounded more like himself.

When the nurses left them alone to wait for the doctor,

Alec pulled his chair up to the side of the bed. He gestured at the bag he'd set against the wall. "I think Harper packed you something to come home in at least."

"Good." Damien tugged at the sleeve of the shirt Alec was wearing. "Isn't this mine?"

"Um. Yes?"

Before Alec had to explain *why* he was wearing Damien's clothes, the doctor interrupted them by entering the room. He ordered a battery of tests that carried Damien in and out of the room constantly over the next couple of hours.

An officer stopped by in between tests to take Damien's statement, but Damien didn't tell them much. Thank the gods Damien had taken Alec's plea for silence to heart until they could talk.

The doctor finally released Damien with a diagnosis of a probable concussion, a prescription for pain relievers if he needed them, and orders to stay home all week to rest and heal. The doctor slipped Alec a sheet with care instructions while Damien was getting dressed. He would have his phone read the sheet to him later using an OCR—optical character recognition—app.

When Damien and Alec got outside, a car door opened, and the scent of autumn leaves reached Alec's nose. Vincent started up the car as Ari called out to them, "Over here, Little Wolf. I have to get back to Tim, but we have time for a few stops."

Alec helped Damien inside the car before sliding in

next to him. Damien listed to the side and rested his head on Alec's shoulder. "Gonna nap for a bit."

"You didn't have to pick us up. I could've called Vincent myself," Alec said as he pulled the door shut.

"Not without your phone, you could not. You left it with your ruined clothes." Ari set the offending device in Alec's hand.

Feck. Even Harper had forgotten to check his pockets. Alec frowned. The same chemical odor from earlier clung to his phone. Had it happened when the creature bumped into him on the stairs? "How is Tim doing?"

"He will be fine. Harper is with him for now at a safe house, and I will send her home when I arrive. We may accelerate his relocation to ensure his safety, however. Jac can handle the police."

"Do you know what happened?"

"We have not spoken yet."

That didn't answer his question. Alec frowned.

"Do we need to stop at the pharmacy?" Ari asked instead, already knocking on the partition.

"Yes, mum?" Vincent asked from the front seat.

"Stop at the CVS before the Arena Crossing Apartments, please."

Why did she ask if she already knew?

Grant Medical Center was close to both the CVS and Arena Crossing. Before long, they had Damien's pain medication, and Vincent pulled into a spot outside

Damien's apartment building and parked the car. Alec nudged Damien awake. "We're here."

Alec frowned, torn. He should help Ari with Tim, but what about Damien? Ari solved the dilemma for him and nudged him out of the car. "Stay with your detective, Little Wolf. I will see to Tim."

"I am fucking exhausted." Damien yawned and ambled over to his bed the second they stepped inside his apartment. Clothing rustled as it landed on the floor. "You don't have to stay, you know."

"Maybe I want to stay." Alec approached Damien from behind and slid a hand up his back, finding skin instead of cloth. He pressed his forehead between Damien's shoulder blades and let out a long, relieved sigh.

Alec pressed a kiss to Damien's shoulder and reluctantly stepped back. "You should sleep."

"Lie down with me, then?"

"I need to make a few calls. It won't take long."

Damien grumbled but still climbed onto the bed. His breathing quickly evened out.

Alec stepped into the hallway to call Harper.

"How is he?" she asked in lieu of a greeting.

"Sleeping. He shouldn't be alone in case the concussion gets worse, so I plan to stay here the rest of the week. How's Tim?" Maybe Harper would have more information.

"He's shaken up, doesn't want to talk yet. Jac arranged for him to go to a 'private hospital.'" Alec suspected Harper was using air quotes. "He told me later it's a shifter safe house. Tim keeps asking for Ari."

"Ari just dropped us off, so she's on her way over now."

"Do you need me to run anything over before I go back to your place?"

"No, I'll stop home in the morning to pick up what I need. I think I just want to get some rest myself. It's been an exhausting day."

After ending the call, Alec double-checked that the apartment was locked tight and pulled the blackout curtains closed. He climbed into bed and curled against Damien.

Damien rolled over, trailing fingers down Alec's cheek. "Thanks for coming with me today."

Alec leaned into the touch. "You're supposed to be sleeping."

Soft lips brushed Alec's in response. His heart nearly thundered out of his chest at the simple touch. There were so many reasons they shouldn't do this. He shouldn't even be there.

Further thoughts scattered as Damien deepened the kiss, his tongue sweeping out and demanding entrance. Alec's mouth opened on a gasp, allowing Damien's tongue to dance and twist with his own. Damien rolled on top of him, his erection brushing against Alec's.

Electricity shot up Alec's spine.

Alec quickly drowned in the musky scent of Damien's arousal as it overpowered his usual vanilla and spice. It was too much.

It was everything.

Damien moaned into his mouth as he laced their fingers together, pinning Alec's hands above his head and grinding harder against him.

The move stretched Alec's spine.

Ice shot through his veins.

His body locked up, his mind flashing back to a different time and place.

No. No. No. Not again.

He had to get away.

A piercing whine tore out of Alec's throat. He twisted, lashing out. A small voice in the back of his head demanded he take care. This was Damien. He didn't want to hurt Damien.

Damien wouldn't hurt *him*.

But it was too late.

The memories sank their claws in deep.

The dark dungeon.

Alec's heart thundered in his ears.

His arms chained to the wall high above his head.

Gods, no, not again. Please.

Endless pain.

He couldn't breathe. Why couldn't he breathe?

His tormentor, laughing. Always laughing.

Air. He needed air.

Damien's voice echoed from far away, bringing Alec back to himself. Damien had positioned him with his feet off the edge of the bed and his head between his knees.

"Alec. Sweetheart. Breathe. Come on, breathe with me." Damien pressed his forehead against Alec's, breathing in deeply through his nose and exhaling slowly through his mouth.

The bands around Alec's chest eased as his breath fell into sync with Damien's.

"That's it, sweetheart. Keep breathing. You're okay. It's okay." Damien rubbed soothing circles up and down Alec's back.

His body shook with the adrenaline and fear pulsing through his veins. It took several tries to speak, his voice coming out rough. "D-Damien."

"Shh. It's okay. I've got you." Damien propped himself against the headboard and pulled Alec against his chest. Alec's pulse shot back through the roof, but Damien immediately relaxed his hold, resting one hand lightly on Alec's hip while he carded his fingers through Alec's hair with the other.

Alec relaxed back into Damien, beyond grateful the man innately understood that he couldn't be held in that moment but still needed the touch to ground him.

He closed his eyes and just breathed.

The scent of blood tickled his nose. Alec tried to turn, but the hand in his hair dropped to his shoulder and pressed back. Alec let out an anxious breath. "Damien, you're bleeding."

"It's nothing. I probably knocked my arm against the nightstand when I rolled away from you."

It smelled like more blood than that. "Are you—"

Damien pressed his fingertips to Alec's lips. "Shh. I'm sure. Just rest, sweetheart."

Something in his voice didn't sound right. Alec tried to turn one more time but stopped when soothing fingers tunneled through his hair again. The touch brought feelings of warmth.

Safety.

Exhaustion seeped into his bones, the events of the day catching up to him.

Vaguely aware that he had a lot to explain in the morning, Alec drifted to sleep.

20

WHAT. The. Ever-loving. Fuck.

Damien stared down at his shoulder. The heavy blanket had taken the brunt of the damage, but ... Alec had claws. Actual fucking claws.

He chuckled bitterly. Why not? It's not like anything else made sense anymore.

Holy hell, his shoulder burned. Alec had definitely broken the skin, but Damien didn't blame him. Not really. It was his own damned fault, grabbing Alec's hands like that and triggering another panic attack.

No. It was a full PTSD flashback.

He hadn't seen one of those in almost seven years.

Damien's heart twisted painfully before he managed to shove the errant thought back into its box. It could wait a few more days before he took that trip down memory lane.

The clock taunted Damien, reminding him he was on the

wrong side of midnight and well on the way to dawn. Despite his exhaustion and the low thrum of a headache from going several rounds with a pillar yesterday morning, he couldn't sleep. His mind raced at the implications of the previous day.

Had that really been a bobcat in Tim's apartment?

Had that bobcat really been *Tim*?

By the time they'd returned to his apartment, Damien had been ready to chalk everything up to a concussion-induced hallucination.

Current evidence begged to differ.

Damien frowned down at Alec, sleeping steadily against his chest. They needed to talk in the morning, and he wouldn't let the younger man distract him from it. Alec had promised answers in the ambulance, and now there were several more that Damien needed.

He didn't even care about the weird shit, really.

Inadvertently sending Alec's mind back to whatever hell he found himself in during that flashback, however, was another story. They'd find a way to work around this.

Damien attempted to shift into a more comfortable position, but his shoulder protested the movement. Fuck. His shirt had glued itself to the wound. He shouldn't have let it go this long, but he hadn't had the heart to move.

He couldn't put off disturbing Alec any longer.

Dawn's first light was creeping through the cracks around the curtains when he finally slipped out from under the exhausted man and padded down the hall to the bathroom. Damien gaped at the rust-colored stain that had spread over half of his not-so-white-anymore T-shirt.

He prodded at the three-inch hole in the shirt's shoulder and winced when fresh blood welled up. He would have to just tear it off like a Band-aid.

This wouldn't be fun.

Gritting his teeth, Damien pulled the shirt away from the wound. He hissed at the sting and carefully lifted the shirt over his head, pulling the torn fabric, so he wouldn't have to move his injured arm until he could get a better look at the wound.

Damien damn near jumped out of his skin when warm fingers prodded the injury while his shirt was still half over his head. He yelped and jumped back, immediately regretting the action when he caught sight of Alec.

The poor man looked like a kicked puppy, just waiting for someone to send him away. Damien's heart broke at the sight. He reached out with his good arm and pulled Alec toward him. "Come here."

A low whine filled the space between them. Alec reluctantly stepped forward into a loose, one-armed embrace. "I hurt you."

Nope. He wasn't going to let Alec beat himself up over the injury.

"Hey. It's just a scratch."

Alec shook his head and burrowed closer against Damien. "But that was hours ago. I can smell fresh blood."

"This?" Damien loosely gripped Alec's hand when the

other man reached again for the wound. He pressed a kiss into Alec's palm before letting it go. "This is my own damned fault. I didn't want to wake you, so my shirt took revenge by gluing itself down to the scab. Let me clean and bandage this, and then we can talk."

When Alec didn't respond, Damien gripped his chin and tilted his head up. He seemed so much smaller in that moment even though Damien barely had two inches on him. "Okay?"

Alec nodded and fled the room.

With practiced hands, Damien cleaned the wound before slapping on a few butterfly bandages. He covered the injury with gauze and medical tape. Good enough. The scratch was deep enough to scar but not so deep that he'd been at any actual risk from leaving it all night.

The new scar would look right at home with the knife wounds he'd received as a beat cop in a dangerous Milwaukee neighborhood. This was nothing compared to taking a knife to the gut and nearly losing his spleen. Bullet-proof vests don't stop all knives.

Damien stepped out of the bathroom and directly into the kitchen. Conversations like this one needed coffee, and it was too early to get any at Stauf's. He popped a pod into his seldom-used cup-at-a-time unit. It wasn't the same but would do for now.

Fortified with the scent of coffee brewing, he turned to find Alec slouched on the couch with his head buried in his hands.

Stepping up behind the couch, Damien leaned down and kissed the side of Alec's head. He finally took in what Alec was wearing and chuckled at the too-large sweatpants and long-sleeved running shirt. "I have to say, I love seeing you in my clothes."

Alec lifted his head out of his hands, and the corner of his mouth twitched into a barely there smile. "They're a little big on me. I should really run home and get some of my own. That is if you still want me here."

He knew Alec was worried about the concussion. While his head throbbed slightly, and there was a bit of a tender lump at the base of his skull, Damien had experienced worse concussions. This one wouldn't be a problem.

That didn't mean he couldn't use the situation to his full advantage, though.

"Now, why the hell wouldn't I want a sweet, sexy man to take care of me while I'm stuck at home this week?" Seeing that he had Alec's attention, Damien went for broke. "Besides, my birthday is in two days. You're not going to make me spend it alone, are you?"

Damien really didn't want to spend his birthday alone again this year.

Alec bit his lip and cocked his head to the side. "I don't understand you."

That surprised a laugh out of Damien. "That's okay. I don't understand me either. Do you want some coffee before we go get your stuff? I just have one of these single-serve units, but I can make you one quick."

Alec scrunched up his nose adorably at the suggestion. "Actually, I have some of Stauf's beans in my apartment. I can make you some there if you want."

"What the hell are we waiting for, then? Let me throw something on quick." Damien's heart warmed at the sound of Alec's laughter chasing him down the hall.

When they arrived at the apartment complex on Vine, Alec paused and turned to Damien. "Harper's been staying with me, and she's probably still asleep. But don't worry about waking her."

"Sound sleeper?"

Alec snorted. "Hardly. She sleeps with noise-canceling headphones. She's not used to the city noise with her new senses yet."

New senses. The phrase echoed in Damien's brain as they headed inside. Alec closed the door behind them, setting an intricate security system. "Let me make you that coffee first. Make yourself at home."

Damien's head hadn't appreciated the walk over to Alec's apartment, but he refused to say anything and make Alec worry again. Instead, he opted to take a seat on the inviting sofa in the middle of the open-concept room.

In the kitchen, Alec pulled down two mugs and started the coffee grinder. Damien's head didn't like that much either.

Watching Alec in the kitchen was fascinating. He moved with precision as he prepared the coffee with a press that Damien hadn't seen before. The brew smelled like heaven, and he couldn't wait to taste it, but Alec repeated the process to fill his own mug before carrying both over.

The first sip elicited a moan from Damien. "Oh, shit. This is fucking good."

A pretty blush painted Alec's cheekbones, and Damien didn't even bother to hide his grin. He tugged Alec closer to him on the couch, pleased when the sweet man tucked himself under Damien's arm and pressed into his side.

Alec took a deep breath before speaking. "How much of yesterday do you remember?"

That was as good a place as any to start. Damien sketched out his memory of the events leading up to his concussion the best he could, starting with the call from Kat and ending at the point where there'd been a ... bobcat? "Honestly, I hit my head pretty hard that first time. For all I know, I hallucinated the rest. I swear I heard someone shout my name after I slipped and fell back against the wall again, but my memory gets fuzzy on the details after that."

"You hit your head *twice*?" Alec's voice shot up an octave. Damien squeezed his shoulder briefly to remind Alec he was okay. Alec settled back against him and huffed out a breath. "That was me you heard shouting. Jac and I were in the hallway when Tim shifted."

"Shifted. Explain that to me."

"Tim is a bobcat shifter."

The fuck? Images from the day before flashed through Damien's head. The shove. Flying through the air. Tim's blurry form. A bobcat taking his place. He hadn't imagined that part? Then again … Alec had claws. The wheels in Damien's head spun as Alec continued the explanation.

"He was born with both forms—human and bobcat— and can shift between the two at will. The injury you described could've been deadly if he hadn't shifted to jump start the healing process." Alec took a shaky breath. "Tim's instincts tripped into self-preservation mode because you were there."

Well, shit.

Damien used to spend time up north in the woods back home on his family's annual camping trips. Bobcats were fucking dangerous when cornered. Were shifters the same way? *Christ, Damien, you're told the man turned into a bobcat and you're sitting here comparing the dangers to a wild one?* Must be the concussion fucking with his head.

Before Damien's thoughts derailed further, more memories popped into his brain. The cat crouched low and ready to pounce. A flash of white fur. Then, nothing. "Something jumped at Tim. I thought it was Frosty at first, but that doesn't seem right. Frosty is larger than it was."

Alec fidgeted against him, speaking into Damien's shoulder. "That was also me."

Come again? The wheels in Damien's head finally clicked into place. He blinked down at Alec. Sharp claws. White fur. *New senses.* "So that means you're a shifter too? And … Harper?" Was he surrounded by these creatures? His heart involuntarily picked up at that thought.

"Not exactly. Harper and I are werewolves—wait, how did you know about Harper?"

Werewolves were real? Damien snorted at himself. He had dead bodies that he was ready to believe were decades older than they ought to be. He was willing to believe Tim was a bobcat, why not werewolves too? Nothing should really surprise him at this point. He glanced down at Alec. Maybe he should fill the man—wolf?—in on his investigation. He might finally find some answers.

Damien's heart dropped as another thought struck him. Collin. Did Alec even know what had happened to the kid?

Alec tensed and tried to sit up. Shit, he'd been quiet for too long. What was the question again? Harper. Damien tugged Alec back against him, running a soothing hand up and down his spine. "Sorry, I didn't mean to go away on you there. You said something earlier about why Harper wears headphones to sleep."

The woman herself chose that moment to step out of the bedroom, cackling. "Alec, how've you kept any secret for so long? Nice to see you awake, Damien."

Alec lobbed a pillow across the room, catching the back of Harper's head and ruffling her long, burgundy hair as she turned to the kitchen. She pivoted back around and blinked down at the pillow and up at Alec before locking her hazel eyes with Damien's. Damien was sure he had an equally fascinated look on his face.

Werewolf. Was that how Alec could so easily hide his inability to see? He pressed his face against the side of

Alec's head and spoke low. "You're amazing, you know that?"

DID *ANYTHING* FAZE DAMIEN?

When Alec had awoke that morning to the scent of fresh blood and an empty bed, his heart had nearly stopped beating entirely. After he'd found the gash in Damien's shoulder, shame had burned through him at the realization that *he'd* been the source of the injury.

His *claws* had been the source of the injury.

Last night's panic attack had been the worst in years. Decades, really. Not since the last time he'd tried to become intimate with someone.

At least that time, the other man was a shifter and could defend himself. Long enough to toss Alec out of his home and onto the cold, rainy New York streets.

Ari had found him there hours later, locked in a flashback in an alleyway. Bruised and bloody from thrashing against a wall, never realizing he could just get up.

Walk away.

Damien had every right to toss him out too. Hell, the man was recovering from a concussion. He didn't need to risk injury creeping through the minefield that was Alec. He definitely didn't need to risk his life stepping into Alec's world.

But that wasn't Damien. Even after learning the truth about Alec, Damien was sticking around.

Damien nuzzled the side of Alec's head, murmuring into his ear. "You're amazing, you know that?"

And he called *Alec* amazing.

Alec turned his head until his nose brushed Damien's. "I think that's my line."

Soft lips captured his in a brief, but sweet, kiss that Alec melted into.

The sound of Harper rattling around in the kitchen pulled them apart. Alec sighed softly. The rest of the conversation that he needed to have with Damien would have to wait until they were back in Damien's apartment. He wasn't ready to share that much with Harper.

Not yet.

Something about Damien's recollection of the events in Tim's apartment was bothering Alec, but he couldn't put his finger on it. "There was something on the stairs when Jac and I arrived. I have no idea what it was. The only scent I could pick up from the creature was artificial. A harsh chemical. I don't think Jac saw it."

"While Jac was busy arguing Tim's way into the safe house, I poked my nose around." Harper made a noise in the back of her throat that Alec couldn't quite interpret. "I saw a picture of Tim on the wall with what I assume was his family. Now, I hadn't met the guy before yesterday, so I could be way off base, but ... the way you and Ari always talked about him, I thought he was younger. Like in the picture."

Alec lifted his head from Damien's shoulder. Where was Harper going with this? "Tim's thirty-three."

"Thirty-three? No way."

Before Harper could say more, Damien swore and extracted himself from the couch. "Aw, hell. I need to call my officers. I knew I fucking forgot something important. I'll be right back."

While Damien stepped into Alec's office, Alec joined Harper in the kitchen. He almost felt bad not telling Damien that he could still hear him in there, but curiosity had gotten the better of him. "Wonder what that's about."

"I guess what I said sparked a memory." Harper hummed thoughtfully before pulling some things out of the refrigerator. She'd stocked it up with food after berating him for always eating takeout. Alec had a feeling that Harper would be more of a den mother than Ari ever was.

The sizzle of frying bacon muffled Damien's voice as he spoke low into his phone. "It's Damien. Yeah, I'm fine. They stuck me on medical leave for the rest of the week, though. Look, I just remembered something important. I need you to interview Tim."

He paused for a few minutes while the other person spoke. With the door closed, Alec couldn't hear the other half of the conversation. "Shit, that's not good. I'll talk to Jac and see if I can get something out of him. I think Tim's attack is connected to the Doe cases. I swear he'd aged thirty years since I saw him last week. This might be the break that we needed."

A sinking feeling settled in the pit of Alec's stomach.

He wasn't positive, but the only Doe cases Damien had been working on were Oliver's and the one from the Conservatory last month. Damien's call implied that something connected the two cases. And now to Tim's attack as well.

Ari hadn't said a word.

She'd been avoiding him. Was this why?

Aged thirty years.

That sounded almost like soul magic if Tim had rapidly aged. Soul magic stole the lifeforce of the victim and fed it back to the caster.

It was also forbidden. Few creatures even possessed the ability to use it anymore.

A shiver of trepidation crept up his spine. He didn't like where his thoughts were heading. Alec tuned back in as Damien was wrapping up the call. "Bring what you can, along with your partner, to my apartment tomorrow. I want to go over everything with a fresh perspective."

When Damien stepped out of the office, Alec took a fortifying breath before turning toward him. "I think I need to hear more about your cases."

"I agree. That's why I asked Andy to bring everything they could smuggle out of the office over tomorrow. Look, there's something I need to—wait, you heard me?"

Alec pointed at himself. "Werewolf."

"I see." Damien didn't sound mad, but he wasn't exactly pleased either. "Maybe you should give me a crash course on what that means."

Harper clapped her hands together a little too cheerfully. "Sounds like the perfect topic for breakfast. Food's ready."

Subtle.

Alec sighed and let the subject change. For now.

DAMIEN WAS A COWARD.

It was imperative that Alec learn what Damien knew about Collin before Candice and Andy showed up tomorrow evening. The last thing Alec needed was for Damien to blindside him with the news in front of strangers.

But he didn't have it in him to bring any more pain to Alec's face.

Not today.

Damien sighed and placed the liquid gold that Harper had sent home with them in his refrigerator—a jug of cold-brew coffee that she'd made using Alec's beans from Stauf's. Harper had promised the coffee would be ready in the morning and taped to the side were instructions on how to use Alec's AeroPress to filter it.

He owed that woman big time. Not only for the coffee but for jarring his memory and then distracting Alec from his phone call. He turned to the sweet man standing nervously in the entryway with a duffel bag in his hands.

Damien was also an idiot.

"If you want to unpack that, I can make some room in my closet for you."

A shy hint of a smile twitched at the corner of Alec's mouth. He dipped his head, biting his lower lip. "I'll just leave it at the foot of the bed for now. Maybe ... maybe I'll unpack later." The unspoken *if I'm still here* lingered between them as Alec hurried to set the bag down.

Alec's insecurity was palpable. Damien hated to see the shy but confident man eclipsed by it. The instinct to hunt down and maim whomever had caused Alec to react this way rose again. They should probably have the conversation that Damien had been avoiding all day, now that they were alone, but he wasn't sure how to bring the topic up without sounding like an asshole.

Damien stepped up behind Alec and pressed a kiss to the side of his neck. Alec shivered and relaxed back against him. That was better. He nipped at Alec's ear, eliciting a soft moan. "I'd love nothing more than to coax more of those sounds out of you for the rest of the night, but I think we need to talk first."

Alec nodded and silently stepped away.

They sat together on the couch. The apartment was dim enough that Alec took his glasses off. What an honor to know Alec felt comfortable enough to do that around him.

Alec removed his scarf, revealing the ropy scars Damien had seen once before.

Slowly tugging one finger at a time, Alec removed the gloves he always wore and placed them on the coffee table. A matching ring of scars circled each of Alec's wrists. Dread crept up Damien's spine at the implications.

This sweet, wonderful man had been imprisoned. The positioning of the scars made it clear his captors had strung him up by his arms with shackles that bit deep into his skin.

No wonder this man suffered from PTSD.

Fuck.

Alec huffed out a soft, self-deprecating chuckle as the silence stretched between them. He hugged himself tightly, effectively hiding the worst of the scars. "This is harder than I thought it'd be."

Tugging one arm free, Damien turned Alec's wrist and kissed the inside of it. He repeated the action with the other one, then pressed a soft kiss to Alec's lips. He didn't linger; his only purpose was to comfort and support.

With a shaky breath, Alec rose from the couch and reached for the hem of his shirt with trembling hands. What would make Alec understand that Damien didn't care about the scars? Well, he did, but not in the way Alec feared.

"Come here." Damien tugged lightly at the waistband of the sweatpants Alec still wore. With the other man standing between his legs, Damien slid his hands up Alec's hips. He stopped when his fingertips brushed just under the hem of the shirt and waited.

Alec nodded and hesitantly dropped his arms away.

Damien pushed the fabric up in gradual increments, enjoying the silky heat from Alec's skin. Leaning forward, he kissed each glorious inch that he revealed. White scar tissue adorned most of Alec's stomach. Some scars had left deep grooves in his skin, but the rest of them were smooth and stretched over toned muscles.

His tongue traced the hard ridges of Alec's abdomen. Lifting his eyes when Alec started panting, Damien found a lovely flush spreading across the beautiful man's face. "You're so fucking gorgeous."

Alec shook his head in denial. "How can you say that?"

Slowly rising, Damien slid the shirt the rest of the way up and off. Alec helped him at the end, so the fabric didn't tangle and constrict him for long. With the shirt out of the way, Damien drank in the sight. He grabbed Alec's hand and pressed it to his aching cock. "See what this is doing to me?"

Nostrils flaring, Alec moaned as his own erection surged, tenting the sweatpants. Damien chuckled and pressed a chaste kiss to Alec's lips. "We're getting distracted. Come, lie with me in bed and tell me what you can."

A low growl rumbled up from Alec's throat. "You're such a tease."

Damien grinned and kissed Alec's nose. "I can't help

what you do to me, sweetheart. But I need to know, so we can avoid more misunderstandings, okay?"

After stripping down to his boxers, Damien tugged Alec over to his bed and leaned against the headboard. Alec instantly curled against Damien's side, wrapping an arm and leg around him and tucking his head against Damien's chest. Alec let out a shaky breath. "Did you know there are no wolves in Ireland?"

That was an odd question. "I ... no, I didn't know that."

Alec smiled sheepishly. "It's relevant, I promise. In the year 1652, Oliver Cromwell signed an agreement with my family to breed our Irish wolfhounds for the Commonwealth to combat the rampant werewolf population. Enormous packs of werewolves were terrorizing all of Ireland and infecting entire villages with the werevirus. By the time I was born in 1755, our family had become highly adept at hunting them."

Damien's head spun with the enormity of the information Alec had just dropped on him. His family had hunted werewolves. Was that how Alec had become one? And born in ... "Wait, you're telling me you're *two hundred and sixty-five* years old? How is that even possible? You told me at breakfast that werewolves aged normally."

To think that Damien had been thinking of Alec as a younger man. By all appearances, he couldn't be much over thirty.

Turning thirty-nine in a few days didn't seem so bad anymore.

"Every werewolf I've ever met has lived slightly longer than a normal human lifespan. The oldest wolf that I've ever known besides myself lived to be a little over a hundred years old."

What made Alec different?

Christ, how long had Alec lived with those scars? Alec had explained in a little more detail how Tim's shift had allowed him to heal rapidly. If werecreatures healed the same way, did that mean Alec had been tortured as a human?

Alec shifted to press a hand against Damien's cheek, distracting Damien from his thoughts. "We're getting a little ahead of my story."

Turning his head, Damien pressed a kiss into Alec's palm. "Okay, but if you keep dropping bombs like that one, expect me to interrupt again."

Huffing out a soft laugh, Alec settled back against Damien and idly traced his fingers through the light coating of hair on Damien's chest. "The last pack of werewolves in Ireland captured me in the spring of 1786. I think they tried to ransom my life in exchange for my father calling off his hounds, but he refused. Their Pack Alpha took his frustrations out on me after that."

That was putting it mildly. Damien traced his fingers over the scars peppering Alec's back. Alec didn't need to relive his torture for Damien. But something about those scars ...

A voice from Damien's nightmares echoed in his mind.

"More o' me wolves have succumbed to de bastard's father's hounds."

Damien studied the scars on Alec's wrists and frowned, the cold sensation of steel biting into his skin. Chains echoed in his memories.

Fuck.

His nightmares.

Pain filled Damien's heart as the reality of what Alec had gone through sank in. The nightmares were real. They just weren't Damien's.

But why did they haunt *him?*

No. The how or why didn't matter enough to reopen Alec's wounds, no matter how curious he was. The important part was that Damien knew, and he could use that information to avoid triggering Alec in the future. And maybe now that he knew, the nightmares would end.

Hopefully.

Damien kissed the top of Alec's head, forcefully silencing his thoughts. "How did you escape?"

"Ari found me at the brink of death. She ... did something that helped the werevirus take hold after ..." Alec held his hand to his stomach. "The virus helped me heal from the mortal wounds, but it couldn't heal everything. It couldn't bring back my sight. That was the day I stopped aging." Alec lifted his head, unseeing eyes burning straight into Damien's. "The day I became the abomination that my family hunted."

Abomination? Is that what Alec thought of himself? "Sweetheart, you're anything but that."

A tentative smile tugged at Alec's lips, but he shook his head sadly. "To our family, that's what werecreatures were. Unnatural creatures that deserved to die."

Oh, to be able to go back in time and slap some sense into Alec's family. Damien sighed and focused on the rest of Alec's story. "So you're still alive because of what Ari did?" Alec had been with Ari all this time. Just who was that woman?

"We don't really know." Alec shook his head. "No, that isn't right. *I* don't really know. Ari might, but she's never told me. Anyway, that isn't important."

It seemed important, but Damien didn't have enough information to formulate the reason he felt that way. The puzzle settled into his hindbrain, and he'd poke at it more later.

"When I completed the change, Ari took me home to my family. The hounds knew what I was. Instead of welcoming me home, my father didn't stop them from chasing me off the property. He threatened to kill me if I ever returned." Alec's voice cracked. Damien swiped the pad of his thumb under Alec's eye, catching an unshed tear before it could fall.

Alec had gone through so much.

So damned much.

Christ.

"We boarded a ship bound for America that same day.

We later heard stories that within a week of our departure, high in the slopes of Mount Leinster, my father's hounds took down the last werewolf in Ireland. They followed my scent straight to his lair."

Damien held Alec loosely after he fell silent, rubbing soothing circles into his back until he fell asleep. Pieces were falling into place, but there were a few that didn't quite fit.

He lay awake most of the night, haunted by the implications.

21

VANILLA AND SPICE SURROUNDED HIM, but the bed was empty of Damien.

Alec stretched and rolled onto his stomach to bury his face in Damien's still-warm pillow. He must've woken when Damien got out of bed. It amazed him he could sleep beside the other man so soundly and not have any trouble with the closeness.

He had never thought he would have this again.

There was a soft curse and a loud crash down the hall. Alec leapt out of bed and rushed toward the sound. "Damien?"

"Shit. Watch your step. I made a fucking mess." Damien was on the floor. As Alec approached, his foot nudged a box in the middle of the hallway.

"What in the world are you doing?"

Damien chuckled derisively. "I was making room for

you in my closet. I lost my balance moving a box, and it all came crashing down. Sorry I woke you up."

Alec frowned. "You didn't hit your head again, did you? Damien, you have a concussion. You shouldn't be doing this."

"I wanted you to feel like you had space here." Damien stood and cupped Alec's cheek. "I'm fine, I promise."

This man was unreal.

Alec pulled Damien into a tight embrace before stepping back, lips twitching into a half smile. "I appreciate the sentiment. But it can wait until you're better."

Damien grumbled and started shoving boxes and other things across the floor. "I guess. Let me at least clean this up a bit."

Not wanting to stray too far away, Alec leaned against the wall. Damien could adapt to just about anything, but Alec was quickly learning how stubborn the man could also be.

After cleaning up, Damien strode to the kitchen. "Can you grab the press from your bag? I'm dying to try Harper's coffee."

Halfway to the bed, Alec stopped and tilted his head. Damien's heart rate had picked up. And this was the second time he'd rubbed his hands on his boxers. The detective that Alec had become so fond of was unusually nervous.

AeroPress in hand, Alec returned to the kitchen. He set it down on the counter before grabbing Damien's bare shoulders and turning him until his back was against the counter. Alec cupped Damien's face in his hands and cocked an eyebrow.

"That obvious, huh?"

"Your heart is racing. Your palms are sweaty ... You're either sick or nervous about something, and I don't detect illness in your scent." Alec dipped his head and lowered his voice. "Werewolf, remember?"

That startled a laugh out of Damien. "Human lie detector, eh? I'll keep that in mind. Sorry, I've been putting this off, and at this point, I feel like you're going to be pissed that I didn't say something as soon as I was sure."

That didn't bode well.

Alec leaned against one of the kitchen pillars while Damien gathered his thoughts and pressed the cold brew into cups for them. He forced his mind to clear—thinking too hard and getting worked up before Damien could even speak would definitely lead to an emotional reaction. The man had taken everything Alec had told him yesterday in stride. The least Alec could do was to keep an open mind in return.

Damien sighed and handed Alec a cup of coffee. "I feel like I need to preface this. Before yesterday, I didn't think you'd believe me, and I didn't know how to bring it up."

Lacing his fingers with Damien's, Alec led them over to the couch. This was probably a conversation they should have while sitting down. "You're stalling."

"I know. I know." Damien groaned and set his coffee down. He tugged Alec closer, wrapping an arm around his

234

shoulders. "Okay. You heard my conversation yesterday with Andy. He and his partner Candice are coming this evening to discuss the John Doe cases and how they connect with Tim's attack on Monday."

Dread crept up Alec's spine. He wouldn't like what Damien had to say at all, would he?

"Until a few weeks ago, we believed we had two John Doe bodies that had died of old age and also a set of disappearances that coincided with the bodies." Alec's head shot up at Damien's words, trepidation holding his tongue. "It was easy to believe that with the first body. I didn't know the man personally and easily discounted the minor things that didn't fit the puzzle."

Oliver had been Damien's John Doe from May. Mike had reached out about the dead werewolf in the morgue. Ari herself had confirmed it was Oliver. But neither one of them had said anything about Oliver dying of old age.

That shouldn't be possible for a thirty-seven-year-old werewolf.

Unless it involved soul magic.

He hadn't connected the dots when Damien described Tim's attack yesterday. *"I swear he'd aged thirty years since I saw him last week."*

If Tim's attack was connected ... Alec stood and paced in front of the couch. "Ari didn't tell me how Oliver had died."

"Wait, you knew Stone?"

"Yes, Oliver was a werewolf." They were getting off

track. Alec stopped pacing and pinned Damien with a glare. "That isn't what you were putting off telling me. What is?"

He had a feeling he already knew. Pain lanced through his chest at the very thought. Damien grabbed his hand, squeezing reassuringly. "Alec, I recognized the body in Franklin Park. It was the spitting image of Collin if you ignored his age."

An anguished cry tore out of Alec's throat. He pulled his hand away from Damien and hugged himself. "She knows, and she's never said a word. Why, Ari? Why did you keep this from me?"

She'd lied to him.

Ari had kept things from him before, but she'd never once outright *lied* to him.

That he was aware of.

What else was she hiding?

"Are you sure she knows?" Damien's soft-spoken question broke through Alec's rampant thoughts.

He laughed bitterly. "Oh, she definitely knows. She's the one who told me Collin had died. I'd assumed it was unrelated to your case and had a preternatural cause instead. That's why I never said anything. Turns out it was both."

Alec swiped his phone off the coffee table. "Call Ari."

The phone rang.

And rang.

Alec's heart sank as voicemail picked up. Static filled

his ears before the message started playing. Bad connection? Either way, she hadn't answered. He ended the call and sat heavily on the coffee table, facing Damien. Alec wasn't ready for touch yet, betrayal burning raw in his veins. "I feel so alone."

"You're not alone, Alec."

"Everyone leaves, Damien. They leave on their own or they die. Even my father turned his back on me once he'd seen what I'd become. Ari has been the only constant in my life." *How pathetic was that?* "And she lied to me. How much has she kept from me over the years that I just went along with because I thought it was in my best interests?"

He'd always thought she kept silent because what she knew couldn't be changed, but what if that wasn't it? What good was there in keeping him in the dark about how Collin had died? She hadn't trusted him to handle it.

"I'm broken. Damaged." Alec let out a pained breath and gestured to Damien's still-healing shoulder. "I even hurt you, Damien."

Damien leaned forward and pressed his forehead to Alec's until they were nose to nose and breathing the same air. "I am right here, sweetheart. I'm not going anywhere."

When their lips met, it was soft and sweet. Damien's sincerity burned through Alec, and he melted into the kiss. This man was everything he'd ever wanted and more.

Everything he'd always thought he didn't deserve.

"*A rúnsearc.*" The whispered endearment fell from Alec's lips as they parted, but he wouldn't take the words back. The truth of them sliced through the last of his restraint.

Alec didn't want to think anymore. He needed to *feel*.

Alec launched himself into Damien's lap, kissing him deeply with his arms wrapped tight around Damien's neck. Damien moaned and skimmed his hands across Alec's bare back, threading his fingers through Alec's hair with one hand. He left his grip open, giving Alec plenty of space to pull away.

Damien slipped his other hand under the waistband of Alec's sweatpants. He teasingly dipped his finger along Alec's crease. Alec moaned into the kiss and pressed down against Damien's clothed cock with his own, seeking friction.

The musky tang of their mixed arousal engulfed Alec's senses. He spread his legs to straddle Damien and grind their erections together.

Sliding his hand between them, Damien pushed Alec's sweatpants down just enough to free his cock, fingers wrapping tightly around its length. Pleasure ripped through Alec. He tugged Damien's lower lip with his teeth as he broke the kiss and dropped his forehead to Damien's shoulder, panting.

Damien seized the opportunity to kiss and nip at the sensitive spot behind Alec's ear as he fumbled with freeing his own cock. Alec batted Damien's hand away to grip them both together, pumping with a tight fist and a twist on each upward stroke.

The dry friction quickly eased as Alec spread the precum from both of them down their shafts.

"Oh, fuck." Damien moaned and threw his head back against the couch, thrusting into Alec's fist. Alec bit down at the junction between Damien's neck and shoulder, causing Damien to cry out again, his cock jerking in Alec's hand.

Each spasm shot sparks along the base of Alec's spine. It'd been far too long since Alec had felt anything against his cock but his own hand. He wouldn't last much longer.

Alec tightened his fist and pumped harder, turning his head for a sloppy kiss from Damien. They were both panting and uncoordinated, breathing too hard for more than just a press of lips and shared breath.

Damien reached behind Alec and traced his finger along Alec's hole again, pressing just the tip of his finger inside. That, along with a few more hard, upward thrusts from Damien, forced Alec's orgasm to shoot out of him without warning. He muffled his cries in Damien's shoulder.

Allowing his oversensitive cock to fall free from his fist, Alec kept up the pace on Damien's cock, spreading his release to ease the way. Alec reached down with his other hand to squeeze and tug at Damien's balls. Damien's hips stuttered, and he cried out as cum splashed across Alec's stomach and chest.

Alec collapsed on top of Damien, sated and emotionally drained. He nestled closer, nuzzling and licking at the bite mark he'd left imprinted on Damien's skin.

Damien threaded his fingers through Alec's hair as they lay there, catching their breath.

What would it be like to feel this man moving inside him? Was it worth the risk?

With anyone else, the answer would be no.

Absolutely not.

But with Damien?

Smiling softly, Alec traced his fingers down Damien's torso. Maybe he could come up with something for Damien's birthday that would be fun for them both but still mitigate the risk.

Alec's mind drifted on fantasies until the cum dried between them. Groaning, he pushed up from Damien's chest. "We should probably take a shower."

Not that he particularly wanted to lose their shared scent just yet, but their bodies were quickly becoming glued together.

Chuckling, Damien patted Alec's shoulder. "Give me a few more minutes. I don't think my legs are ready to hold me up yet."

"Okay."

DAMIEN PRODDED at the bruise on his neck from Alec's teeth, body heating all over again from the memory of the sensation the bite had triggered before turning away from the mirror. No broken skin. He had to get dressed, so they could get an early dinner in before his officers arrived in a few hours.

Stepping out of the bathroom, Damien drank in the sight of Alec lounging on his bed in a pair of dark wash jeans and a long-sleeved, jade green shirt that brought out the emerald in his eyes. The scarf and gloves sat nearby, waiting for Alec to put them on before they left the sanctuary of the apartment. Alec's lips twitched with a sly smirk.

The progress they'd made in just over a day was leaps and bounds from that of the past several weeks. Damien loved this confident side of Alec and made it his new goal in life to draw out more of it. "What are you chuckling about over there?"

Alec made a show of flaring his nostrils, amusement dancing across his expressive face. "You always smell like vanilla and spice to me, but it's the third scent that I love the most." He dropped his voice into a seductive growl. "It lets me know when you're turned on."

In two long strides, Damien stood with one knee on the bed and one hand next to Alec's head. He leaned down and kissed the man soundly before dipping his head to kiss the sensitive spot he'd discovered behind Alec's ear. "You always turn me on."

Alec moaned and tried to pull Damien further onto the bed, but Damien resisted. "Nope. We're leaving to get food." Damien tugged his arm out of Alec's grip. "Damn, you're strong."

"Sorry, I'll try to tone it down a bit." Alec shrugged sheepishly.

Damien nipped at his ear. "Don't you dare. I love it."

The thought of Alec pinning him down with all that strength shot straight to Damien's groin. Alec hummed knowingly as Damien stepped back from the bed before he gave in, and they spent the rest of the day there.

They could do that tomorrow.

Damien glared at the pile of boxes on the floor outside his closet, still irritated that he'd lost his balance this morning. While he didn't have much of a headache with this concussion—well, no more of one than he'd been battling for several weeks now—the occasional vertigo and distortions in his vision told him he should probably be more careful than he'd been.

His outpatient paperwork had prescribed rest and limited physical activity. Did orgasms count as limited physical activity? Damien shrugged and grabbed a pair of jeans and a T-shirt out of the closet. They did now.

Since driving was also out, Damien had suggested they walk a few blocks to an Indian bistro on Spring Street for something different. Not that he didn't enjoy Sister's every day of the week, but the noise level inside wouldn't be ideal right now. They could sit outside at the bistro.

When they were ready to leave, Alec donned his protective gear. Damien understood why he wore those things, but it made him sad that Alec wasn't comfortable enough in his own skin to go without them in public. He wrapped his arm around Alec's waist as they walked. "So. I'm not going to turn furry if you bite too hard, am I?"

An adorable flush filled Alec's cheeks. "What? No. That wouldn't happen unless I was in wolf form, and the bite was fatal."

Good to know.

Damien chuckled. "Just making sure."

After the host seated them outside, Alec tilted his head. "I haven't eaten at this place before. What's on their menu? The lamb smells amazing."

Damien read off the various lamb dishes for Alec to choose from before selecting a shrimp dish for himself. They ordered several appetizers and bread dishes to share. After the server left, Damien laughed. "I think our server is questioning our sanity given all the food we just ordered."

"I can't help it. We skipped breakfast, and I should really eat more than I already do."

Maybe Damien should have some groceries delivered, so Alec had something to snack on between meals while he was at the apartment. He hadn't really thought about it, but it made sense given what he'd learned yesterday about werewolves.

Was that only yesterday?

Damien's life had taken a drastic turn.

Alec nudged him with his foot. "You're thinking hard over there."

"Sorry." Damien glanced around. There was only one other couple braving the July heat by eating outside. The patio was private enough, but he kept his voice low to be safe. "We talked a lot about the basics yesterday, but I still have a lot of questions."

"Ah. I imagine you do. Ask away."

"The cases I'm working on have me curious. Who does your community go to when they need help? Who polices them? I can't imagine a fugitive shifter would quietly go to a human jail."

Laughter lines crinkled around Alec's eyes. "This certainly isn't light dinner conversation, is it? You're right, they wouldn't, and if they did, it would be catastrophic."

That was putting the situation mildly. It could be a fucking bloodbath. Damien's only experience so far included people he knew hadn't intentionally hurt him, and he had still walked away with a concussion and a shiny new scar.

He'd been lucky.

So damned lucky.

Alec pressed his foot to Damien's again. The comforting gesture slowed the racing heart he hadn't noticed while lost in thought.

"The key factor you have to remember is that all of us are actively working to keep unaware humans, well, unaware. As such, the community often polices itself. There are still aware humans who hunt the creatures that get out of hand. If all else fails, the Fae Lords step in. And no one wants that."

"Why is that?" They'd discussed the Fae yesterday, but

not Fae Lords. The name said enough. They didn't sound friendly.

"The last time they stepped in, the solution was to eradicate every last wolf and werewolf in Ireland."

Damien blinked. "You said your family's Irish wolfhounds did that."

"They did as a part of the Wild Hunt. Oliver Cromwell was a Fae Lord."

Holy shit. That gave a whole new perspective on the bloody history of the British Isles.

Alec had also neatly sidestepped Damien's question. Before he could call him out on it, the server arrived with their appetizers and bread.

They ate in silence for a few minutes while Damien gathered his thoughts. After they finished the bread, he verbally pounced. "What about crimes that don't risk the big secret? Or the ones that end up in the legal system anyway?"

A complex series of emotions flashed across Alec's face as he considered the question. Finally, he sighed and shook his head. "They often go unsolved. As for the ones who land in your lap, so to speak? Well, I think you've experienced this yourself. Bodies disappear, evidence gets misplaced. I suspect they called a certain Fae lawyer to come in this time when the other options were no longer viable."

Damien cocked an eyebrow at the low growl that had

seeped into Alec's voice. Fae lawyer? "Are you telling me Jac is Fae?"

"Half Fae, I believe. Scott is full-blooded."

The low thrum of a headache formed at the base of Damien's skull. Had the preternatural surrounded him his entire life?

His mind spun throughout the rest of their meal.

DAMIEN HAD GIVEN Alec a lot to think about at dinner. Sure, there were Pack Alphas and Pride Leaders that the shifters and werecreatures could go to for help, and he and Ari did all they could for the Independents. But Ari had limits for what she could do, and Alec relied on her to decide what to take on.

Maybe too much.

Who did the rest of the preternatural community have? The answer was alarming.

They had no one.

Unless you counted the Fae, whose interests lay solely in keeping humans unaware. Or, gods forbid, the shifter enclaves. Communities where they didn't allow humans and highly discouraged them from entering through physical or magical means. But there was a reason he considered those places a cult.

Collin had been lucky to get away.

But his luck had run out.

Alec sighed.

Damien squeezed his shoulder briefly before threading his fingers back through Alec's hair. They'd spread out on the couch after returning from their meal. All the food had left Alec sated and sleepy.

Down the hall from Damien's apartment, a female voice that Alec recognized spoke softly to her male companion. Alec lifted his head from Damien's lap and stretched. "I think your officers are here."

"Yeah, I buzzed them up a minute ago from my phone." Damien went to greet them at the door. He opened it before they could knock. "Come on in, guys."

The woman sucked in a surprised breath. "Geez, Damien. Did you install cameras in the hallway or something?"

"Not exactly." Someone closed the door, and Damien led them further into the apartment. "Let's set up in the living room. I cleared off the coffee table, so we can spread out. Sorry, I don't have a better space."

If Alec had been thinking, he would've offered his own apartment for this. They could've used the breakfast bar. Nothing to do about it now, though.

Damien wrapped a loose arm around Alec's shoulder. "Alec, I'd like you to meet Candice Lawrence and Andy Jones. These officers often work with me on cases and have been working on the John Doe assignments with me. They're both studying to take the detective's exam in a few months."

"It's nice to officially meet you, Alec," Candice said. Alec held out his hand, which Candice shook briefly. She wore a light perfume that reminded Alec of a field of wild-flowers. At least it didn't make him want to sneeze. Underneath that, she smelled completely human.

Her partner, on the other hand, wore a cologne that didn't do enough to cover up his scent. It was so subtle that if Alec hadn't been looking for it, he would've missed the hint of rosewood that signified witch blood. Andy wasn't a practitioner—the scent wasn't strong enough for that—and it was entirely possible the man didn't even know about his heritage. But the witch blood meant that Andy would see things that most humans wouldn't notice. Alec would need to tread carefully around this officer.

"I thought we were going to go over the details of the case?" Andy asked.

"We are. Consider Alec a consultant for now. He's the fresh perspective that I'd like to use." So Damien hadn't told them anything yet. Good. They'd gotten so distracted earlier that Alec had forgotten to ask what the officers knew.

They settled around the coffee table. Alec perched on the couch while the rest sat on the floor to review the items the officers had brought with them. If this was soul magic, then there would be a ritual or pattern to the deaths. "Damien already gave me some general details, but can we start with Ol—the first John Doe?"

These officers were willing to speculate that the bodies

were Oliver and Collin, but Alec hesitated to confirm it. Nothing he could say would stand up in the eyes of the law.

Besides, if this was preternatural, it wouldn't matter in the long run. The CPD wasn't equipped to handle a preternatural creature themselves. That wouldn't stop Alec from helping Damien solve this, however. He wanted answers, and this was the only way he could get them.

When he knew enough, he could confront Ari.

"Okay. I was the responding officer when the initial call came in." Andy flipped through his notes. "We received the call on John Doe 0522 on Friday, May 22nd, at 8:17 a.m. after the neighbor's dog ran into the house. Victim was an older male in his late seventies to early eighties. After my initial sweep of the scene, I made the call to bring in homicide."

"Which meant no doughnuts for me that day." Damien sighed dramatically as he picked up on the recounting. "I arrived while Emily, the medical examiner, was working the scene. She pointed me to the driver's license that identified the homeowner as Oliver Stone, age thirty-seven. There were some distinct physical similarities between the body on the bed and the license photo, including unique hair coloring and a scar above the man's eye. My initial thought had been a stalker situation with emulation tendencies."

It always amazed Alec how the human mind could rationalize the impossibilities of what they witnessed. If something didn't fit into what they expected, their mind conjured up justifications that were more palatable—even to the point of being impossible. These rationalizations enabled a werewolf—in fur—to walk right past a person in the middle of town, and that person would coo over what a gorgeous dog they were. They didn't even stop to consider whether the creature was a wolf, much less a werewolf.

Candice hummed thoughtfully, drawing Alec's attention back to the discussion. "They didn't involve me much with the initial scene. After I arrived, one of the senior officers assigned me to watch the door and prevent any further incidents of that ridiculous dog racing around the house."

Alec snorted. "Fluffy is a hellhound. She'll show her belly to me, but that dog absolutely hates Ari. I thought she left Oliver mostly alone, though. It's strange that she wanted inside his house that badly."

"Mrs. Stevenson mentioned that Fluffy didn't care for the 'lady friend' who regularly visited Mr. Stone." Did Andy mean Ari? There weren't many people in Oliver's life as far as Alec was aware. "CSU found no signs of a break-in, but she reported the door was open when she followed Fluffy inside. Maybe Fluffy was interested in an intruder."

That was a possibility.

"Let's stick a pin in that for now." Damien shuffled some things around on the table before finding whatever he was looking for. "The ME report suggested that John Doe 0522 had been sleeping when he died from a heart attack. Time of death occurred between the hours of five and seven in the morning. Emily's autopsy gave us mixed signals on the victim's apparent age. Much of the soft tissue results concurred with the visual age, but the skeletal structure was more consistent with a man in his late thirties. After that, the fucking body got mixed up at the morgue, and that forced us to work with what evidence we already had."

Alec had to hold in his laughter at the indignation in Damien's tone when he talked about the disappearance of Oliver's body. He would keep what he knew about that to himself for now. Maybe he'd share it later if it became relevant. Maybe.

Andy blew out a frustrated breath. "The trail ran fairly cold after that. Mr. Stone's background check came back flagged six ways from Sunday, and prior to December, it was as if the man didn't even exist. Fingerprints for John Doe 0522 returned as a match to Mr. Stone, which made little sense, so we had the FBI run them instead. Those results came back as a match to one Frank Oliver Stonewell, who'd already died in a hiking accident in Montana. By that time, Captain Saunders had shuffled the case over to BCI to track Mr. Stone down. But I haven't heard or seen anything come from it."

"On Saturday, June 13th, a pair of teenagers discovered a Jane Doe along the shore of the Scioto River." Candice tapped her pen against the coffee table as she spoke. "At the time, the case had no bearing or connection to the John Doe cases, but we learned differently during the Franklin Park investigation, where we identified Jane Doe as Mindy Hawthorne. Ms. Hawthorne had severe lacerations to her back and shoulders. She bled out from a slice clean through the carotid artery."

That almost sounded like Harper's attack, only she'd sustained more damage to her lower legs from her attempts to run away. That'd happened only a few days later in Indianapolis. Alec furrowed his brow. "How is this connected to the rest?"

Damien tilted his head back against Alec's leg, squeezing his ankle in a comforting gesture. "We found Ms. Hawthorne's home address while looking into John Doe 0621. She'd been scheduled to work with Collin at Franklin Park, but she wasn't alive at that time. It appeared someone had abducted her from her home before she died. Her place was a disaster, but we found no traces of blood from her injuries. We never found the entry point into the river."

Alec leaned forward and gripped Damien's shoulders when the detective swore and swayed forward. "Damien, what's wrong?"

"Fuck me, it's the damned headache I started getting every damn time I try to focus on certain events surrounding this case after I got sick." Damien snapped his fingers and popped his head up suddenly, cursing at himself for the action. "The public housing center across from the Scioto next to all that new development. The one that had those overdoses last year. That's what was listed on the original forms. Candice, write it down before I fucking forget again."

"Okay, I made a note. Do you mean the forms supposedly in that envelope of yours?" What did Candice mean by that? Alec filed the question away to ask Damien later.

It was highly concerning that Damien still had headaches from whatever had triggered his fever at the beginning of the month. Between those and his concussion, the poor man had to be in pain. Alec slipped off the couch to find Damien's pain medication in his bag and returned with the pills and a glass of water, tapping the bottle against Damien's shoulder. They were strong pills, but the pharmacist had said they shouldn't cause drowsiness.

After shaking a pill out and swallowing it, Damien handed the bottle back to Alec. "Thanks, sweetheart. Yes, I meant those forms. But we're getting ahead of ourselves. Let's back up to the body in Franklin Park."

"Okay, here we go. According to the log, the call for John Doe 0621 in Franklin Park came in at 7:57 a.m. on Sunday, June 21st. Mr. and Mrs. Daniels were out for an early jog with their German shepherd. Their dog found the body under the decorative bridge on the path just off the amphitheater. The body had sustained damage, but Emily ruled that it was all caused by the German shepherd dragging it out of the bushes."

"Right. She also gave us an estimated time of death between four and seven in the morning. I think she narrowed that down in her autopsy report."

Candice hummed an affirmative after shuffling through some papers. "She narrowed the TOD down to between six and seven during the autopsy, but her notes here mention that oddities with the internal organs may've skewed her estimates."

Oddities with the internal organs. That didn't surprise Alec. Since shifters were never human, they sometimes inherited traits from their animal counterparts. Modern medicine posed certain risks to the preternatural community as a whole, but most of the time, the anomalies coincided with traits of human diseases. The human brain quickly latched on to the more believable reason and ignored anything that didn't align.

"This John Doe appeared to be in his late eighties. I could've sworn I recognized him when I saw him, but what really got me was that Collin's wallet and ID badge were in his pocket, along with some watches, a tube of lipstick, and several coins."

A small, involuntary whimper escaped Alec at Damien's description. A tiny part of him had still hoped, but this John Doe was definitely Collin.

Candice sighed. "After that, Andy and I spent a considerable amount of time fighting with the Conservatory over the name of the employee who Mr. Wilde had been working with. Both of them had gone MIA, but they stonewalled us until we could get a warrant."

"Turned out they didn't have the paperwork, and no one could remember the woman's name. I ended up at PackForce Staffing to get the information directly from them. That was the day I got sick. We didn't find much after that, except for Ms. Hawthorne's identity."

Alec frowned. Collin had never mentioned he was working for a shifter company. It made some sense, but that seemed like something Alec should've known. Had Ari known? It was hard to believe she hadn't if he were honest with himself.

It also explained why Alec had scented a wolf on Damien that day.

"Which brings us to the attack on Damien's downstairs neighbor on Monday morning." Andy shoved some things around until he found what he was looking for. Alec could just imagine the mess that the table had become. "Looks like the call came in at 5:59 a.m. Candice and I couldn't really smuggle much out of the office on this one. There's been a bit of a dispute with the higher-ups about jurisdiction of the case since you were also technically a victim."

"Of course, there is. Okay, someone or something was in that apartment when I got there. Unless Tim dyed his hair, there was a lot more gray in it than there'd been a few weeks ago when I saw him last. I have someone who can corroborate this. I interrupted whatever was happening, which caused the intruder to slash at Tim before escaping. Let's assume that all of these have been attacks, but there was no interruption with the others and therefore no reason to physically damage any of the prior victims."

Alec bit his lip. This was treading dangerous waters, but every detail mattered right now. "Monday was a new moon. You should double check me, but I think May 22nd and June 21st were as well. Moonrise is in the early morning on the new moon. I'm also willing to bet that the deaths occurred within a brief period after moonrise. It could be ritualistic."

The death of the moon was a powerful time for soul magic.

The only person that he knew would have answers was Ari.

"Good catch, I didn't think of that." Damien must've read something on Alec's face. "Let's let this all sink in tonight. The pills I took are kicking in, and I'm exhausted. See what else you can pull from Tim's case and look into the dates, see if Alec is onto something. This is sounding serial to me, so let's look into unsolved deaths during the new moon prior to May with similar unexplained disappearances. Pull in Sorensen and Young from special ops if they're available. Let's meet back here on Saturday."

With Mindy's and Harper's attacks so similar and close together, was Harper's attack connected to all of this? Perhaps even Oliver's initial attack in Montana? They didn't fit the new moon pattern, but ... "Besides Columbus and the greater area, you might want to look at Indianapolis from the beginning of the year to May and the region of Glacier National between Browning and Kalispell prior to January."

After the officers left, leaving the mess of papers behind at Damien's insistence, Alec cocked an eyebrow at him. "Those pills don't cause drowsiness."

"What are you thinking?"

"I think there's more to this. Someone attacked Harper in Indianapolis around the same time that Mindy died, and she had similar injuries. I'd like to scent Mindy's home tomorrow if that's possible. And Oliver really was hiking in Montana when he was attacked in December. I promise I'll explain further, but I need to talk to Ari first." Alec pulled out his phone and instructed it to call her. It rang several times and went to a staticky voicemail again. He hung up without leaving a message. She would know he'd called. "She didn't answer. I'll text Harper and see if she knows where Ari is."

Harper's reply came immediately. *"Ari is in Kalispell with Tim. They want me to ship his things after they release the apartment as a crime scene."*

Damien swore.

So much for answers.

"I'll keep trying."

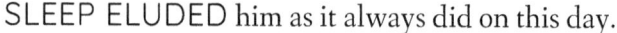

22

SLEEP ELUDED him as it always did on this day.

Damien glanced away from his phone and smiled down at Alec, sleeping curled tight against his side. Birthdays were always bittersweet, but this time he had someone special to take the edge off.

Seven years.

It was hard to imagine that much time had passed already.

Alec yawned and stretched before throwing an arm around Damien and propping his chin on Damien's shoulder. "You're thinking very loudly this morning. What are you doing awake already?"

"Yeah. Funny thing about memories, they don't really care what time it is, and they don't like staying in their boxes." Damien sighed and threaded his fingers through Alec's hair, taking comfort in its softness. "My birthday is a lonely affair these days. I know I made light of it the other day, and I'm grateful you're here, but ..."

"You don't have to talk about it."

Said the man who had bared his soul for Damien several times already. Alec was too sweet. "There isn't much to tell, really. According to my mom, my dad was never the same after Vietnam. He came home with severe PTSD and panic attacks. Mom never could get through to him, but I could."

"You do the same for me." Alec's murmured words settled something inside Damien. If anyone would understand, it was this man.

"I was away giving a seminar at the academy. It was my birthday, but all we had time for was a quick phone call before I had to get back. My dad fell into a bad flashback right after that call. Someone with shitty timing broke into the house after the flashback was triggered. Or maybe something they did triggered it. I don't know."

Damien draped his arm across Alec's lower back and sucked in a shaky breath. "The only reason anyone knows that much was because the intruder tripped the alarm, and the recording caught everything. Dad attacked the man, but he didn't know who he was fighting. The bastard killed him, and then he killed my mom. He got away. They never found him."

He'd listened to that tape repeatedly for weeks on end. It'd haunted Damien for years but had also given him a sense of purpose. He'd talked to his sergeant about the detective's exam that night. Even if he couldn't get justice for his own family, he wanted to bring it to whomever he could.

Alec rolled fully on top of Damien and held him tightly. "I'm so sorry."

Squeezing Alec's shoulder, Damien moved to sit up. He just had to keep moving forward and leave the past where it belonged. He didn't think about his family often anymore.

It hurt too much.

Lifting his head, Alec pressed his lips to Damien's. The kiss lasted a sweet, fleeting moment, but the gesture warmed Damien down to his soul. Alec was right. People left on their own, or they died. It didn't matter whether they died naturally or their lives were stolen away.

They left all the same.

Someone you loved could be gone in an instant, a year from now, a decade, a lifetime, or more. He saw it every single day.

But they were both here.

Now.

And he would make the most of what he had.

Damien cupped the back of Alec's head and brought him down for a deeper kiss. Alec settled between his legs and wrapped his arms around Damien's neck, parting his lips to Damien's tongue. Alec smelled and tasted like the forest.

Of wild things, just waiting to be unleashed.

Alec pulled back from the kiss, dipping his head to nip

and lick at the purpling bruise at the junction of Damien's neck and shoulder. Damien moaned and tilted his head to give him better access.

Alec kissed his way up to Damien's ear. "I want to try something. Put your arms behind your head and leave them there for me."

The whispered request shot straight into Damien's groin. He moved to comply, curling his fingers around the shelf in the headboard. Alec rewarded him with a deep, demanding kiss. A lovely blush stained his cheeks as he pulled back with a shy smile.

Alec slid his hands down the planes of Damien's chest, carefully avoiding the bandages on Damien's shoulder. He slowly shifted down Damien's body, kissing and trailing his tongue along the way. Alec's whispered words against Damien's skin stoked the flames of his arousal. "I want to see all of you."

He swirled his tongue around one of Damien's nipples, pinching and rolling the other one with his fingers. Damien arched into the touch.

"I don't need my eyes to see you." Alec kissed across Damien's chest to lave at the other nipple, tugging it gently between his teeth. Damien's breath caught as Alec dipped his fingers lower, toying with the waistband of Damien's boxers.

Damien ached to reach down and touch Alec. To run his fingers through that silky hair. He settled for watching Alec's thorough exploration of his body through hooded eyes.

He groaned in a combination of frustration and arousal as Alec continued his journey downward, sucking bruises onto the surface of his skin along the way.

Every wet pop as Alec released his skin ratcheted Damien higher and higher.

Alec paused at various scars, but he didn't question them. Instead, he lingered at each one, kissing and tracing them with his talented tongue.

"I just need to touch you." Alec nuzzled at the beginning of Damien's happy trail, a rumble of a sound that almost could've been a purr vibrating through his frame. Alec sank lower to mouth along the wet spot quickly forming on Damien's boxers.

Damien moaned as Alec nudged his nose along Damien's length through the fabric. Damien's cock jerked at the attention, and he couldn't stop the whimper that escaped when Alec pulled away.

Grinning, Alec tugged Damien's boxers downward. Damien lifted his hips to help remove the offending garment. Once freed, his cock bobbed to his stomach, purple and leaking.

Ignoring it completely, Alec moved lower, sliding his hands up Damien's hips and his tongue along the crease of his inner thigh. Damien's hips jerked off the bed. "Oh, fuck, Alec."

Repeating the action on the other side, Alec breathed deep and continued his whispered assault against Damien's skin. "I know what I'm doing to you by the way your scent changes. The heady musk, quickly overpowering your vanilla and spice."

Alec trailed his tongue along Damien's balls, sucking each one into his mouth and pulling off with an obscene pop. Alec kissed downward along his taint, encouraging Damien to lift and open his knees. "I could become addicted to this scent."

The first tentative brush of a wet tongue along Damien's hole made him cry out and bite down on his arm. The sound must've been all the encouragement Alec needed, as he speared his tongue inside, licking and nipping until Damien was nothing but a writhing mess on the bed, his cock leaving a pool of precum on his stomach.

Alec chuckled as he pulled back and finally, finally, traced his tongue up the underside of Damien's cock with one final whispered enticement before he closed his lips around the head. "I'm already addicted to how you taste."

With an arm banded across Damien's abdomen, Alec sucked Damien's cock down to the root, opening his throat to take him deep. Alec struggled for a moment to control his gag reflex but stayed there, swallowing and humming his pleasure once he had it under control.

Damien's scream echoed across the apartment, his blood on fire from Alec's ministrations. "Fuck, Alec!"

Alec bobbed his head, tonguing along the sensitive vein before taking Damien deep again.

Finally coming up for air, Alec pressed his forehead

against Damien's hipbone, panting. "Gods, it's been a while since I did that. I love the sounds you make."

Damien had to swallow twice before he could speak, his voice just as wrecked as Alec's. "Sweetheart, feel free to do that any time."

Alec nuzzled along Damien's hip. "Lube?"

Damien blindly patted along the shelf above him until he found the bottle he was looking for then groaned. Fuck. No condoms. "I don't have—"

Alec shot up and silenced him with a kiss. Damien tasted himself on Alec's tongue and moaned into his mouth. Nipping at Damien's jaw, Alec hesitated and cleared his throat. "We don't need them. If you're comfortable with that. Werewolf, remember? I can't catch or transmit human diseases."

Damien shot his hand down to grip the base of his cock, discarding the order to keep his hands above his head in an effort not to shoot right there. Just the thought alone was enough. "Shit, sweetheart. Think you could've mentioned that before we started?"

Alec laughed and dropped kisses to Damien's shoulder before picking up the bottle that Damien had tossed on the bed. "So ... is that a yes, then?"

"Fuck, yes."

After squirting lube onto Damien's fingers, Alec sat up and removed his sweatpants. He leaned down, kissing Damien again and climbing back on top of him. Alec's thick erection bobbed between them as he settled into a position on his hands and knees over Damien. "Then, get me ready. I want to ride you."

Fuck. Yes. Damien had to clamp down on the base of his cock again, panting until the renewed surge settled down enough for him to focus on the task at hand. He trailed his hand down to Alec's crease, dipping his lubed fingers along Alec's hole.

Moaning into the kiss, Alec pressed back against Damien's hand. "Hurry. Need you now, *a stór*."

Despite the demanding words, Damien still took his time. Alec was so tight, and he didn't want to hurt him by rushing. By two fingers in, Alec was fucking himself back on Damien's hand. Damien pressed a third finger firmly inside.

Alec dropped his head to Damien's neck and bit down, leaving a matching bruise to the one on the other side and muffling his cry at the same time. "I'm ready. Please."

Damien grabbed the bottle and slicked himself up.

With one hand planted on Damien's shoulder for balance, Alec reached back and positioned Damien's cock, so he could sink down onto it. After a slight wince, a look of pure bliss washed over Alec's face when Damien breached the tight ring.

Gorgeous.

The man was fucking gorgeous like this.

Damien's thoughts fled as Alec rocked back and forth, taking him inch by slow inch until he was fully seated.

Alec leaned down to kiss Damien.

Then he leaned back and began to *move*.

Each graceful roll of his hips shot through Damien's core. Damien moaned and threw his head back, holding Alec's thighs and joining Alec's rhythm by thrusting up on each downward roll.

Flames licked along Damien's spine as he sank into Alec's heat over and over again.

Alec dropped his hand to his cock, rocking up into his fist and back down onto Damien in an erotic dance.

He stroked and rolled his hips faster and faster, grunting and biting his lip.

Alec was damn near bouncing on Damien's cock by the time he threw his head back and growled out his release, painting them both with rope after rope of cum.

The sight shattered the last of Damien's control, and he thrust up hard into Alec, crying out his own release.

Collapsing on top of Damien, Alec peppered soft kisses to the new bite mark.

Eventually, Alec climbed out of the bed, disappearing into the bathroom. He returned with a warm washcloth to clean them both up.

Afterward, Alec set the cloth aside, crawled back on top of Damien, and cuddled close, murmuring sleepily into Damien's neck. "Happy birthday, *a rúnsearc*."

Laughter rumbled through Damien, the orgasm leaving him high and satisfied.

Happy birthday indeed.

TODAY WAS NOT GOING the way Alec had anticipated.

He'd planned on a lazy morning in bed. Had even convinced himself that he could freely explore Damien's body without fear of triggering something if they were careful, and Damien kept his hands off of Alec.

Alec's fantasy had involved waking Damien while he mapped the wonderful man's body with his tongue.

He hadn't expected Damien to already be awake, or the heavy emotions that preceded the events. It had explained a lot about Damien's personality and how easily he could navigate Alec's issues. Alec's heart hurt for all the man had gone through to find his easy-going outlook on life.

And once they got going? Alec definitely wasn't ready for how much of a rush controlling Damien's body like that had been. Or how revved up it would make both of them.

Most of all, he hadn't predicted that they would be breaking into Tim's apartment immediately after they woke again and got out of the shower.

But when had anything with Damien ever been predictable?

Alec followed Damien into the apartment after the detective bypassed the police seal on the door. The tingling warmth of an active glamour washed over him. Jac's power lingered throughout the room, likely still hiding parts of the scene from mundane eyes. "What are we looking for exactly?"

"Not sure yet. If my officers can't get the casework out of the precinct, I'll have to wait until Monday to read through the first responder's report. In the meantime, I'd like to get fresh eyes on the situation myself." Damien pressed a hand to Alec's chest to stop him from following further. "We have to be careful not to contaminate the scene. There's still dried blood everywhere."

While Alec could mostly tell where the blood was, it was probably best for him to stay back near the door. He tilted his head and took in a deep breath, sifting through the scents in the apartment.

Underneath the earthy scent of Jac's glamour, there were traces of the awful chemical scent lingering in the air. Alec frowned. It was too strong to be a residual odor from three days ago. "Check the bathroom. Something in there reminds me of what the creature on the stairs was saturated with."

Damien grunted an acknowledgement before rifling around through the bathroom. "I found a purse hidden behind the towels, and it looks like something's leaking inside it."

That explained why the chemical odor was still so strong. "Can you tell what it is?"

Damien stepped out of the bathroom. "I can barely smell it. I never would've found the purse if you weren't here. The smell is familiar, but I'm not sure why.

Doesn't look like CSU went through the bathroom yet—no reason to, with everything out in the living area. I'll shoot my officers a text to 'revisit the scene' and bring some techs by as soon as possible, so they can document it before going through the contents of the purse. Hopefully they can get in before the higher-ups decide whose scene it is."

Now that his heart wasn't pulsing with adrenaline and fear for Damien's safety, Alec focused on the scent. Would Tim have been able to smell it this strongly? Or was it just Alec's oversensitive nose? There was no way someone would've caught Oliver unaware if he could detect the odor to this degree.

He'd recognized it in the stairwell, and the scent had clung to his phone for several hours after Ari had returned it to him at the hospital. Where had he encountered that scent before?

Had Harper noticed it while she was in the apartment with Jac?

Nothing else caught Alec's attention while he stood near the door waiting for Damien to poke around the apartment. They left a short while later, with Damien muttering to himself about sloppy evidence tags.

Alec called Ari's driver to take them over to Mindy Hawthorne's house. Damien had another few days before he should be driving, though the detective seemed to be bouncing back from his concussion just fine.

Damien sighed as they approached the house. "As far as we've been able to find, Ms. Hawthorne inherited this house from her late grandmother. All the bills are on autopay through a trust. No one ever noticed she had gone missing."

With a hand on Alec's back, Damien guided him efficiently around the evidence tags still littered throughout the house, murmuring occasionally about the mess and to watch his step. Once they arrived in the middle of the living room, Alec searched for familiar scents in the air.

He shook his head after a minute. "You said the door was open when you found this house? I think any trace of lingering scent down here faded away from the constant flow of air. I can pick out traces of your officers and several people I assume are crime scene techs, but there's nothing that gives any indication of what happened down here. Can we go upstairs?"

"Sure. It's less messy up there, and the techs cleared the rooms quickly, so don't worry about contaminating evidence. Stairs are directly behind you. The railing is on the right side."

Upstairs, the rooms were permeated with fading scent memories, but anything the house could tell him had dissipated too much. Alec blew out a frustrated breath and turned to Damien.

"There are traces of something that I recognize, but it's impossible to pick out among the more recent officers and techs. I'm sorry. This was a waste of time."

Damien squeezed Alec's shoulder. "Everything about this is a long shot. There's one more place I'd like to go today, and that's the apartment complex I remembered yesterday."

The housing development where Damien thought Collin might've lived. Alec took a fortifying breath and nodded. "Okay."

Maybe they would have better luck there.

LOCATING Collin's apartment within the building proved easier than Damien had feared. They arrived while a pair of burly men from a moving company were fighting with pushing a couch out through the front door of the building.

Alec tilted his head in the manner Damien was quickly associating with the other man scenting the air before rushing up to the two men. "The apartment you're clearing out. Where is it?"

One mover grunted and gestured roughly down the left hallway. "Ask the super. He's the asshole tapping his foot in the hall down that away. Can't miss 'im."

Damien caught up with Alec as they slipped inside the other doorway that the mover helpfully opened for them. "What's up?"

"That couch belongs to Collin."

Shit. "Always one step behind. Andy's right, this case is cursed."

Alec stopped short in the hall, and Damien nearly ran into him, when a thin, raven-haired woman stepped out of an apartment door and approached a man with a perpetual scowl etched onto his face. The man must be the super, but who was the woman?

Groaning under his breath, Alec leaned back into Damien to speak privately. "That woman is with the enclave. We have to tread carefully here. Let me take the lead on this, okay?"

Enclave? "You're going to explain that later, right?"

With an affirmative hum, Alec slowly approached the woman. "Hello. I don't believe we've met. Does Ari know you're here?"

Alec was lucky he couldn't see the withering glare that the woman pinned him with. Damien cringed and held back to avoid drawing her ire. She pursed her lips. "Ms. Fushimi has no power here."

Fushimi? Damien's fingers itched for his notebook. That name sounded familiar.

A piece of the puzzle fell into place, shining a light on more missing pieces. Ms. Fushimi had hired Jac to represent the Conservatory and, more than likely, the staffing agency.

She was also Alec's Ari.

Ari Fushimi.

Damien put a mental pin in his swirling thoughts and tuned back in as a low growl rumbled out of Alec's throat. "You can let us look around for a few minutes. We won't get in the way. What's the harm?"

"What is your goal, exactly?"

"As I told you, we're looking for someone who's putting the entire community at risk of exposure. The police are investigating several bodies that were left to be found in the open, including Collin's. The more we know, the faster we can stop it. I promise we won't involve the enclave."

Alec was exaggerating the truth a little there, but Damien bit his tongue. He was so out of his depth here that it wasn't even funny.

Before Monday, Damien would've approached this differently. But did the preternatural community even care about his badge and gun when they could do so much more? How many of them could heal from otherwise life-threatening injuries like Tim had in the apartment?

Damien's life hadn't only taken a strange turn, it had missed the detour and gotten lost in a portal to another dimension.

The woman pinned Damien with her piercing golden eyes, lip curling in disgust. "But you will involve *him*?"

Almost as if he sensed the danger, Alec sidestepped enough to block the woman's view of Damien. "Please, just a few minutes."

"If you must, but *he* will stay in the hallway. Do hurry along. I'm on a schedule, and you are putting us behind."

Alec's shoulders tightened at her tone, but he turned back to Damien with his lips pressed into a tight line. "What should I look for?"

"I could call this in, get a warrant."

Alec shook his head. "We do that and she'll pull strings

to make it all disappear before anything happens. You don't know the extremes the enclave will go to, Damien."

They didn't have much of a choice but to go along with this, did they?

Damien fished an evidence bag out of his pocket. Good thing he'd remembered to grab some this morning. He handed the bag to Alec with a sigh. "It'd be ideal if you could find something that I can give to Em for a DNA match. Hair with the follicle still attached is probably the best thing at this point, and it'll be circumstantial at best since you're the only one that'll know it's his."

Alec nodded, stepping around the movers as they returned for more furniture, and disappeared inside the apartment.

The woman glared daggers at Damien the entire time Alec was gone.

Unease slithered up his spine.

Just who was she, and what the hell was the enclave? It sounded like some kind of cult.

A spike of pain shot through Damien's head, and for the second time today, his vision blurred. For just a moment, he could've sworn the woman's golden eyes turned an unnatural, bright yellow. After blinking to clear his eyes, the color returned to normal.

The concussion must be affecting his vision again. The first time had been while he searched in Tim's bathroom, just before he'd found the purse. He hadn't mentioned it to Alec, not wanting to worry the man.

When Alec returned, he held up the evidence bag that now contained a comb with hair woven through the teeth. With any luck, the age regressions would be back by the time Damien returned to the office, and they could corroborate the results with a DNA match. It was better than nothing.

But what did he even do with the results?

23

"ALSANDER, 'ould ye fetch the pups from the field?"

Alsander halted in his tracks at his father's call and sighed. Konnyer waited for him behind the barn. A shame he would be late once again. "Aye, Athair."

Fiery red and orange lit up the horizon as the sun began its descent behind the rocky slopes of Mount Leinster, ready to birth the next moon the following day. Prickles of power still danced across his skin from the black moon's sacrifice that morning.

He found the pups, young wolfhounds not yet a part of the Wild Hunt, where they spent their days on the hillside protecting the land. The pack would be ready to join the Hunt by the end of the season. Alsander would join them after his coming of age in the autumn.

His attention shifted to a pair of women arguing near the forest border at the same time that the pack took up a hunting cry. The smaller woman turned her head sharply as the wolfhounds descended upon them.

With no time to think, Alsander raced on an intercept course between the women and the hounds, shouting the commands for the pack to yield.

Too late, his vision wavered as the radharc na fírinne flared to life, revealing glimpses of fur in place of the women. The first creature, standing proud in a coat of brilliant gold and white, watched him intently while the second, adorned in deep red and black, crouched low with its white teeth glistening in the fading sun.

These women were other. What were they doing here?

Alsander frowned and skidded to a stop in front of the women. While he was distracted, the pack leader rammed into him, knocking him off his feet.

With a high-pitched screech, the taller woman dropped to the ground, and Alsander's vision became reality. The other woman jumped back from the hounds, eyes wide, and raced alongside the twin-tailed fox into the forest.

ALEC STRETCHED BEFORE CURLING TIGHT around Damien, burying his nose in the crook of Damien's neck and relishing in his scent. It wasn't often that he dreamed of the time before his change. Why now, and why remind him of a power he would never wield again?

The radharc na fírinne, roughly translated as sight of truth, had been passed down through his mother's bloodline. The rare power revealed a preternatural creature's true form, be it Fae, shifter, were, or anything in between. His family had used the gift to hunt the werewolves more efficiently. It was also the reason Alec never should've turned into a werewolf in the first place.

The witch blood should've made it impossible, but somehow Ari had found a way.

Damien turned and brushed his lips along Alec's, more of a caress than a kiss, but enough to scatter Alec's thoughts. "Morning, sweetheart."

With the last tendrils of his dream fading, Alec cupped Damien's cheek and drew the sleepy man in for a deeper kiss. They'd enjoyed a lazy day in bed the day before. It had been, as the detective had so aptly pointed out, to make up for working on Damien's birthday.

They needed to get up and have breakfast before Damien's officers arrived. They were going to brief Damien about what the pair had uncovered over the past few days. Instead, Alec snuggled deeper into Damien's warmth. "Good morning, *a stór*."

"Your treasure, hmm? That one I know. One of these days, you'll have to tell me what the other one means." The fondness in Damien's voice warmed Alec's heart at the same time as embarrassment heated his cheeks.

A rúnsearc. The phrase escaped him in the heat of the moment when Alec wasn't overthinking. When his heart overruled his head.

He wasn't ready for those words just yet.

But he would be someday.

They finally got out of bed when Damien's stomach started growling, and Alec's agreed wholeheartedly. Damien laughed and kissed the side of Alec's head. "We're out of the coffee that Harper sent over so how about breakfast at North Market? I haven't had my doughnuts all week."

Damien was addicted to those doughnuts. Alec chuckled and shook his head. "We better feed the stereotype, then."

"Hey, now, I broke the mold when they made me. The stereotype begins and ends with coffee and doughnuts."

The corners of Alec's lips twitched as Damien wandered down the hall to get ready. "If you say so."

After stepping out of the bathroom, Damien pressed up behind Alec to nip at the sensitive spot behind his ear. Alec couldn't help but moan at the sensation.

"You should probably try to bite me a little lower next time, or I'm going to have to buy stock in collared shirts. Or steal some of your scarves," Damien said.

Ears burning, Alec turned and buried his face in Damien's neck. Sure enough, Damien's skin was hot just above the junction of his neck and shoulder, where Alec had bitten last night. "Why didn't you tell me I was leaving marks?"

He knew he'd been biting Damien regularly during sex. Feck, Damien had even asked him about it. But biting hard enough to leave lasting bruises wasn't something he'd ever done with other lovers.

Not that he'd had much of a chance, but the urge had never been there before regardless.

But with Damien? Alec turned into a growling, possessive wolf. He wanted to mark and claim this man as his own.

Strong fingers gripped Alec's chin, lifting his head for a deep kiss. "Sweetheart, if I didn't have to look professional during the day, I'd wear the marks proudly."

As Damien's musky scent filled the air, a feral part of Alec wanted to take him back to bed and mark him some more. They had to stop talking about this, or they'd never leave the apartment for breakfast. "What time are Officers Lawrence and Jones coming over?"

Cackling at Alec's not-so-subtle change in topic, Damien ushered them out the door. "Around lunchtime, I think."

"You should tell them to meet us at my apartment. We can spread out more on my breakfast bar. I'd also like Harper to listen in from the bedroom, so we can talk after. She has good instincts. Unless you can convince your officers to involve another consultant."

"No, I don't think I can without telling them why." Damien remained silent on the way down the stairs and across the street to North Market.

Alec didn't blame him for needing to think over the matter. He was pushing a line with this request, and while

Harper's instincts astonished him, she didn't know enough to contribute directly. But she was the only one he felt he could trust with this outside of Damien.

Ari's betrayal still stung.

She'd disappeared when he needed her the most, taking the only lead Damien had on this case with her. Alec's calls remained unanswered.

There might come a time when they had to bring Damien's officers in further, but despite the witch blood that Andy possessed, they were both still unaware humans. Alec could explain, should he ever have to, why he'd brought Damien into their world.

He wouldn't be able to explain involving the CPD.

Standing in line for doughnuts, Alec could tell that Damien had come to some kind of a decision. He pulled Alec close and nuzzled the side of his head. "The reason I became a detective was to find closure for the victims and their families. Closure might look a little different in this case, but I'll do whatever I can to help. Even if it means coloring outside the lines this time."

Alec turned his head and kissed Damien softly. "Thank you."

"But I'd like to call in Jac too. He has to know something about what happened after you left with me to the hospital. Maybe he can help shed some light on a few things. I think I can get away with inviting him to the party."

An involuntary growl rumbled in Alec's throat. Just the

thought of allowing the Fae lawyer into his territory brought his hackles up. But Damien was right; Jac knew something. Alec tamped down the growl and took a deep breath to calm himself. "Okay."

THIS WAS A TERRIBLE IDEA.

Damien should've figured that out after sharing their plan with Harper. Her eyes had quickly shifted to Alec when he mentioned that Jac would be joining them. After a moment's pause, she'd nearly tripped over herself while laughing all the way into the bedroom without saying a word.

The minute he arrived, Jac made himself right at home in Alec's living room. Twice, Damien caught the soft rumble of a growl catching in Alec's throat. Turned out he hadn't been hearing things earlier in North Market.

It was hard to ignore the growling with Alec pressed against Damien's side on the couch, putting in his best effort to glare daggers into Jac with eerie precision. Jac just raised his eyebrow, mirth dancing in his eyes.

Damien would have been more amused at the situation if he had any idea what was triggering such a reaction in his usually timid boyfriend.

Boyfriend.

Warmth rushed through him at the thought. Their lives had clicked together so easily this past week after dancing around each other for months. He couldn't imagine his life anymore without Alec in it. A soft smile twitched at Damien's lips, and he pressed a kiss to the side of Alec's head, nipping playfully at the sweet man's ear despite their audience.

Alec visibly relaxed, proverbial hackles dropping. Damien blinked at the sudden change.

Jac chuckled. "I see you two have gotten better acquainted. I'm happy for you, Damien."

Before Damien could ask what Jac meant by that, Alec's alarm system alerted them to Candice and Andy's arrival. Alec stood to let them into the apartment while Damien and Jac moved to the barstools surrounding Alec's kitchen island. Damien had already spread out everything the officers had left at Damien's apartment into rough piles related to each case.

Candice immediately started straightening the piles and adding new folders to the mix. "How are you feeling, Damien?"

He shrugged. "Ah, you know how doctors are about concussions. They always make them seem worse than they are."

Candice smiled softly, shaking her head at him for the nonanswer. She pressed her lips into a firm line, raising her eyebrow. Damien escaped her censure when Andy dropped a heavy box at the end of the counter and blew out a frustrated breath.

"So they assigned the Singer case to another precinct.

We're completely locked out." Slumping on a barstool, Andy eyed Jac warily. "What's the lawyer doing here?"

Was Tim's case assigned to another precinct, or did this qualify under Alec's "misplaced evidence" explanation? His new perspective on everything was turning Damien into a cynic. The brass didn't know enough to connect the cases, and with a detective technically labeled a victim of the crime, it made sense that their precinct would have a conflict of interest.

Given what he knew, did it really matter? Either way, he would end up coloring outside the lines like he had told Alec earlier. Whether or not they solved the case in an official capacity, there would be closure. The victims deserved that much at least.

To Damien's thinking, the only remaining issue was how much more he should involve Candice and Andy. If the case officially turned serial, it could make or break their future careers as homicide detectives. The only problem? There was no way to explain, much less prove, how the victims had died.

Alec still hadn't shared what he suspected, adamant that he had to talk to Ari first. That alone was enough to tell Damien that no one would believe the truth.

Shaking himself out of his spiraling thoughts, Damien glanced at Jac before answering Andy. "I'd like Jac's take on the Singer case since he was there that day. Assigned to a different precinct or not, it's still relevant to our Doe cases. What's in the box?"

"It's everything that Sorensen and Young helped us dig up that even remotely resembles the MO. We haven't been able to go through them yet, but ..."

Damien cocked an eyebrow when Andy trailed off. The box they had brought in could easily hold a hundred file folders. Just how far back did this go?

When the silence stretched too long, Candice plucked the lid off the box and handed the top folder to Damien. "We haven't found anything in Montana or Indiana yet though we're still looking. Damien, these cases are all from Ohio and easily stretch back to the late 1970s. There are still more files that aren't digitized yet that are on the way from other precincts."

Alec sucked in a sharp breath at that statement, face draining of all color. Jac pursed his lips and shook his head when Damien opened his mouth to ask what was going on. Snapping his mouth shut, he filed the questions away until the officers left.

Instead, he flipped open the file that Candice had handed him. It contained a cold case file from June 29th, 2003, referencing a John Doe that CPD had found in a homeless camp near a rail yard. Male, approximate age of seventy-five to eighty-five. Presumed heart attack. No identification found on the body. Autopsy never performed. Body disappeared. Case cold.

The next file in the box was nearly identical, two months later, in a different precinct. He met Candice's eyes. "What can you tell me so far?"

"All of them died on the new moon, though we didn't find a case each month. Given that they found most of these in low-income areas, I wouldn't be surprised if some cases never saw the light of day. We didn't detect any sort of pattern when pulling the case files beyond the loose MO we used as our criteria."

Not that they had much of a modus operandi to compare to. Not yet anyway.

"What about recent cases before John Doe 0522 in May?" Out of their current cases, only Collin qualified as low income, but they'd found his body in a public park—therefore, a high-profile location. Stone and Tim were both well off, and someone would've noticed if they'd gone missing.

What had changed?

"We found several cases scattered across Cincinnati. Sorensen tried to sweet talk his way into the case files, but they don't want to play."

It was probable they'd never see most of the case files. What the officers had dug up in such a short amount of time took Damien's breath away as it was. "Good work on this. We'll start digging into these soon. What did the techs say about the purse I found in Tim's bathroom? Or did we get locked out before the results?"

"You found a purse?" Jac's eyes lit up. No one stopped him when he grabbed one of the folders that Candice had added to the pile nearest him. "Saturated in hunting spray. Huh, so that's how she does it."

Jac had murmured the last part so softly that Damien barely heard him. She? Did Jac know something he hadn't shared? "Hunting spray? Like the stuff deer hunters use to mask their scent?"

Alec made a face. "That stuff smells awful. It's any wonder that it actually works."

"That might just be you, Alec." Grabbing another folder from the pile, Jac settled in to read what looked like the Stone case file. The officers followed his lead and distributed the rest of the files from the box to the rest of them. Grilling Jac would have to wait until later.

Even Alec discretely grabbed a few of the folders, popping an earbud in his ear. Damien caught him lifting his phone a few times over the files, but Candice and Andy were too engrossed in taking notes to notice.

He should've thought about the OCR option before and asked Alec to read through the files at his apartment. Resting his hand on Alec's knee below the counter, Damien settled in to read.

AFTER A FEW HOURS of going through the case files, patterns started to emerge. Bone-chilling patterns that forced Alec to take deep, steadying breaths to settle himself before a whine could escape his throat.

He and Ari had moved to Ohio in the winter of 1970. With the help of his phone, Alec had gone through all twelve files that were in the box from both 1973 and 1975. There were few details in the files, which wasn't surprising. It'd been far easier to hide evidence before computers and modern investigative techniques came along. He should know.

Would there be more in Vermont from 1940 to 1970? Or in New York from 1910 to 1940? That far back, it was more likely that a death wouldn't have been investigated at all. Illness and old age had been easy ways to quickly dismiss any death back then. If no one claimed the bodies, then unmarked graves had awaited the poor forgotten souls.

Alec knew about several of the cases in the files he read. Each of them had been shifters or werecreatures. Each of them had died of old age long before they should have. He'd helped cover up their deaths himself. Never questioned how they'd died, just helped make the bodies disappear before the investigations could gain any traction. All in the name of keeping the great secret.

What a fool he'd been.

How many others in that box were preternaturals whose deaths Alec had helped cover up? How many more had never made it into that box?

Only Damien's hand, occasionally rubbing soothing circles on Alec's thigh, kept him calm enough to wait for the unaware officers to leave. By the end of the evening, whispers of the past rang in Alec's ears. Taunting him.

Blaming him.

The officers spoke in low tones near the apartment

door, and before he knew it, only Damien and Jac remained.

Harper stepped out of the bedroom minutes later. She paused in the doorway before joining Damien and Jac in the living room. Damien asked Harper questions, but his words barely registered with Alec. Numbness spread through Alec's thoughts, blanketing them until the past fell silent.

Vanilla and spice surrounded Alec moments before a gentle hand landed on his shoulder. "Doing okay, sweetheart?"

Leaning into the comforting warmth of Damien's body, Alec took a deep breath to ground himself back into the here and now. He nodded slowly and turned his head toward Jac. Accusation hardened his words. "You know something."

The Fae lawyer grunted in acquiescence. "I'd hoped to avoid this part."

Damien tensed behind Alec. "When you read the report from Tim's apartment, you said, 'that's how *she* does it.' Who is *she*?"

With a frustrated hum, Jac remained silent. Alec arched his eyebrow. "Did you know what the creature was when we ran into it on the stairs?"

"I wasn't sure at the time."

If Alec had picked up anything over the years with Ari, it was the art of detecting a nonanswer when he heard one. Unable to wait any longer for Ari to provide explanations,

Alec weighed his wording carefully. "This creature has been performing rituals on the new moon using soul magic. Using the death of the moon to steal the life essence from preternatural creatures and leaving them for anyone to find. They started in Ohio the same month I moved here with Ari. But that isn't where it starts, is it?"

"You have the answer to that."

"Dammit, Jac. Just answer Alec's question." Damien tensed, presumably in preparation to move toward the Fae.

Alec snaked his hand out to twine his fingers with Damien's, effectively stopping him midmotion. Shaking his head, he addressed Jac. "You foolish Fae."

A grin laced Jac's response. "Smart wolf."

"It isn't that he won't answer me, Damien. He can't."

"What do you mean?"

He should have explained this to both Damien and Harper when they had discussed Fae earlier in the week. The minute he realized he was dealing with a Fae lawyer, really. Though what would he have told Damien back then? Alec snorted. So much had changed in so little time.

"A Fae's word is power. Not only are the old stories true that a Fae can tell no lie, but if they give their word, they are honor bound to it. Ari tricked you into silence about this case, didn't she? It binds you even with your diluted blood."

"As I said, smart wolf." Humming thoughtfully, Jac approached the kitchen island. He tapped the counter three times before turning and heading to front door. "You have everything you need. I cannot stay."

It didn't pay to stop him from leaving. Alec turned to Harper and Damien, who stood silently nearby. "What pile of folders did he indicate?"

Paper rustled as Damien picked up a set of folders and handed them to Alec. "These. Do you think we'll find something?"

Alec nodded and chewed his lip before blowing out a heavy breath. "I think I might. I—can you give me some time? To go through these alone?"

"Are you su—"

"I need to think." And process what he had learned.

"Okay." Disappointment filled Damien's voice, but he squeezed Alec's shoulder and kissed his temple. "I'm here. When you're ready."

"I'll walk you out," Harper said as silence filled the room.

When the door closed behind them, Alec clutched the folders to his chest. He had some reading to catch up on.

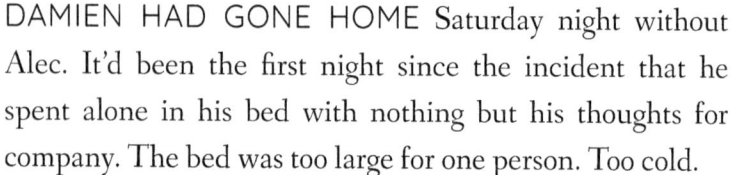

24

DAMIEN HAD GONE HOME Saturday night without Alec. It'd been the first night since the incident that he spent alone in his bed with nothing but his thoughts for company. The bed was too large for one person. Too cold.

He hated it.

But without the distracting werewolf around, Damien's brain had finally caught up with reality. A reality where he used the word "werewolf" to describe his boyfriend. One where magic was real, and there really were things that went bump in the night.

Damien snorted at himself, taking a swig of his coffee as he sat in his SUV outside the precinct and stared at the front door apprehensively. First day back, and just thinking about going inside sat heavily in his stomach. The little bubble he'd created for himself over the past week had finally popped.

Now he had to go inside and work on a case he would never truly solve. The lack of possible closure ate at him. Coloring outside the lines meant that he had to let these cases go cold at the end. Or find some way to reconcile his new reality with what the law would believe.

What was the point of that? It was like he'd lived his entire life wearing a veil over his eyes. Now that the veil had been ripped away, the world he found himself in was foreign and dangerous. There was no need for police officers or detectives in the preternatural world.

He hadn't become a detective to find closure for himself but for others. The living and the dead both deserved answers. Deserved justice.

No matter what form that justice took.

But what did justice look like in a world where it was acceptable to just sweep everything under the rug and forget about it? Or solve issues with tooth and claw? Alec hadn't outright said it, but Damien could read between the lines.

Alec had defaulted to sharing minimal information and keeping his cards close to his chest. It made sense given the world he lived in, but the man was suffering, and Damien could do nothing until Alec was ready to share. Something about what Alec had learned on Saturday had rattled him, but the sweet man had pulled in on himself again.

Even asked for some time alone.

Harper had caught little of value from the bedroom that night but had promised to help Alec decipher what Jac had meant. Harper was good for the reticent werewolf and wouldn't let him get too far lost inside his own head.

With a weary sigh, Damien dragged himself out of the SUV and went inside.

"Welcome back, Detective." Janice greeted him with a bright smile as he walked past her desk. "Captain Saunders would like to see you in her office straightaway."

Naturally, Kat would want to see him. He'd ignored her demand to wait for backup, and it had resulted in a head injury. But it could've been worse. Absently rubbing the still-healing scratch on his shoulder, Damien shook his head.

So much worse.

"Thanks, Janice."

Candice glanced up from her desk as Damien stepped into the bullpen. She tapped her partner on the shoulder and lifted a stack of folders, gesturing toward the conference room that had quickly become their de facto meeting room, eyebrow raised in question.

Damien nodded toward Kat's office. "I'll meet you two in there. Have to get my ass handed to me first."

Laughter danced in Candice's eyes while Andy grabbed a box from his desk and followed her out the door. Damien sighed after they were far enough down the hall. He either needed to fully read those two in soon or cut them loose.

Before he could lift his hand to knock on the door, it

opened. Chief of Police Rodney Anthem stepped out with his trademark frown etched on his face. Damien gritted his teeth and stepped aside before the man could plow him over.

Ice clawed at Damien's spine when a woman stepped out behind Chief Anthem. Piercing golden eyes shifted to Damien as the woman from Collin's apartment pursed her lips at the chief's back. Did that woman have any other expressions?

Damien blinked as everything grew too bright, shooting through his head like an ice pick to the brain. Even a week later, the fucking concussion was still taunting him.

Bright yellow eyes blinked back at him as his vision cleared and sharpened. For a moment, the woman's raven black hair spread out into wings spanning the hallway. "What the ..."

"Are you going to stand out there all day, Damien, or are you going to come inside, so we can all get back to work?" Kat's glacial voice broke Damien out of the staring contest that he'd inadvertently fallen into with the woman.

Normal golden eyes narrowed as the woman slowed to a halt, but Damien turned his back before she could speak.

One problem at a time.

Rubbing his eyes, Damien stepped inside the office and closed the door behind him, leaning against it rather than taking a seat. The solid door felt secure at his back as he took in the press of Kat's lips, her stiff posture, and the irritation radiating from her in waves. Her eyes locked onto something over his shoulder through the frosted window next to the door.

Damien's shoulders released their tension. Chief Anthem was the source of her ire, not him. Maybe he'd get through this unscathed.

As he waited silently, his boss pulled herself together, and the cool professional slipped back into place. Ice blue eyes dropped to his, slicing daggers into him.

Or ... maybe not.

"I see you're in one piece."

More or less. "I'm—"

Kat held up her hand and talked over him. "I should suspend you for disobeying orders. Not to mention breaking an official police seal while you were off duty. And don't get me started on the waste of department resources on a case that we don't even have jurisdiction over."

When she put it that way, Damien couldn't help but wince. He waited for her to bring up the cold cases—the ones he'd asked his officers to pull Sorensen and Young in on—but her tirade stopped just short of that. Well, if she wasn't planning to bring it up, then neither was he.

Instead, he stood patiently waiting near the door for her to either dismiss him or rip into him further. He didn't have to wait long.

Kat let out a long-suffering sigh. "I'm going to level with you, Damien. We're getting pressure from on high to wrap up the Franklin Park case or pass it along to BCI. I don't like it any more than I enjoyed letting that case from May go cold. Do what you need to do to solve this thing but be discreet about it. Get back to work."

Damien twitched his lips and turned to open the door. So that's why the chief had been in her office. Although that didn't explain the presence of the woman who he and Alec had seen at Collin's apartment. Kat called after him as he stepped into the hallway.

"And Damien?" He glanced behind him to find a rare grin on his boss's lips. "Welcome back."

Damien blinked. Apparently, Kat's heart wasn't quite so frozen over after all.

Shaking his head, he sought out Candice and Andy in the conference room.

The officers sat among a sea of files. Damien whistled as he sat down, glancing over what had to be at least twice as many as they'd brought to Alec's apartment on Saturday. "This is quite the spread here."

Candice shoved a small stack toward him. "Age regressions came back this morning. They're in the top folder."

Flipping open the folder, Oliver Stone's somber face stared back at him. At least a relatively close interpretation of him anyway. The rendition of Collin was damn near perfect, however. Damien sat back with a sigh. What did he even do with this?

When he'd requested these through Emily, Damien had been grasping at straws. Even then, a part of him had known that the results wouldn't get him anywhere. On their own, the renditions didn't qualify as concrete evidence to connect their two Doe cases to the two missing person cases.

What would someone on the outside think when they saw these? Perhaps suggest that they somehow related the victims to the missing persons but not necessarily that they were the same people. Even if the DNA match that Emily was working on for Collin came back positive, it was plausible that a match could still point to a family member instead.

Who would believe that the cause of death was magic in both cases? Soul magic as Alec had called it. Whatever that meant.

Rubbing his temples, Damien glanced up at the worried faces of the two officers across from him. He had to decide soon, but for now, he would keep turning over every stone until he found the missing piece. And pray the officers didn't ask questions he had to lie to answer.

"What else do we have?"

Andy gestured around the room. "Cincinnati PD still isn't playing ball, but we got files fitting the MO from Dayton, Springfield, and Akron that fill in several gaps in the timeline. We've been sorting them on most-likely matches to the criteria."

It was as good a place as any to start. Maybe something in these files held the key Alec needed. Damien grabbed the next folder from the stack that Candice had given him. "All right. Let's get to work."

"ARE you sure you're ready for this?"

Harper paused outside Sister's Bar and Grill and patted Alec's shoulder affectionately. "I'm pretty sure you're more worried about this job than I am, and I'm the one who has to perform it. Exposure is the only way I'm going to get used to the overload. Hiding in Ari's house or your apartment isn't helping."

She was right and had used the same argument with him several times now. Besides, Deci would run interference if Harper needed a break. "Okay, but I'll be at my usual table all evening. Damien should be here within the hour."

Harper let out a long-suffering sigh and gripped Alec's shoulder. "Stop fretting and relax. I've got this."

The confidence in Harper's voice released the last of Alec's apprehension. Why was he so worried about this? Perhaps it was residual guilt from what had happened to Oliver. It didn't help that he'd spent the weekend repeatedly reading Oliver and Collin's case files, looking for the link that Jac had alluded to.

It would seem he was becoming something of a masochist with as much time as he'd spent beating himself up lately. Spending time with Damien over the last week had been akin to shaking off the fog after suddenly waking up from a dream.

Or a nightmare.

Alec had been walking around as an empty shell before all of this had started. Barely living and blindly following Ari's whims without a care for the consequences. When the realization had struck him over the weekend, he had felt the impact deep in his chest.

It hadn't helped that each time he'd tried to engage in life again, something had pushed him further and further into his shell until there was nothing left to come out for again.

Damien and Harper's appearances in his life had changed all of that.

For the first time since he'd become a werewolf, Alec wanted to *live*. But before he could do that, he needed to confront Ari about what she knew and how long this had been going on underneath his nose. If his instincts were correct, the incidents started further back than the fifty years they'd lived in Ohio.

Much further.

How many more had to die before someone put an end to it?

None—if he had any say in it.

Even if he had to go to the Fae Lords to stop this.

With a heavy sigh, Alec made his way to his usual table near the bar and pushed aside his spiraling thoughts. He couldn't help his grin at Deci's warm greeting after Harper stepped into the kitchen.

"Harper! I'm so glad to see you tonight. I'm sorry it took me this long to get you on the roster. I know you wanted to start sooner. Now, I understand you have waitressing experience, so let's just dive right in, shall we?"

Tuning out Harper's cheery reply, Alec turned his attention toward his phone. "Call Ari."

Why he even bothered was beyond him. After seven rings, an apologetic electronic voice answered the call instead of Ari's usual voicemail message. "We're sorry, but the person you contacted does not have voicemail set up. Your call cannot be completed at this time. Please try again later."

Alec dropped his head into his hands and groaned. He'd first heard the error message when he had tried calling last night. Either something had happened, or—

Who was he kidding? Disabling her voicemail was a deliberate act. He'd even tried her answering service, but it was also disconnected.

Why would Ari disappear like this?

"You look troubled, child." Alec startled at the gravelly, contralto voice beside him. Only after the woman had spoken did he notice the scents of rosewood and belladonna that always surrounded Deci's older sister, Marta. He didn't know how, but the woman often snuck up on him when she visited the bar.

With a self-deprecating laugh, Alec lifted his head. "You could call it that."

Marta hummed thoughtfully. "You know, Deci has been working on a tapestry for some time now. She ended up with too many threads in one place a while back. Every time she thinks she has it sorted out, a new distortion appears in the piece."

Before Alec could ask what that had to do with anything, Deci placed a glass of iced tea in front of him. "Oh, come now, Marta. It would've been fixed ages ago if you would stop cutting the surrounding threads too short."

"Well, if Naomi had spun the colors that I requested in time, I could have."

"Yes, blame the sister who isn't here. That is so typical of you."

"You didn't need to leave all those threads in the piece either."

"Oh, so now it's my fault?"

Harper leaned down to whisper in Alec's ear. "What in the world are they on about?"

Alec shook his head and shrugged helplessly, momentarily distracted by the scent of vanilla and spice. Warmth rushed through him as Damien approached the table and took a seat.

Deci didn't seem to have noticed him as she continued arguing with her sister. "Do you know how hard it is to find preternatural dog owners? It's harder than it should be, Marta."

What did dogs have to do with a tapestry?

Damien leaned into Alec and kissed the side of his head. "Hey, sweetheart. What's going on?"

Alec couldn't help his grin, turning his head to steal a quick kiss. "Hey, you. This is Deci's older sister, Marta."

The sisters halted their argument mid-tirade. Deci quickly recovered and slipped her professional bar-owner persona back into place. "Detective O'Connor! Can I get you a rum and Coke to start off with?"

"Uh, sure. That sounds great, Deci." Damien cleared his throat and shifted away from Alec. "Marta, it's a pleasure to meet you."

"Oh, you are always such a charmer, Connor. Oh! My bad, it's O'Connor now. Damien, I believe?"

Did they already know each other? Alec opened his mouth to ask, but Damien beat him to the punch. "I'm sorry. Have we met?"

"Oh no, not recently, dear." Mirth filled Marta's voice as she stood and clapped her hands. "Now, I just dropped by for a moment. I've so much to do and so little time. Ta!"

Chuckling, Alec shook his head and sipped his iced tea. He'd never met anyone quite as eccentric as Marta. Given he'd lived in New York in the thirties, that was saying something.

Damien draped his arm across Alec's shoulders and settled in at the table while Deci and Harper stepped behind the bar to prepare Damien's drink. "Sometimes I wonder if I'm missing some subtext in these conversations."

"Don't worry, I think I missed it this time too."

"You okay? You sound stressed."

Alec sighed. Now that the distractions were gone, he couldn't help but think about Ari. "When I called Ari last night, her voicemail was disconnected. So was her answering service. This isn't like her, Damien. I'm worried."

Harper returned with Damien's drink and squeezed Alec's shoulder. "I'm sure there's a reasonable explanation, sweetie. Are you two ready to order, or are you good for now?"

Just the thought of food made Alec nauseous. "Maybe in a little while unless Damien wants something."

"Nah, I'm good." After Harper had left the table, Damien leaned in and kept his voice low. "We spent the day sorting cold cases from around Ohio that filled some gaps in the timeline, but nothing really stood out aside from the sheer volume of them. Any luck on the files you read over the weekend?"

Alec hadn't found whatever Jac had hinted at, even after reading the files forward and back several times. The CPD had very little to work with on these cases. Considering their nature, it wasn't surprising.

He'd found something else, however. Curiosity got the better of him, and Alec tilted his head. "Not really. But I have to ask, why did you have an envelope full of leaves in with the file folders?"

The envelope had been at the bottom of the box left at his apartment, saturated in a scent he felt like he should recognize, but he still couldn't place it.

"Oh, shit. I was going to tell you about that and completely forgot." Damien shared the story of how the envelope of leaves had come into his possession.

It had happened the same day that someone had tampered with Damien's memory.

And there were few creatures whose illusions utilized dried leaves. Only one of those could alter memories.

Kitsune.

One of whom he knew like a sister.

Or he had thought he did.

Alec's heart sank. He had to know. Through numb lips, he breathed the words that would change everything. "Were there leaves found with Oliver's or Collin's bodies? Or in Tim's apartment?"

When a kitsune hands something over to a person, there's a high probability that the item will turn out to be nothing but dried leaves, an illusion that would fade after the kitsune left. Even food shouldn't be trusted unless the kitsune was eating it herself.

And of course, she would rarely share anyway.

But only the yōkai kitsune were malevolent tricksters.

Ari wasn't yōkai.

Was she?

"Now that you mention it, I think so. I'll have to double check the evidence log to be sure, and I haven't read the first responder's report on Tim's case yet. I'll do that tomorrow."

Alec dropped his head into his hands.

Damien's arm tightened briefly around Alec's shoulders, and warm lips brushed against his ear. "I'm here. Whenever you're ready to share."

The cold abyss opened wide before Alec, ready to carry

him back into his blissful, ignorant shell. Only Damien's warmth kept him from falling back in. He nodded silently as he pressed into that warmth, desperately clutching the tiniest thread of hope.

Oh, Ari. What have you done?

25

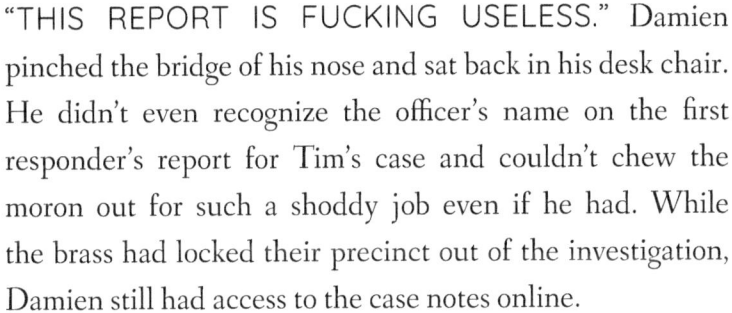

"THIS REPORT IS FUCKING USELESS." Damien pinched the bridge of his nose and sat back in his desk chair. He didn't even recognize the officer's name on the first responder's report for Tim's case and couldn't chew the moron out for such a shoddy job even if he had. While the brass had locked their precinct out of the investigation, Damien still had access to the case notes online.

Not that there were any.

Guess he wasn't such a cynic after all.

The only part of the report that read true was that an officer on the scene—Damien—had sustained a head injury when falling back against the pillar in the kitchen. Tim's injuries were fabricated, and there was far less blood mentioned than Damien knew had been throughout the main room of the apartment.

Even when he'd returned with Alec, there'd been more blood than the report mentioned. No one had made notes about the bloody paw prints that had been all over the apartment either.

Scrolling through his phone, Damien stopped on a photograph of Alec that he'd taken on his birthday; the man was sleeping peacefully curled around Damien's side. "Oh, sweetheart. Why won't you talk to me instead of keeping it all bottled up inside?"

It broke his heart to see the man in so much pain.

Further down, Damien found the picture he'd taken that clearly depicted four distinct sets of paw prints in the apartment last Friday. The prints he didn't recognize stood next to the larger canine prints Frosty had left behind and slightly smaller canine prints Damien assumed belonged to Alec. The largest prints were Tim's.

The unknown prints were too small to be a bobcat's and nothing like a dog's or a wolf's. They had outer pads set further back and in toward the heel compared to Frosty's and Alec's. Damien had hoped there would be a CSU report on what kind of animal had left the prints, but that didn't look like it was going to happen. He shot a quick message to a friend of his back in Wisconsin who specialized in tracking animals and attached the photo.

While he waited for a reply, Damien grabbed the evidence printouts on his desk, along with his coffee, and headed down the hall to the conference room. Shuffling through the pages, he found the images he was looking for.

The first photograph displayed Stone's wallet with the contents spread out around it. Next to the note with the dried leaves attached to it, Damien's attention latched onto the money with the unique folds. The same folds Alec used to count his money. "That's where I saw that before. Now, why would you have money folded like this? Did Alec give this to you? Or maybe it was Ari?"

Either option wouldn't be out of the realm of possibility. Alec had known Stone and had mentioned the man was a werewolf. Was Collin also a werecreature or shifter of some kind? The incident at Collin's apartment gave Damien reason to believe that was the case. In a sample size of two, both of the perpetrator's targets were part of the preternatural community. Was that what made these cases different?

Or were all the victims preternatural?

Sticking a pin in that thought, Damien studied the second photograph. In this instance, dried leaves had worked their way inside Collin's ID badge for Franklin Park Conservatory. Given that a German shepherd had dragged the body out from under a small footbridge, the team had all assumed the leaves had come from the ground.

But the other leaves in the photo were green and brown. These were red and yellow as though they'd fallen off a tree in autumn and not late June. He'd have to check the envelope at Alec's apartment to determine if those were also autumn colors.

A brief knock at the door interrupted Damien's musings. He turned and waved Candice and Andy into the room. "Come on in, you two. I have a new needle for us to dig out of this haystack."

"What've you found?" Andy asked, taking a seat across from Damien. Candice set a file folder on the table before perching nearby.

Damien gestured to the photos in front of him. "I want to explore a new angle with the cold cases. Alec reminded me last night of the envelope full of leaves that'd made its way to his apartment, and it got me thinking. We've run into leaves in each of these incidents. While they seemed innocuous at the time, I'm not so sure now."

"Now that you mention it, I vaguely recall leaves attached to the blank forms in the Conservatory's records for the second PackForce employee."

Andy's sharp memory would serve him well as a detective. Damien nodded approvingly. "You're right. Those forms were also full of debris. So I want to see if we can spot any more unassuming leaves in the evidence for the cold cases. Let's stick with the past year or so, and we don't have to dig too deep. I just want to confirm they're relevant."

Maybe if they were all autumn colors, that would mean something when he brought it up again with Alec. Whether that would allow the man to open up to Damien remained to be seen, but the least he could do was come armed with facts the next time the topic came up.

Damien nodded at the folder Candice had brought in. "What's this?"

"DNA results are back on that comb you found. It was a perfect match to John Doe 0621." Candice tilted her head, studying Damien carefully. "You're not surprised by this."

Damn. Candice could read Damien like a book. Not sure how else to answer, Damien hedged. "You mean after everything we've seen on this case? No, I'm really not. I already threw everything I thought I knew out the window to preserve my sanity."

She pursed her lips but let the nonanswer slide and settled in to go through the files.

Damien's phone buzzed. Glancing at the image attached to the text message, Damien hummed thoughtfully. He returned to his desk to do a little research of his own, leaving the officers to their task in the conference room.

He was finally getting somewhere.

A CUP of coffee appeared under Alec's nose.

He took the offering from Harper with a murmur of thanks. Wrapping his hands around the cup, Alec held it to his lips but didn't take a sip, lost in his thoughts.

Almost a week had gone by since he'd last heard from Ari. Even Harper seemed worried, masking it with an extra-chipper attitude.

Would Ari ever come back?

Or had she left for good with the knowledge that Alec was close to discovering the secrets she'd kept from him all these years? Close to learning the truth about how Oliver and Collin had died. How their deaths could've been prevented if she'd only confided in him.

Eyes burning, Alec blinked away the wetness as the knife of betrayal slid even deeper into his soul.

Everyone left.

Even the only constant in his life.

What would he do if he lost Damien and Harper too? Alec sighed. He knew what would happen. It would shatter what was left of him. And if his lifespan continued its current course, he would one day outlive them both.

Would his sanity survive that loss?

"We should invite him on Monday." Harper's warm voice broke through to him, melting Alec's melancholy thoughts.

He took a sip of his coffee and frowned in confusion. "Him?"

Concern bled into her response. "Damien. Have you even been listening?"

How long had she been speaking? Invite Damien where on Monday? Monday was ... "You mean for the full moon run?"

"Alec, what's gotten into you? You've been in a constant daze for the past few days. Now you're missing entire conversations, even when you participated in them."

Blinking, Alec set his coffee down on the table. "I've been answering you?"

Growling out her frustration, Harper stalked into the

kitchen and pulled several pans out of the cupboard, presumably to start preparing an early dinner before her shift at Sister's. The scent of frying peppers and onions filled the room while Alec considered her suggestion.

Harper was right, Alec had been in a daze. He'd even turned down spending more time with Damien these past few days, hadn't he? Inviting Damien to the run made sense, in a way, and would give Alec a means to make up for the distance he had put between them. So far, Damien's only exposure to the preternatural had been Tim's survival shift and Alec's panic attack. Everything else had been theoretical. Stories.

How would he react to seeing Alec as a wolf?

Would that be the reason Damien left?

Stamping down the flicker of panic before it could take hold, Alec pulled out his phone. Damien had texted earlier to apologize. Something had come up at work, and he needed to stay late and wouldn't make it to Sister's tonight.

Biting his lip, Alec considered calling. But if Damien was busy, he didn't want to bother him. Sighing, he instructed his phone to compose a text message instead. "Damien. I know you have to work on Monday, but I was hoping you could join us in the evening for the full moon run. We're probably going to Highbanks Metro Park again."

Harper hummed her approval from the kitchen as she started mixing spices. "Meatballs sound okay tonight?"

"Meatballs sound great." Grabbing his coffee, Alec

moved to the kitchen island to sit with Harper while she worked. It would also keep his mind off his phone's silence.

Damien was working.

And who knew where Ari was.

Gods, he hated this.

"So the cleaners are scheduled to sanitize the apartment on Thursday. I think I'm going to move in this weekend. Let you have your space back."

Alec's heart dropped. He'd known she still planned to move into Tim's apartment, but he'd gotten used to having her around. But she couldn't stay in his bedroom forever. They both needed more space. He took a sip of his coffee to stop a whimper from escaping.

Harper dropped a hand on his arm, perceptive as always. "Hey, we're still our little pack of two. I'm moving into the same building as Damien, so it isn't like I'm going far. Besides, someone has to make sure you have food in your apartment."

Pack.

The word filled him with warmth and hope for a future he had never thought he would have. Alec grinned and tilted his head. "What, I can't survive on burgers from Sister's? You work there now. That's even more reason to eat there."

"Try it, and you'll be served vegetarian."

"Ouch, hit me where it hurts, why don't you. Next, you'll try to serve me soy sauce and rice." As soon as the words were out of his mouth, Alec's good mood plummeted.

If Harper started showing up with food unannounced, would it forever remind him of Ari?

Before he could sink too deep into that thought, his phone buzzed with the pattern set for Damien. *"How about Alum Creek instead? We can rent a cabin."*

"I like how that man thinks. Let me see if they have anything available." Harper washed her hands before stepping into the living room. "Monday to Tuesday is all booked up. Let me text Deci and see if she'll let us use the shifter cabin instead."

"There's a shifter cabin in Alum Creek?"

"Yeah, the sisters own it and use it as a safe house for their patrons. I'm surprised you didn't know that."

Alec knew all the safe houses in the greater Columbus area. Alum Creek wasn't one of them.

Harper's phone buzzed. "Deci says it's not a problem, and we can use it every month if we want unless something else comes up. The cabin is a six bedroom, and the rooms are soundproofed for privacy."

That was incredibly generous of her. Just who were those witches? "Well, all right, then. Send me the info, and I'll forward it to Damien."

26

AFTER DOWNLOADING the last of the articles on Japanese folklore that he planned to read tonight, Damien glanced at the clock and swore. He was running late and still had a half hour's drive ahead of him to meet Alec and Harper at Alum Creek.

Pieces of the puzzle were dropping into place thanks to his friend back home, shining a new light on the entire investigation. Between that and the new set of dreams he'd started having instead of those damned nightmares, he had a pretty good idea where to start looking.

If only Alec had spoken up, Damien would be so much further ahead by now.

No, that wasn't fair.

Something had triggered a regression in the progress they'd made during Damien's recovery. They'd barely spent any time alone together after Damien had left Alec's apartment. They always met at the bar and never ended the evening back at either of their apartments, though not for a lack of trying on Damien's part.

Granted, Damien had been busy with work and often arrived late, but it was Alec who'd made the excuses each night.

The sooner he could wrap this all up into a presentable case, the better. Who he was going to present it to was another question entirely, but high on his list was the suspiciously absent Ari.

That was if she returned at all. Damien would have a few choice words for her; that was certain.

"Heading out, Damien?" Candice asked from her desk, working late with Andy to track down Damien's latest hunch. It was getting harder to dodge her questions, but he needed just a little more time. An idea had taken root in the back of his mind that he was allowing to develop before he brought it forward to consider more fully.

There had to be a way to solve the case and still give the credit to his officers. It would make their careers, and he owed it to them to try. Especially given how much they'd had to put up with, with his misinformation and redirection over the past few weeks.

Two weeks remained before the next new moon. They were halfway there, and with any luck, this would all be over long before then.

"Yeah. I might be in a bit late tomorrow."

"You deserve it after working so hard lately. Enjoy the extra time. We'll cover for you."

"Thanks, Candi. You're a doll."

Taking the stairs two at a time, Damien rushed down to the parking lot and hopped in his SUV, firing off a quick text to Alec. *Running late. Leaving the office now. See you in thirty.*

Before hitting send, Damien's thumb hovered over the "L" on the far-right side of the keyboard. He frowned and shook his head, not quite ready to let those words free.

Not unless he wanted to send Alec even deeper into his shell.

Alec's reply, *We are too*, popped up just before Damien could drop his phone in the cup holder, followed quickly by a second message. *See you soon if Harper doesn't kill me on this death machine first.*

Cocking an eyebrow, Damien started his vehicle and pulled out onto the road. Just what did that mean exactly? The werewolves were sharing a ride out to the park since Damien would drive Alec back in the morning, and Harper planned to stay at the cabin until she had to work again. He'd assumed they would take Ari's driver.

The invitation tonight was welcome, though unexpected under the current circumstances, and anticipation buzzed through Damien. Although he'd finally gotten used to thinking of his boyfriend as a werewolf, this next step would cement the idea into reality.

Technically, he'd seen Alec as a wolf once already. But did it really count when he was about to pass out from a concussion? It'd been a flash of white fur and little more.

Hell, he'd seen Tim more clearly, and even that felt like a dream now.

Too bad Tim had disappeared right after that. The man had to have known who was in the apartment with him that day well enough to allow them inside so early in the morning. Or had it been an overnight stay?

Ari showing up and whisking him away before even Alec could find out the truth was damning.

The sins piling up at Ari's feet would soon drown the tiny woman.

If she was even a woman at all.

Or if Tim had even left willingly.

Damien glanced briefly at his laptop bag and allowed that branch of thought to grow until the GPS alerted him to his turn, and he shoved it into the back of his brain to process with the rest of his growing suspicions.

Slowing for the turnoff, Damien pulled onto the small service road that would take him to the cabin. Twilight had fallen during the drive, and the woods were already dark. Damien flipped on his headlights as he drove further in.

He'd used the camping grounds on the other side of the park a time or two but hadn't known this cabin existed. As he pulled into a small clearing, it quickly became apparent why. The cabin was brand new, with some of the construction materials still set off to the side of the drive. Parking his SUV, Damien hopped out.

What the hell?

The rumble of a motorcycle echoed through the woods,

followed by a lone headlight pulling into the same clearing. Damien shared a long look with Harper as she pulled off her helmet and assessed the cabin in much the same way he had.

Before he could ask about it, however, Alec hopped off the bike. Damien caught a brief glimpse of the green tinge to Alec's skin in the motorcycle's headlight before the poor man threw his helmet at Harper and launched himself at Damien, burying his nose in the base of Damien's neck and taking a deep breath.

Damien blinked down at the shaking man. "Hi there."

Alec responded with a disgruntled growl.

Harper shook her head with fond exasperation. "He doesn't do so well on the bike. If Vincent had been available, we would've taken the car."

"Why wasn't he available?"

"Not sure. The car was gone when we stopped by Ari's place on the way here."

When Alec lifted his head, Damien leaned in to capture his lips in a soft kiss. There was a moment where Alec tensed before he melted into Damien, parting his lips on a sigh of pleasure and wrapping his arms around Damien's neck. Damien released a breath of relief as he deepened the kiss.

In that moment, the walls that Alec had built between them fell away.

But it wouldn't last.

Not yet anyway.

Harper stepped away to give them privacy without so much as a quip. Damien glanced up briefly to catch a small smile curling her lips. She winked at him before turning to head inside. Breaking the kiss, Damien pressed his forehead to Alec's and soaked the other man in.

Overhead, the moon broke through the trees, bright and full of promise. The light reflected off Alec's glasses as he lifted his head to smile shyly at Damien. "Sorry about that."

Damien traced the smile with his fingertips before reaching up to remove Alec's glasses, revealing the sage green he loved so much. Bending down for another soft kiss, Damien let Alec feel his grin. "You never need to apologize to me, sweetheart."

Alec was nearly vibrating with energy as the moon rose higher in the sky. He threw his head back and took in the night breeze, looking more himself than he had all week.

In the cabin, Harper cried out in pain.

Damien took a step toward the door, but Alec's hand on his arm stopped him. "The shift isn't without pain for werecreatures."

Frowning, Damien glanced toward the cabin's front door while memories of that morning in Tim's apartment played like a reel in his mind. "Tim seemed to struggle to shift, but I don't remember it being particularly painful for him." Although the man had been in a considerable amount of pain beforehand given his injuries.

"The innate magic to change forms is different with shifters. They were never human, Damien. To them, it's almost as simple as breathing. Tim's shift may not have been as smooth if he was fighting it. Which he likely was for your sake."

The idea that Alec was about to put himself through something painful didn't sit right with Damien. The cries from the cabin trailed off into a tired yowl shortly before a beautiful gray-and-red timber wolf appeared around the side of the building and flopped down with her chin on her paws.

A tiny part of Damien's lizard brain tried to scream that the wolf was dangerous, but Alec's hand was still on his arm, and Damien's worry for his boyfriend quickly overrode that sentiment. But where had Harper come from? Hadn't she gone inside?

Damien led Alec around the back of the cabin toward where Harper had appeared. She picked her head up and watched him with mirth in her eyes and her mouth open in canine laughter. He quickly found the source of her amusement in the form of a doggy door installed in the cabin's back door.

It was large enough for a wolf.

"What's so funny?" Alec asked when Damien chuckled.

"There's a doggy door."

Alec blinked slowly. "Come again?"

"In the cabin's back door. You said this was a shifter safe house?"

"Well, that's what Deci said, but ..." Alec trailed off and

tilted his head, scenting the air. "We're the only ones who've been here. This place doesn't hold traces of any scent but the woods."

Right, Alec hadn't seen the building materials outside. "You don't smell the renovators either? There's extra lumber and stone over by where we parked. I don't think this cabin has been here long."

"Just who *are* those witches?" The murmured question was barely loud enough for Damien to make out. Unsure if he should've heard it at all, he let it go for now.

Besides, he was starting to have the same thought.

Alec shivered and wrapped his arms around himself. It wasn't exactly cold outside, being summer in Ohio, but goosebumps raised along what Damien could see of Alec's skin. Pressing his hand to the small of Alec's back, he opened the door to lead them into the cabin. Flashing a grateful smile, Alec stepped forward and hesitated for a moment just inside the threshold before making room for Damien to follow him.

The back of the cabin held a hallway that contained three doors on either side and a large archway that appeared to lead into a dining room of some sort. Most of the doors were closed, but one lay partially open, just wide enough for an animal—or Harper in wolf form—to fit through. Another door across the hall had been left wide open to reveal a rustic bedroom.

"Harper took that room." Alec gestured behind him, confirming Damien's suspicions, as he stepped into the open bedroom and strode toward the bed. "She left my bag in here."

Alec paced in front of the bed for a moment before he huffed out a frustrated growl and tugged methodically at his gloves, one finger at a time, to remove them. Quickly crossing the room, Damien placed a hand on Alec's arm, and the man nearly jumped out of his skin. He turned his head toward Damien, worrying his lip between his teeth, but didn't speak.

"Do you want me to leave the room while you ..." Damien trailed off, unsure of what word to use. Shift? Change?

Turn furry?

Startling out of his thoughts, Alec quickly shook his head and spoke rapidly. "No, no, you don't have to leave while I change. I'd like you to watch. If you're comfortable with it. Which you might not be. If you're—"

Damien pressed his lips to Alec's in a swift, reassuring kiss and cut his boyfriend's nervous babble off mid-tirade. Although it was nice to see that side of him again—at least, it was far better than his melancholy silence—the night wasn't getting any younger. Outside, Harper yipped in what almost sounded like exasperation.

Stepping back, Damien sat on the bed and grinned at Alec's bewilderment. "Sweetheart, I wouldn't be here at all if I didn't think I'd be comfortable with it. That wouldn't be fair to you."

"How are you real?"

"Says the werewolf to his human boyfriend."

A lovely blush spread across Alec's cheeks, followed by a brilliant smile that lit up the emeralds in his eyes. Was that the first time Damien had spoken that word out loud? Surely not. If so, he was an idiot.

Certifiable, even.

While Damien continued to mentally chastise himself, Alec began stripping with renewed purpose. He folded his gloves and scarf and set them carefully over the top of his bag before unbuttoning his shirt.

Alec's movements were methodical, but with each inch of skin he revealed, Damien's interest grew. Hooking his fingers in Alec's belt loops, Damien tugged until the other man stood between his legs. Leaning forward, Damien nuzzled at the scars on Alec's stomach, planting kisses and sliding his hands under the hem of the shirt.

Breath hitching, Alec dropped his hands to Damien's face. "We don't really have time right now, *a stór*. I don't have much longer before the change will be forced on me."

"Mmm. Think of this as a preview for later, then." Damien reached for Alec's waistband and unbuttoned his jeans, kissing lower as he revealed more skin. Alec whimpered as his arousal grew, and Damien mouthed along the wet spot on his briefs.

"Gods, Damien." Alec shoved halfheartedly at Damien's head but didn't step away as Damien slipped his fingers inside the briefs to pull Alec's length free. "You're such a tease."

Outside, Harper yipped again, followed by a growl. Alec spun his head toward the sound, heat crawling up his cheeks as he groaned in embarrassment. "You didn't close the door?"

Chuckling, Damien released Alec and sat back again. "I guess I forgot. You distracted me."

Soundproofing didn't work very well when the room wasn't sealed.

Grumbling to himself in Gaelic, Alec quickly finished stripping out of his clothes. There was a good chance the man was cursing heavily at Damien. *Ah, well. It worked.* Despite the blush and untimely interruption, the distraction had helped settle Alec's nerves.

It had also helped Damien forget what Alec was about to put himself through until Alec contorted in pain. Alec's spine stretched out like ... Damien curled his fingers in the comforter on the bed to stop himself from rushing to Alec's side as phantom pains from his nightmares surfaced with Alec's cry.

Every bone in Alec's body seemed to pop at once as he dropped to his hands and knees. Damien's eyes twitched, and he blinked rapidly as the room grew too bright. Between one blink and the next, Alec shifted between human and wolf.

A beautiful, pure white wolf with brilliant green eyes. A golden pattern swirled across the wolf's forehead before sinking into the fur and disappearing without a trace. The overbright light in the room dimmed a heartbeat later.

The wolf stood before him, whining softly as the silence extended between them, distracting Damien from the strange sight.

Damien let out the breath he hadn't realized he was holding and slid to the floor. "Holy hell, Alec. You're stunning."

Hesitantly, the wolf stepped forward and pressed up against Damien's side. Incredibly soft fur brushed Damien's arm, and Damien couldn't help but tunnel his fingers into the thick coat. Alec pressed his head encouragingly into Damien's hand.

"Like that, do you?" Scratching Alec a bit behind the ears where he was sensitive even in human form, Damien had a moment of disconnect. This animal was still Damien's boyfriend.

Before he could dwell on the thought too long, Harper made another impatient yip. "We better get out there before she storms in here and drags you out."

Alec huffed out a breath and led the way back outside. He stopped at the door and waited for Damien to open it. Damien chuckled and held it open for him. "Too good for the doggy door?"

Snorting and shaking his head, Alec raced around the cabin to nudge Harper to her feet. Side by side, Harper as a timber wolf stood a good head taller than Alec, even though the man was taller than her in human form. The lithe white wolf was unlike any wolf Damien had ever seen.

Harper nipped at Alec, dancing around him playfully

before glancing up at Damien. Intelligence shone out of her amber wolf's eyes. There was more human in there than animal, but a wildness surrounded both wolves that called to their other nature.

It was an honor to bear witness to this event.

In this form, a weight seemed to have lifted off Alec. It had given him a respite from his human worries. Why, then, didn't he change more regularly? Of course, the mental anguish the change must cause him at first would be a deterrent.

Setting those thoughts aside until he could discuss it with Alec—someday, at least—Damien grabbed his laptop and overnight bag out of the SUV and turned back toward the cabin. The wolves tussled and chased each other around the clearing.

Harper howled, and Alec took up an echoing cry.

With one last glance backward, they ran off into the woods.

Damien stepped back inside, his grin fading.

Time to get back to work.

27

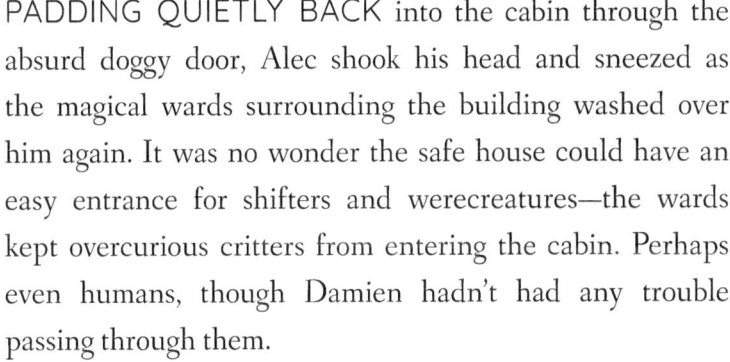

PADDING QUIETLY BACK into the cabin through the absurd doggy door, Alec shook his head and sneezed as the magical wards surrounding the building washed over him again. It was no wonder the safe house could have an easy entrance for shifters and werecreatures—the wards kept overcurious critters from entering the cabin. Perhaps even humans, though Damien hadn't had any trouble passing through them.

The magic was warm and welcoming to him and Harper as they slipped into their respective rooms and nudged the doors closed behind them. Inside their bedroom, Damien's slow heartbeat and rhythmic breathing confirmed the man was fast asleep.

Following the scent to his bag, Alec cursed himself for not orienting himself in the room earlier before his change. As his claws clacked on the tiled floor, he paused and huffed out a laugh. Ever thoughtful, Damien had moved Alec's belongings into the adjoining bathroom.

That man was too good to be true.

With the moon song losing her strength, long past her peak for the night and well on the way to morning, Alec pushed the wolf back inside. Fur rippled along his back as it receded, followed by the flash of familiar pain.

Returning to skin was always easier.

Exhausted from the run, Alec stumbled to his feet and found the shower in the corner with the glass door open and waiting. Adjusting the water, he stepped inside and let the heat soak into his sore muscles. The pain would fade in an hour at most, but for now, he stood gratefully under the hot stream.

He and Harper had nearly bitten off more than they could chew with the buck they had taken down tonight. It'd put up a good fight, and a misplaced step had allowed the buck to toss Alec into a tree. They'd feasted well in triumph, however.

Alec could've done without the aftertaste coating the back of his throat and tongue. He should've rinsed his mouth out before getting in the shower.

The shower door opened a moment later. Damien slipped inside, slid behind Alec, and caressed his jaw. Resisting the pressure of Damien's hand as he tried to turn Alec's head for a kiss, Alec stepped free instead.

Damien sighed in disappointment. "I'm sorry, I shouldn't have assumed—"

"No! No, that isn't it." Cheeks heating, Alec caught Damien's arm before the man could step back out of the shower. Worrying at his bottom lip, Alec stepped close again, sliding his hand up Damien's arm. "It's just ... is there a mouth rinse close by? We sort of went hunting tonight and ... um, there's still ..."

Well, this was awkward. What did he plan to say? *There's still blood in my mouth? Maybe some entrails stuck in my teeth?*

"Say no more. I think I have a bottle in my shaving kit." Damien stepped out of the shower and pressed a small bottle into Alec's palm when he returned. While Alec fought with the thrice-damned child lock on the cap, the scent of Damien's vanilla body wash filled the shower.

After swishing some of the mouthwash, Alec raised an eyebrow. "Vanilla mint mouthwash?"

"What can I say?" Damien all but purred as a soapy hand slid up Alec's back, followed by a washcloth. "I like vanilla."

No argument there. Alec had developed an attachment to the scent himself. He lo—was quite fond of vanilla. Really, he should invite more of it into his life.

Closing his eyes and tilting his head forward, Alec's muscles relaxed as Damien massaged his neck and shoulders with the washcloth. Damien chuckled softly. "Like that, do you?"

Arousal warred with exhaustion as Alec hummed in

agreement. "The buck tossed me. I'm lucky I didn't land in the river."

Damien's hands stilled. "Shit. Are you okay?"

Alec turned, cupping Damien's cheeks and kissing him affectionately. "Werecreatures heal just as easily as shifters, *a stór*. I might've cracked a few ribs, but I'm just a little stiff and achy now. Another hour, and I'll be right as rain."

Pressing close, Damien captured Alec's lips in a deep kiss. Alec opened for the questing tongue tracing along his lips, the kiss turning heated and reigniting the arousal from before Alec's shift. Damien threaded his fingers through Alec's hair, tilting Alec's head back slightly for Damien's tongue to delve deep and twist around Alec's.

Cool, wet tile met Alec's back, conjuring memories of damp stone. Damien grunted his disapproval and flipped their positions without breaking the kiss, leaning back against the shower wall and encouraging Alec to lean against him instead.

It was almost as if Damien had known the tile would trigger a flashback.

But how?

Thoughts and memories washed away under the hot spray of the shower, swirling down the drain as Damien slid his hands down Alec's back to anchor at his hips, aligning their cocks and sparking flashes of pleasure up Alec's spine. One hand traveled further until soapy fingers dipped into Alec's crease and circled his hole teasingly. Alec moaned into the kiss, grinding against Damien's cock.

Damien grinned against Alec's lips as his hands disappeared, followed by the sound of a cap popping open. Alec broke the kiss and rested his head against Damien's shoulder, panting as a slick finger returned to his hole, pressing inside to the first knuckle and slowly pumping in and out. Damien wrapped his other hand around Alec's cock, gripping the base tightly.

A second finger joined the first, curling until it found its target. Alec moaned and thrust his hips in counterpoint as the fingers scissored and stretched him. Damien tightened his fist, moving it with Alec rather than allowing his cock to slide through, drawing a desperate whimper out of Alec.

Nipping at the sensitive spot behind Alec's ear, Damien chuckled softly. "I don't think I can safely hold you up in here. Don't want you coming before we make it to the bed."

Fumbling behind him, Alec shut off the water. Damien's chuckle morphed into a laugh as he opened the door and stepped out, enveloping Alec in a fluffy towel when he followed. Capturing Alec's lips in another scorching kiss, Damien haphazardly dried them both and tossed the towel somewhere.

Between heated kisses, they stumbled toward the bed. Falling onto the comforter, Damien encouraged Alec to roll onto his side with his back facing Damien. Hooking his knee under Alec's leg, Damien pressed against him, slick cock sliding along Alec's crease. Damien snaked his arm under Alec's side and gripped his cock as Damien lifted his knee to open Alec's legs.

Damien paused and pressed a kiss to Alec's shoulder. "This okay?"

This man.

How was he real?

The position allowed Alec to feel Damien's heat against his back without feeling trapped. Turning his head, Alec looped his arm backward around Damien's neck and pulled him in for an awkward kiss, pushing the depth of emotions swirling inside him into the kiss.

Breaking the kiss, Alec pushed back against Damien's cock in invitation, threading their fingers together against his hip as Damien took the hint and adjusted his hips to press insistently inside. Damien trailed heated, open-mouthed kisses on the back of Alec's neck, humming his pleasure as he rocked his hips, sliding deeper inside inch by inch until he was fully seated.

Damien stroked Alec's cock in time with the slow, sensual dance of his thrusts. Alec pressed his head back into Damien's shoulder, moaning as each inward stroke lit sparks inside him until the tingle at the base of his spine set off a cascade of pleasure.

Alec cried out when Damien bit down on the back of his neck, an intense flare of heat and bliss washing through him as his release spilled out into Damien's fist. Damien let go of Alec's hand and gripped his hip instead, thrusting deeper to chase his own release until his hips jerked, and his cock pulsed in hot spurts inside Alec.

Drifting on the afterglow of his orgasm as exhaustion

seeped back into him, Alec barely felt Damien's softening cock slip free. He dozed lightly when Damien disappeared from the bed, returning a short while later with a warm washcloth to clean them both up and manipulate them under the covers.

Alec rolled over to wrap around Damien as the man silently stroked Alec's back. Contentment washed over him as sleep claimed him, even as something in the back of his mind whispered a word that should scare him. A word that sat just at the tip of his tongue, but that he couldn't quite reach.

What could have been minutes or hours later, Alec jolted awake to a heartrending scream. Damien thrashed under him, back arching and twisting enough to throw Alec off. Another nightmare? Gods, what was Damien dreaming about?

Alec reached for Damien, determined to wake him up this time. Damien lashed out, grabbing Alec's arm. If Alec tried to break the hold, he could hurt him. "Wake up, *a stór*, you're having a nightmare."

"No, no, please." Damien shoved at Alec, trying to push him away, finally releasing Alec's arm. "Not again."

Damien's next scream was filled with pain. A whimper escaped Alec as he reached for Damien again. Damien didn't fight him, gripping his stomach instead as his voice turned hoarse. He curled up into a tight ball, protecting his middle.

Alec stroked Damien's face, tears pricking at the back of

his eyes as Damien flinched at the touch. What could he do? Damien wasn't waking up.

"No. Just let me die."

Die?

Alec's throat clogged. Damien couldn't die. He couldn't. Why would he say that? Panic threatened to sink its claws into Alec, but he pushed it away.

A whisper escaped Damien's lips that stopped Alec cold. "No good deed goes unpunished ..."

Ari's voice from long ago drifted through Alec's memories, words he had all but forgotten. *"A saying that has never been more true. I am sorry, Little Wolf. For returning my soul, I grant you this boon. You shall live until this wrong is right, and you find a mate to share your life."*

Were Damien's nightmares about ... Alec? He shot a shaking hand up to his mouth and bit down hard to prevent the pained cry from escaping his throat. Had he caused this? Just like with Oliver, Alec had brought nothing but pain to Damien's life.

His eyes burned as the tears threatened to fall.

Desperation bled into his voice as he tried again to shake Damien awake.

To end this.

"PLEASE WAKE UP, *A RÚNSEARC.*"

Damien jerked awake as Alec shook him with a note of

desperation in his voice. Scrubbing a hand down his face, Damien struggled to shake off the heavy fog that came with waking suddenly from a dream.

Cold sweat pricked the back of Damien's neck.

No, it'd been a nightmare.

One of *those* nightmares. Alec's memories.

"Shit." Guess the two-week reprieve wasn't meant to last. It'd been too much to hope that once he'd determined their origin, they'd be gone for good and replaced with something different. His throat was sore. Had he been shouting in his sleep? "Christ, I'm sorry, sweetheart. Did I wake you?"

Collapsing against Damien with a sigh of relief, Alec laughed almost hysterically. "Wake me? Gods, Damien, you've been twisting and shouting in your sleep for the past ten minutes. You scared me half to death when you wouldn't wake up."

Fuck, he wasn't kidding. Alec was trembling. Rubbing soothing circles on Alec's back, Damien leaned up a bit to press a kiss to the side of Alec's head. "Hey, now. I'm okay. It's okay."

Silence stretched between them for so long, Damien almost checked to see if Alec was still awake. When he finally spoke, his voice was wounded and soft. "What were you dreaming about?"

Given Alec's tone, it was clear Damien had said something in his sleep to give it away. Damien sighed and pushed himself into a seated position on the bed. Alec sat back warily as he waited for his answer. "I've been having nightmares for months now. It started back in May, the same day the Stone investigation started."

"So the day you met me?"

Was that the same day? Damien frowned as another memory surfaced. "I think I met Ari that night too. She was outside Tim's apartment when I got home."

Alec stilled, shock and sadness flashing across his face. He pressed his lips into a grim line and scrambled to get out of the bed, stalking over to his bag to get dressed. "Were you ever going to tell me?" he asked quietly, his back to Damien.

Not if Damien could help it. There was no point in opening that wound if he didn't have to. Sighing, he shook his head. "I thought they were gone. They stopped two weeks ago."

Nodding as if that made sense, Alec packed his things in silence. Finished, he turned back to Damien with an unreadable expression. "Take me home."

Harper was still asleep in her room when they left the cabin. Damien left her a brief note on her door, so she wouldn't worry, before he and Alec climbed into his SUV. Tense silence filled the car for the full thirty-minute drive back to the city. Alec was understandably upset, so Damien didn't try to talk.

One step forward, ten steps back.

Damien had to stop keeping things from Alec. Glancing in his rearview mirror at his bag, he amended that thought. After the investigation, no more secrets between them.

He was so close to the end that he could taste it.

When they arrived at Alec's building, there were two police cars sitting outside with lights flashing, but no officers were in sight.

Damien released his seatbelt and unlatched the door. When Alec opened his mouth to protest, Damien silenced him with a hand on his arm. "The police are here. At least let me come in with you. Please, sweetheart?"

"What are the police doing here?"

"Not sure. There isn't an ambulance, so it's likely a routine call in."

Alec nodded and bit his lip. "Okay. Do you ... have time to stay for coffee?"

Taking the olive branch for what it was, Damien leaned over the center console and captured Alec's lips in a quick kiss. "Absolutely."

As they exited the stairwell and approached the door to Alec's apartment, a uniformed officer hurried over to stop them from entering. "Sir, this is an active crime scene."

Just a glimpse inside the apartment dropped Damien's heart to his knees. The living room was a mess, with cushions and drawers strewn across the floor. He dug his badge out of his pocket and flashed it at the officer. "Detective O'Connor. What happened here?"

"Sorry, Detective. I'm Officer Kent. The alarm system reported an unauthorized entry. It looks like it waited at least an hour before notifying the police. We just arrived to find, well, you can see what we found. We haven't reached the renter yet. Is that either of you?"

"That's strange. I should've been notified first." Alec slipped his phone out of his pocket and furrowed his brow. He glanced back up toward the officer. "This is my apartment."

"Could you come inside and see if anything is missing?"

"Of course." Alec stepped inside and immediately coughed into his arm. He let out a soft curse and turned to Damien, stepping close and burying his nose at the base of Damien's neck, speaking softly, so only Damien could hear him. "There's an awful chemical scent in here, like that hunting spray we found in Tim's apartment. Can you smell it?"

The officers further into the room shared a glance with raised eyebrows at the display, but thankfully they kept their mouths shut. Damien glared at them before taking a deep breath through his nose. But instead of the chemical that Alec claimed he could smell, all Damien could smell was something sweet ...

A spike of pain shot through Damien's eye, and a groan escaped him as he doubled over. "Ow, fuck me."

"Damien? Are you okay?" Alec led Damien over to the nearest stool at the breakfast bar, massaging the back of his neck soothingly. "What can I—"

Out in the hall, Officer Kent shouted as someone entered the apartment despite his protests. Alec froze as the intruder spoke softly to herself. "Foolish girl made such a mess. Did she think I would just leave it out in the open?"

Damien cracked an eye open and stared at Ari in disbelief. Her timing was suspect to say the least. When the tiny woman noticed Damien watching her, she took an involuntary step back before she could stop herself. Straightening her spine, a frown tugged at her lips. "It would seem that while my arrival is far too late, the Little Wolf and his mate are early. I am sorry you had to witness this."

A low growl rumbled up Alec's throat, and Damien placed a placating hand on his arm, hoping it would be enough to stop him until the officers left. After that? Ari deserved anything the wounded wolf had to get off his chest.

Nodding approvingly, Ari turned to Officer Kent. "There appears to be a bit of a misunderstanding here. There has been no burglary, and there are no charges to press. I would ask you to leave."

A soft glow surrounded Ari as she spoke, passing between the officers in the room and Officer Kent, whose demeanor changed rapidly. Gone was the aggressive gatekeeper, and in his place stood a receptive shell. He blinked a few times and nodded, almost to himself. Within moments, all three officers had left without so much as a single word.

What the hell?

Alec stepped protectively in front of Damien and growled again. "Tampering with more memories?"

"Oh, come now, Little Wolf. You know as well as I do that the officers would only complicate matters." Stepping back into view, Ari studied Damien carefully. "It seems that I am indeed partly to blame for the headaches afflicting your detective, however. May I fix them?"

Damien frowned. "Fix them how? You know why I've been getting these headaches?"

"You have not told him?"

Deflating, Alec stepped aside. "It hasn't come up."

Humming her disapproval, Ari approached cautiously. "You are afflicted by a geas that is actively disrupting your memories, Detective. Much like I just did to those officers."

"Except you had long-term memories associated with what the geas is trying to erase. It made you sick and caused all those headaches whenever you tried to remember something related to them. How are you only partly to blame, Ari? You did this to him." Hurt and anger laced Alec's words. Damien snaked out a hand to comfort him.

Ari paused and tilted her head. "I did not place the geas."

But she'd done something else.

Did that mean she'd caused Damien's nightmares? No wonder Alec had fallen silent at the cabin; he'd known the moment that Damien had mentioned Ari's name. But how? Why?

Ari stopped with her arm outstretched just short of touching Damien. Damien's eyes burned, forcing him to blink several times. The room—no, *Ari*—grew brighter with each blink, and the braids atop her head morphed into … tails? Ten white tails tipped with gold fanned out behind her, and her eyes had taken on a distinct vulpine shape.

Just like the creature from his dream the other day.

Damien sucked in a sharp breath as warmth spread through him, and his headache finally subsided, bringing a clarity he hadn't felt in months. Would her paws match the prints Damien had found in Tim's apartment? His friend had confirmed that those prints belonged to a Vulpes vulpes Linn: the common red fox.

But Ari's fur held no red.

He'd suspected this, pouring over the lore over and over again after he'd discovered the source of the prints, but to have it confirmed … "You're kitsune."

Alec tensed and turned toward Damien. "How did you know that?"

"Interesting. I had not foreseen this." Ari tilted her head, a slow grin spreading across her lips. "But it is a good sign. I am relieved your mate is so astute." Tapping her lips, she shook her head. "And no, Detective, I am not the kitsune you seek."

There was another kitsune? Right, the red fox with two tails in his dream. So that *was* also one of Alec's memories.

With a wistful sigh, Ari turned to Alec. "Little Wolf, this is a long story. May I have some tea?"

Alec's spine grew rigid. "Why, Ari? So you can lie to me again? Did you think you could just come back here after disappearing for two weeks, and everything would just go back to normal? If you aren't doing this, then who is?"

Ari took a startled step back, blinking. "I have never lied—"

Shaking his head, Alec laughed derisively. "That I cannot see is no excuse for me to be blind. The things I've done for you all these years. The deaths we've hidden away under the guise of keeping the great secret. How many of them, Ari? How many could've been avoided?"

Just what did Alec mean by that? Covered up what deaths? Surely, he didn't mean all of those cold case reports that Damien had poured through with his officers. Although ... in each report with photographs, they'd found leaves. Crisp autumn leaves.

And Alec had pulled back into himself after reading some of those reports. Even more when Damien had explained the origin of the envelope full of those same leaves.

Ari pressed her lips into a thin line, but she didn't immediately respond.

Her silence could write a book.

Damien studied the kitsune before him as the grand glow surrounding her faded away. She appeared ... exhausted.

Defeated.

But only Damien could see the devastation in her eyes. Alec pointed toward the door. "I think you should leave, Ari."

"It would appear the Fates are laughing at me." Ari closed her eyes to hide the resignation in them. "Even now, you continue to defy them."

Alec frowned. "What does that mean?"

Tears streamed down Ari's cheeks as she opened her eyes, but her voice held steady. "For what it is worth, I am sorry, Little Wolf. I am the blind one. I could not foresee this outcome, but that is no excuse. There is only one way to set this to rights now that I am sure. When the time comes, you will understand."

Without a backward glance, Ari left the apartment.

Damien stepped forward to stop Ari, but Alec's despondent voice stopped him in his tracks. "Let her go. She was telling the truth when she said it wasn't her."

"How do you know?"

Alec simply tapped his nose.

Right. Werewolf. But did that work on kitsune as well?

Glancing around at the devastation in the apartment, Damien could believe that Ari wasn't responsible for this at least. If it had been her, Alec's alarm wouldn't have gone off at all. And given his dream, he believed there was a second kitsune somehow related to Ari. Fuck, there was too much that he still didn't know.

Damien sighed and focused instead on Alec, standing stoically with his arms wrapped around himself. If someone else was doing this, then Alec wasn't safe either. What he had to say was going to go over like a lead balloon. "I think I should stay with you until the next new moon."

"What? No. Don't be ridiculous."

"I'm being ridiculous? Alec, someone broke into your apartment, and you didn't even know about it. The police were here, for fuck's sake!"

"Which is exactly why I can't let you stay here. What was I thinking, involving you in all of this? I should've kept you unaware." Alec shook his head frantically. "First the headaches from the geas, then the concussion in Tim's apartment, and now this? Not to mention the nightmares! It's getting too dangerous for a mere human. Just go, Damien. You're not safe with me."

"But—"

"No!" Alec's shout rang throughout the room, and he turned his back. "Everyone leaves, Damien. This time, I'm going to leave first. If you were to get hurt because of me, I—I don't want to see you again."

"Alec ..." Damien sighed, shoulders slumping. What could he say to that? "If that's what you really want."

"It is."

"All right, then. I'm just a phone call away. If you change your mind."

"I won't."

Back to square one.

Outside the building, Ari stood waiting expectantly next to Damien's SUV. Damien raised an eyebrow at her, and she sighed. "You should not let him push you away so easily. It is what he does, wounded wolf that he is."

"He needs time."

"Time is a luxury we cannot afford, I fear."

What the hell did that mean?

Ari clearly expected to go somewhere with him, but there was information Damien needed first. "Why the nightmares?"

"Nightmares were not my intent, Detective. I had seen the potential mate bond between the two of you and had only meant to give it ... a little push. It would seem I pushed too far. He ... I did not expect it to take this long for him to find you."

Mate bond. That was something Damien preferred to discuss with Alec.

If they ever spoke again.

"Why did you ignore his calls?"

Ari blinked. "He did not call me."

Damien shook his head. "Alec called you and your answering service several times. Both were disconnected."

"See for yourself, Detective." Ari slipped a well-worn set of business cards out of her pocket and handed one to him. The cards simply contained two numbers and a tiny wolf's print in the corner. "The entire preternatural community in Columbus has one of these. Feel free to ask Jac to show you the one I gave to him. The first number is my answering service."

Shaking his head, Damien dialed the numbers. Both connected immediately. Damien shared a look with Ari as she silenced her phone. "Why wouldn't Alec's calls go through?"

Ari's lips turned down into a confused frown. "I do not know. He last called just before I left with Tim."

"How is Tim, by the way?"

"He is settled into Kalispell with a new name. The local Independents will keep their eyes on him. I will give you his contact information later. You can ask him yourself." Ari tucked her phone away and steeled her spine. "Let us go someplace private, Detective. We have much more to discuss. Perhaps we could grab some sushi on the way?"

Maybe—just maybe—Damien would finally get some answers.

28

SHOVING *the pack leader off him, Alsander stood and brushed himself off. One of the hounds growled and snapped something up in his jaws before taking off on a tear toward the barn. Frowning, Alsander took a step to follow when the last of the sun's rays caught on another object.*

Picking up the small, white-gold ball, Alsander spun it around in his hands. The ball was warm to the touch and began emitting a soft, golden glow the moment he picked it up. Had the women dropped this?

With the sun set below the horizon, it was foolish to enter the forest, but Alsander called for the women anyway. "I think ye dropped something."

"It would seem you have something of mine. Would you return it?"

Startled by the soft voice behind him, Alsander whirled around. Behind him stood the shorter of the two women, warily watching the ball in his hand. He held it out to her. "Aye. Apologies for the hounds, lass."

Though she was other, he felt no ill will from her. A smile twitched her lips, and she swiped the ball up, twisting it artfully among the seven white-blonde braids piled atop her head. "For that, I shall grant you a boon. What is it you wish from me?"

A boon? Just what was this creature? Taking a boon could be dangerous indeed.

Before he could decline, a low growl rumbled to Alsander's left, the twin-tailed fox changing back into the tall woman with a pair of long red braids. "And what of mine?"

Taking a step back, he held out his hands. "I only found the one. A hound may have taken off with the other one."

"Fool!" The red-haired woman lunged at him, only to be held back by the shorter woman. "Release me, Mother."

"Easy, Ina. We shall find yours now, yes?" With a sparkle in her eye, the woman nodded toward Alsander. "When the time comes, you shall receive your boon."

Following the ominous portent, the women disappeared in a cloud of leaves.

ALEC SWATTED at the hands shaking him awake and rolled over to cover his face in the pillow. "Leave me alone."

Harper growled at him. "I'm not letting you waste away

in bed. You're having lunch with me today, remember? It's already midafternoon."

When had he promised that?

The pillow was jerked away from him, and before Alec could swipe it back, his curtains were opened to stream bright afternoon sunlight into his bedroom. Wincing in pain, he unsuccessfully felt around for his glasses.

"Get out of bed, and I'll give them to you."

"That's low, Harper, even for you." Alec kicked the blankets out of his way and slid out of the bed. Harper pressed his glasses against his chest, and he fumbled to put them on before stalking over to his dresser to pull out some clothes.

Humming her approval, Harper left the room. "It worked, didn't it?"

They ended up eating lunch at Sister's Bar and Grill since Harper's shift started in half an hour. Guilt slithered down Alec's spine as they sat down. He hadn't meant to forget about lunch. Hell, he hadn't meant to sleep so late either.

But ever since Alec had kicked Damien out of his apartment a week ago, he'd felt … wrong. Like a part of him had walked out that door with Damien.

Tightening his resolve, Alec clamped down on that thought and sipped his iced tea while Harper headed to the kitchen to put in their lunch order. He wouldn't let Damien fall victim to this mysterious kitsune.

He wouldn't let another person die.

How long had another kitsune been in Columbus? Had Ari known? She'd said she couldn't see the outcome, but how was that possible? For as long as Alec had known her, Ari had possessed an eerie sort of ... prescience.

What made this different?

For that matter, how had Damien known about Ari? It went without saying that she was a shifter of some sort, but few who met her ever knew exactly what—or who—she was. Jac knew, but the Fae's promise to Ari held his tongue. Whatever that promise entailed.

But Damien had figured it out.

The lemony scent of spring swirled around Alec as someone sat to his left. Naomi's soft, lilting voice whispered across Alec's skin, startling him from his thoughts. "Stubborn wolf, always insisting on taking the unthreaded path. We will warp a new frame soon. Try not to disrupt this one, as it has taken us quite some time to fix the last one."

He'd only met the youngest of the three witches once, but her scent was unlike any other he'd come across. "You spend too much time with Marta. Neither of you ever makes any sense."

"We make perfect sense to those who listen."

Right. Like Alec did anything *but* listen.

"You hear, but you do not listen."

Alec's head shot up. "I didn't say that out loud."

"That is because I listen even when I do not hear." Naomi huffed out an exasperated breath. "It doesn't matter. My point remains. One way or another, the weave shall be repaired, and the impossible fox returned to her den when the moon is black. And this time? We will not allow a disruption. The question that remains, however, is what to do with her messenger?"

For such a young witch, Naomi's manner of speaking reminded Alec of times long past. And what had she meant by *this time*?

"That's enough of that, sister. We didn't go through all this trouble to have you back out now, and there's still much that needs done." Deci set another tea in front of Alec as Harper sat down with their lunch.

"As you say. I suppose it could've been worse."

Deci chuckled. "Oh, very much so. Marta had big plans for this year."

The women disappeared into the kitchen with Naomi's soft, mirthful response lost behind the door. Something about a plague?

"I swear, that whole family is insane." Harper shoved a plate toward Alec. "Eat."

Alec shook his head and picked up one of the burgers in front of him. "I've never met so many witches who speak in riddles like they do."

"I wonder what she meant by impossible fox?"

"It wouldn't surprise me if she meant Ari." Alec sighed, what little appetite he had fading. He tossed his burger back down and shoved his plate away, dropping his head into his hands. "Gods, Harper. This entire year has been a mess."

"Why would you think she meant Ari?" Harper hummed thoughtfully after several minutes passed, and Alec just shook his head without answering. It wasn't his story to tell. "Naomi also mentioned a black moon. Did you know that the next new moon is supposed to be a black one? It's been in the news lately. I can't read anything without seeing something about black moon this, black moon that."

Alec sucked in a sharp breath. "The new moon this month is black? Which kind?"

"I take it that means something more than four new moons this summer?"

"The one where there's two in a month is virtually irrelevant. Astrologists just wanted to slap a fancy name on it and reused an existing one. But the true black moon is the third new moon in a season with four new moons. The third death can be used to perform magic that is not normally possible. Witches always use it as a time of significant change."

And soul magic would be at its most potent. Dread crept down Alec's spine as his resolve to keep Damien away grew stronger. There was no way he could allow the kitsune anywhere near the Damien on that day.

Or Harper for that matter.

STEPPING into the lobby elevator for Chase Tower, Damien punched the button that would take him to the

PackForce Staffing floor. He stepped back to watch the numbers climb alongside his heart rate. He'd almost expected a spike of pain upon entering the building, but he hadn't had even the slightest hint of a headache since Ari had lifted the geas or whatever it was.

Walking into the lion's den where someone had fucked with his memory was a terrible idea, but what other choice did he have? A smart man would've asked someone to come with him, but who should he have asked? His officers had no clue about the dangers that lay behind the mysteries of this case.

Jac? His old friend had come along the last time, and now that the fog had cleared, it had become increasingly obvious that there'd been no legal reason for Jac to be there. Ari "hiring" him was a complete sham, and the VP had even tried to send Jac away, but it hadn't worked.

Hell, Jac had come on his own to reacquire the paperwork that had disappeared. Jac had done what he could to keep Damien out of this and safe. Just like Alec was trying to do by pushing him away.

Too damned bad.

The kitsune had been toying with him here. With all of them.

But now he knew who she was.

Damien's officers had followed his hunch with skepticism and grace, but they'd found the link. It all came back to this place. He just needed confirmation.

With a fortifying breath, Damien stepped through the

doors to PackForce Staffing. Behind the front desk sat an older, unfamiliar woman. She smiled at him warmly. "Good afternoon. How can we help you today?"

Damien frowned. "What happened to the other woman?"

"I'm sorry. I don't quite know who you mean. This has been my desk since this branch opened."

What the hell? "No, there was someone else here the last time I came."

The woman blinked up at him but said nothing further. The look on her face almost reminded Damien of the empty gaze on the officer's face in Alec's apartment before Ari had sent him away. Had the kitsune done this to her?

"Is there a problem out here, Mary?" Suzanne poked her head out of the doorway leading to the back offices. "Oh, hello, Detective. I'm afraid if you're here to see Mr. O'Rourke, he has left for the Portland offices. We don't expect him back anytime soon, but he left instructions to cooperate if you were to stop by again. Is there something I can help with?"

Well, this wasn't going how Damien had expected, but he would take it. If the kitsune wasn't here, he could get what he needed to help his officers build a plausible case and leave. Even better that he didn't have to deal with the VP again. "I'm actually looking for the woman who was working the desk when I stopped in for the Franklin Park case."

A flash of something akin to anxiety crossed

Suzanne's face. Rubbing the bridge of her nose, she waved Damien to follow her to the back offices. "I'm afraid Miss Meadows stopped coming in a few weeks ago, Detective."

Right after her failed attack on Tim, perhaps? "That's okay. Maybe you can help me then. What is her usual role here, if not at the front desk?"

"Miss Meadows is contractual. Sometimes she helps out around here when Mr. O'Rourke requests her." Suzanne sat at her desk and woke her computer. "Is there something specific you need, Detective?"

"Could you pull up her contracts for the year for me?"

"Of course. Give me a few minutes to print them out." Suzanne stepped out for a moment and returned with a hefty stack of papers. "Would you like an envelope for these?"

Damien absently nodded as he leafed through the stack, pausing at the employment contract. So they were right. Trisha Meadows. If only he could hand this woman over to Candice to repay his debt for making her deal with "the bubbly bitch" on the phone instead of just handing her information after the next new moon.

Trisha had worked at the storage facility with Stone for nearly a month and had left two days after his death. She'd then picked up the contract at Franklin Park Conservatory at the last minute when Ms. Hawthorne had failed to show up for work. Damien glanced up at Suzanne. "Why wasn't Miss Meadows listed on the Franklin Park paperwork in

June? What I received indicated Mindy Hawthorne had been assigned to the job."

Ms. Hawthorne, who'd already died at that point. They wouldn't have determined who she was if it hadn't been for that paperwork.

"She should've been. We were having some problems with our database this summer. Perhaps I pulled the information from the backup file for you without realizing it. I'm sorry, Detective. Would you like me to double-check now?" The lie flowed off Suzanne's tongue easily, but she failed to mask the fear in her eyes.

A sense of wrongness permeated throughout the entire agency, and Damien had stepped right into the deep end. Ensuring the next contract in the pile belonged to Tim's company downstairs, he shoved everything into the envelope Suzanne had set aside on her desk for him and shook his head. "No, I think I have everything I need."

Confirmation that the kitsune had been stalking her victims.

But why?

Out in the SUV, Damien shoved the envelope between his seat and the center console and climbed inside. With any luck, there would be no envelope full of leaves this time around. "Did you find what you were after?" he asked a moment later.

"Their minds are wounded." Ari sighed sadly as she slipped into the passenger seat. "I found it, but only because it holds no power. She lives on stolen time. I have failed her as a mother."

Mother? So the kitsune causing all this mayhem *was* the same one from his dreams.

Damien glanced over as Ari pulled a small, dark ball out of her hair and held it up for him to see. The object looked nothing like how she'd described it would during their discussion last week and even less like the one in his dream. "So that's Ina's?"

Ari blinked at Damien. "How do you know the name of my daughter?"

She didn't know? "What, you didn't give me those dreams too?"

Tilting her head, Ari studied Damien for a moment. "The bond between you and the Little Wolf is already so strong. I am glad. My promise to him is nearly fulfilled. I believe you can help him correct the rest."

"I don't understand."

A tear slid down Ari's cheek as she tucked the ball away. "There are pivotal points of Fate, Detective. Anchors in time that do not—that should not—change." Ari turned her head and stared out the window. "Nearly two and a half centuries ago, our Little Wolf rescued my daughter and me from a pack of Irish wolfhounds. It should never have been possible. I was meant to die that day."

When Alec had intervened and stopped the hounds from attacking.

"It set off a sequence of events that have fallen entirely

outside of the Fates' control. My daughter should have inherited my power. Instead, she turned her back on me and ... traded her boon to help the Alpha that had taken our Little Wolf. I now believe the Alpha betrayed her and stole her power for himself instead. I began to suspect that she had found another way to live by using the death of the moon to steal the life force of preternatural creatures."

And causing them to age as they died.

What a way to go.

Damien frowned. "So this is your daughter doing all of this? How has it gone on so long without you knowing for sure? That's a lot of bodies over two-hundred-plus years."

"I believe so. Understand, Detective, I cannot see her. My powers do not affect her in any way. We are but two parts of the same whole. The preternaturals that have died were all old, and ... I could not see as it directly affected Ina." Ari's voice cracked, a forlorn expression on her face.

"Why didn't you stop her after you began to suspect?"

Ari turned back to Damien with a sad smile. "A mother will do much to protect her daughter. I had hoped I could save her, Detective, but she is beyond saving."

Including covering up the deaths of ... hundreds if not thousands of preternatural creatures over the course of two-and-a-half centuries, unwittingly or not. Ari might not have done the crimes herself, but she was still guilty. If she were human, he would arrest her.

But she wasn't human, and he wasn't foolish enough to try.

Damien was so far out of his depth here.

Fuck.

"Why haven't you shared this with Alec?"

Closing her eyes, Ari shook her head. "By the time I realized, it was too late to stop the events. We are heading to another anchor point, Detective. Even the gods fear the wrath of the Fates. The Little Wolf could not be allowed to interfere again."

"How did he do it in the first place?"

"Even the Fates do not know."

Ari fell silent. Guess that's all she was willing to share. Who the fuck were the Fates? And was Damien just supposed to accept all of this? What other choice did he have? With Alec refusing to speak with him, he could only follow his own instincts.

And those instincts told him that Ari's hands were genuinely tied.

Well, fuck that.

"Back in Alec's apartment, you said there was only one way to set this to rights. Are you ready to tell me how?" Damien would do everything he could to end this.

"Ina will have one last chance to absorb my *Hoshi no Tama*—my Soul Ball—when the black moon rises in one week. I am afraid we have all run out of time. Kitsune are only meant to have nine tails."

And Ari now had ten.

What did that mean?

Something told Damien that Ari wouldn't answer that.

"So how do we stop her from killing anyone else?" he asked instead.

Ari hummed. "Perhaps you *can* help. Yes. But first ... there is much we need to do that we cannot accomplish sitting in your vehicle. Let us go somewhere to grab dinner. I believe I owe you for all the trouble I have put you through these past few months. Let me help you close your cases, Detective. It is the least I can do."

And just how did she plan to do that?

29

"YOU LOOK like you could use a drink."

Alec chuckled mirthlessly at Deci's declaration. Before his change, he and Konnyer would occasionally share a good bottle of whiskey under the stars. He didn't drink anymore because it dulled his senses. But tonight? The numbness the whiskey always brought with it sounded like a taste of heaven. "How about a bottle of the strongest thing you have?"

He would try anything to just ... forget everything. Blissful ignorance for an hour before the alcohol metabolized in his system. Even Harper had given up on him this week after he'd forgotten plans with her three days in a row. She kept trying to make him eat.

The food sat heavy in his stomach each time.

But he'd felt cooped up in his apartment. His skin had itched to be anywhere else. After wandering for hours, his feet had eventually brought him to Sister's. Harper was off tonight, and Damien hadn't stopped in all week. Alec could be alone even here in this crowd.

It was a good thing.

Someday, Alec would believe all the lies he told himself.

Deci hesitated, a frown in her voice. "If you're sure that's what you want."

"Oh, listen to the wolf, Deci. This is perfect." A sudden rush of belladonna flooded Alec's senses. He turned warily toward Marta as she slid onto the barstool next to him. Perfect for what? "Fetch him a bottle of mead."

"If you say so, Marta." With a sigh, Deci returned with a bottle and a glass, setting them both in front of Alec. "This is troll mead. Drink it slowly, Alec. This isn't meant for humans."

Troll mead? Alec poured a glass and held it to his nose before taking a sip. Honey and spices bloomed on his tongue, and within moments, he felt a rush of warm calmness fill him. Why hadn't he tried this stuff before?

"That should do the trick quite nicely." Marta took the glass from Alec's hand and filled it again. "I haven't seen your mate recently. Where is he off to?"

Alec frowned as Marta took a sip of the mead, but his mind latched on to the other phrase. "He's not my mate. That's just a phrase humans throw around anyway." Wasn't it? A piece of Alec rebelled at the thought. Even Ari had used the term.

Pushing Damien out of his life was the right thing to do.

Humans had no place in a world where they couldn't protect themselves. He wouldn't be able to live with himself if Damien got hurt again because of him.

Or, gods forbid, died because of him.

A wounded whimper pushed out of Alec as he once again stood at the edge of the cold abyss. There was no warmth this time to hold it back. The Fates were cruel, allowing him to wake up and *feel* again, only to yank it all away.

Marta hummed and handed him another glass of mead. "Poor wounded wolf. You brought yourself such unnecessary pain. I almost regret what we have to do."

Deci's voice cracked. "I know this leads to the best outcome, but … I still don't like this." What did she mean by that?

"Do not waste your breath, sisters. He hears, but he still does not listen." Alec twisted his head at the whisper of Naomi's voice on the other side of him, but he'd missed her scent behind the honey and spice in his glass. All three of them were here?

"I listen," Alec said, shocked at how slurred his words were. He'd heard humans call each other a lightweight, but he was a wolfwere. Werewolf.

That.

Alec shook his head as ringing filled his ears, and he listed to the side on his barstool. This was a mistake. Why had he thought this was a good idea? A delicate hand grabbed his arm, and before he realized what was happening, the tiny woman yanked him unceremoniously to his feet. The scent of cinnamon and autumn leaves touched his nose before his hand tangled in the short stack of braids atop her head. "Ari?"

"He is quite intoxicated, isn't he?" she asked. If anyone answered, Alec didn't hear it through the ringing in his ears, but Ari's voice remained clear. "Let's get you home, Alec."

Frowning, he tried to shake off Ari's grip. "Leave me alone, Ari. I'm still angry with you."

She merely laughed at his words and shoved him toward the door. "Oh, don't be that way. Surely, I couldn't have hurt you that badly. You're my favorite wolf, after all."

Something was wrong.

Wasn't there?

The new moon was tomorrow. Why had he gone out again? He should've stayed in tonight, figured out what the kitsune had been looking for in his apartment two weeks ago.

Alec's mind whirled as he stumbled along in Ari's grip, back toward his apartment. Inside, Ari pushed him toward his bedroom. "Why don't you rest for a while? Sleep off the mead, hmm? We can talk when you're more awake."

Yes, sleep sounded like a good idea.

DAMIEN SAT BACK from the seldom-used breakfast nook where he'd set up his laptop and rubbed his eyes. This was coloring a little further outside the lines than he'd anticipated but few options remained. No one would believe the truth, but at least this way, not *everything* had to be swept under the rug.

Stone and Collin would have justice. As would the poor forgotten souls from the boxes back at the precinct. Those cold cases would change Candice and Andy's careers for the better. It was the least Damien could do after all they'd gone through these past three months.

His apartment door opened after a soft knock. Damien leaned back to greet his guests. "Everything set up?" he asked.

Ari handed Damien a small thumb drive. "Add these to your records. In a few weeks, an FBI agent will contact your captain. He will ensure your officers get the credit for closing these cases after spinning the story we discussed."

Stone and Collin would forever remain missing, but with Ari's help, Damien had found a way to spin a serial case spanning back over fifty years. The FBI agent was a member of the preternatural community and would "find" the body of Trisha Meadows—or some acceptable substitute —and trace the killings back to her family, starting with her "grandmother."

It was the best he could do, but it was enough to jumpstart Candice and Andy's careers.

Damien plugged the drive into his laptop. It contained the Cincinnati files that no one else had been able to obtain. How had Ari gotten her hands on these?

He shook his head in disbelief. "You're sure this will work?"

"As sure as I can be."

"That doesn't instill me with much confidence." Damien shook his head when Ari simply closed her eyes and shrugged. As the days had flown by, Ari had become more withdrawn and only answered his questions when it suited her. He turned his attention to his other guest instead. "How is he?"

Harper set a coffee next to Damien and leaned against the counter in the kitchen, gesturing north. "Who, the stubborn, stupid wolf who would rather be a martyr than be happy? He's moping. Barely eating. Ari suggested I just give him space."

Heart sinking at Harper's words, Damien cursed at himself for not pushing harder. He'd thrown himself into work, following the leads that Ari had set out for him. She'd promised it would wrap up neatly in the end but insisted it all needed to be put into motion before the new moon. Just in case.

Besides, Alec would've thrown a shit fit if he knew what Damien and Ari had planned.

Ari reached up and pulled the ball she'd retrieved from PackForce Staffing from her hair, setting it on the counter between them. As she stared at the ball, a faint white glow pulsed within it. Harper and Damien glanced at each other in awe.

"What did you call this again?" Damien asked.

"The balls are known as *Hoshi no Tama*, or Soul Balls. I have made this object resemble mine, which remains safely hidden with our Little Wolf." Shaking her head, Ari handed the ball to Damien. It pulsed in his hand, and a brief flash of Ari's radiant tails spread out before him. When the light faded, Ari appeared older.

As though her own light had faded.

Their plan was to trap the murderous kitsune so Ari could stop her ... somehow. Ari still held enough secrets to last several lifetimes and refused to tell him how. Just that he would know when it was time.

Damien would play the bait, and Alec would be safe.

He held up the ball. "You're sure she'll come here for this?"

Turning back, Ari studied Damien before answering. "She will come for my *Hoshi no Tama* tonight, yes." Without another word, Ari slipped out of Damien's apartment, with a frowning Harper on her heels.

Why did it feel like Ari had left something out?

With more questions than answers, Damien slipped the ball into his pocket and turned back to his computer. He picked up the coffee Harper had brought him, downing half the cup in one long sip.

He was in for a long night.

30

"WAKE UP, ALEC."

Alec groaned and tried to roll over but couldn't get his limbs to cooperate. Was the mead still affecting him? The voice penetrated the cotton in his brain as hands grasped his wrists. "Ari? What are you—"

"You still don't realize it, do you?" Ari sneered. "It's your fault. Everything has happened because of you."

Because of him? "I don't understand."

She pulled his arms tight above his head. At the first brush of bindings, Alec's brain caught up with what was happening. He tried to wrench his hands free, twisting his body to break her hold.

But he was too slow.

No.

Oh gods, no.

Blood rushed to Alec's ears as they began ringing once again. His heart hammered, adding a staccato thrum, deafening him as his mind spun. Why was Ari doing this? *What* was his fault? *What* had happened because of him?

He'd only followed her wishes.

Done exactly as she'd said.

He'd never questioned her.

Until recently.

Was that why she'd turned on him? Because he'd turned his back on her? She'd lied to him. She'd known about Oliver and Collin. How they'd died. Why they'd died.

Was that his fault?

Had he failed them more than he realized?

Ari slapped Alec, drawing him out of his spiral. Her hand held faint traces of a harsh chemical scent. He knew that scent. Ari slapped him again. "Listen to me!"

"Wh-why—"

"It's your fault she still exists. Your fault *he* enslaved me and forced me to keep us both alive month after month, decade after decade. You should've retrieved my *Hoshi no Tama* from those blasted hounds, not hers. Instead, you stole her power from me! It's *mine!*"

"Ari—" A scream of rage cut Alec off, followed by another slap that stung his face.

"My name is *Ina!*"

Ina. Not Ari.

They shared the same scent. The same voice.

Pain blossomed behind Alec's eyes as his memories sharpened, finally understanding Ari's moments of confusion. The times she seemed to start the same conversation twice.

Ari had never called Alec by his name in all the years he'd known her. It had always been "Little Wolf," from the very first day.

Until recently.

Ina had been here for months now, messing with him, the same way she had altered Damien's memories. Twisting his perception. Of everything.

How had Alec not known?

He'd never escaped her.

Panic rushed through his body as Ina laughed gleefully. "Oh, you remember me now, do you?"

The past bled with the present, and it carried Alec back to the days he had spent in that dark, cold cave. Damp stone replaced the bed at his back. The soft bindings turned to shackles, holding him upright when his body could no longer support him.

Ina caressed Alec's face, leaning forward to whisper into his ear. "But do you remember *him?* We've both followed you. All. This. Time."

His heart pounded a staccato beat.

Gods, he couldn't breathe.

Alec's tormentor's voice from the past echoed in his ears, followed by Ina's menacing reply.

"Tch, 'e's no fun anymore. How am I ta take me frustrations out on 'im now? More o' me wolves have succumbed to de bastard's father's hounds."

"Oh, I may have some ideas."

But his father's hounds had killed that Alpha.

Hadn't they?

Before he succumbed completely, Alec reached for the only thread of hope he had left, forcing air into his lungs to speak. "A-Alexa. C-call Damien ..."

He could only pray that it worked as his past claimed him.

DAMIEN POUNDED on Harper's door, praying like hell that she still had her keys to Alec's apartment. The fucking leaves that he'd found in his pocket were still in his hand, his gun in the other. He had no time to grab a holster, but he'd be damned if he went over there unarmed.

Ari stepped into the hallway, face grim. "Let us hurry. I will get us inside."

"You lied to me," Damien spat, throwing the leaves at her.

Ari sighed bitterly. "The Fates would not allow me to intervene, remember? This was the only option they offered."

Again, with the fucking Fates. "Then why give me a fake Soul Ball?"

"So I could keep you alive, Detective. It was the only way to honor my boon to the Little Wolf and still set this right." Ari shook her head. "We do not have time for this."

Damn her, she was right. The call from Alec had shaken him. This was like Damien's family all over again, but instead of a recording, he'd listened live as Alec fought off his attacker. He wouldn't lose Alec too. "He's locked in a flashback. He managed to call, but she disconnected it."

"Then what are we waiting for? Let's go." Harper pushed through the door, closing it behind her. The three of them raced down the stairs and out into the darkness of the early morning, bypassing Damien's SUV and heading toward Vine street. They'd get there faster on foot.

Ari stopped Damien with a hand on his arm outside Alec's building, tears in her eyes. "Whatever happens, it is not your fault, Detective. And please, do not let him push you away again. He will need you now more than ever. I need to know he will be cared for."

Damien studied the grim determination in Ari's eyes and nodded once. He'd let Alec push him away, and now all hell had broken loose. Saving Damien at the expense of Alec's life was not an option. "I promise."

"I do too. He has pack now. Whether he wants it or not. Our little pack of three." Harper patted Damien on the back.

"Right, then. Let us go end this. The death of the black moon draws near. When the time comes, do as I say, and my debt to the Fates shall be paid in full." Ari turned and opened the door to the apartment complex as though there were no lock. Damien blinked but moved when Harper pushed him forward, and the three of them raced down the hall and up the stairs. What had Ari meant by that?

Alec's alarm beeped as they entered, but Ari silenced it as she hurried toward the bedroom. She stopped short, a pained cry falling from her lips. "Oh, Ina. What have you done?"

Harper gagged, squaring her shoulders with a growl. "I smell blood. A lot of it."

Fuck.

From behind Ari, Damien peered into the room and clenched his jaw. "Christ. Why? Why do this?"

Alec lay strapped down to his own bed with leather cuffs, his scars flayed open beneath his torn shirt. Damien gripped his stomach with his free hand as memories assaulted him.

Claws.

Teeth.

The rattle of chains.

Alec twisted in pain, lost to his nightmares.

Damien shook his head. No. Not now. He raised his gun, aiming it at the woman standing over Alec. A woman who appeared identical to Ari. Hell, they could be twins.

As Ina turned to face them, Damien's eyes burned, and the braids atop her head shifted red and morphed into four flaming tails tipped with black. In her hand, she held a Soul Ball, shining brightly with white and gold, dripping with blood.

Alec's blood.

She'd pulled it out of him.

Damien's gorge rose, his heart thundering in his ears.

"How can I help you today, Detective?" Ina asked in a mocking, bubbly voice as her appearance shifted, so she looked similar to Trisha Meadows at the staffing agency, only taller and with bright red and black hair that matched her tails. Her lips spread into a fang-filled grin as she turned her attention to Ari. "I came for what is mine."

Ari stepped further into the room and out of Damien's line of sight, voice cracking as she addressed her daughter. "This was not the way, Ina. I could have helped you."

Rage flashed in Ina's eyes as she stood over Alec. "Helped me? You and your foolish wolf *did this to me*."

The Soul Ball flared to life in Ina's hand, a blinding light filling the room.

A tether of smoke or ... *something* shot from the ball to Alec's chest, creating a circuit with Ina. Alec coughed, thrashing wildly as the orb turned bright gold.

Damien aimed his gun, but what the fuck did he shoot?

Ari screamed and launched herself at Ina. "I cannot allow you to harm him!"

As the pair crashed to the ground, Ari grabbed hold of the Soul Ball and twisted, so they faced Damien, the ball clutched tight to her chest.

The circuit with Alec shattered. A pain-filled shout tore from Alec's lips, his back arching as though something had shocked him.

Harper tried to run to him, but Damien held an arm out

to stop her. He couldn't risk Harper breaking his line of sight. She whimpered helplessly but remained behind Damien.

Outside, the first tendrils of dawn crept over the horizon.

Moonrise.

Ari met Damien's eyes with cold determination. "Shoot it, Detective. Shoot the *Hoshi no Tama*. Shoot it now!"

Fuck.

This was it.

Damien took aim, finger reaching for the trigger.

But if he shot, he would hit Ari as well.

Damien froze.

This had been what Ari meant. Destroying the Soul Ball was the only solution. The kitsune both lived on stolen time.

An eerie calm stole over Damien.

It didn't matter if he shot Ari.

Shooting her Soul Ball would have the same effect.

Alec, forgive me.

Damien pulled the trigger.

Harper screamed and launched herself into the room.

But it was too late.

The bullet shattered the Soul Ball and continued through both Ari and Ina's chests, lodging itself into the dresser behind them. Hatred flashed in Ina's eyes as she gasped for breath and blood pooled around them both.

Ari simply closed her eyes, a peaceful smile on her face.

Damien's breath exploded from his burning lungs.

Fragments of the Soul Ball swirled around the dying kitsune, weaving in and out of their bodies. A blinding light filled the room once more, and Damien could just make out two proud foxes standing tall before they merged into one awe-inspiring being with ten multicolored tails and deep, limitless voids for eyes.

The creature nodded at Damien before turning its gaze to Alec.

Fuck. Alec.

Damien dropped his gun and rushed to Alec's side, forcing himself to calm down as he reached for the man. Harper joined him, undoing the bindings on his wrists, tears streaming down her face. Alec thrashed his freed arms, slashing at both of them, but Damien ignored the sting and pulled Alec into a sitting position while Harper released his legs.

"Sweetheart, come back now. You're safe. It's over." Damien held Alec's head between his trembling hands, pressing their foreheads together. Calm and steady. Freak out later. Alec needed him now. "Breathe, sweetheart. Breathe with me. Please, come back now."

Alec sucked in a harsh breath, his unsteady arms coming up around Damien's shoulders. "D-Damien?"

Oh, thank fuck.

Damien sagged against Alec as the light in the room faded.

When Damien looked back, the creature and the kitsune were gone.

TOO BRIGHT.

What was that light?

"No good deed goes unpunished. I am sorry, Little Wolf ... This is goodbye."

Alec came back to himself slowly. It felt as though he had been scattered, and only now had someone decided to put the pieces back together, but something was missing. Something important.

Voices echoed around him, but the words were still too far away to make any sense. Someone was crying. What had happened?

Everything hurt.

"Please, come back now." Damien's worried voice finally penetrated, and Alec sucked in a deep breath, wrapping his arms around Damien.

Alec's throat felt full of broken glass, and words took several tries to form. "D-Damien?"

Darkness filled the room.

"Oh, thank fuck, sweetheart." Damien kissed Alec's forehead. "It's over."

Memories rushed back to him. The bar. The alcohol. Ari—no, *Ina*—dragging him back to his apartment.

She'd tied him up.

The moon song was silent within him. The black moon had risen. Alec pulled away from Damien as the potent scent of blood and gunpowder reached his nose. Someone had been shot?

Harper's whimper drew Alec's attention. He reached for her as Damien stepped away, turning on the faucet in Alec's en suite. "What happened? Are you bleeding?"

"It's over, sweetie." Harper gripped his hand. "Don't worry about us. It's just a little scratch."

Damien returned with a warm washcloth, wiping Alec's stomach. He hissed and pulled back. The blood was his? But what about the gunpowder? No, it was his and … "Ari?"

Silence followed his question.

"Where is Ari? And what happened to Ina?"

"They're gone, Alec." Damien's voice cracked. "Ari … Ari's gone."

Something was missing.

The only constant in his life.

Alec reached for Harper and Damien, pulling them into a tight hug as silent tears fell from his eyes.

They were all he had left.

EPILOGUE

MEMBERS of the preternatural community traveled from all over the country to attend Ari's funeral, filling every open space surrounding the Irish Run Natural Bridge in Wayne National Forest. Her loss would be felt in the hearts and minds of every single one of them.

The urn seated in the center of the bridge held what was left of Ari's Soul Ball, as no other traces remained of her or her daughter. Surrounding the urn were various dishes made with rice or tofu. All things that Ari had loved.

Alec had insisted.

Damien stood back as the pair of wolves took up their position at the base of the bridge. As the full moon crested over the trees, Alec and Harper silenced the crowd with a mournful howl. One by one, each shifter and werecreature in the crowd took on their animal form while others stood by silently with tears in their eyes.

It was a sight to behold.

The wind picked up, carrying a maelstrom of leaves throughout the clearing as the animals joined their voices in the haunting melody.

Goosebumps prickled along Damien's skin.

As the leaves swirled around the urn, Damien could just make out the shape of a tiny orange fox in the center. It picked up a small, glowing object in its mouth and turned away. Without a backward glance, the fox bounded off into the trees.

Silence descended upon the forest, and the leaves settled to the ground.

Everything on the bridge was gone.

"NO MORE PUSHING EVERYONE AWAY?"

Alec sighed. "I shouldn't have done that."

"I would rather you turn toward me. Let me hold you together when you feel like everything is falling apart." Damien kissed Alec affectionately as a smile twitched at Alec's lips for the first time in weeks.

Alec rested his head on Damien's shoulder as the others who had gathered in the clearing gradually dispersed. They were back on even footing, but it was like a minefield, where one wrong step could shatter them both into a million broken pieces.

Ina was gone, but she'd implied that the Alpha who'd

broken Alec all those years ago remained out there. Somewhere.

If he was, they would find him.

The only way forward was through.

Together.

THE STORY CONTINUES ...

... in Silence of the Moon, Secrets of the Moon Book Two.
Available April 13th, 2023.

AFTERWORD

Thank you so much for reading my debut novel, *Death of the Moon*. This is the first in a planned trilogy, *Secrets of the Moon*, and some side characters, both current and future, are whispering to me, asking for their own books as well. Poor Alec has been through so much already, but I promise that he and Damien will find their HEA by the end of Book Three.

I'm a binge reader. In 2019, I exhausted my well of MF PNR and urban fantasy and decided to seek out something new. J.R. Ward's *Lover at Last* introduced me to a whole new world of romance that I didn't know I needed, but once I started, I was hooked. I read over three hundred books that year—though I'll admit that includes rereading some new favorites. At least twice.

Then 2020 happened. And with it, I could not find that exact *something* I needed to distract myself from real life. So I started writing again. Before I knew it, Alec and Damien were born. I am so happy to be able to share them with you.

I'm hard at work on the next book, *Silence of the Moon*. To stay up to date, please follow my page on Facebook. Join my reader group, Pavlik's Pavilion, for extra teasers and to just hang out and have fun with other readers and authors.

Please consider leaving a review on Amazon and Goodreads. Reviews help indie authors like me by encouraging readers to take a chance on self-published books.

ABOUT THE AUTHOR

S.A. Pavlik writes what she wants to read but that doesn't exist ... yet. An avid reader, she first discovered and promptly devoured hundreds of M/M romance novels in 2019, and it rekindled her desire to write. She started her debut novel, Death of the Moon, the very next year.

She was born and raised in Wisconsin, where it's too cold, but she loves it there anyway. She lives with her husband and her little chaos demons: a pair of kittens the universe found just for her. When she isn't reading or writing, she's obsessively playing video games or proving that an introvert can be an extrovert on the internet after all.

Join her Facebook reader group, Pavlik's Pavilion, or follow her on:

linktr.ee/sapavlikwrites

A TRILOGY OF SECRETS

Secrets of the Moon

01 - Death of the Moon

02 - Silence of the Moon

03 - Fury of the Moon (*TBA*)

Secrets and Lies *(Working)*

01 - Lie With Me (*Working - TBA* 2024)

SECRETS COMPENDIUM NOVELLAS

Chronicles of the Redwood Pack *(Working)*

01 - Title TBA (*TBA* - 2024)

SECRETS UNIVERSE SHORTS

01 - Peachville Haunted House (Death of the Moon Prequel)

02 - A Quiet Night in with Alec and Damien

SNEAK PREVIEW

S.A. PAVLIK

I

ALEC COULDN'T BREATHE.

No. No. No. Not again. He yanked at the binds holding his arms. Couldn't move. *Must get away. Not safe. Not safe here.*

A fire-tipped claw traced his scars, flaying Alec open all over again. He screamed, throat raw and filled with glass. Twice he tried to speak, but words remained locked in his chest. His heart hammered. The bands around his lungs squeezed tighter.

Oh, gods, stop.

"Alec."

Please stop this.

The creature thrust her hand into his chest, leaning over to whisper menacingly in his ear. "You should have saved *me* all those years ago."

"Alec. Sweetheart. Come back to me now."

It was Alec's fault. Everything that had happened. All his fault. He whimpered and tugged desperately at the bindings ... but they were gone. His arms flailed forward and smacked into a hard body just inches away.

What? That wasn't Ina ...

"Breathe with me, Alec. Please breathe."

A cool sensation washed over the back of Alec's neck as the comforting scent of vanilla and a hint of spice finally penetrated his senses. Home. No, not home. He didn't have a home anymore. But safety. He was safe. And sitting on the edge of the bed. Not lying down.

Not bound.

Alec sucked in a cleansing breath, coughing as his lungs burned from not enough air. Reality rushed back like a tidal wave, washing away the rest of the panic attack. "D-Damien?"

Damien heaved a shaky sigh of relief and pressed his forehead to Alec's, kneeling on the floor between Alec's legs. "Oh, thank fuck." The cool washcloth on Alec's neck disappeared. Damien wrapped his hand around the back of Alec's head, peppering kisses all over his face. "I'm here. I'm right here."

Here.

Damien's studio apartment in Arena Crossing. Ever since the incident two weeks ago, Alec hadn't returned to his own apartment. He barely had anything here to call his own aside from the clothing that Harper had retrieved for him after ... after ...

Tears burned the back of his eyes. He choked back a sob and launched himself forward, wrapping his arms around Damien as the tears fell helplessly. Damien knew better than to hold Alec in return. Instead, he kept one hand in Alec's hair and rubbed soothing circles into Alec's hip with the other.

"Shh, sweetheart. I know. Let it out. I'm so sorry. I—" Damien took a shaky breath and kissed the side of Alec's head, saying nothing more. He'd apologized so many times for reasons unknown over the last two weeks.

Alec had his suspicions, however.

They should discuss the why at some point, but ... not today. Today, Alec needed to honor his best friend and mentor in the only way he knew how. And that meant getting out of bed and facing the local preternatural community with his head held high.

The community needed him now, with Ari gone.

Gods, she was gone.

Conflicting feelings welled up inside him. She'd abandoned him toward the end. Put a distance between them that had never been there in all the years they'd known each other. Feck, she'd gone as far as disconnecting her phone.

As well as the preternatural helpline.

He'd never had the chance to ask her *why*.

Now he never would.

None of that erased the history they shared. Tainted it, certainly, but he still missed her. Gods, he still missed her.

With a deep, unsteady breath, Alec pulled out of Damien's arms, plastering on a smile he didn't quite feel and knew wouldn't reach his eyes. He swiped his wraparound sunglasses and fingerless leather gloves from the table, donning them like armor. He and Damien had a lot to accomplish today and should probably get going. Alec tilted his head. "What time is it?"

Darkness shrouded the apartment, but that didn't mean anything. Damien kept the blackout curtains closed throughout the day now, granting Alec a comfortable sanctuary for his oversensitive eyes. Even after everything they'd endured, Damien remained too good to be true.

The curtains allowed Alec to forgo his sunglasses inside the apartment—he could perceive light and dark through the scar tissue over his eyes, like an afterimage, but everything else was lost to a painful haze.

A frown laced Damien's reply, his voice hesitant. "Right before noon. I let you sleep. Harper and Jac are picking up the takeout all over town for us. They'll meet us down at the Archers Fork Trailhead, where everyone is planning to park."

"Almost noon? Damien, we need to arrive before four." Alec stood and started rummaging through his bag for something to wear. Sandalwood tickled his nose, and a hysterical laugh forced itself out of his throat. Gods, he'd never replaced his bag.

And now he never would.

The interior still smelled like Ari's incense from the … from the last time he'd traveled to Wayne National Forest. The place used to be his sanctuary.

Now it was a place of mourning. Taken from him just as surely as the lives of those close to him these past few months.

Back in May, Alec had failed a young werewolf named Oliver. Ina—a ghost from Alec's past and Ari's kitsune daughter—had cut Oliver's life off far too soon. Ina had stolen Oliver's remaining time to keep herself alive just a little bit longer.

Alec and Ari, along with Collin, had traveled to a place of power within the forest to say goodbye to Oliver. In the same place they planned to say their farewells tonight for Ari herself.

One month after Oliver's death, Alec had failed Collin as well. He hadn't known back then, but the young squirrel shifter had escaped an enclave—a horrible shifter cult where no humans were welcome—only for Ina to rip his remaining life away for herself.

Before them, thousands of other nameless souls had lost their lives to the same sinister cause. All to right a wrong that had occurred over two hundred years ago, when Alec had unwittingly rescued Ari instead of her daughter and changed the course of Fate.

Every single life lost was his fault.

Tears burned the back of Alec's eyes again, threatening

to fall. He bit his lip hard to keep them at bay. It should've been him. *He* should have died instead, all those years ago.

Damien rested a gentle hand on Alec's trembling one, pulling him out of his spiraling thoughts. "There's plenty of time, sweetheart."

Time? Time for what?

Oh.

To get to the forest. Right. Alec nodded and finished dressing. A stoic calm fell over him as he wrapped his scarf —his last piece of armor—around his neck.

He was ready to face the world.

2

MEMBERS of the preternatural community traveled from all over the country to attend Ari's funeral, filling every open space surrounding the Irish Run Natural Bridge in Wayne National Forest. Her loss would be felt in the hearts and minds of every single one of them.

A loss Damien felt responsible for.

He had pulled the trigger, after all.

It didn't matter that Ari had demanded the outcome. Or that destroying Ari's Soul Ball had been the only way to stop her daughter from stealing her power, killing Alec, and doing who the hell knows what afterward. The minefield of damage left in that morning's wake still haunted them all.

Ina's actions had reignited Alec's panic attacks. Alec

had admitted one night that the attacks were worse now than they'd been in the past two hundred years. Because Damien's boyfriend was a two hundred and sixty-five-year-old werewolf that appeared no older than thirty-one.

Christ, life had taken a strange turn. A couple of months ago, Damien had been more worried about turning thirty-nine, and his job as a homicide detective made sense. He investigated suspicious deaths, found the assholes responsible, and put them away. That was the theory anyway.

He'd carried on unaware of the preternatural community surrounding him his entire life until the Stone case in May. Nothing about that case or subsequent cases made any sense until the event that ripped the veil from Damien's eyes. He'd suddenly found himself in a world where he wasn't quite sure where he even fit anymore.

He still wasn't.

What did he do when the perpetrator turned out to be preternatural and would cause absolute havoc in the human justice system? The community's answer was to handle these situations themselves, hide the evidence, and sweep everything neatly under a rug.

But did that bring closure to anyone?

Bringing closure to victims was the entire purpose behind Damien becoming a homicide detective. Closure he never got for himself when someone had brutally murdered his parents seven years ago. Just another cold case sitting at the bottom of a never-ending pile.

These cases would've fallen to the same fate if not for Ari. By next week, the plan he'd put in place with her help would move forward, and over fifty cold-case files would be closed as a result. With any luck, at least.

A thick Boston accent pulled Damien out of his musings. "Thinking hard over here. It's nearly moonrise. They're about ready to start."

Damien blinked over at Jac. Damn, his old friend and former lover looked tired as hell. Dark circles surrounded the Fae lawyer's silver eyes, and his blond hair stood up as though he'd run his hands through it one too many times. "You look like shit," Damien said.

"Yeah, well, not being able to help much these past few months hasn't been sitting well with me. I'm here now and will do everything I can to make it up to you and your wolf."

They still needed to discuss Jac's absence, but there hadn't been an opportunity over the past two weeks. Jac had disappeared right before everything had gone down in Alec's apartment, and Damien hadn't heard from him again until they'd finalized Ari's funeral arrangements.

Movement pulled Damien's attention to the natural stone bridge close to where he and Jac stood. He'd kept as far away from the preternatural community as possible, given the number of them in attendance tonight. Wary and sometimes hostile eyes still watched the only human among the crowd, sliding over him like predators stalking their prey. He shuddered involuntarily. With this lot? He was absolutely prey. Thank fuck for Jac's presence nearby while Alec and Harper were busy shifting into wolf form.

The urn seated in the center of the bridge held what was left of Ari's Soul Ball since no other traces remained of her or her daughter. Surrounding the urn were various dishes made with rice or tofu. All things that Ari had loved.

Alec had insisted.

Damien stood back as the pair of wolves assumed their position at the base of the bridge. Alec's lithe white wolf was a breathtaking slip of a creature, much smaller than Harper's gray-and-red timber wolf, standing proudly next to him. Bright, sage-green eyes glinted in the moonlight, and while the scars over Alec's eyes left him blind even in wolf form, his other senses allowed him to perceive more than anyone else Damien had ever met.

As the full moon crested over the trees, Alec and Harper silenced the crowd with a mournful howl. One by one, each shifter and werecreature in the crowd took on their animal forms while others stood by silently with tears in their eyes.

It was a sight to behold.

The wind picked up, carrying a maelstrom of leaves throughout the clearing as the animals joined their voices into the haunting melody.

Goosebumps prickled along Damien's skin.

Whispers of words floated on the breeze.

We sing for those who came before us.

We anguish for our sister that watched the world change.

We call out to the ancestors to welcome her home.
We stand vigil until she returns.

As the leaves swirled around the urn, Damien could just make out the shape of a tiny orange fox in the center. It picked up a small, glowing object in its mouth and turned away. Without a backward glance, the fox bounded off into the trees.

Silence descended upon the forest, and the leaves settled to the ground.

Everything on the bridge was gone.

"NO MORE PUSHING EVERYONE AWAY?"

Alec sighed. "I shouldn't have done that."

He'd shoved Damien out of his life to keep him safe. It had killed him to do so, taking away what little joy in life he'd found over the past few months. And for what? To lose the only constant in his life instead.

Ari had been with him since he'd become a werewolf.

And now she was gone.

But he wasn't alone.

"I would rather you turn toward me. Let me hold you together when you feel like everything is falling apart." Damien kissed Alec affectionately as a genuine smile twitched at Alec's lips for the first time in weeks. Damien was right, of course.

Alec rested his head on Damien's shoulder as the others

gathered in the clearing gradually dispersed with the coming dawn, allowing Damien's vanilla-and-spice scent to comfort and ground him. Behind him, he caught an earthy scent along with diesel and wolf. Jac and Harper, standing a few paces away. Waiting.

With another heavy sigh, Alec turned to them. "I suppose we should head back."

Harper sucked in an unsteady breath. "Yeah, we should."

Alec tugged her forward into his arms, offering what comfort he could. She, too, knew better than to return Alec's embrace and instead patted his shoulder once before stepping away. The threat of panic always stripped away any peace a simple hug could bring him. He didn't like to be constrained or to feel like he couldn't get away. Not after what he'd endured all those years ago.

Even if he desperately needed a hug.

Damien silently linked his fingers with Alec's as the four of them made their way back to the trail that would lead them out of the forest and back to their respective vehicles. As they traveled along, songbirds welcomed the new day with a bright, refreshing melody that washed over Alec like a balm.

After saying their goodbyes, Alec and Damien climbed into Damien's SUV. The warmth of the sunrise enveloped Alec as they pulled onto the road for the three-hour trip home, his sunglasses already in place to keep the light from reaching his eyes.

They drove in silence for a little while before Damien tangled his fingers with Alec's again, squeezing gently. "How are you feeling?"

If Alec only knew. He gripped Damien's hand tight, keeping it in his lap. "Numb, mostly."

"It's okay to feel numb." Damien traced circles on the back of Alec's hand with his thumb. "I'm here when you're ready to talk about it."

A bittersweet smile twitched at Alec's lips, and he rested his head against Damien's arm. "I know. Thank you, *a stór.*" Damien truly was Alec's treasure.

"North Market will be open when we get back to town. Do you want to stop there for breakfast before we go inside?" Damien asked hours later, waking Alec from the light doze he had fallen into against Damien's arm.

Far be it from Alec to keep Damien from his obsession with coffee and doughnuts, but ... "You have to work today though, yeah?"

"We have time. I told them I'd be in a bit late since I could only swing the one day off." Damien squeezed Alec's knee, concern bleeding into his voice. "You going to be okay? I'm sorry I couldn't get more time. I can try to—"

Damien swore as a ringtone Alec knew all too well echoed over the speakers of the SUV. It was exclusive to Kat Saunders, the captain of Damien's precinct. Damien pulled his hand away to answer the call with the button on his steering wheel.

"O'Connor."

"Are you home?" Kat asked without a greeting, irritation threading through her stone-cold voice. Alec frowned at her tone. Did that woman ever say hello first?

"Not quite. I'd say another twenty or—"

"Make it ten. We have a pair of victims at the Hilton across from the Convention Center. The ME and CSU are delayed. They'll arrive as soon as they can. Check in with Officer Kent when you arrive. The manager is complicating matters and demanding his room back. Kent could use the backup ASAP."

When the line cut off moments later, Damien sighed wearily, and the SUV's engine roared as he stepped on the gas. "That hotel's only a block or so from the apartment. I'll drop you off first."

So much for breakfast.

Thanks for reading!